WHAT THE HEART WANTS & SEALED WITH A KISS

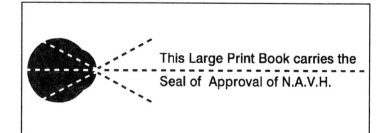

This Large Print Book carries the
Seal of Approval of N.A.V.H.

WHAT THE HEART WANTS & SEALED WITH A KISS

DONNA HILL
AND
NICKI NIGHT

THORNDIKE PRESS

A part of Gale, a Cengage Company

GALE
A Cengage Company

Farmington Hills, Mich • San Francisco • New York • Waterville, Maine
Meriden, Conn • Mason, Ohio • Chicago

LIBRARY OF CONGRESS CIP DATA ON FILE.
CATALOGUING IN PUBLICATION FOR THIS BOOK
IS AVAILABLE FROM THE LIBRARY OF CONGRESS

ISBN-13: 978-1-4328-6981-6 (hardcover alk. paper)

Published in 2019 by arrangement with Harlequin Books S.A.

Printed in the United States of America
1 2 3 4 5 6 7 23 22 21 20 19

CONTENTS

5

This novel is dedicated to my mom,
Dorothy Hill.
You were always my biggest cheerleader
and made me believe I could do
anything!
I love and will miss you forevermore.

Dear Reader,

Thank you so much for taking this journey with me. If this is your first Donna Hill book, I hope it will not be your last! For those returning readers, welcome back. I'm excited to introduce my new family series, The Grants of DC. Franklin, Montgomery and Alonzo Grant — all tall, dark, handsome, successful and, best of all, available!

The debut title, *What the Heart Wants,* features the eldest of the Grant trio — Franklin Grant, chief cardiothoracic surgeon at Jameson Memorial Hospital. I really wanted to stretch myself a bit with the profession of my main character Franklin. So why not a surgeon?

Franklin Grant is driven, devoted to his craft and dedicated to his patients and his family, which leaves him little time for a full-fledged relationship. I knew that the woman to capture Franklin's heart had to be able to stand toe-to-toe with him. Enter Dr. Dina Hamilton, his equal on every level and then some!

I do hope that you will enjoy every page as

Franklin and Dina sidestep all the relationship land mines and realize once and for all *what the heart wants.*

Until next time,
Donna

Chapter 1

"Yo, the game is getting ready to start!" Franklin Grant shouted from his prime spot on the eight-foot sectional that dominated his living room. The skyline, defined by the nation's capital and the iconic shadow of the Washington Monument, provided the backdrop beyond the terrace windows. The sky was clear, barely a cloud in the sky, and everywhere one looked the riot of cherry blossoms signaled that spring had arrived. He took a beer from the cup holder embedded in the couch.

Alonzo, brother number two, strode in from the kitchen with a platter of hot wings, his secret special dipping sauce and hand-cut seasoned fries that he'd whipped up upon his arrival. "Maybe if you would actually *buy* food and learn to cook . . ." He let the inference hang in the air.

Franklin took a long swallow of the golden liquid. Dewdrops slid down the bottle neck.

"Hey, I provide the space, the sixty-two-inch *with* surround sound *and* my company," he said with a chuckle, but was dead serious. "Besides, you're the big-time celebrity chef. It's what you do, bruh. You need emergency surgery, heart replacement, then I'm your guy." He wiggled his long, tapered fingers. "Can't risk these babies."

"What is the point of having an HGTV chef kitchen that you don't or can't use?" Alonzo set the platter down on the low rectangular glass-and-wood table. "At some point you're gonna starve to death."

"That's why they have takeout and delivery." His thick, dark brows drew together. "Where's Monty? Should have been here by now." He put his bare feet up on the ottoman.

"Probably buying another hotel."

They both chuckled and bumped fists.

The Grant brothers were equally successful in their chosen fields, highly competitive in their professions and with each other. Franklin Grant was one of the country's most renowned cardiothoracic surgeons, traveling the world lecturing on cutting-edge techniques, but his home was in DC, as chief of cardiac surgery at Jameson Memorial Hospital. The man in the middle was Alonzo, whose love for food and cook-

14

ing led him to pursue a career as a chef and ultimately chef to the stars. At any given moment he might jet off to some exotic location to prepare a sit-down dinner for Oscar and Grammy winners or private parties for the A-list. Montgomery, the youngest, had counted and saved money since he started getting an allowance. *Shark Tank* was his go-to television show. His love for business and spotting potential moneymakers led him to the hotel industry. To date he owned two boutique hotels and three B and Bs. However, as wealthy and successful as they were, they remained grounded by the love of family. Their parents, Louis and Ellen Grant, nurtured them on the importance of family first and foremost, and they made it their business to always be there for each other.

Alonzo plopped down on the couch and snatched up a beer from the ice bucket. "Yeah, we need to nail down the details for this anniversary party."

The doorbell rang.

"Speaking of . . ." Franklin said, swinging his feet to the floor and going to the door. "Thanks for coming," he joked when he opened the door for his youngest brother, Montgomery.

"With the jokes." They quickly did the

Grant brother embrace: a combination of one-arm hug and backslap with a fist. "I smell some wings," he sang out, doing a half shuffle, half hop dance across the floor.

"Hey, man." Alonzo drew Monty in for their greeting. "Whatsup?"

"Taking over the world," he said with a chuckle. "Think I might have another deal lined up." He sat down and was joined by Franklin.

"Another hotel?" Franklin asked.

"No, another B and B, right outside DC, in Silver Spring."

"Seriously?" Alonzo asked.

Montgomery nodded yes. "Working out the details. Have to see how it goes, but at the moment it's looking good."

"Damn, bro, you really are gonna take over the world," Franklin teased.

"That's the plan." He lifted his bottle of beer and the three brothers toasted.

As if given a signal, all three brothers turned their focus to the jumbo screen and whooped with delight at the move by LeBron James that defied physics.

They fell all over the couch hollering at the move and whooped again at the instant replay, with Alonzo jumping up to reenact it.

As they always did when they got together

for "game night," they dished on their work and their love lives. On that note, Franklin generally remained mute, which became the topic of discussion.

"You can't come stag to Mom and Dad's anniversary party," Montgomery said after finishing off another wing. "Damn this sauce is the bomb." He wiped his mouth.

Alonzo lifted his chin in thanks. "Exactly. There has to be some unsuspecting nurse that would be willing to spend the evening with your ornery ass."

Franklin grumbled under his breath and continued to ignore his brothers. His relationships or lack thereof were always fuel for debate and dissection. Easy for them to razz him. Lonzo ran through women the way he ran through party nights with celebrities, and Mo lined up women the way he lined up and moved from one property to the next. Those weren't his visions for relationships. He dated, but it wasn't his top priority and he had his reasons. If he was going to get involved with anyone long-term it would be with someone who could go with him toe-to-toe. Someone who could turn him on mentally as well as physically. With the hours he spent at work and on research in his field, well — he just didn't have time.

"The party is coming up quickly. We good with everything?" Franklin asked, turning the topic away from himself.

"Working with Monica the party planner," Montgomery said. "The space is all set at the MG Empire in Alexandria. I've kept all of the six bedrooms at my connected B and B for overflow, free for anyone that wants to stay over. And I have a block of rooms at the venue as well for Mom and Dad and family." He winked at his brothers. "I'm letting Monica handle all the setup details for the party, decorating and all that, and the entertainment."

"Yeah, and my team has the menu and the liquor," Alonzo added. "We'll take care of everything on that end. I got extra folks on board to help with serving and whatnot."

Franklin nodded as he listened. "Well, just stay on top of the invoices and send me the bills. I'll take care of the expenses, along with the limo for the night for Mom and Pops." Why did that sound empty? Funny, searching deep into the pumping heart of a patient on his operating table, performing microscopic surgery on tiny veins, was a walk in the park compared to navigating the intricacies of this people-to-people stuff. That's where he felt lost. *Better to know your strengths.* So he left all that to his brothers and did what he did best, look at the big picture and pay the bills. Alonzo playfully slugged Monty in the shoulder as they shared a joke. He envied them even as much as he loved them. He envied their ease in the world, the way they charmed and cajoled, skills that seemed to have bypassed him. But, he could do what neither of them could — save lives. He satisfied himself with that.

"So who are you gonna bring to the prom, big bro?" Monty asked dragging him back into the conversation.

"You know the folks will flip if you come alone to another family function, especially this one." Lonzo tucked a pillow behind his head. "I can hook you up if you want," he hinted with a wink.

"Thanks, but no thanks. I can get my own date." Not sure where, but damn if he would let his baby brother hook him up.

Alonzo and Montgomery murmured under their breath, but turned their attention back to the game.

"Speaking of dates," Monty began. "Who are you bringing, Lonzo? The one from the party a few months back?"

"Doubt it. Didn't work out too well."

"Another one bites the dust," Franklin tossed in.

"Let's just say that she wanted more than I was willing to put in."

"At some point, the both of you are gonna have to get serious. You can't keep running through women like socks."

"Says the man who thinks a date should only be one every decade," Monty teased.

"Not funny. I have expectations."

"Yeah, that will never be met unless you can cut it open, examine it and make it better," Alonzo said.

Franklin pushed to his feet. "Wanting something more than a one-night or one-week stand isn't a character flaw." He strode off to the kitchen and returned shortly with another six-pack for the ice bucket and a plate of nacho chips and dip.

"Since I'm a gamblin' man," Monty said, "how 'bout we set a friendly brotherly wager?"

"I'm in," Alonzo agreed while scooping dip onto a large nacho chip.

"You don't even know what the bet is," Franklin said and lightly shoved him in the shoulder.

"Don't need to," he mumbled over a mouthful of nachos. "I bet it has to do with you, big bro." His broad shoulders shook with laughter.

Franklin's eyes darkened as they slid

toward Montgomery.

Montgomery shrugged. "He's right." He sat up straighter in his seat. "The bet is that Franklin won't have a date for the anniversary party and if he does it's only for show."

"How much we going in for?" Alonzo asked.

Montgomery pursed his lips in thought. "Five big ones?"

"Light stuff. A half hour's work for me."

"Don't I get any respect as the oldest?"

"Hell naw," the brothers sang in unison then cracked up with laughter.

Franklin scorched them both with a look. "Fine. You're on. And we're doing double or nothing. When you two lose, you'll double your bet and it goes to my favorite charity."

"You're on!"

Franklin snorted feigned annoyance. He had no intention of paying his brothers a dime. Winning the bet, however, was the problem. His self-imposed all-work-and-less-play regimen left him short on the playing field. But there was one woman who came to mind — Dr. Dina Hamilton.

CHAPTER 2

It was Dina's first day off in nearly a month. Her limbs were lead weights and her eyelids developed a mind of their own — the off position. Rest was on the agenda, but when she rolled over in her queen-size bed and her eyes squinted open, tempting sunshine curved a come-hither finger.

Tossing the pale peach sheet and light floral quilt aside, she basked for a moment in a bath of warm light. Bright sunny days were her Achilles' heel. Some people loved chocolate, others potato chips or a glass of wine at the end of the day. For Dina it was sunshine, as much of it as she could get. The memory of her six-year-old self, crying as the sun set, brought a smile of nostalgia to her lips. She could still hear her mother's soothing voice, telling her that the sun always rises and it would be back, that it needed to go to bed and rest just like she did. Her mother's assurances quieted her tears and calmed her worries. And as Bettye Hamilton promised, the sun rose again. She internalized her mother's words and pulled them out during those times when she felt alone, afraid and uncertain, like now.

Sighing, she swung her legs over the side of the bed and winced when her toes touched the cold wood floor. She still hadn't grown used to the roller-coaster weather of the East. One of these days she was going to get a carpet for her bedroom. She'd been telling herself that since she'd moved to DC from the West Coast — land of sunshine. But she knew she never would. Her allergies were not fans of carpets, cats or dogs. Since carpets were out, she'd settled for sheepskin slippers that mysteriously found their way under her bed during the night instead of beside it where she put them.

She got down on her knees, felt for her slippers and pulled them toward her. "Possessed," she muttered and shoved her feet into the cushioned warmth. She shuffled into the bathroom, took care of her bladder then turned on the shower.

Refreshed and moderately caffeinated, she picked at her toasted everything bagel while scanning the front page of the *Washington Post.* Religion and politics were two topics that could make the good go bad, break up families and friends and incite wars. All very good reasons why she didn't engage in those conversations. However, as she fumed from one headline to the next, one image after another, it was impossible for her to contain her horror over what was happening in the world. If only the fix to all things that were wrong in society could be repaired like a bad heart she would jump right in. But that was a pipe dream.

She finished off her coffee and the last bit of her bagel and hopped down from the stool. The great outdoors was calling her. Yoga pants, sneakers, oversize sweater and infinity scarf, and she headed out with no particular destination in mind.

The sun bounced off the windshields of parked cars and squinted the eyes of morning walkers and joggers. She held her face upward, smiled, then began her stroll. In the months that she'd been a transplant to Chocolate City, she'd made it a point to seek out places of interest and there were many. She decided to walk over to the National Mall — or the Great Lawn as some called the long expanse of green, flanked by museums, memorials and history — maybe buy a giant salty pretzel from a street vendor or if she was lucky find the artist who drew caricatures for fifteen dollars.

She stopped at a curbside vendor that advertised an extensive list of smoothies that promised to help everything from exhaustion to improving eyesight. She opted for a green smoothie that claimed to boost her energy and continued her stroll along the pedestrian walkway. Even midweek the Great Lawn teemed with hand-holding couples, moms pushing strollers and children too young for school rolling and tumbling on the emerald-green grass. Coming from a place like California, she was accustomed to Rollerbladers on sidewalks, to scantily-clad women in open-top convertibles heading for the beaches, to the designer-suited businessman ready to close the next deal all within the space of a few feet of each other. But the first time she'd sought the sunshine of the North and found the National Mall, nothing could compare to seeing the Washington Monument rise toward the cloudless sky, against the backdrop of the US Capitol on one side and the Lincoln Memorial on the other. It took her breath away, leaving her with a sense of humility mixed with anger over America's tumultuous history, especially when she visited the National Museum of African

American History and Culture for the first of many times. She made a point to take the tour at least once per month to reinforce her commitment to make a difference in any way that she could.

Today, however, she simply wanted to bask in the sunshine, inhale the aroma of hot dogs and spicy mustard, listen to muted conversations and lilting laughter.

She spotted the perfect vantage point and walked off the concrete path, strolled up the emerald slope and settled beneath an unoccupied tree. Leaning back against the ancient knotted bark she jabbed the plastic straw through the hole on the cover of her smoothie and took a long sip. Not bad.

Her gaze slowly roamed along the rolling landscape. It seemed like such a short time ago that this very lawn was covered with a mass of humanity that stood for hours in the bitter January cold to witness the first African American president being sworn into office. She'd stood side by side with her colleagues in the doctor's lounge, some stoic, others brought to tears, but all awed by the spectacle, and filled with hope in their hearts for the future. That was then. Much had changed since then including her leaving the life she'd known to move across the country.

A soccer ball bounced off her foot and snapped her out of her musings.

"Sorry about that." A long sweater-covered arm reached down for the ball.

Dina's gaze rose. She squinted against the sun, cupped her hand over her eyes. "Dr. Grant?" Her pulse raced.

He straightened, tucked the ball under his arm. His eyes widened in surprise. "Dr. Hamilton . . ."

"Hi." She rose to her feet in one fluid movement. "Playing soccer? Didn't know you had kids."

"I don't. Unless you want to count my younger brothers," he said, hooking his thumb over his shoulder.

Dina's gaze followed his direction and spotted two men, one more gorgeous than the other. *Must run in the family.* "Oh."

"You here alone?" He scoped out the immediate area.

"Yes. Actually. Needed to get out of the house."

He nodded, shifted his weight. "Well I'd better get back to the game. Enjoy your day. See you . . . at work."

"Sure."

He lifted a hand in a wave and jogged off. "Have a good game."

He glanced over his shoulder. "Thanks."

■ ■ ■ ■

"Took you long enough," Monty groused and grabbed the ball from Franklin.

"Who was that?" Alonzo asked, lifting his chin in the direction of Dina.

"Doctor from the hospital."

"She could cure my ills any day," Alonzo said and that earned him a fist bump from Montgomery.

"We gonna finish this game or what?" Franklin asked.

"She single?" Monty quizzed.

"Don't know. It's none of my business whether she is or not."

"You should find out. You do need a date for the party," Alonzo reminded him.

Franklin snatched the ball from his brother. "Let's play."

Whatever peace and tranquility she thought she'd find beneath the yawning branches of the tree was totally upended. Her heart still raced. Working with Franklin Grant in the hospital setting was difficult enough. Seeing him out of his element added another layer that she wished she could peel back. But it was clear from his near-indifferent manner that there was no interest on his part.

She finished off her smoothie, took a final gaze at the trio of brothers as they made looking ruggedly sexy as easy as breathing, then headed in the opposite direction, taking the long way to the exit.

CHAPTER 3

The reserved parking space in the hospital's underground garage was one of the perks that Franklin truly appreciated, especially on a day like this one. Even at 7:00 a.m., the horizon remained in darkness, heavy gray clouds trolled the heavens emptying themselves in sheets and swirls. Flooding alerts dominated the forecast with no end in sight for the rest of the week. Days like this not only flooded the streets but also the emergency room, filling it with weather-related accident victims. Good day to stay in bed with a medical journal, but he had surgery in three hours.

The private elevator hummed softly as it rose to the cardiac wing on the third floor. The instant he stepped onto the hospital floor a surge of energy flowed through his limbs. He'd never get enough of that rush, fueled by the beep of machines, the hushed steps of cushioned feet and the sense of urgency and purpose that pumped like a heartbeat.

"Good morning, Dr. Grant," the head nurse greeted.

"Morning, Grace. Is Dr. Hamilton in yet?"

"She's in with a patient. Six B."

"Thanks." He continued down the corridor lined with glass-fronted rooms occupied by patients in various stages of pre and post heart surgery. The clanging of metal carts being rolled down the hall by orderlies were the daily music to his ears. He either conducted the surgeries himself or oversaw the work of Dr. Hamilton, Jameson Memorial's newest fellow. She was a skilled diagnostician and brilliant surgeon, he'd give her that. But she was also opinionated and too often she questioned and tested his decisions. The fact that she was the best cardiac surgeon he'd worked with in much too long made up for her lack of regard for hierarchy. None of that was his real issue with Dina Hamilton. The real issue was that she was sexy as hell and threw him off his game with her very presence. That ticked him off and turned him on at the same time.

Franklin shrugged out of his jacket, hung it on the hook in his office in exchange for his white lab coat, then went in search of Dr. Hamilton.

"Everything looks good, Mr. Vincent." Dina checked the flow of fluids and the stats on the machines monitoring her patient's vital signs. "I want you to rest for the next day. Then we're going to get you up and walking." She patted his shoulder. "I'll check on you later this evening."

She turned, stopped short at seeing Franklin Grant standing in the doorway. Her stomach fluttered. He had an uncanny ability to unmoor her with those penetrating looks that dipped down into her soul and stirred all kinds of things that she couldn't pin down. The fact that he towered over her five-foot-six-inch height only added to the feeling of being swallowed whole.

"Dr. Grant." She stuck her laser pen in the pocket of her lab coat, and gripped her iPad.

"Dr. Hamilton." He lifted his chin toward the patient. "How is he?"

"Came through surgery fine. Vitals look good. How did the game go yesterday?"

He almost smiled. "Same as usual. Cheaters." He checked his Rolex. "I thought we could take a few minutes to go over the chart and the plan for the surgery."

"Your office?"

Why does the question sound more like an intimate invitation than a request for a meeting? He cleared his throat. "Sure."

Dina made notes to the patient's chart on her iPad, hit Send to upload to medical records and walked with Franklin toward his office on the opposite side of the corridor.

It was faint, the soft scent of her that dared you to draw closer and experience it. Franklin shoved his hands into the pockets of his lab coat. How was he supposed to concentrate on a complex surgery when she wore that scent? Something new? He wasn't sure, just annoyed. Suddenly seeing her yesterday, out of the hospital, totally shook him. Gone was the starched professional. In her place was a carefree, sexy woman. And all night long he couldn't get the image of her out of his head. The way her eyes lit up in the sunlight, the light coating of something glossy on those full lips or the white T-shirt that outlined the lushness of her breasts, those skin-hugging pants . . . He pushed the images away.

Franklin opened the door to his office, held it open for Dina and when she passed he couldn't help but inhale her. This time it was her hair. His lids drifted down. He started to close the door but left it partially open.

Dina made herself comfortable in the chair next to his desk and crossed her legs.

Franklin came around his desk, sat and turned on his computer. Within moments the medical history, films, test results, visits and recommendations came up on the screen. The surgery would take at least four to six hours.

"I'd like to use the robotics for the first half of the procedure."

Franklin looked across at her, brow raised. She gazed back, unblinking. "You're more than ready."

She smiled and nodded. "That I am."

"You'll have an audience of interns in the theater."

Her eyes lit up. She gave a half shrug. "Won't be the first time. That's how we learn, right?"

He half grinned. "Let's hear your plan . . ." He turned the screen toward her.

Dina pulled her chair around to Franklin's side of the desk and leaned in for a closer look. Franklin's jaw clenched. She pointed to several areas of the patient's heart projected on the screen while detailing the plan for reconstruction of the damaged valves and how she would use the robotics to initiate the laser incisions.

Franklin nodded and murmured in his throat, but if someone were to ask him what she'd said, he was pretty sure he wouldn't be able to recall. She was too close. That scent too lush. The way the waves of her hair framed her face, too appealing.

"What do you think?"

He adjusted the screen to give him a moment to reclaim his thoughts. "Our patient is in good hands."

Dina grinned, looked into his eyes. "Thanks for the vote of confidence. It means a great deal."

An awkward silence went up like a wall between them.

"So . . . what do you do to unwind after a grueling surgery?" Dina finally said. "Me, a martini usually does the trick."

"I'm more of a bourbon guy."

She tilted her head to the side in appraisal, then nodded. "Yep. Bourbon fits you."

"How's that?"

"Well, when I'm drinking alone, which I usually am, guys like you drink bourbon."

His lips twitched a moment. "First, why are you drinking alone and two, guys like me?"

She held up a steady hand, long slender fingers, short nails — a surgeon's hand.

"Second question first." She looked him straight in the eye. "What I meant by guys like you was men who know who they are, sometimes the strong silent type. They don't make waves, just make moves." She licked her bottom lip. "And to your first question I know that drinking alone may make me look desperate, but to be honest, I don't know many people here in DC to hang out with when I need to hang, and drinking alone in my apartment is definitely not a good look." She blinked rapidly, glanced away, then back at him.

That would explain why she was alone in the park, why he rarely saw her engaged in any way other than in some professional capacity with any of the other doctors, and apparently she wasn't seeing anyone. Coast clear. Franklin cleared his throat. "We can't have that. Uh, maybe you'd like to come with me to an anniversary party." Did he sound casual or creepy? "Still a few days away, but you'd get to meet a bunch of cool people and still have that martini." What did he just do? "I mean you don't have to feel obligated to go or anything . . ."

"I . . . I'd really like that. Thank you." Her brows knitted together. "Whose anniversary?"

"My parents' fiftieth wedding anniversary."

"Wow!" Her eyes widened. "Fifty years. I think my longest relationship was six months. And that's a generous estimate." She laughed.

"Commitment issues?"

"Hmm." She frowned. "Not really."

He waited for some kind of clue to what she meant, but she didn't elaborate.

Dina slid her chair back, then pushed it to its place beside Franklin's desk. She jammed her hands into the wide patch pockets of her lab coat. "I should get ready." She picked up her iPad from the desk and walked to the door. "Open or closed?"

Franklin blinked. "Uh, open is fine."

"See you in the OR."

Once Dina disappeared from the threshold of the doorway, Franklin plopped against the cushioned backrest of his chair. He pushed out a deep breath. He didn't even realize he'd asked her to the party until he'd heard her answer. The words tumbled out of his mouth like some dazed school kid smitten by the prom queen. Now he was stuck. He couldn't very well rescind the invitation. Working with her was becoming more difficult by the day. She was a distraction. Thankfully it wouldn't be for too much longer. When the time came in the next couple of months, he'd sign off on her work at Jameson Memorial and she could move on. The upside was that he'd gotten a date out of the deal and he'd win the bet with his brothers. At least there was that.

CHAPTER 4

Dina walked back to her office in a bit of a daze. The last thing she'd expected was to be asked out by Franklin Grant. Dr. Grant was as inaccessible as the cure for the common cold. Aloof, some would say. She attributed his standoffish persona to more of a defense than offense. Then again, she was probably projecting her own issues onto him.

She unlocked her office door and stepped inside. Fantasizing about him was one thing while they roamed the halls together and conferred on cases in tight spaces, complemented each other's skill in the operating room, but a night out with him was something different. She wasn't even sure why she'd agreed. The last time she'd been on a "date" was before she'd left Los Angeles to come to DC. Paul Greene. It was a disaster. After months of beating around the bush and flirting he'd finally asked her to dinner.

Sometimes fantasies are best left alone.

She could always change her mind. A woman's prerogative. Then again that was a problem in itself. The last set of adjectives she wanted to be associated with was indecisive and flighty. The world of surgery was still dominated by men. They existed in a special kind of rarefied air that women still struggled to inhale. She wanted, no, demanded, the respect that was due her and she didn't want her gender and all the "isms" associated with it to cloud the perceptions of her as anything other than a brilliant surgeon.

So, if she couldn't say no, guess she would have to find something to wear. In the meantime, surgery awaited.

After nearly five hours of open-heart surgery she felt energized rather than exhausted. The procedure was a resounding success. She replayed every minute in her head. Damn she was good. Having Franklin nearby overseeing her every move, encouraging and directing, could have been nerve-racking for someone else. For her, she rose to the challenge.

"Nice work in there."

She glanced over her shoulder while getting out of her surgical garb. "Thanks." She dumped her gown and gloves in the bin, then turned to look up at Franklin.

He swiped his cap from his head.

Her heart thumped. "I'd like to lead the team on the robotic training."

"Really?"

"It's what I came to Jameson for, isn't it?"

"I'm sure that it is, but I decide when you're ready."

She folded her arms. "I think I proved that today." Her chest rose. "So when are you going to 'decide' when I'm ready?" She cocked her head to the side.

He studied her defiant stance, the half-taunting smile on those damned pouty lips. Typical. It annoyed him to no end and shot him with need at the same time. "If you think you can handle it." Did that come out the way it sounded?

"I know I can."

He bet that she could. "I'll take it into consideration," Franklin said, finding himself conceding to her — again.

"Fine."

They faced off.

Franklin cleared his throat, lifted his chin. "About the anniversary party . . . I don't want you to feel obligated."

"No. Not at all. I'd really like to go. It'll be fun."

"Okay, then. It's Saturday night, by the way. Seven o'clock."

"I'll be ready, or should I meet you there?"

"I can pick you up."

"Perfect."

"Good job, Dr. Hamilton," he repeated, then left through the swinging doors.

Dr. Hamilton. Hmm, clearly he was trying to keep it professional, but she'd watched him twist and untwist his cap between his fingers while he was talking to her. He was actually nervous! She smiled. The great Franklin Grant. Who knew?

CHAPTER 5

"Hey, Dina."

Dina stopped with her hand on the knob of her office door, glanced over her shoulder. "Hi, Anna. I've got a minute, come on in." She opened the door. Anna walked in behind her.

"How did the surgery go this morning?" She plopped down on the side chair.

Dina shrugged out of her white coat and hung it on the wooden rack — a gift from her mentor in Los Angeles, Dr. Fulton, then sat down behind her desk. "Exhausting. But . . . Kicked butt!" She beamed with pride.

"I wanted to be in on the viewing, but an emergency came in. All the hands were on *your* deck, so they called me."

Dina wanted to like Anna Lorde. She was one of the few doctors with whom Dina talked outside work. With the two of them being the only females of color on the surgical team, it should somehow bring them together. But it was comments like that one that raised the hairs on the back of her neck. Anna never came right out and said anything foul, but the scent of it often hung in the air. Instead of relying on her skills to get ahead, she all too often used her exotic Latina looks and even at times playing the victim which garnered more sympathy than respect. She'd known women like Anna all through med school, throughout her life, actually. Sonia Fleming for example. Third-year medical student, talented, smart, easy on the eyes but every chance she got she played the victim or would kick the unsuspecting intern under the bus. Passive-aggressive. They never quite said what they meant, but the implication was evident. With Anna, she was never sure if she was friend or foe. Even though she'd only been at Jameson for six months, she'd figured out the best way to deal with Anna's insecurities. Feed her ego.

"Really? What was the case?"

Anna waved her slender hand in a dismissive motion. "Nothing as medical journal worthy as yours."

Dina inwardly rolled her eyes. "Everything we do is important. Did you save the patient's life?"

"Of course," she said as if there could be any doubt.

Dina gave a light shrug. "See."

Anna poked out her lips, sighed. "Of course you're right." She tucked a lock of sleek dark hair behind her right ear revealing a tiny gold stud. "I don't know how you do it, Dina."

Here we go. "Do what?"

"Stay so upbeat and positive. It's totally cutthroat. And it's so much harder for women to rise up the ranks, like we aren't qualified." She lowered her voice as if letting Dina in on some secret. "That's why we need to stick together."

Dina's right brow lifted. "Stick together?"

"Yes. Us. Me and You. Women."

Dina cleared her throat. Hmm, umm. "Well, tell me about the patient," she segued.

Anna's sandy-toned face lit up as if she'd been stroked with a warm hand. Dina leaned back in her chair and set her expression to "interested." What she would rather do is talk to a real girlfriend about the out-of-the-blue invitation that Dr. Grant had presented. Talk over drinks about what it really meant, if anything at all; what she should wear and most important, what should she do when he took her home? The

45

problem was, she didn't have any real girlfriends. She wished she could blame it on having relocated from Los Angeles to DC, but she knew that wasn't the issue. The issue was that as much as she dreamed of the camaraderie of friendship, she didn't trust anyone to actually get that close. She was her own example of passive-aggressive, which was why she could spot it in others. At least with hers, she wasn't destructive to others, just herself.

"I heard the robotics were a big hit. Everyone is buzzing," Anna said.

Dina blinked Anna back into her train of thought. "Hey," she said, nonchalant, "everything is always a big deal in the beginning. Once it becomes part of our everyday routine —" she shrugged "— we'll be wondering what the big deal was."

"I still say we should celebrate. Plus, I am dying to hear what it was like having the great Dr. Grant zoomed in on your every move."

Her belly tightened. She could feel the heat of his presence, an almost-there scent of his maleness that clung to her long after they'd parted ways and kept her body on simmer. "Like working with any other gifted surgeon," she said with cool detachment.

Anna leaned back and crossed her legs.

"But you have to admit Franklin Grant is hot!"

Dina smothered a smile. That he was, but she would never admit that to Anna. "I have two patients to see and a consult," Dina said while she rose to her feet. "I'll leave the assessment of Dr. Grant to you."

"Not. A. Problem. How about that drink later? I should be done here by six."

"I'll text you," Dina said. She took her jacket from the hook, and picked up her iPad from the desk.

Anna followed her out into the corridor. "See you later?"

"No promises."

They walked in opposite directions. Maybe she would take Anna up on her offer. She did have her moments when she could be fun to be with. It was those other times that were the problem.

CHAPTER 6

Grant scanned the X-rays on the wall-length monitor, moving methodically from one slide to the next. None of the images registered. He'd lost track of how long he'd been looking but not seeing. He wanted to blame it on exhaustion from the hours in surgery, but surgery wasn't the culprit. When he walked into the OR, the power to heal, to cure, to save a life was a feeling akin to euphoria. He never took what he did for granted. The ability, vision and skill to repair a heart, the centerpiece of life, was given to a chosen few. His mentor, the renowned Dr. Elliot Pratt, who had perfected the artificial-valve technique in the lower chamber of the heart, had ushered him toward cardiothoracic surgery. During his surgical rotation, Dr. Pratt singled him out to assist him on a groundbreaking procedure. He was scared as hell, but Dr. Pratt never wavered in his confidence as he guided him through the intricate surgery. The overwhelming sense of achievement was a drug that seeped into his veins and he couldn't kick the habit. That day he discovered his destiny, and every move and decision that he made since had been to fulfill that destiny. Knowing that didn't explain his disconnect from his work. The explanation was Dr. Hamilton.

He flipped a switch on the side of the monitor and the lights went out leaving behind the ghostly halo of a patient's heart. He massaged the bridge of his nose. The first rule of healing was to accept that you had a problem. Dina Hamilton was a problem. From the moment she arrived at Jameson Memorial and was assigned to his team, he hadn't been himself — at least the self he knew. Anytime she was in the vicinity it was as if some kind of brain fog came over him. Clarity escaped him and in its place was a tension that even got under his skin. He knew how skilled she was, the best he'd seen in years. But because of his mixed feelings about her, he rode her harder, made her fight for every inch, as if by doing so, he'd shield himself and the rest of his team from the fact that he favored her, was turned on by her. And now of all the screwed-up things to do, he'd asked her out.

The truth was he'd wanted to ask her out from the moment he'd spotted her in the lecture hall nearly six months earlier. The room was filled with eager talent, all hanging on his every word, all wanting the opportunity to hone their skills under his supervision. Yet, in the sea of faces his gaze landed on Dina Hamilton. Her hair was pulled back that day, which widened her eyes. She'd stared right at him, defiant almost, and lifted her chin as if daring him — to what he didn't know. For an instant the subtle tease short-circuited his train of thought. He'd repeated himself. He knew he did but it was the only way he could gather his thoughts. At the end of the lecture he was surrounded by young interns. He barely heard their questions.

He shook away the memory. That didn't help. If anything it sent his thoughts into disarray. This was why he worked so hard to keep walls up, at work and in his personal life. Relationships were distractions. Relationships drained you; they went wrong and then you had to recover. He turned to face the window, slid his hands into the pockets of his navy slacks. Drained you the way Lindsay had drained him, shook him loose from his anchor, then set him adrift. But one thing that he'd always prided himself on was learning from his mistakes.

Attraction was one thing, consensual sex was another, but what the heart often wanted could never be planned. After Lindsay, his plan was never again to mix feelings with pleasure.

CHAPTER 7

Dina gripped the silver-plated handle of the entry door to The Bottom and hoped that she hadn't made a mistake in deciding to meet up with Anna. She pulled the heavy door open and was greeted by the sound of tinkling glasses, muffled conversations and bursts of laughter. A blend of mouthwatering aromas reminded her that the she hadn't eaten since breakfast.

Her eyes adjusted to the dimly lit interior as she scanned the space for signs of Anna. The Bottom, the go-to spot for the doctors and nurses at Jameson, could seat maybe eighty customers at the long, family-style rectangular wooden tables that were laid out in various configurations of rows. When Dina came there for the first time the setup reminded her of the cabin turned dining hall at sleepaway camp when she was eleven. Growing up as an only child — at least the early part of her life — she was pretty traumatized by camp. Sharing a room with strangers, community bathrooms and eating meals in a room full of laughing, screaming preteens was pure sensory overload. The first week she cried every single day, and it wasn't until Marian Lewis decided to make Dina her friend that life at camp not only became bearable but one of the best experiences of her life. She often wondered what happened to Marian. They'd stayed in touch for a couple of years after that first summer, but life and cute boys got in the way. But it was the deaths of her parents that changed everything for her.

"Hey, sorry to keep you waiting." Anna slid up behind her.

Dina put on her smile. "No worries. I just got here."

"Oh, good. I'm starving. So, let's get a table." She hooked her arm through Dina's as if they were besties.

"Sure." She made out that she needed to search her purse. Anna unhooked her arm. "Here it is." She pulled her wallet from her purse. "I had a vision in my head that I'd left it in my other bag." She laughed lightly.

Anna angled her head to the side in question and squinted. "Are you okay?"

"Yes. Fine. Guess I'm hungry *and* tired."

The hostess approached. "Bar or table?"

Anna looked to Dina.

"Table is fine," Dina answered for them both.

"Right this way." She scooped up two menus, then led them across the wood plank floor to a table that sat six in the rear of the space. She placed the menus on the table. "Your waiter will be with you shortly."

Dina shrugged out of her pearl-gray trench car coat, hung it on the back of her seat, then sat down. Anna sat opposite Dina.

"Aren't you hot in that sweater?" Dina asked and picked up the menu.

"Girl, I'm always cold." She stretched her hand across the table and clasped Dina's fingers.

Dina flinched. "Damn, Anna, you're like a vampire or something."

"See." She gave a light shrug. "*Cold hands, warm heart* my mother used to say."

"I guess. But you're a doctor. You know better. Could be a vitamin deficiency. Poor circulation . . ."

Anna held up her hand. "I am not going to dissect my health. I'm here for girl talk, drinks and food."

"Okaaay."

The waiter arrived and they shouted out their drink and menu orders over the wave of voices and music from the jukebox.

"So we really haven't had much of a chance to talk outside work," Anna began.

Dina gave a slight shrug. "Busy lives."

Anna shifted in her seat. "I pick my associates wisely and friends even more so. Especially at the hospital. It is truly cutthroat unless you have a patron." She leveled her gaze at Dina.

"That's pretty much how it is all over. If you want to advance your career you need a mentor."

She leaned across the table. "It's why I said earlier that we need to stick together."

The waiter arrived with their drinks, and hurried off, while the hostess seated a trio at their table.

Dina and Anna gave the newly seated group a quick cursory smile and returned to their drinks.

"So . . . Your fellowship is finishing up pretty soon. What are your plans?"

Dina took a sip of her martini. "It depends on if I get an offer to stay at Jameson. Otherwise, there's a spot open back in LA. I only need to decide if I want to take it."

"Nice to have options."

Dina rolled her eyes in her mind. "We all have options, Anna. It's up to the individual to decide what to do with them."

"Easy for you to say. Look at you. You

55

have it all going on. And apparently you've fallen under the good graces of Dr. Grant."

Dina linked her fingers together and leaned forward, lowered her voice. "Anna, the victim role is not a good look."

Her neck jerked back. "What?"

Dina lowered her voice and looked intently at Anna. "No matter what success you accomplish, you find some way to diminish it and act as if everyone else has one up on you. That is so far from the damned truth. You're such a skilled doctor, Anna. Own it." She frowned and reached for her drink. "But, hey, if that's your MO." She shrugged her right shoulder. "I'm just saying it's wearing thin."

Anna pursed her lips.

The waiter arrived with their orders. "Can I get you anything else? Refills?"

"Yes," Anna said almost too quickly.

"For you, miss?" he asked, directing his question to Dina.

"Sure. Thanks." She gazed across the table at Anna. "If I offended you, I apologize. It wasn't my intent. I know I can be blunt sometimes." She licked her bottom lip. This whole girl-talk thing was so out of her comfort zone. She'd always been awkward when it came to expressing her feelings, especially when it came to small talk and conversation to cultivate a friendship. She learned early in life that if you hitched your feelings to another person no matter how simple and innocent, you were bound to be hurt because relationships don't last. She reached for her glass and finished off her drink, but no matter how many drinks, how many successful surgeries, how many accolades, none of it mattered because the ones she loved and trusted left her.

Anna tugged in a breath. "Nothing came easy for me."

Dina raised her gaze from her plate of grilled zucchini and pasta. "Meaning?"

"Oldest of six." Her lips pinched together. "Always had to be the responsible one. Got a job after school when I was only thirteen. My mother was rarely home. My father —" she reached for her glass and her eyes narrowed "— he could be any number of people." She snorted a laugh, drew in a breath, then leveled her gaze on Dina. "Sad. Huh?"

"I'm sorry," Dina gently said. "But look at what you've accomplished, Anna. Despite tough beginnings."

"I suppose I should count myself lucky." She pushed her salad around in the bowl, then stabbed the lettuce with her fork.

Dina winced. "So where . . . did you grow

up? Here in DC?"

"Philadelphia."

"Hmm." She chewed slowly.

"Oh look who's here." Anna lifted her dimpled chin in the direction of the door.

Dina glanced over her shoulder and her pulse quickened. Franklin Grant. "Everyone gets hungry." She turned away and focused on breathing.

Anna waved to signal him.

Dina wrapped her fingers around her glass, but didn't dare lift it to her lips. She swore she felt him approach. But he stopped at the table three rows over and began talking to one of the doctors she recognized from the hospital.

"Wow," Anna snapped. "Talk about being ignored."

Inwardly Dina rolled her eyes. "Probably didn't see you. Stop taking everything so personal," she said, relieved that he hadn't come to their table.

Anna leaned in and lowered her voice. "I guess all the rumors about Dr. Grant are true."

"What rumors?"

"Elitist and smug."

Dina set down her fork and rested her forearms on the table. "Do you believe everything you hear? He's smug and elitist because he didn't notice us in a crowded and, might I add, dimly lit restaurant?" She wanted to tell her how off base she was about Franklin Grant. Anna hadn't seen the fun-loving, athletic man that she'd viewed in the park playing with his brothers, or the suddenly uncertain man who'd asked her to accompany him to his parents' anniversary party. She had, and she wasn't going to be the one to inform Anna otherwise.

Anna sighed. "You're probably right. But speaking of sexy if not 'smug' men, anyone special in your life?"

Dina kept her gaze focused on her food. "Really don't have time. I didn't travel all the way across the country to find a love connection," she said, trying to lighten her tone. "I'm here for work."

"Of course there's that, but come on, Dina. You're still a woman."

That she was, and keeping her attraction to Franklin Grant under wraps was becoming more difficult on a daily basis. She had to keep reminding herself that her goal was to finish her fellowship and land an attending position. She'd been down the relationship road before; it was a painful distraction and a reminder that people you care about leave. She couldn't let that happen again, no matter how tempting the "smug" Dr.

Grant was.

Dina filled her fork with zucchini and lifted it to her mouth. "Yes, a woman with a focus. What about you?" She chewed slowly.

Anna tucked a stray strand of silky hair back into her trademark topknot hairstyle. "Well, nothing steady, but there is a guy that I've been seeing."

"Doctor?"

"Hell no." She sputtered a laugh. "Too much ego in one relationship. I try to steer clear of men in the medical profession. Although from time to time when the chemistry was right I have made an exception." She winked.

"Do tell." Dina caught movement in her peripheral vision. Her heart thumped. She saw Anna's lips moving, but the only thing she could process was his presence.

"Dr. Lorde . . . Dr. Hamilton. I thought it was you two."

He was standing directly behind her. His large fingers rested on the back of her chair. If she moved even in the slightest, his fingertips would brush the back of her neck.

"I noticed you when you came in. That's Dr. Fischer isn't it?" Anna asked, all teeth.

Franklin briefly glanced over his shoulder. "Yes, it is." He cleared his throat.

"You're welcome to join us. I'm sure the

waitress can make room," Anna said.

"Thanks for the offer, just wanted to say hello. Have a good evening."

The flutter in Dina's throat kept her from responding. She barely glanced up offering only a tight-lipped smile. The hairs on the back of her neck electrified as he walked away.

"You, too," Anna called out. She turned her attention to Dina. "If you were any more disconnected you wouldn't have been here," Anna said.

Dina settled her gaze on Anna. "What does that mean?"

"You acted like he wasn't even here. Playing nice will get us ahead."

"I was nice. We just saw each other a couple of hours ago — long hours I might add."

Anna blew out a breath. "Whatever. Now, Dr. Grant would make the perfect mentor. With him as a patron . . . Anyway . . ."

Anna prattled on, but Dina wasn't really listening. All she could think about was how turned on she'd gotten with Franklin standing so close. It was crazy. He was a colleague, and she didn't get all worked up over a man — at least she hadn't until now, and that was a problem.

CHAPTER 8

Franklin returned to his table and settled in his seat. He didn't make it a habit of frequenting the local hospital hangout. After one drink too many the lines of the personal and professional generally collided and not always for the best. However, today he'd made an exception when Dr. Fischer asked if he'd listen to an idea he had for a prototype for heart valve replacement. Fischer suggested The Bottom. The last person he'd expected to see there was Dina. He'd gotten the impression from her that she wasn't the crowd-gathering type either. Obviously he was wrong.

The waitress brought them their drinks and Fischer launched into the details of his idea that he said he'd been working on for the past two years.

Franklin listened, or half-listened, nodding and ummhmming at all the appropriate places. His thoughts kept shifting to

Dina. Subtly he stole glances in her direction, maybe to catch her eye; he wasn't sure. He watched the way she lifted her glass, tilted her head, tucked stray hair behind her ears and pensively chewed her food while it appeared that Anna prattled on nonstop. What if she did suddenly turn and look at him, caught him staring?

"So do you think I have a shot presenting to the board?"

Franklin blinked Fischer back into focus. "I don't see why not." He took a long swallow from his glass. "Sounds very promising. There would have to be clinical trials."

"Of course. Of course." His voice lifted with excitement. "A word from you would definitely give me the push I need with the board," he said, his pale cheeks flaming red.

So that's what this was really about. Franklin blew out a breath, wrapped his hands around his glass and leaned in. "I . . . don't make a habit of endorsing experimental procedures or prototypes. The waters can get very murky when that happens. I can't have every surgeon or resident on my team coming to me asking for a 'get me in the door' ticket. What I will do is take a look at your research and when you —" he pointed a finger at Fischer "— are ready to present, if it is all that you claim it is, I'll give you my support."

Fisher bobbed his head, his ginger hair gleaming under the light. "Fair enough. I didn't mean to overstep. I just thought —"

Franklin raised his hand to halt any apology. "It's okay." He picked up the plastic menu. "Let's order. I'm actually hungry." He lifted his gaze above the top of the menu and collided with Dina's smoldering eyes. It was only an instant, but long enough to send a jolt through his system. She was alone and almost looked as if she smiled at him — almost. Anna returned, momentarily blocking his view of Dina and severing the electric wire.

Franklin cleared his throat, tossed back the rest of his drink and set the glass down. "On second thought I'm going to have to take a rain check on dinner. I have a surgery in the morning."

"Oh. Uh, sure."

Franklin pulled out his wallet and put a twenty on the table. He pushed his chair back and stood. "Keep me posted on your progress."

Fischer nodded. "Thank you. I will."

Franklin gave a short nod, grabbed his jacket from the back of the chair and walked toward the exit. Briefly he looked toward the table where Dina was seated. Anna was turned away talking to two doctors. Dina slid out of her chair and walked over to him.

"Leaving? Did you even get a chance to eat?" she asked looking him in the eye.

"Early day tomorrow."

Dina pressed her lips together and nodded with understanding.

"How long are you staying?"

Her eyes sparkled. She ran her tongue across her bottom lip. "I'm actually ready to call it a night myself." Her gaze slid back to her table. Anna was in full conversation mode.

"I'm probably going to grab something on my way home. This place is a little too crowded for me. There's a great diner not far from my house. Reds."

Her eyes widened. "I know the place. Delish burgers."

Franklin chuckled. "That they do." He slid his hands into his pockets to keep from touching her like he'd wanted to do from the instant he stood behind her chair.

"The food here isn't all it's cracked up to be. I'm still hungry."

Franklin swallowed. Snatched a look in Anna's direction. He and Dina were blocked from view by a large group that was standing around with their drinks. "I'll probably be there for an hour or so if you decide to drop in. I'll save you a seat."

"I just might do that."

He gave a short nod, turned and strode out.

Dina sucked in a shaky breath. What she wanted to do was slide her hand in his and walk out into the balmy spring night with him. She wanted to nestle under his arm while they strolled along Constitution Avenue and inhale the intoxicating scent of him. But she'd settle for a cheeseburger with all the fixings and a side of sweet potato fries.

CHAPTER 9

Dina returned to her table and slid into her seat moments before Anna's laughter ended and she swung back around to her table mate, her face beaming.

"Isn't Kara hysterical? She has that Nurse Ratched attitude perfected, down to the arching right brow every time you ask her a damned question." She snatched up her glass and took a swallow. Her eyes caught the light.

Dina didn't engage. She pushed her pasta around on her plate while mentally counting how long she should wait before she made her exit. Besides, the last thing she wanted was to get dragged into a conversation dishing on some other woman. She knew from experience what that felt like, being on the listening end of a group of interns virtually tearing her to shreds simply because she chose to work a third shift knowing it was the toughest and would challenge her. She was called all kinds of butt-kisser names. The experience wounded her in a way that she, at first, couldn't process. She naively believed that these young women whom she stood shoulder to shoulder with every day, battling life and death, were not only colleagues, but her friends. Lesson learned. She took her napkin and dabbed at the corners of her mouth.

"Hey, listen, I'm beat. I'm going to call it a night. Early call in the morning."

Anna blinked. Her glass held in midair, inches away from her lips. She tipped her head to the side, her brows pinched. "Really? I thought you didn't have to go in until noon?"

Dina didn't flinch. "Earlier than the late shift." She smiled, put her napkin down and reached for her purse. The last thing she was going to do was explain herself to Anna. She took out her wallet.

Anna held up her hand. "No. I got this. I invited you." She flashed a smile.

"I always pay my share." She pulled out two twenties. "That should cover my end plus a tip." She pushed her chair back and stood. "Thanks for the invite. I need to get out more."

"Sure. Anytime. I'll probably leave in a little while myself." She gave a short shrug.

"Guess I'll join Kara and company for a bit."

Dina nodded. "Get home safely and thanks again. I'll see you tomorrow." She hooked her bag over her shoulder and took her jacket from the back of her chair, draped it across her arm.

Anna stretched her neck, looked around Dina. "Looks like Dr. Tall-Dark-and-Handsome has left the building." Her gaze slid to Dina's.

"Who?"

"Dr. Grant."

"Oh." Dina feigned a glance over her shoulder. She drew in a breath. "See you tomorrow," she said, leaned down and patted Anna's hand before turning and walking out.

Once outside she slowly shook her head and pushed out a breath of relief. What was she thinking in agreeing to have dinner with Anna Lorde? The past hour was more of a strain than surgery. She proceeded down the block to where she'd parked her car. It wasn't that she didn't like Anna. She did have good qualities. She could be funny. She was smart, a good doctor. It was . . . there were just those little snarky things about Anna that rubbed her the wrong way. The way she was always ready to undercut someone, and her deep-seated "us against them" mentality. She frowned. The chirp of her car alarm disengaged the locks. She looked right, left, then opened the door, an old habit from growing up in the hood.

She slid behind the wheel, dropped her purse on the passenger seat and engaged the locks before putting on her seat belt. If she remembered correctly, Reds was an easy fifteen minutes away. She turned on the ignition and the sound of Childish Gambino's "This Is America" pumped through the speakers. When the song was released, it took the music industry and the world by storm. The messages were raw and unapologetic. Long after its debut the lyrics and the images still resonated. She put the track on a permanent place of honor on her go-to music playlist.

Dina eased out of her parking space and into the light evening traffic. She stopped at the intersection. At the mouth of the horizon, the light from the Washington Monument lit the sky. A beacon of hope or a spotlight on the rubble that was becoming America?

She made a left.

CHAPTER 10

Franklin had been at Reds nearly forty minutes. He'd ordered a drink and waited to choose his meal in the vague hope that Dina would actually show up and join him. Why was he even doing this? Taking up with a colleague, albeit a hot, sexy, brilliant one, was not his MO.

He slowly rotated his glass in a circular motion and watched the ice swim in a pool of warm amber. It was probably best that Dina didn't show up. It was enough that he'd been so foolish to ask her to attend the anniversary party. What the hell was it about Dina Hamilton that made him —

"Hi. Took forever to find a parking space."

He looked up from the depths of his drink and his gut seesawed at the sight of her. He started to get up to help her into her seat, but she'd already slid into the booth before he'd gotten to his feet.

"Glad you could make it," he said, hoping

to sound casual.

She smiled and linked her slender fingers together on top of the table. "Me, too." She took a quick look around. "Kind of crowded for a Tuesday night, huh." Her gaze swung back to him. "Did you order?"

"No. Figured I'd wait."

Her long, lowered lashes shielded her eyes. "And what if I didn't come," she asked, her voice suddenly smoky.

Franklin's jaw clenched. Her words were loaded with innuendo. At least he thought so. Maybe he was hearing what he wanted to hear. The right corner of his mouth lifted. "Now that you've come . . . we can order."

Her tongue peeked out and laved her bottom lip. "I'm beyond hungry." She picked up the menu.

Her face was hidden behind the menu and it was just as well. It gave him a minute to pull himself together. He felt like he'd been body snatched. This was so out of character for him. Of course he was no monk. He enjoyed the company and pleasures of a woman like any other man, but on the job flings rarely turned out well. And when they didn't there was always the awkwardness of still having to work together. Besides, after her fellowship was done, she'd leave. So, what was the point in starting something that already had a time stamp on it?

"I think I'll have my go-to," she said, jerking him out of his wandering thoughts. She put the menu down and turned her focus all on him.

His groin tightened. He shifted in his seat. "Burger and fries?"

"Yep. You?"

"Same."

As if on cue the waitress came to take their order.

Dina linked her long fingers together on top of the table and slowly glanced around. "When I first got here from California I must have trolled the restaurants and burger spots for about a month before I found Reds." She grinned at the memory. "From then on this was my spot."

"I'd think all you West Coasters would be vegans," he said with a light chuckle.

Her brows rose to an *Oh really* arch. "Don't believe everything you hear. I mean I do make every effort to eat healthy on a regular basis, but I can't do the vegan thing because I love a good thick burger from time to time."

Franklin swallowed. Was she messing with his head? Everything she said seemed to have a double meaning, like she was baiting him, reeling him in. That's crazy thinking.

Must be him. Letting his imagination run wild, seeing stuff that really wasn't there.

"I saw on the board that you have a pretty complicated surgery tomorrow."

Franklin lifted his glass of water, took a swallow. "Yes, a reconstruction."

"I'd like to scrub in if that's okay."

His lips quirked. "I don't see that as a problem."

"Great."

"I didn't know that you and Dr. Lorde were . . . friends."

"I wouldn't exactly call us friends . . . colleagues, yes." She pushed out a breath, lowered her gaze. "Like I mentioned before, I don't really know anyone here outside work. I'm not what most would call outgoing." She laughed lightly. "And I'm pretty picky when it comes to friends or anyone getting close to me."

On that note they were very much alike. Other than his brothers he was short on the close male friend scale and as for women, once burned twice shy. He chose slow and wise. Her gaze suddenly landed right on his and a shock jolted up his back. He moved his water glass in a slow circle on the table.

"Anna . . . Dr. Lorde has been asking me for weeks to come have a drink or lunch or whatever. I finally gave in." She pointed a

74

finger in his direction. "But I really didn't take you as someone that would go to The Bottom. You don't come across as the mix-and-mingle type."

"Touché. I'm not. Dr. Fischer wanted to talk outside the hospital. That was the closest place."

"Guess we both got wrangled into doing something we wouldn't normally do by people we wouldn't normally hang out with." She tipped her head to the side and smiled at him. "And here we are. Together. Funny how things work out."

His gaze slowly moved over her face. He wanted to touch her, see if her cheek was as soft as it was flawless, or if her lips were as sweet as the glossy fruits they appeared to be. "Yeah, funny," he finally said.

The waitress arrived with their food and the moments of any awkwardness were filled with the clicking of silver against plates and murmurs of pass this or that across the table.

Dina's eyes closed with pleasure as she slowly chewed on her first bite of the burger. Her tongue peeked out to grab a crumb from the corner of her mouth. She hummed deep in her throat and Franklin thought this was the most erotic thing he'd ever witnessed. His nostrils flared as he sucked in air and forced himself to concentrate on the food in front of him, not across from him.

"Did you see the news today about the latest immigration debacle?" Dina asked out of the blue.

Franklin speared a French fry and groaned. He slowly shook his head in disgust. "I can't wrap my head around what's going on. It's horrific what's happening to those families."

Dina put down her fork and leaned forward. The intensity in her eyes held Franklin immobile.

"As a health care provider and understanding trauma — that's not always physical," she added, pointing her finger, "my heart breaks knowing what they're dealing with. What happened to our humanity?"

"What's most disturbing is that what is happening at the borders is symptomatic of much deeper issues that we have in this country."

Dina heaved a heavy sigh. "Exactly."

Their conversation, fueled by their individual passions, touched on politics, gentrification, books and movies. There were so many things they had in common from their love of burgers to sci-fi and horror novels, and really scary movies. They both enjoyed bike riding and were avid gym members. Surprisingly after talking and laughing for more than an hour they hadn't spoken one word about work. They laughed at the same things and like mischievous teens they bent their heads together and whispered sweet and all-too-funny fictional stories about the customers who came in that cracked them up to a point that they had heads turning in their direction. They snickered under their breaths and mouthed apologies, then laughed some more.

"This was . . . really nice," Dina said. "Thank you for the invitation."

She looked across at him with an expression that Franklin couldn't define other than it stirred him like a spoon swirling in a simmering pot. Franklin pushed his empty plate aside. "We work pretty much side by side every day. I've even gone so far as to ask you to my parents' anniversary party." He paused. "And to be honest . . . until tonight I really didn't know anything about you."

"Now that you do, are you taking the party invitation back?"

His eyes picked up the sparkle from the overhead lights and crinkled at the edges. "To be honest . . . when I asked I wasn't thinking. At all. I considered taking it back, but knew that was totally not cool. Now . . ."

He watched her tug in a breath and her breasts rise and fall. "I'm glad I asked and that I didn't take it back."

She waited a beat. "So am I," she said softly. "I don't care what they say about you," she teased, "you're a really great guy."

He tossed his head back and chuckled. "Really, and what are they saying about me, that I'm a cold, hard-assed, tunnel-visioned workaholic, and that I don't accept mediocrity?"

Dina scrunched her face. "Sort of. But —" she held up her hand and her amused expression sobered "— I can testify that none of that is true — well, almost none of it," she said with a half smile. "I can easily say when you get to know him, he's smart and funny, has a quirky sense of humor, is family oriented, has a myriad of interests . . ." She stopped in midsentence, lowered her head for a moment. "I'm sorry. Rambling."

"What are the parts that are true?"

She glanced up. "You *are* a workaholic. You *don't* accept mediocrity. I totally get it. I'm the same way. My work, my career are the centerpieces of my life. I can't tolerate people who make excuses." Her expression tightened. "Don't have the luxury of family to take the edge off, I guess."

The sliver of vulnerability that hitched her voice caught Franklin off guard. He cleared his throat. "Well, after you meet my family you may want to be careful what you wish for," he teased, hoping to lift the light veil of uneasiness that settled between them. That got him a smile.

Franklin wiped his mouth one last time and pushed out a breath. He checked his watch. "Wow. It's nearly eleven."

"What? We've been here for three hours? I'm surprised they didn't throw us out."

He signaled for the waitress. "How 'bout that?" he murmured as he reached for his wallet inside his jacket pocket.

Dina went for her purse.

He held up his hand. "I got it."

She leaned back and studied him from beneath her lashes. "That would make this something like a date, Dr. Grant."

He pulled his black card from his wallet and slid it inside the slim leather portfolio with the check. "What if it is?"

Well just damn. She was speechless. She blinked. Tried to think of something smart and funny to say. She had nothing. Going with him as his plus-one to an anniversary party as a colleague was one thing — a date was completely different. But she knew it was what she wanted — for it to be something different, even if only for a little while.

CHAPTER 11

"Where did you park?" Franklin asked as they stepped out into the night.

His hand rested at the small of her back and sent waves of tingling heat flowing through her. Her thoughts fogged. It took her a second to process what he'd asked her. He needed to get his hand off her as much as she wanted it to stay put.

"Um, on the next block." She fiddled with adjusting the strap of her tote up on her shoulder. That hand was still there. She wanted to turn right into him, press herself against him. Her breathing kicked up a notch as she inhaled the subtle scent of him.

"I'll walk you to your car."

With his hand firmly in place they started off in the direction of her parked car.

The DC streets had finally settled down for the night, with only a few determined nighthawks out and about. It was that perfect kind of night, unusually clear skies dusted with stars, a light breeze — a night for lovers.

Hmm . . . when was the last time she was out with a man — who mattered to her — on a night like this? She couldn't remember. But if she allowed herself to imagine that this really was a date . . . with Franklin Grant, then she could imagine everything that came with it: the searing parting kiss, the hesitant invitation to come in for a nightcap, followed by some soft music and . . .

"The surgery tomorrow is at ten."

She blinked out of her fantasy. "Yes. Of course. I'll be there." She stopped in front of her car. "Thanks again for this evening. I don't think I realized how much I needed to get out and actually have some fun."

"Neither did I."

She held her breath and felt her heart pounding.

He angled his head to the side, smiled. "Do you have your keys?"

She sputtered a short laugh. "Yeah, guess I'm more tired than I thought." She dug in her purse for her car keys.

Franklin nipped the keys from her fingers, pressed the unlock icon on the fob. The car chirped. He leaned in, reached around her and opened the door.

He was so close she could almost bury her face in his chest. Every nerve ending was on high alert. Somehow she managed to get behind the wheel without making a fool of herself. She looked up at him. He was smiling like he was thinking the same things she was. She should ask him . . .

"See you in the morning. Drive safe."

She managed to nod her head. "You, too."

He handed her the keys, stepped back and closed her door.

Her fingers shook ever so slightly as she inserted the key into the ignition. She pressed the button in the armrest and lowered the window. "Thanks again," she softly said.

He gave a short nod, tapped the roof of her car and walked off in the opposite direction.

CHAPTER 12

Under the beat of the shower Dina replayed her evening, specifically all the parts that had Franklin Grant in them. She reached for the almond butter shower gel, dropped a dollop on her loofah, closed her eyes and lifted her face to the cascade of water. Steam enveloped her. Slowly massaging the lathering gel across her skin she envisioned the moment she saw Franklin walk into The Bottom. That funny fluttering feeling began in the pit of her stomach, spread to her limbs and clouded her thoughts. All of that only intensified when she sat across from him at Reds. She slowly rubbed the loofah across her breasts and down her belly, the soapy water sluicing between her thighs, along her legs; she was relishing the sensual feel. Franklin Grant affected her that way, seeming to effortlessly enter her space, heighten her awareness, touch her in secret places. Her hands were his hands. A tiny shiver shimmied down the curve of her spine. Her eyes flew open. What would Franklin's very skilled hands feel like exploring her body?

She'd watched him during surgery, self-contained, totally in control while subtly commanding the best from everyone in the room. Tunnel-vision focus, steady, strong hands, able with the pads of his fingers and eyes closed to locate exactly what needed to be healed.

Dina drew in a shaky breath, turned her body round beneath the water and rinsed the suds away. Would he be as thorough with the parts of her that needed to be soothed, reawakened, healed?

She turned off the water, stepped out of the shower, determined for the moment to satisfy herself with possibility.

Franklin stood in front of the floor-to-ceiling window of his condo that looked out onto the DC skyline. He held a glass of bourbon in one hand. Smiled. She'd said she'd pegged him for a bourbon kind of guy. He took a swallow. His lids fluttered closed as the amber liquid lit a small fire in his belly. She knew him — intimately — not the strip-out-of-your-clothes-and-hop-into-bed kind of intimate, but the kind that knew your mind, read your thoughts, anticipated your needs, could be by your side in absolute silence and still communicate. Surgery, having the power of life and death in your hands and depending on the person next to you birthed a particular kind of intimacy. You had to get to know each other in ways that were inexplicable to outsiders. It wasn't often that as the team leader you found the perfect one. When you did it was pure magic. He took another swallow and turned away from the twinkling lights that presented the illusion of a fairy tale.

Dina Hamilton. He steered clear of office flings, but this thing he had for Dina threw his rule right out the window. But at the end of her time at Jameson, he'd simply sign off on her fellowship paperwork, give his recommendations and she'd move on and so would he. So . . . what would be the harm in stoking the embers? It was bound to end anyway.

"Amazing work in there, Dr. Grant," Dina said as they pulled off scrubs and deposited them in the bins the next day.

"I have a great team." He tugged off his surgical cap. "Glad you're part of it, Dr. Hamilton," he added.

She glanced up at him. Her insides shifted

when he stared back at her. "So am I."

He gave a short nod, tossed his cap in the bin and walked out.

Dina released a breath she hadn't realized she'd held.

Claire, one of the surgical nurses, came up alongside her at the sink. "He can be a little stiff at times, but he's great to work for." She lowered her voice and glanced over her shoulder to ensure they were alone. "Every nurse on this service has the hots for him, but he doesn't give any of us the time of day. Strictly professional."

"Hmm," Dina murmured, secretly pleased but undaunted. Dina washed and dried her hands. "Probably for the best."

"Probably. Some of the other doctors around here could take a lesson from Dr. Grant on keeping the lines of business and pleasure separate." She shook her head and rolled her eyes. "The stories I could tell." She huffed, tossed her gown in the bin. "Have a good day, Doctor."

"You, too."

Dina stared through the glass partition that opened onto the operating theater. Franklin Grant was as complex as the surgeries that he performed. He gave off the impression that he was aloof, cold, a strictly by-the-book professional, one who would never become involved with a colleague. She saw a different Franklin Grant, someone who laughed, loved good music, enjoyed a strong shot of bourbon, was a surgical genius and was willing to cross that invisible line. At the same time downplaying the crossing as no more than business as usual. Why did he allow her to get a look behind the walls that he'd erected around himself?

Franklin returned to his office to unwind from the grueling four-hour surgery. He dimmed the lights, booted up SiriusXM on his computer to classic jazz, then stretched out on his office couch. He threw his arm across his eyes and drifted along with the music. Music always soothed him going as far back to when he was a kid. As the eldest, a lot of responsibility was put on him to look after his brothers and keep them in line. Alonzo and Montgomery did everything in their little powers to make his life miserable. Music was the one thing that put them on chill. They mimicked Boyz II Men, New Edition and Jodeci and swore they were going to be stars.

" 'Round Midnight" by Thelonious Monk filtered through the small desk speakers. Franklin felt his body unwind along with the melody. It was one of his favorite pieces, copied by several jazz masters but none could match Monk's original. He'd been in a debate with his brothers about that very topic during a hospital fundraiser when Lindsay Gray entered the conversation siding with Franklin. *A beautiful woman who was a jazz aficionado.* He had no other choice than to ask her to dance. She fit perfectly in his arms and moved with him as if this was something they'd always done. She was beautiful, a skilled dancer and she was also the CEO of Media Corp., the organization that controlled the public relations messages and managed foundation galas for a string of hospitals in DC, Jameson Memorial being one of them.

That night was the first of many. Through the next two years he strengthened his career, built one of the most renowned thoracic surgery departments in the country and fell in love with Lindsay. At least he thought it was love.

He jerked at the sound of knocking. Inwardly he groaned, swung his legs to the floor, got up and went to the door.

"Dina . . . Dr. Hamilton." He cleared his throat. "Something happen with the patient?"

Soft music floated out to greet her. She dipped her hands into the pockets of her lab coat. "No. Patient is out of recovery. I just came from his room."

He stood in the doorway . . . waiting.

"Um, I wanted to ask about Saturday night. The anniversary party."

"Oh." His brows shot up. "Yeah. Come in." He finally stepped aside and wished he'd had the presence of mind to turn up the lights. He shut the door behind her.

Dina turned in a slow half circle taking in the relaxing ambiance. "Nice music. Was that ' 'Round Midnight' that I heard?"

Franklin smiled. "Yeah. As a matter of fact it was. Good ear."

"Hmm, my dad was a would-be trumpeter. I've been listening to jazz long before I could even talk," she said laughing lightly.

"Guess we didn't get that far last night."

Dina swallowed. Her gaze settled on him, wouldn't let him go.

"So about the anniversary. I thought I could pick you up about seven."

"That's fine." She held out her hand.

He frowned in question.

"Phone. I'll put in my number."

He walked around her to his desk, stealing looks along the way. There was something softer, more vulnerable about her in the low lighting. He picked up his cell phone and came to stand in front of her —

close, very close.

"Password."

He tapped in his password, then handed over his phone.

Dina put in her number and gave the phone back. "Text me for the address." She brushed by him, stopped and turned back around. "I'm really looking forward to Saturday." She opened the door. "See you at seven."

Franklin sat on the edge of his desk. He was looking forward to Saturday, too.

CHAPTER 13

Dina hadn't been to a formal-type gathering in longer than she could remember. Franklin wasn't the best in terms of details on what to wear. But since it was being hosted at one of the ritzy boutique hotels, she opted to go semiformal with a cocktail dress. She'd had to buy a pair of shoes, since her repertoire consisted of soft-soled shoes for work and sneakers for jogging and the gym. After trying on the sexy sling-backs and walking through her apartment, she wasn't sure if she'd make it through the night, but at least she would look good.

With a full two hours before Franklin was due to pick her up, she took a long relaxing bath before getting ready. When she'd been dress shopping — she knew her selection would make Franklin's eyes pop — she'd made a stop at Victoria's Secret in Union Station. She leaned back against the lip of the tub, closed her eyes and smiled. If he was lucky enough to get beyond the slinky fabric and angel-hair straps of her dress he would be in for an extra treat.

Seated on the side of her bed, wrapped in a towel, she massaged her legs, hips and thighs with body butter and thought about how long it had been since she'd been touched by a man. Maybe that was why she was projecting so hard onto Franklin. Sure, he seemed interested, but he'd made no real effort to do much about it, and the word throughout the hospital was that he was a stand-up guy. Even his invitation to this party didn't seem to be romantically motivated, but rather out of a sense of pity for her.

With these thoughts running through her head, she moved on to applying makeup. Finally, she put down the tube of lipstick and stared at her reflection in the mirror. She refused to be pitied. For the past twenty years she'd done everything in her power to move beyond a sad history that seemed to mark her as an object of sympathy. Her fledgling family and fair-weather friends all felt sorry for poor Dina Hamilton, yet they'd done little to lift her burden. She blinked away the past. She wasn't that girl anymore.

By the time she'd dressed, done her hair

and makeup, that dark mood of earlier had dissipated, replaced with a giddy excitement, even as her good senses told her not to make more out of it than it was.

When her doorbell rang at seven on the dot, her stomach actually did the butterfly flutter. She drew in a breath, schooled her expression to cool and opened the door. *Hot damn.* She sucked in a short breath. There was nothing like a good-looking man in a tux. But this good-looking man took it to the next level. Franklin Grant transformed from simply desirable to must have. His hard-roped frame encased in black was as sexy as it was dangerous. Black-panther sleek, strong, in control, ready to pounce at will.

"Hi," she managed.

Whatever he expected it wasn't the woman standing in front of him. *Man.* This was supposed to be a simple evening out with a colleague who was helping him out as his date. How the hell could it be simple when she looked like that — sexy, classy and edible all at once? That dress, all slingy straps and shimmering black beaded fabric that hugged her waist then flared above her knees showcasing legs, incredible long — wraparound-you legs.

Her soft greeting drew him to her mouth,

her eyes. He cleared his throat. "You look . . . incredible."

"We both clean up nicely."

Franklin chuckled. The tight knot in his belly unwound. "You certainly do." He slipped his hands into the pockets of his tuxedo slacks.

"Thank you. Umm, you have a minute to come in? Just need to get my things." She stepped aside.

"Sure." He walked in behind Dina into the front room.

"Be right back."

He watched her swirl away; the swish of delicate fabric lifted around her knees drawing his eyes back to those dancer legs that begged him to follow. His groin tightened. *Trucks, trucks, trucks.* He strolled fully into the room. The off-white area gave the impression of space, clean lines, plenty of books, a decent-looking sound system and music collection. The gray sectional dominated the center of the room. What seemed to be missing was anything personal. There were no photos or anything that indicated an extension of herself — family, friends. Nothing out of place, almost too perfect. Did it always look this way or just tonight? *Oh, right, she only cleans up because you are coming.* Probably because she has no long-term plans to stay here. No point in making a place home if it's not going to be.

"Ready."

He turned toward her and once again was awestruck. Dina stood in the doorway and his gaze was magnetically drawn along the soft curves of her body perfectly draped in this crazy black dress that played hide-and-seek with her body and his mind. Was that some kind of halo floating around her? Crazy. "Yes." He checked his watch to clear his head. "We should get going."

Dina led the way to the door. Franklin opened it and they stepped out into early evening, that time of year that held on to the light breeze of spring while reaching for the long lazy days of summer, bordering on perfect.

He turned to take her hand as she descended the three steps to the landing. Felt good, holding her hand and seeing the way her eyes seemed to light up when she looked at him. But he had to keep his head on straight, couldn't get ahead of himself. This was just one night.

Franklin held open the door to the midnight-blue Jaguar and Dina slid onto the butter-soft fabric that gently cupped her like a sweet dream. He got in behind the wheel, turned the key in the ignition; the seat belts slid into place and a whisper of music brushed around them.

"Air or window?" he asked.

"Window is fine. Beautiful night."

That's not all. He pressed a button in the armrest and the windows lowered halfway. The distant sound of a siren mixed with car horns, compliments of inner-city living, echoed in the air. They pulled off.

"I've heard good things about the MG Empire," Dina said.

"Really?" He hid a smile.

"The rooms are sleek, totally upscale. The service is top-notch." She adjusted her black clutch purse on her lap.

"I'll introduce you to the owner. I'm sure he'd be happy to hear."

She angled her body toward him. "You know the owner?"

"Yeah." He chuckled, snatched a look at her then back on the road. "My younger brother Montgomery. You could say he's into real estate."

"Wait." She held up her hand. "MG? That's a chain of boutique hotels and B and Bs, right? MG . . . Montgomery Grant. He . . . your brother owns all of them?"

"Yep."

"I'm totally impressed."

Franklin snorted a laugh. "He'll be happy

to hear that, too."

"So . . . surgeon, land baron. What does your other brother do?"

"Chef. No. Let me correct that. Celebrity chef." He chuckled.

"Hmm, celebrity chef." Her arched brows rose.

"He travels all over cooking for clients. He put the menu together tonight."

"Your parents must be incredibly proud."

"We owe a lot to them."

"I'm looking forward to meeting them."

He made a turn onto Seventeenth Street NW, then headed toward the George Washington Memorial Parkway.

"It's a short ride into Alexandria," he said, bearing right onto his entrance to the parkway. "Barring traffic we should get there in about twenty minutes. According to Monty festivities are scheduled to start at eight-thirty. Schmoozing and elbow rubbing first," he added.

"Owww, schmoozing." She laughed. "Nothing like a good schmooze to kick off the night."

He liked the airy sound of her laugh, the way her mouth curved and her eyes squinted. There wasn't anything that he didn't like about Dina Hamilton. That was the problem.

The hotel was up ahead. He still hadn't decided on what charity would benefit from him winning the bet. He couldn't wait to see Monty and Zo's faces when he walked in with Dina. They should never bet against him. And as long as he kept it in the back of his mind that this whole night was no more than a business transaction, he would be just fine.

CHAPTER 14

When they pulled in front of the MG Empire one would have thought it was a premiere for the Hollywood elite. Spotlights posted at the entrance on either side of the red carpet fanned the starlit sky. Six-foot urns overflowed with calla lilies and baby's breath.

Franklin exited the car, handed off his keys to the valet and came around to help Dina out of the car.

"If this is the prelude to the rest of the evening . . ." Dina said, stepping out, clearly enjoying the ambiance. She stood inches from his chest, looked into his eyes and smiled.

He lifted his chin. "Definitely went all out," he said, taking in the scene while guiding Dina along the red carpet. This was the kind of high-end event that put Lindsay on the map. It had her signature all over it. His jaw clenched. But he knew better, Monty and Zo would never hire Lindsay after the way things went down between him and her, no matter how good she was.

"Everything okay?"

Franklin blinked, looked into Dina's concerned chocolate-brown eyes. "Yes. Fine."

"Your face got all tight for a minute."

He brushed aside the observation with a flick of his left brow. "Just wondering about the price tag."

"Price tag?"

"Monty took care of the venue, travel and room reservations for guests in and out of town. Alonzo handled the menu, liquor and staffing. I foot the bills."

"Well —" she slid her arm through the bend of his as they crossed the threshold of the hotel "— maybe you need a new profession," she teased.

Franklin chuckled. "May-be."

The doors were opened by another red-vested attendant and they were greeted in the sprawling lobby by a hostess carrying a tray of champagne. Franklin took one for himself and another for Dina.

"Fan-cy," she teased.

Franklin touched his glass to hers and took a sip of champagne as they crossed the lobby that had been repurposed into the main reception area. Gone were the patterned, overstuffed couches, chaise lounges and low wood tables. Instead the gray marble floors were topped with waist-high tables draped in heavy white linen tablecloths and scented votive centerpieces. Waitstaff, who looked like they'd been pulled from the pages of *Vogue,* decked in black and white, moved seamlessly around the room carrying silver trays of mini appetizers of sea scallops, all manner of pâté, oysters on the half shell, Mediterranean vegetables, imported cheeses and sliders.

"They can't be *all* family," Dina said, taking in the sparkling and tuxedoed gathering.

Franklin chuckled, took a sip of his drink, looked around. "A pretty healthy mix. Cousins, aunts, uncles, but mostly friends and former coworkers of my folks. My mother is a member of three or four community organizations. I lost count *and* she's a Delta. And my dad is an Alpha man so plenty of frat brothers in place." He lifted his hand and waved to someone across the room. "Aunt Celeste," he said under his breath.

"Mother's or father's side?"

"Neither. She's what we call a 'play auntie.' One of my mother's childhood friends."

Dina smiled. "Ohh. I've heard of those."

"No play aunties in your family?"

She took a sip of her champagne. "No. Can't say that there were." A play aunt that loved her because she wanted to rather than had to because of blood may have changed her life and eased the pain. Her aunt Jean was her father's half sister. Did that make her a half aunt? Jean was still young, barely ten years older than Dina when she took her in. She wasn't uncaring; it was more that she still wanted to party, not babysit a teenager. For the most part Dina was left on her own. Books, studying became her comfort and her friend. She could trust science. People . . . debatable.

"There's my brother."

Dina blinked, put her smile in place.

"Let me introduce you." He placed his hand at the small of her back and guided her across the room, stopping every few feet to kiss a cheek or shake a hand.

Dina had to bite her lip to keep from laughing out loud at the side comments Franklin made about the guests, and to keep her mind off the heat of his hand, resting inches above her ass. He had a raw sense of humor that he hid beneath his cool exterior. This was a whole other side of the impenetrable Dr. Grant. And oh my God was he sexy. Effortless. She squeezed her thighs together.

"There you are." Monty beamed, set down his glass on the tabletop and stepped up to embrace his brother.

Franklin kept his arm around his brother's wide shoulder. "Monty, this is my colleague Dr. Dina Hamilton. Dina, my brother Montgomery."

There could be no doubt that they were related. Montgomery Grant was a younger version of Franklin. They shared the same hot-chocolate complexion, penetrating eyes and intriguing smile. Where Franklin was lean and muscular, Montgomery was thicker, a little broader.

"Pleasure to meet you," Dina said.

A slow smile lifted the corners of his mouth the same way that Franklin's did when he was amused. His dark eyes grew inky as he tossed Franklin a quick look. He tipped his head slightly to the side and extended his hand.

"Dr. Hamilton." His fingers enveloped hers. "I thought you looked familiar. I rarely forget a face."

"Familiar?"

"The park, a few weeks ago."

"Oh." She laughed. "Good eyes."

"Hmm, need a good eye in my line of work. Glad you could join us."

"Your hotel is amazing. I've heard nothing but good things."

"Thank you. I aim to please." He stroked the tapered shadow of his beard, clapped Franklin on the back. "Listen, bro, need to go do my host thing. The folks should arrive about eight."

"Cool. Where's Zo?"

"Working his ass off," he chuckled. "He was here a few minutes ago. Just missed him. He's supervising all the moving parts."

Franklin snorted a laugh. "Getting to see baby bro do his thing is worth the price of admission."

"Speaking of price," Monty said, "cash or check?" He winked, patted Franklin's upper arm. "Enjoy the evening, Dr. Hamilton."

"Dina."

Monty gave a short nod. "Dina." He strode off.

Dina sipped her champagne. "Thought you were footing the bills."

His dark eyes cinched in question.

"Your brother said 'cash or check.' I . . ."

Excited voices cut off any response, and a smattering of applause drew their attention toward the entrance.

In the instant of reprieve, he leaned

toward her ear, his lips mere inches away from her bare shoulder. "The guests of honor have arrived."

Dina turned her head ever so slightly, lifted her chin until they were eye to eye. She moistened her bottom lip with a tiny swipe of her tongue.

Franklin's jaw tightened. He took her flute of champagne and placed it on the tray of a passing waiter, then possessively placed his arm around her waist. "Come, I'll introduce you."

CHAPTER 15

Franklin and Dina crossed the room, so close that they moved as one. At least that's how she felt and that made it difficult for her to focus on anything but the feel of his hard body brushing rhythmically against hers, the sensation of his palm on her back, the heady scent of him that made her dizzy with need.

She heard his voice introducing her to this one and that, but nothing fully registered. Her ability to accept and retain information escaped her. Finally they reached his parents.

"Mom, Dad, this is Dr. Dina Hamilton. We work together."

"So nice to meet you both. Congratulations on your anniversary," Dina said. "That is a beautiful gown."

Ellen Grant's smile was slow before blooming into a beam of light and warmth. She took Dina's hand and encased it with both of hers. "Dr. Hamilton." She did a quick assessment. "Thank you so much for coming *and* the compliment." She reached out and cupped Franklin's chin. "She's perfect for you."

"Ellen." Louis Grant gently scolded his wife. He turned eyes identical to Franklin's on Dina. "Thank you for coming, Dr. Hamilton. You must excuse my wife. She thinks any woman with our elusive Franklin is the one."

Dina felt Franklin's body grow rigid. Subtly she rubbed his arm.

"It's so rare that he brings anyone around." Ellen sidled next to her son, barely reaching his shoulder. Her champagne-colored gown, embossed with rhinestones, shimmered under the lights of the chandeliers. She placed her delicate hands on the pleats in his white tuxedo shirt. "I want him to be as happy as we are, Louis." She lifted up on her toes and kissed Franklin's cheek, then rubbed the coral-colored lipstick away with the pad of her thumb.

Dina watched Franklin's tense expression relax under his mother's warmth.

"Are you a surgeon as well?" Louis asked.

She blinked, smiled. "Yes, I am. Specialist. I'm here on fellowship, actually."

"Where are you from originally?" Ellen

asked. She patted her coiffed silver hair that sparkled like the diamonds in her ears.

"California by way of Chicago."

"Your family must miss you," Ellen said.

"I think we'll get a drink before dinner," Franklin cut in. "Otherwise my mother will grill you until she has your birth weight. Excuse us."

She snatched a breath of relief. "Pleasure to meet you, Mr. and Mrs. Grant. Congratulations again."

"Thank you, dear." Then she added in a pseudo-whisper, "I do hope we'll talk again." Her eyes widened in delight as she was approached by a group of her sorors and was quickly enveloped in hugs and air kisses.

Franklin clasped Dina's upper arm, steered her away. "Sorry about that," he said as they walked. "My mother can be a bit much."

Dina laughed. "No problem. Really. I think she's wonderful. You have your mother's smile but you look like your dad. Same eyes, jaw . . . expression."

"So I hear."

"What did your mother mean about you never bringing anyone around?"

"I don't think she said never." He stepped up to the U-shaped check-in desk that had been converted into a bar. "Bourbon," he said to the bartender, then turned to Dina.

"I'll have an apple martini, please."

"No. She said *'rarely,'* " Dina said, picking up the conversation. She angled her body to face him. Did his bringing her to something as important as this mean something — anything? Or was she foolishly hoping?

He half shrugged. "Can't argue with that." His eyes rolled down her body, then back to settle on her lips that were slightly parted. "I have my reasons. Work is my priority. My research. Most women can't or won't deal with that."

Inwardly she winced. "I'm sure there's someone . . ."

The bartender put their drinks in front of them just as the music from the live band stopped.

"If everyone would gather in the main ballroom," came a voice through the microphones. "Dinner will be served. Please look for your assigned tables. *Bon appétit.*"

Franklin bent his arm. "Dr. Hamilton," he gallantly intoned.

She slipped her arm through his, took a quick look at his sculpted chocolate profile and her clit twitched. She wasn't sure at exactly what moment she'd decided that she was going to sleep with Franklin Grant.

What she did know for sure was that the evening was young.

CHAPTER 16

The banquet hall was located beyond the hotel bar and bank of elevators. The modulated, smiling directions of the staff to the guests were mixed with the click of heels on marble floors, the rustle of silk, satin and tulle, over bursts of musical laughter and deep baritones.

The throng of a hundred-plus guests poured like expensive wine into the glittering flute of the room that sparkled from the chandeliers above and the gleaming silver and crystal below.

The guests were greeted at the entrance by white-jacketed waiters who controlled the flow of traffic to the reserved seating where lush bowls of watercress salads already dotted the linen-topped tables.

Franklin and Dina were seated at the family table with Montgomery and his current bae Vanessa Lang — introduced as a Wall Street broker — Franklin's parents, Louis's brother Donald and his wife, Patricia, and Ellen's best friend from high school, Lisa Forde and her husband, Brian. There were two empty seats at the twelve-seat table until Alonzo strolled over with his date on his arm.

"Welcome, everyone," Alonzo greeted with an exaggerated bow.

"You outdid yourself, bro," Monty said.

Alonzo winked, adjusted his white tuxedo jacket. "It's my thing. Hey, everyone, this is Angela Moore. Angela, this is the fam. The guests of honor, Louis and Ellen, my brothers, Franklin and Monty, and their dates." He gave Franklin an extra long look. "My uncle Donald and aunt Patricia, and our play auntie and uncle Lisa and Brian Forde." The gathering at the table laughed at Alonzo's quip, even Dina.

"Nice to meet you, Angela dear," Ellen said. "So glad you could join us."

"Thank you."

Alonzo helped her into the empty seat next to his uncle and aunt. He stood behind Angela's chair. "The menu tonight is going to blow you all away. Guaranteed. And have as much as you want. Franklin's got this," he joked. "Well, duty calls." He leaned down and kissed Angela lightly on the cheek. "I'll be back for the main course. Enjoy."

"So now I've finally met all the Grant brothers," Dina said and placed the napkin on her lap. "Your parents *and* aunts and uncles." She smiled.

"Haven't scared you off yet?" He speared some salad.

"Not at all. Do you want to scare me off?" The fork was suspended between his mouth and the plate. His teeth toyed for a moment with his bottom lip. Dina watched, fascinated.

"Not anymore." The right corner of his mouth almost curved upward. His focus swung back to the task at hand.

Dina couldn't breathe. At least she thought she couldn't breathe. The air was stuck somewhere in the center of her chest. Conversation floated around her. She caught some words ". . . fifty years . . . looking good . . . beautiful . . . remember . . ." but couldn't put much together. It was a momentary out-of-body experience.

A waiter appeared and began refilling water goblets. She blinked the world back into focus. She was surrounded by love and laughter everywhere that she looked. There was a fairy-tale quality to the evening and when she stole a glance at Franklin — animatedly talking with his uncle Donald — she wondered if she was the princess for

114

the night who would go home with the prince.

From the moment that Franklin showed up on her doorstep he'd taken her breath away. Tall, richly dark, dangerously sexy, he had her giddy as if hundreds of tiny ballerinas were dancing and twirling inside her. She felt fluttering and girlish, fragile almost, under the total maleness of him that oozed from the depths of his dark eyes, the ruggedness of his voice, the electricity pulsing from the tips of his fingers. He moved with the same controlled grace out in the world — commanding his space — as he did in the operating room. In all the fairy tales, the unlikely pair always found their happiness together.

Silly woman. This was real life. But for now, she would pretend. She drew in a breath, turned her head. Franklin was staring at her with a look of hunger in his eyes. Her heart tumbled. She squeezed her thighs together.

A waiter appeared, swept away the salad plates while another waiter set the bowls of lobster bisque on the table. When she dared to look up from her bowl, Franklin was in conversation with Montgomery. *Silly girl.*

One dish after another, each more delicious than the next, was placed in front of them. Conversation and laughter bubbled, fueled by fine wine, incredible food, good company and the backdrop of the live band.

Alonzo, after seeing to the entrées and checking in on all the guests, finally joined the family table.

"Toast time," he announced after they'd finished their meals, lifting his hand to signal his brothers to their feet.

Franklin and Montgomery got up and followed Alonzo to where the band was set up at the front of the hall. The music slowly stopped. Alonzo took the mic.

"Good evening, everyone. I hope you all are having a fabulous time. Thank you for joining us in celebrating the fiftieth wedding anniversary of the greatest parents a bunch of hardheaded boys could have."

The room broke out in cheers, applause and laughter.

Alonzo passed the microphone to Montgomery.

"Mom, Dad . . ." He raised his glass of champagne. "You two are the example that I live by. Thank you for everything." He took a sip from his glass and the gathering followed suit. He passed the mic to Franklin.

Franklin looked down for a moment, then out into the crowd. "Monty, Zo and I are the men we are because of you both. Mom, your wise counsel has never failed me. Dad, your work ethic and dedication to your family showed me what a real man is. My only wish for you both is that you have many more years of health, love and happiness. Congratulations!" He lifted his glass. "To fifty more years."

"Fifty more years!" the gathering shouted.

Franklin turned to the band and mouthed a request. They launched into Luther Vandross and Gregory Hines's "There's Nothing Better Than Love," his mother's all-time favorite.

Louis rose from his seat, extended his hand to his wife and escorted her onto the dance floor. One by one other couples joined them, swaying to the music under the slowly spinning lights.

Dina looked up to find Franklin standing over her. "Dance with me." He held out his hand.

She placed her hand in his and swore her knees wobbled when she got to her feet.

Franklin guided her onto the floor and eased her close. She felt her heart bang and wondered if Franklin felt it, too.

"Enjoying yourself?"

She swallowed. "Yes. Very much. Thank you for inviting me. You have a wonderful family."

His hand moved slowly up and down the center of her back. "Did I mention how beautiful you look?"

Her eyes flew up to look at him. A half smile graced his face.

"You can tell me again."

He chuckled softly. "You look beautiful tonight."

"Thank you," she whispered. Her cheeks were on fire.

He held her a bit closer until she was one with the hard outline of his body. She rested her head on his shoulder, closed her eyes and drifted effortlessly to the music that she never wanted to end.

She longed for him. Plain and simple. So what if she only had a few months left on her fellowship? So what if they would inevitably end? Not to know him, feel him, share herself with him was a scenario that she could not imagine, no matter how brief.

The tips of his fingers brushed the back of her neck. She bit her lip to keep from moaning.

He lowered his head, teased the shell of her ear with his lips.

"Come home with me," they said in unison.

Dina's long-lashed eyes widened. Franklin grinned. "Guess the operating room isn't the only place where we think alike." He took her hand. "Get your purse. I'll get the car and meet you out front."

"Aren't you going to say good-night to everyone?"

He looked over her shoulder to his parents who were totally into each other. "They won't even notice." He gently squeezed her waist.

"See you out front." She spun away, and her pulse fluttered like crazy. Maybe fairy tales did come true.

CHAPTER 17

When Dina stepped out into the cooling evening, Franklin was at the curb waiting in front of his car looking like an advertisement for everything sensually elegant.

Damn, damn, damn he's fine.

He opened the passenger door. She inhaled a shaky breath and slid into her seat.

Franklin came around the front of the car and got in. "My place is closer," he said, turning the key in the ignition.

Dina swallowed. "Okay."

He angled his body to face her, reached out and cupped the back of her head, eased her toward him. The world disappeared as his lips touched hers, captured them, made them his.

Her body ignited from the tips of her toes to the top of her head. He groaned against her mouth, teasing her lips open with his tongue to dance with hers.

Then it was over.

Franklin pulled back, checked the mirrors and eased into traffic.

Dina ran her tongue along her bottom lip. It was still hot, still held the taste of him. She drew in a steadying breath. It didn't help. Her insides continued to flutter like loose leaves during a windstorm. She gripped her purse, stole sideways looks at him. He seemed totally unmoved as if what had just happened hadn't happened at all. Once again he was laser focused only on what was in front of him. A moment ago it was her, now it was the road. She wasn't sure how she felt about that — that he could turn off and on in a blink. It may work well in surgery, but —

"I'm pretty sure I have some wine, not big in the food department. If you want anything, we can stop on the way or order something."

"No. I'm fine."

"Okay." He pressed the button on the armrest and lowered the windows, then turned on the music.

Dina leaned back, let her body unwind to Anita Baker's "You Bring Me Joy."

"Love her," she murmured.

"I think I read somewhere that she was back on tour and coming to DC."

"Really? When she was in LA a few years

ago, I missed her. Had a surgery."

"Maybe we can make up for that."

Her lips parted, but no words came out. She blinked back her surprise. She wasn't going to read anything into what he said. But what did he mean "make up for it?" She swallowed. "Sounds . . . like a plan."

Franklin slid her a short look, half smiled, then turned his attention back to the road.

Franklin's building, the Kipling House, was on the corner of Eleventh Street SE, across from a high-end apartment building braced on either side by the Bearnaise French Bistro, an Italian deli, and Senart's Oyster and Grille Room.

Dina took it all in, trying not to look like a tourist or someone who had grown up on the south side of Chicago, surrounded by burned-out buildings, empty lots, over-priced grocery stores and violence. It was the only life she knew for fifteen years. Her mom did the best she could, worked two jobs, kept her in private school, but couldn't protect herself from what eventually killed her. Dina shook away the images. She was here. Now. She'd worked. She'd earned her life.

Franklin drove down into the under-ground garage and parked in his reserved space, next to a silver Mercedes and behind a Lexus. He came round, opened her door and helped her out.

"Need to make a stop in the lobby before going up," he said. "This way." He took her hand again. They walked to the elevator.

The doors slid soundlessly open. Dina stepped in first and when she turned, Franklin was right in front of her, surrounding her. The doors closed.

His thumb stroked her cheek. He leaned in, slid an arm around her waist, pulled her close.

Dina held her breath.

The doors opened.

Franklin bit back a laugh, guided her out.

They entered what resembled a hotel lobby complete with tan leather seating, glass tables topped with overflowing vases.

"Good evening, Dr. Grant, ma'am," the concierge greeted.

"Evening, Mark. How are you? How's the shoulder?"

Mark instinctively rubbed his left shoulder. "Getting better. I've been going to that therapist that you recommended."

"Excellent. Make sure you take your meds. Keep that pressure under control."

Mark nodded his salt-and-pepper head. "Absolutely."

"Take care." He tapped the desk, took Dina's hand again and walked over to the bank of mailboxes discreetly located around the corner from the concierge's desk, checked for his mail.

"Real good guy," Franklin said as he took his mail out. "Looks out for everyone."

"Seems like you do, too."

His sleek brows drew tight.

"His shoulder . . . the meds . . ."

"Oh." He blew it off. "It's nothing."

"It's a lot to him."

They walked to the elevator, and Franklin pressed the button for the top floor.

"The more I learn about you, the more I don't know."

He took her hand, walked back to the elevator. "Maybe it's for the best."

There were only two apartments on the fifth floor. One on either end. Franklin put his key in the lock. Motion sensors turned on the lights when they walked in.

The floor-to-ceiling windows faced them, framing the breathtaking view of the DC skyline under the stars.

Dina's gaze swept the expanse of open space from the large living area that led to the stainless steel kitchen. The furnishings were fully contemporary and totally Frank-

124

lin — sleek, defined, a cool control.

"Really nice," Dina said. She put her purse down on the couch.

Franklin walked over with a bottle of wine and two glasses. He opened the door to the terrace.

They stepped out. He handed her a glass and poured.

"Thank you. This view is incredible. How long have you lived here?"

"Almost five years." He took a sip from his glass. He eased beside her, leaned his hip against the railing. "What are your plans when you finish your fellowship?"

"Much of that depends on you."

He tipped his head to the side. "Me?"

"Yes, Dr. Grant. You hold my future in the palm of your hand," she said, looking into his eyes.

"What if you get to stay?"

"What if I don't?"

"I shouldn't have let my guard down with you," he said, and stepped closer. "Business . . . pleasure . . . never a good move." He kissed her behind her ear.

She hissed in a breath. "I'm a big girl —"

He kissed her again, longer this time. His lips trailed along her neck. "No guarantees."

"For however long it lasts . . . and no more," she said against his mouth.

"And no more." He pulled her fully against him and sealed their deal.

CHAPTER 18

Under the starlit sky Franklin stoked the embers that sparked and bloomed in her center with brushes of his fingertips across her tingling skin. The rough groans of his need heightened her sighs. Hot, barefoot, simmering with anticipation, they moved along the balcony, and Franklin slid open the door to his bedroom. The sheer drapes blew lightly in and out of the terrace door, buffeted by the night breeze.

Between sweet kisses to her eyelids, cheeks, her mouth, neck, the swell of her breasts, Franklin feasted on every inch of her that was exposed to his will.

"I want to see you," Franklin breathed hot into her ear. "All of you." He wrapped an arm around her waist and unzipped her barely there, little black dress.

The zipper soundlessly slid down its track. Dina trembled. Franklin laved the hollow of her neck, slipped one strap off her shoulder then the other. The featherlight fabric fell with a soft rustle to the floor, pooling at her feet only to reveal the body-hugging ribbon-and-lace teddy with its cut-out sides, satin straps and V-string bottom that showcased the perfect orbs of her rear and nearly did him in.

Dina reveled in the simmering look of hunger in his eyes when he feasted on what was in front of him, knowing that it was worth every penny.

Franklin reached behind her and un-snapped the teddy before burying his face deep in the valley of her breasts. He cupped the weight of them in his palms and teased the lacy covering away with his teeth.

Her nipples tightened into hard, sweet points that Franklin eagerly took into his mouth, drawing them in between his teeth. She gasped and grabbed his shoulders to steady herself.

Franklin moved down her body, peeling away the last barrier between him and what he wanted. His mouth seared her skin followed by his expert tongue that cooled it. The erotic mix of hot and cool got her slick and wet and wanting.

He was on his knees now, her hips steadied in his large hands. Dina whimpered. Her inner thighs trembled. Franklin pressed his face against the flutter of her belly, kissed her there — then lower. She gasped. Her fingertips dug into his shoulders.

His thumb slid between her wet folds, parting the glistening lips; he brushed the hard kernel of her clit with the tip of his tongue, gently suckled it.

"Ahhhh . . ." Her knees buckled but Franklin held her firmly in place. Tremors rippled through her like jolts of electric shock.

In one swift motion, Franklin lifted her off her feet. She wrapped her legs around his waist, her arms around his neck, her lips sealed with his. Their tongues dipped and danced.

He carried her to his king-size bed. Kneeling above her, he pulled off his shirt, tugged off his belt and unzipped his slacks, tossed them all to the floor.

Dina scooted back on the bed, rose up on her knees and helped relieve him of his black silk boxers.

Her breath hitched at the sight of his erection: thick, stiff, utterly beautiful. She reached for him, wrapped her fingers around the breadth of him. Franklin hissed air between his teeth.

Dina ran the pad of her thumb across the swollen head, teasing out the first dew drops while she cupped the weight of his sack in her palm.

Franklin groaned from the pit of his stomach, grabbed her hand and covered it with his.

"I want to feel you," Dina whispered, "inside me." She slid back on the bed, propped up by the thick pillows. She bent her knees, parted her thighs, extended her hand in invitation.

"Damn, woman."

On his hands and knees he moved up her body, placed kisses along the way until he was braced above her, her knees tight against his waist. He lowered his head and kissed her, long, deep and slow.

There was no turning back now. He reached into the nightstand and took out a condom packet, ripped it open.

Dina's breathing escalated. She took the condom from him. "Let me," she whispered, looking him deep in his eyes. Slowly she rolled the thin sheath along the length of him, barely covering him halfway. She smiled, tossed the empty packet aside and slid her arms around his neck. She searched his expression in the moonlight, stroked his lip with the pad of her thumb.

Franklin pressed against the wet slit of her opening. Dina gasped, held him tighter. Her eyes squeezed shut. He filled her in one long stroke that rocked them both, pushed the air out of her lungs.

Dina wrapped herself around him, wanting to melt into him, give him all of her. The feel of Franklin inside her, moving within her, was pure bliss. She whispered his name over and over as waves of pleasure rose higher and higher. She clung tighter, dizzy from the power of his thrusts. Her body was on fire, every nerve tingled.

Damn, it felt good, deep-down-to-the-soul good. He was as skilled in the bed as he was in surgery. He left no part of her unattended. His hands, his mouth pleasured her flesh while the rhythmic strokes pleasured her soul.

"Dina . . ." he groaned. "So good, baby." His movements quickened. His fingers raked through her hair, pulled her mouth against his mouth.

She could barely breathe as their pace intensified, the thrill flashed and popped. She never wanted this feeling to end, but the wave grew, gained strength. She couldn't stop it as it crested, engulfed her, pulled her under with its power. Her insides seized the full length of him, gripping and releasing him as he pushed them both over the edge.

CHAPTER 19

The force of his release stunned him, left him shaken. He wanted to stay buried deep within the velvet of her warmth. Put the world on hold. He gently stroked her hip, kissed her lightly swollen lips. Her heart pounded against his chest until his seemed to merge with hers into a single heartbeat.

He lowered his head between her neck and the pillow. Just sex. Good sex, but that was all. Simply because it felt damned good didn't mean that it was anything more than two consenting adults fulfilling a physical attraction. This was merely the endgame to a bet. Her insides flexed around him. Dammit. He was still hard. She lifted her hips.

"I need you again," she whispered in his ear and draped her legs around his back.

He lifted his head and looked at her. The wet walls gripped him again. He bit down on his lip to keep from hollering.

Dina wound her hips again.

Franklin moaned in pleasure. "Whatever you want . . ."

Dina listened to Franklin's steady breathing, felt the weight of his leg that was flung across hers, holding her in place. His heart thumped against her palm. She wasn't sure what she expected other than to have sex with a man whom she found utterly tempting. But something else happened. Maybe it had been so long since her last roll in the hay that she was thinking and feeling more than what was really happening. Sure, she'd flirted with him, just a little. She found Franklin Grant sexy, mysterious, complex and those things intrigued her. There was the rebellious part of her that wanted to break through the reserved wall he built around himself. She had no delusions that they could be "a thing." That wasn't what she came to DC for. So, whatever this was that she thought she was feeling was no more than afterglow, a fairy tale.

Her lids fluttered, grew heavy. She slept.

Franklin sat shirtless at his kitchen counter nursing his first cup of coffee while reviewing case notes on an upcoming surgery. It was complicated; the patient was high-risk but the patient along with the family —

major hospital donors — insisted that the surgery be done. He didn't feel good about it, but he was confident that the operation would be successful — difficult but successful.

He sipped his coffee. Surgery, at the moment, was the least of his concerns. This thing with Dina was a different story. Should have never happened. He'd crossed his own invisible line. Not only was she a colleague, now she was a colleague that he was falling for. Double the trouble. If things went wrong it could be problematic for them working together. But he couldn't escape the fact that it was more than good sex, scratching an itch or winning a bet.

"Good morning."

He turned halfway on the stool and was hit right in the center of his chest when he saw her. Damn. She was sexier in his oversize shirt than in that turn-on dress from the night before. She had a glow or maybe he was imaging things.

"Hey. Good morning."

She slowly crossed the room. He tried to ignore those incredible legs that had been wrapped around him. Failed. Images of her moving beneath him flashed in front of him.

"Coffee," she said, inhaling the aroma. "Please tell me there's more."

He chuckled, hopped down from his perch. "You're in luck." He took a mug from the cabinet and filled it. "Here ya go." He placed the mug in front of her. "Half-and-half and sugar right there," he said, pointing to both on the counter.

"Thanks." She slid onto a stool and fixed her coffee.

"Sleep okay?"

She glanced at him from beneath her lashes. A teasing smile lifted the corners of her mouth. She leaned her elbows on the counter and slowly brought the cup to her lips. "Like a baby. You?"

"Best night's sleep I've had in quite some time."

She sipped her coffee, studied him over the rim. "I probably should get going."

"Oh, I thought we could have breakfast." He needed to let her leave. "We can go to the restaurant downstairs. They make the best Belgian waffles."

She laughed. "And have me do the stroll of shame?"

He frowned.

"Prancing around for breakfast still dressed in my party outfit."

His eyes widened. "Ohhh. Yeah. There's that." He hesitated. "We could order. Have them deliver. Pretty sure I have a menu."

"In that case, I'm starved!"

He chuckled. "I'll find the menu." He got up.

"Um, do you mind if I use your shower?"

A vision of her naked and wet materialized in front of him. His groin tightened. "Yeah, yeah sure."

She finished her coffee, set the cup down and stood.

"Let me get you some clean towels." He led the way to the bathroom that was more like a spa.

"This bathroom is almost as big as my living room," she joked.

He chuckled. "Growing up with two brothers and having to share bath time and bedrooms, I always promised myself I'd make up for it when I had the chance." He opened a closet and took out a thick towel and washcloth.

She took the towels from him. "Seems you've come a long way on a lot of fronts."

He studied her for a moment, reached out and tucked her hair behind her ear. His finger drifted along her jaw. Her lips parted ever so slightly. "It's been a while since . . ."

"Since?"

"I woke up with someone in my bed."

He watched the pulse flutter at the base of her throat.

Her fingers went to the buttons of her shirt, unfastened them one by one without taking her eyes off him.

His jaw flexed.

She parted the shirt. Her breasts enticingly rose and fell as her breathing elevated.

He slid the shirt off her left shoulder then her right. She let it glide to the floor presenting her nakedness.

Franklin hummed with pleasure deep in his throat, taking a moment to truly feast on her in the light of day.

"You. Are. Incredible." He leaned in for a kiss.

Dina looped her arms around his neck, curved her body to seal with his. The need that they'd felt the night before to explore, discover, unwrap was now replaced with a hunger from knowing what to anticipate. Knowing what was in store, knowing what the other was capable of, the heights that could be reached. This knowing fueled their need.

Franklin's mouth, his hands took back what had been his the night before. The feel of her skin beneath his fingertips, the soft scent of her, the sensation of her hair dusting across his chest, the wet welcome between her legs, had him crazed with need. His erection was almost painful, and he nearly burst when Dina began a steady stroking of him. But it took all his self-control not to explode when she slid down to her knees and took him into her mouth.

Franklin groaned in exquisite agony. His long fingers raked through her hair, held her head as he reared back and gave himself over to her. But only for a moment. What she was doing with her mouth was pure witchcraft.

He pulled her to her feet, spun her around, leaned her over the sink and entered her in one deep thrust.

Dina cried out with pleasure, reached behind her and cupped his rear to pull him even tighter.

Their reflection in the oversize mirror was one straight out of a book of erotica and a total turn-on. Their hot, naked, sweaty bodies, wild hair, bouncing breasts and bulging muscles all created the tableau, raised their temperatures and steamed the room.

Moans, sighs and whimpers blended with the sound of damp flesh slapping against damp flesh, the tempo rising.

Franklin grabbed her hips, his fingers digging into her flesh as he pounded into her, riding toward release.

Dina grabbed the edge of the counter,

lifted up on her toes and threw him a twerk move that shot them both over the edge.

Their cries echoed off the porcelain walls.

"Damn," Franklin groaned, leaning over her. He kissed the back of her neck, slid his arms beneath her to caress her breasts.

Dina sighed as the quickening in her walls calmed and they finally released their hold on Franklin. She slowly turned herself around to face him, looked into his eyes that still held a look of hunger. "I think I'll take that shower now." She kissed his lips and sauntered off to the shower, making a show of bending and turning and testing the water.

Franklin savored the perfection of the body that had him still hard with need, and knew he was in deep trouble.

CHAPTER 20

"You were right," Dina said, closing her eyes in euphoria. "These are the best waffles I've ever tasted in my entire existence."

Franklin tossed his head back and laughed. "Could it be that we worked up an appetite?"

She gave him a sideways look, wagged her fork at him. "There's that, too."

He pushed up from the table and took his empty plate to the sink, then refilled his mug of coffee. He offered more to Dina, but she waved him off.

She picked up her cell phone and checked the time. "I really do need to get home."

He took her empty plate to the sink. "I'll drive you."

"I can take an Uber."

"I know. But I'll drive you. Give me ten minutes." He came around, gave her a light kiss, then walked off toward his bedroom.

Dina drew in a long breath, looked around

and tried to take everything in. There was a secret part of her that had imagined herself with Franklin. But nothing prepared her for the actual experience. Franklin was unlike other men she'd been with. He wasn't the kind of guy who used his status as some sort of magical potion to attract women. If anything, he seemed to downplay who he was and what he'd achieved. It was easy to see why he'd been mislabeled as standoffish, elitist even. Franklin Grant was none of those things.

She rested her chin on her fist. Falling for him did not fit into her plans. Should she be offered a position at Jameson, she didn't ever want it to appear that there was favoritism because she was sleeping with a powerful man, even if on paper they were equals. She was an outsider and that alone could be seen as an issue for some, combined with an on-the-job relationship. That was not the reputation she wanted for herself. She'd seen what it could do to a career. Her one friend in California, Sydney, was a great doctor with so much potential, but much like Anna, she second-guessed herself. Sydney always believed that as a woman the only way to get ahead was to have the backing of a man, preferably a man in power. The scandal that resulted from Sydney's affair with the chair of the department led to her dismissal and a slap on the wrist for the chair. She feared the same thing for Anna, and she had no intention of going down that road, which would mean that there was no way that whatever this was between her and Franklin could ever get out. Besides, Franklin didn't give her any indication that he wanted more, and that was fine with her, which meant that it had to stop.

Her stomach knotted. Being with him, thinking of him, making love with him . . . how could she stop?

"Ready."

Her head popped up. He was swinging her sling-backs off the edge of his fingers, and when her gaze landed on him that seesaw, giddy feeling took over. *Damn.* She got up and nipped the shoes from his hand. "Thanks." She stepped into her shoes and took her phone from the counter. Her hands were shaking.

"Safe and sound," he said when they pulled to a stop in front of her house.

"Thank you." She focused on her purse because if she looked at him . . .

"Um, I know that we both agreed that this was temporary —"

She held up her hand. "No. Look, like I

said, I'm a big girl and I knew what I was doing. You don't have to worry." She forced herself to smile.

He looked at her through narrowed eyes, gave a slight shrug. "All right then." He pressed a button in the armrest and the seat belt disengaged.

She gripped the door handle, kept her face away from him. "See you at the office." She hoped she sounded light and airy, and not the way she actually felt. She opened the door and walked down the short path to her house without looking back.

Franklin sat in the Jag for several minutes, waiting for what, he wasn't sure. Maybe hoping that she would come back out and tell him she didn't mean any of what she'd just said. That was not going to happen.

He put the car in Drive and pulled off. From the moment he'd asked her to the party he kept telling himself that it was only a bet with this brothers that he'd wanted to win. Thinking of it that way kept feelings at a distance, made it all very surgical. But he knew how easily even the best-planned surgery could go wrong. Ten years later and that day still haunted him. He thought he'd been prepared. He'd studied the charts, knew the procedure inside and out; the patient was the perfect candidate. None of that mattered. Bad reaction to the anesthesia. He did everything he could to save him.

The board cleared him of any wrongdoing, and the malpractice suit fell flat when the wife revealed that her husband had not been totally honest in his medical history so that he would be eligible for the surgery. Nevertheless, the loss shook him. He questioned not only his skills but his decision-making, his ability to read people. Mastering those skills had been the hallmark of his success. Back then, all that came into question. What that devastating loss did accomplish, however, was to force him to add another layer of distance between himself and others and to be hypervigilant in his assessment of anyone who came into his life. That was the plan. He'd stumbled once, with Lindsay, dusted himself off and returned to Plan A.

Then came Dina Hamilton. Every rule he'd carved out for himself he broke when it came to her — especially the rule of not getting involved with a colleague. The image of their reflection in the bathroom mirror flashed in front of him. His penis jumped to attention. He groaned deep in his throat.

The blare of a car horn jerked him to attention. He was sitting at a green light. He lifted his hand to signal his apology to the driver behind him and quickly drove across the intersection.

CHAPTER 21

Dina stretched out on the couch, mindlessly television surfing. She should have asked him to come in. She bit down into an apple, chewed slowly. There were a little more than two months left of her fellowship. The right thing to do was to simply toss last night up to a fling and forget about it.

She couldn't. She couldn't ignore the memory of his fingers stroking her skin, the way he tasted or looked at her with such wonder in his eyes, the way she felt with him inside her, the way her chin fit right into the hollow of his neck or how their bodies were pieces that each other needed to be complete.

If anything, being with Franklin last night, the entire evening, actually, right up to when he dropped her off, only solidified the feelings that she'd been trying to ignore for months. But it was clear that he fully expected that there was nothing going on, no commitments, no expectations. She'd agreed — in the beginning. At first it was fun to flirt, to challenge him, to see him react to her. Now she wanted to believe that what they shared last night was more than just a roll in the hay between consenting adults.

She sighed heavily and curled on her side. The *Sex and the City* movie is on, the part when Miranda is alone on New Year's Eve and her bestie Carrie travels by train from Manhattan to Brooklyn in the snow to be with her friend. That scene always got to her. That was true friendship, a friendship she longed for.

Today was a day when she really needed a girlfriend, someone to pour her heart out to about Franklin Grant and get some girl-friend advice on what to do. The closest person to remotely fit that description was Anna.

The movie was up to the part when Carrie and Big finally said "I do," and he surprised her by inviting her besties to the justice-of-the-peace ceremony. The final joy-filled reception scene of the girlfriends and their significant others at the restaurant had her wondering which of the four women she most identified with.

Something deep inside jumped as if startled. That's what she wanted right there in front of her — true friends, a man who loved her, a family.

For years she'd convinced herself that medicine, her career, would fill all the empty spaces. But she'd never left any room for those spaces. When she thought of spaces to be filled all she could see were the two six-foot holes that they put her mother and father in. To her the holes were dark, bottomless pits, opening up to take into their bellies the two people who had loved her unconditionally. She never wanted space, openings, uncharted territory to ever enter her life again. Everything and everyone in her life must have a reason for being. No ambiguity. No unknowns. Her world from that day forward would allow no spaces in her life. Until now, and it scared her.

Franklin pried them all up. With the skill of a surgeon he made the tiniest of incisions, slipped inside and now here she was in totally unchartered territory, looking down into the space that was opening by degrees.

The credits rolled. Dina swung her bare feet to the floor. Doing nothing beyond watching romantic movies was definitely not going to make her feel better, but a run around the park would help.

■ ■ ■ ■

Franklin finished up his last set of reps, hoping that maybe total exhaustion could erase what happened to him on his way to the gym. His spotter retuned the two-hundred-pound weight back on the rack. Franklin's breath heaved in and out as he pulled himself to a sitting position. "Thanks, man."

"You got it." They did a quick one-hand, one-arm parting thing and the spotter walked away.

Franklin grabbed his towel and mopped his face and neck. He'd been in the gym for nearly three hours. Weights, the track, elliptical, the punching bag, the bike. Every muscle bounced, flexed, hummed.

He made his way around the machines and the grunting, sweating men to get to the showers. He was one of few black males who frequented this gym. Most of the time, that reality didn't faze him one way or the other. He was well-spoken, financially secure, lived in the best part of town and he was a surgeon. But lately he'd been giving his melanin-deficient brothers second looks, wondering if today would be the day when they'd feel "uncomfortable" or if the female hostess suddenly questioned his member-

149

ship. In the blink of an eye a black man, woman, boy or girl could become suspect or worse.

Lately social media and the news outlets were flooded with scenarios of "call the police on black people because they dare to live and breathe." For so long he'd been somewhat insulated from that reality, but it didn't diminish his understanding that at any minute it could be him, especially in the current cultural climate, and being pulled over, yet again, on his way to the gym, had solidified that reality.

No different from the half-dozen other times he'd been pulled over, even with his MD plates. Today simply *felt* different. *Where are you coming from? There's been a rash of robberies in the area. Your car fits the description.*

He turned the shower on full blast, turned his face up to the steamy water and closed his eyes. They always let him go, never apologized. He should consider himself lucky, he supposed.

He lathered his body and took his time rinsing off as if somehow he could wash away that feeling of violation. When he'd been with Dina, all the bullshit, the stops, the surgeries, the life-and-death decisions had disappeared. He, for the first time in much too long, felt connected, a part of someone. He wanted that feeling again, needed it, even for a little while.

He turned off the water and snatched the towel from the hook. Dina was what he needed.

Dina did something that even surprised her. She called Anna.

Anna in one of her many monologues had mentioned that she enjoyed jogging around Rock Creek Park on her day off. She said that while it was great exercise and a stress reliever, the real reason was that there was an endless stream of hunky guys who had turned out to be more than "exercise" on a couple of occasions.

"See that guy over there," Anna huffed as they approached a guy doing some stretches on the bench.

"Yeah," Dina breathed.

"Connor. Real estate. Not bad if you know what I mean."

As they passed him, he turned. Anna waved. Connor smiled and waved back.

"See." She laughed. "You should try it."

Dina didn't want to get into how inappropriate, not to mention dangerous, it was to pick up men in a park. But she kept that little aside to herself. "Hmm, maybe some other time."

Typical for a Sunday afternoon, the park teemed with joggers, bikers, strollers. On the rolling hills camped out on patches of emerald-green grass, picnickers made the most of the sunshine and clear skies. Roller-bladers and skateboarders whizzed by in single file and groups. Squeals of laughter floated along with the light breeze.

They came around a curve, then took the short incline. There were teams on the field to the right of them setting up the stage and equipment for a concert.

"Wonder who's performing." Dina huffed.

"Pretty sure it's Jill Scott, not sure who else." She sucked in some air as they rounded another bend. "All I know is that I'm on call for tonight so I totally put it out of my mind." She lightly elbowed Dina. "See now, if you'd take up with one of these fine specimens out here you might have had a date for the concert."

Dina smirked, shook her head and kept on running.

They finally slowed to a stop near the pond, purchased two bottles of water from a vendor and plopped down on the grass.

"Thanks for running with me," Dina said. "I definitely needed to get out of the house."

Anna took a long swallow from her bottle

of water. "Anytime." She wiped her forehead with a small, checkered hand towel. "Listen, um, I know sometimes I . . . might come off the wrong way. I don't want you to think I'm some kind of slut. Because I'm not."

"Of course not." She shrugged her right shoulder. "Not for me to judge. You're a grown woman, Anna." She sipped her water.

"It's just that sometimes I know I can come off a bit . . . strong. And things I say get taken the wrong way."

Dina turned to look at her. "Something specific?"

Anna gazed off toward a group of kids skipping rocks across the pond. She wrapped her arms around her legs and rested her chin on her knees. "Let's just say that sometimes when you lay your cards on the table you find out who a person really is."

Dina's brows lifted. "I'm sure that's true. But isn't it best when you know?"

"I suppose." She finished off her water and pushed to her feet, checked the time on her phone strapped to her upper arm. "I'm on duty in like three hours."

"Sure." Dina got up, as well.

They walked side by side to the exit from the park.

"So when are you back on?" Anna asked

when they reached the parking lot.

"I totally lucked out. I go back day after tomorrow."

"Wow. Lucky you. See, it pays to be the favorite of the head guy in charge."

Dina inwardly rolled her eyes. "Doubt that is the case."

"Anyway . . ." She lightly squeezed Dina's arm. "I'm parked down the street."

"Okay. I'm the other way. Listen, thanks again for today."

"Anytime. See you on the floor." She walked off toward her car.

Dina sighed. Anna was a strange bird.

Now that she'd gotten her exercise in, she was starving and went in search of something to eat after a quick shower. While she was chopping up some leftover chicken for a salad, her cell phone rang. She licked her fingers and dug her phone out from her back pocket.

Her heart jumped when Franklin's name popped up on the screen. She swallowed. "Hello."

"Hey. Busy?"

"Um, not really. Trying to fix a salad."

"Oh. Listen, there's a concert tonight. Rock Creek Park. If you're not busy, thought you might like to go."

She smiled so hard her eyes hurt. "That is so funny. I just came from there. Running."

"Really? So, is that a yes, or just a funny?" he teased.

Dina laughed. "I'd love to go. Jill Scott, right?"

"Yep."

"I'm all in. What time?"

"First act is at eight. I figure if we get there by sixish we can get a decent spot."

"Perfect."

"I'll have the restaurant downstairs put a basket together."

"I can bring wine."

He chuckled. "Sounds great. I'll see you about five thirty. That good?"

"I'll be ready."

"See you then."

She said her goodbyes and finally breathed. A date. She was going on a date. She hop-skipped to her bedroom to find something to wear, her salad totally forgotten.

CHAPTER 22

By the time Franklin arrived Dina was certain she'd worn out a path from her window to the door. It wasn't as if she hadn't been out with him before or slept with him. She took a quick peek out the window. This was different, not like the anniversary party where it was part feeling sorry for her and part wanting someone on his arm. The sex part was beyond mind-blowing and she didn't want to make more out of it than it was. After all, he'd reminded her that it was a no-commitment kinda thing. So . . . what was this?

She leaped at the sound of the doorbell, squeezed her eyes shut for a second, then pulled the door open.

"Hey," she said with all the casual tone that she could summon. This was yet another version of Franklin Grant. Fitted black T-shirt that defined his hard chest and carved abs, denim jacket and totally sexy short-brimmed straw hat, dipped at just the right angle. And damn if those jeans didn't fit too much like right. "Come on in."

She whirled away. Her heart pounded. "I didn't know if there was seating or if we'd be on the grass. I have a blanket and a small cooler," she called out over her shoulder.

"Definitely a grass night." He followed her into the living room area. "Let me get those," he said, taking the cooler and blanket from her. "Anything else?"

She took a quick look around. "Nope. All ready." She walked around him and opened the door.

"Seen Jill Scott before?" he asked when they stepped out.

"No, but I love her music."

"You're in for a treat." He opened the trunk and put the cooler and blanket inside, next to the basket from the restaurant. "I saw her a couple of years ago at the Kings Theater when I went to New York." He came around, opened her door, then got in behind the wheel. That trip to New York to hang with his frat brothers was the perfect cure to soothe the sting of what happened between him and Lindsay.

Dina settled in her seat. "Long way to go for a concert," she said, amused.

"The trip was double duty. Fraternity

reunion. The concert was one of our hang-out events." The rest she didn't need to know. Until he'd said it out loud he'd almost forgotten how much that trip and being with his brothers had helped take the edge off. They all knew about his relationship with Lindsay, and between drinks, laughter and swapping stories of relationship wins and losses, he got his head back in the game and his eyes back on the prize — his work.

"You said you were out at the park earlier." He checked the mirrors, then pulled off.

"Yep," she said on a breath. "Went running with Anna."

He glanced over, mildly surprised. "You two are getting pretty tight. After-work drinks, jogging in the park . . ."

Dina laughed. "Does kinda seem that way."

"Hmm."

She frowned and turned toward him. "Something you're not saying?"

His brows knitted, but he kept his focus on the road. "Not at all."

Dina watched the lines of his face tighten, his full lips thinned. Anna didn't have the best effect on most people. She could attest to that, but she got the feeling that it was something else happening here. Anna's asides and references about Franklin from how sexy he was, what a great catch he would be, to his standoffish personality flipped through her head. Anna often gave off the impression that she believed she was not getting her due and somehow Franklin could or should change that. What little Dina did know about Anna always had a way of raising the hairs at the back of her neck. Had Anna been hinting that she knew Dina and Franklin had something going on? But tonight was not the night to concern herself with Anna Lorde. Tonight it was all about her, Franklin, chilling under the stars and drinking in Jill Scott — along with some wine. Whatever happened after . . . She shifted her bottom in the seat. She bit back a smile, more than ready.

"Hope you don't mind, but we're probably going to have to park a few blocks away. Folks start showing up at midday," he said, chuckling.

"Have on my walking shoes." She flexed her sneakered foot. "How often do they have concerts out here?"

"Hmm, during the summer, there's usually something going on every weekend, with special events during the week. Honestly, it's been a while since I've been out there. Usually working."

"Then we really need to celebrate."

He slid a glance at her. A half smile was on his lips. "Yes, we will."

Her stomach did that funny butterfly thing when she saw the penetrating look in his eyes and the way his tongue idly laved his bottom lip. She swallowed hard.

"So . . . what's in the basket?" she asked to get her mind on her stomach and not what was happening between her legs.

"Well, Felix, my main contact, put together a feast fit for a king and queen. I think you'll be pleased."

"Your main contact?"

He didn't even try to look embarrassed. "Yes, my go-to guy. As you may have noticed, I don't cook."

She bit her lip, her eyes wide in feigned surprise.

Franklin cleared his throat. "Anyway when I moved in about five years ago, I ordered in all the time, or ate out. I got to know Felix from going in the restaurant so often and he got used to my voice on the phone. Knew what I liked, how I liked it and I tip really well." He smiled.

"I see," she said, holding back laughter. "Good to know folks."

Franklin cut her a glance. "So back in LA . . . you get to go out much?"

"Not really. Definitely not as much as I'd have liked. Crazy hours at work," she added. "And I was really focused on getting the fellowship to come here, hone my robotic skills. Not much time or energy for much else," she said, trying to rack up as many reasons as she could for why her life was pretty much a one-woman show.

"No siblings?"

"No," she whispered. She felt him look at her.

"What about your folks? We never really talked about your family. Are they in LA?"

Her throat clenched. "My parents died in a car accident when I was fifteen."

"Oh, wow. I'm sorry. I didn't —"

She held up her hand. "It's okay. Been a long time." She lowered her head.

"Did they get who did it?"

She glanced out the window, drew in a breath, then turned toward him. "My parents were on their way home from a weekend getaway. They were driving . . . My dad . . . had a massive heart attack, lost control of the car and then hit the median. My mom lasted about a day in intensive care. My dad was pronounced on the spot." She blinked away the burn in her eyes.

He reached over and squeezed her balled fists. "I'm really sorry."

She nodded. "Thanks," she murmured. "It's why I wanted to be a heart surgeon."

"I totally get it."

She drew in a deep cleansing breath. "What about you? Why medicine?"

He gave a slight shrug and laughed lightly. "Would you believe that out of the three of us, me and my brothers, I was the nerd?"

Dina burst into laughter. "Get out. Seriously."

He nodded. "Yep. Black-rimmed glasses, pocket protector." He chuckled some more.

She slapped his arm. "Stop lying."

"I'm not. There is photographic evidence."

"Those I have got to see."

"They are on lockdown."

"I think your mom kind of likes me. She might let me get a peek."

His brow arched. "Oh, you're in good like that — after one night."

"I make a very good impression." She paused. "It can be more than one night," she said and wanted to take the words back the instant they were out of her mouth.

They pulled to a stop at a red light. "I'm going to park on the next block. The walk isn't too far from there," he said.

Dina wanted to disappear. Her fists tightened.

He parked the car and got their things

from the trunk. Dina tucked the blanket under her arm and moved to pick up the mini cooler when Franklin stopped her.

She looked up at him, feeling totally foolish.

"About that more than one night thing . . . I'm with that if you are."

Her heart slammed in her chest. Her whole body heated. "I am."

Franklin leaned down, tilted her chin up and slowly pressed his lips to hers. He moved back, stroked her cheek. "Let's go listen to some Jill."

"Let's. Plus I want to see what's in that basket. I'm starved!"

CHAPTER 23

The night was pure magic. The park was a kaleidoscope of color and sound and scent. Blankets and brightly clothed bodies carpeted the grassy hills and slopes. Laughter rippled along the warm night air beneath a sky dotted by pinpoints of light, peeking through the arms of heavily leafed trees. While many couples sought the sanctuary of the shadows, groups of friends boldly took on the night, singing along to Jill's standards and dancing to the beat.

As promised the dinner basket was truly fit for a king and queen: crackers and assorted dips, Swedish meatballs to die for, fresh fruit, Mediterranean panini sandwiches, arugula salad and mini cheesecakes.

"Oh. My. Goodness." Dina gushed on a breath and collapsed against the leather of the car seat after it was over. "Everything was fabulous. The show. The atmosphere. The food . . ." She turned to him. "And the company." She leaned across the gearshift. Franklin came to her halfway until their mouths met.

He slid his hand through the satin of her hair, cupped the back of her head and held her to him.

She moaned softly into his mouth.

Reluctantly he eased back, ran his thumb along her bottom lip. "Your place or mine?"

She grinned. "What do you like for breakfast?"

He chuckled. "Touché."

"Where do you want this?" Franklin asked, holding up the cooler.

"Oh, that goes under the sink." She took the blanket and put it on the top shelf of the hall closet then plopped down on the couch. "If you would empty out any water, then just leave it on the floor by the washer," she called out. "I want it to dry."

"Yes, ma'am." He strolled off to the kitchen and deposited the cooler as requested, then returned to the living room. "There's still some cheese and crackers."

"Hmm, I'll get the wine. I think I have another bottle in the fridge." She started to get up.

"No. Sit. I can get it. If you don't mind."

She smiled. "Not at all. Knock yourself

out." She stretched her arms high over her head and yawned. She picked the basket up from the floor and set it on the center of the coffee table, just as Franklin returned with the wine.

Dina took off her sneakers and wiggled her toes. She tucked her feet under and curved her body into the corner of the couch.

Franklin poured them each a glass of wine, handed one to Dina and sat next to her. "To a wonderful night." He lifted his glass.

"Totally."

They both sipped.

Franklin leaned forward, set down his glass on the table, then angled his body toward Dina.

"So . . . now we've had an 'official' date," Dina said.

He draped his arm along the couch, ran a finger down the back of her neck. Dina sucked in a breath.

"Seems like we have." His gaze moved slowly over her face. "It isn't often that I find something or someone to distract me from my work . . . my patients."

Her heart galloped.

The corner of his mouth curved upward. "There've been a lot of things I determined

166

I'd never do . . . and then *have* since I met you."

She tilted her head, licked her lips. "Things like what?"

He let out a slow breath. "Getting involved with someone I work with for starters, especially someone whose work I oversee." The skin tightened around his eyes.

"You said *'for starters.'* "

He looked at her with something resembling wonder in his eyes as acceptance dawned and found its way to his lips. "Caring again." He turned away, got his glass from the table and took a long swallow of wine.

Dina curved herself closer to him. "What made you stop . . . caring?"

He leaned his head back against the couch, closed his eyes. He'd never really talked to anyone about everything that happened between him and Lindsay, not even his brothers. They knew they were seeing each other, and then they weren't. He'd refused to get into the bits and pieces and eventually they let it go. All they knew for sure was that he didn't want to talk about Lindsay. His frat brothers knew that something had gone down, but they didn't know it all either.

"A couple of years ago I met someone at

a fund-raiser given by the hospital. Lindsay Gray. She's the CEO of Media Corp. Her company handles all of the public relations and fundraising galas for a string of hospitals in DC, Maryland and Virginia, including Jameson Memorial. Not Jameson at first, but eventually." He sat up, leaned forward and rested his forearms on his thighs. "It lasted about two years."

Dina waited for more. Her pulse quickened.

"It didn't work out," he finally said.

"I kind of got that."

He snorted a short laugh.

"Do you want to tell me why?"

He pushed out a breath. "I wish it was something simple like someone else, or moving away." He gave a slight shake of his head as if still grappling with the past. His brow furrowed. "We were both ambitious — still are — tunnel vision when it comes to our careers. The difference between us is that Lindsay has no problem using the people in her life to get what she wants." He refilled his glass.

"I'll have to stock up on bourbon for next time."

He gave a half smile and took a swallow of wine.

"What did she do? Being ambitious is not

a fault."

"No. It wasn't the idea of wanting to get the most out of your career, to be recognized for your achievements, to succeed when others in your position had failed. That wasn't it." His nostrils flared. "Lindsay wanted an inside track to securing the multimillion-dollar account from the hospital. She saw me as her way in." He shook his head. "I introduced her to all the right people, from the head of the board of directors to the janitor." He exhaled slowly. "To make a long story short, she landed the deal and our relationship ended soon thereafter. She said it wouldn't seem right for the two of us to be together under the circumstances. Not only did she get the account, she has a seat on the board of directors."

"Ouch. Wow, I'm really sorry."

"Yeah. Anyway, water under the bridge. Once burned, twice shy as the saying goes. I stay out of her way and she stays out of mine."

"Makes sense why you wouldn't want to get involved, especially with someone from work."

"Lindsay is smart, shrewd and controlling. She may not want to be in a relationship with me for her own personal reason, but she isn't too keen on anyone else having that role either. She spearheaded the push for HR to ramp up harassment criteria on the job."

"You think she did that because of the two of you?"

"I don't know. Timing of it all was pretty suspect." He shrugged. "Like I said, water under the bridge. But the reality is there will be an opening for an attending. Your fellowship will be finished soon. I want to recommend you for the position. Thing is, if it ever got out that you and I —"

She held up her hand. "I totally understand."

He reached out and cupped her chin in his palm, scored her face with the sweep of his eyes. "I don't want your chances compromised because of my own wants."

"What is it that you want?" she asked on a whisper. Her heart thundered in her chest.

"You. From the moment I saw you at the seminar." The memory came to life with a slow smile. He ran a finger down the side of her cheek. "But I knew what we were up against."

"What changed your mind?"

He twisted his lips to the side. "A bet."

She frowned. "A bet? What bet?"

Hesitantly he told her about the bet between him and his brothers.

Dina's brows rose higher and higher as she listened. "So how much was a date with me worth?" she asked with more bite to her words than she intended. She inched away from him.

"Listen. It's not the way it sounds."

"Yeah, it actually is." She pushed to her feet.

Franklin grabbed her hand. "Dina. My brothers know that since Lindsay, dating . . . has been on the back burner. They also know that I was never one to hop from one woman to another. They told me there was no way I could show up at the anniversary party single. Again. They bet I wouldn't find anyone."

Her body slowly relaxed. She looked down into his perfectly sculpted face.

Franklin took her hand in between both of his. "I took the bet and the only person that I wanted to make good on that bet with was you."

She lifted her chin in that defiant way of hers. "How much?"

"Two grand."

She plopped down on his lap, looped her arm around his shoulders. "That's it?"

"It was double or nothing," he said in earnest.

Dina bit back a smile. "Was it worth it to

you, Dr. Grant?" She placed a light kiss on his cheek, then his eyelids, then his lips.

He grinned against her mouth. "Every dime and then some. And just think you helped to fund my favorite charity."

"Is that right?" she purred. Her fingertip trailed down the center of his chest until it reached the top of his belt. "I'm feeling a bit charitable myself."

Franklin gathered the hem of her soft cotton T-shirt and lifted it over her head, tossed it aside. He placed a featherlight kiss at the shadow of her collarbone. Goose bumps bloomed across her belly. Her hands clasped the bulge of his biceps. His mouth trailed down to the swell of her breasts, and then to her stomach that fluttered like butterfly wings. He ran his fingers around the band of her shorts. She squeezed his hands to stop him.

"Let me," she whispered deep into his ear.

Slowly she unwound her legs and stood, paused a moment, then wiggled out of her shorts and black lace panties. She kicked them to the side.

"Damn," he uttered, grabbed her hips and pulled her against him. Deeply he inhaled her, licked and suckled her until her cries wrapped around them both, her body trembled on the verge of release. Her fingertips dug into his shoulders as the first wave slammed against her.

"Ahhhhh, Frank . . . Ohhhh, God . . ."

With one hand he deftly unfastened his belt, unzipped and shoved his pants down below his hips.

Dina straddled him, cupped his face in her palms and slowly lowered herself down, the throbbing hardness of him filling and nearly sending her right back over the edge. Her mouth closed over his while they wound and ground against each other. Franklin fisted her hair, drove up into her and groaned out his pleasure. Her wet walls gripped him, released him and gripped him over and again until they collapsed in giddy exhaustion.

CHAPTER 24

Dina listened to the steady beat of his heart, the rhythm of his breath. Images of the two of them floated through her mind. The deep timbre of his voice vibrated in her veins. Her body still hummed from the feel of him. She snuggled closer and wanted to burrow beneath his skin. The riot of feelings she had for Franklin unnerved her. He murmured her name in his sleep. A bubble of joy filled her, scared her. She knew that allowing herself to tumble down this unknown valley with Franklin had all the markings of trouble ahead.

They had to keep their relationship under wraps, but if she was honest with herself she wasn't sure that she wanted to stay in DC, even if the position was offered to her. After nearly eight months in Washington, she still felt like an outsider. The only person she'd connected with was Franklin. She'd enjoyed meeting his family, experiencing the laughter and love they shared. Yet, at the same time it reminded her of all that she missed for so many years, what she desperately wanted for herself. But her career, everything she'd worked and sacrificed for was what mattered. Her work never ran out on her, died on her, left her.

She closed her eyes, smothered a sigh. Love, family and happiness were all part of the fairy tale — someone else's. She'd ride the dream for as long as she could. She pressed a light kiss on his chest and drifted to sleep.

Franklin rolled over. He blinked against the dim light seeping through the blinds. The sound of rain beat against the window. It took him a second to realize he wasn't in his own bed. The space next to him was empty. He turned toward the imprint that Dina left in the bed and smiled as the memories of the night ran through his head. Dina Hamilton was incredible, brilliant, beautiful, sexy, funny, worldly and she turned him on in ways he didn't know were possible. He hadn't thought he could feel this way. Whatever he'd had with Lindsay was a teenage crush compared to this.

He sat up, swung his feet to the floor, looked around for his pants and remembered he'd discarded them in the living room. He padded across the cool wood floors to the bathroom, grabbed a towel and tucked it around his waist, then followed his nose to the kitchen.

Dina was at the stove with her back to him, barely covered in a tank top, slowly swaying her hips to some slow jam that he almost recognized. Her hair was in a messy topknot, her long bronze legs on full display. She reached for the glass of orange juice on the counter beside her and took a short sip while she flipped bacon in the frying pan. Thunder rolled in the background. Standing there, watching her, he was hit straight in the heart with the realization that he was in love with this woman. And standing in this moment was something he wanted to do over and over again.

"Hey, good morning," he softly greeted.

Dina glanced over her shoulder. A smile bloomed on her face, lit her eyes. "Hey yourself."

They stared at each other in a private moment of realization.

"Hungry?" she managed.

"Starved." He slow-walked toward her. "Need some help?"

"We've already determined that you are

not the handy one in the kitchen," she teased.

"True," he conceded, and slid his arms around her waist, pulling her flush against his rising erection. "But I set a mean table."

She slid her hand down between them, rubbed him until he groaned.

"Guess you need to decide what you want for breakfast," she said and tugged the towel away.

He reached around her, turned off the jets, then lifted her into his arms and backed her against the wall. Dina wrapped her legs around his waist and he pushed up inside her with a hunger that rattled him.

Dina gasped at the force of his entry and held on for dear life as he lost himself and she gave him what he was seeking.

After the breath-seizing romp, and stuffing themselves with blueberry pancakes, turkey bacon and a feta cheese omelet, they were headed to the shower when Franklin's beeper went off. He frowned.

"What is it?"

"Emergency code from the hospital switchboard." He stalked off into the living room in search of his pants and cell phone. Dina followed.

"This is Dr. Grant . . . Yes. Is Dr. Hines

on staff today? Get Dr. Lorde. I'll be there in twenty minutes. Have them prep the OR and the transplant team." He tugged on his pants, dropped his phone in his pocket while explaining to Dina what was going on. "Major accident on I-95. The victim is a donor and a perfect match for my patient Harold Finch."

"Oh my God. That's incredible."

He tossed her a quick look. "I'd like you in the room." He fastened his belt, scoured the floor for his sneakers.

"Uh, of course. I'll get ready." Her eyes danced around the space and found her pants on the couch along with her bra, but no panties. No one but Franklin would know that she was going commando. She slid her feet into Crocs and less than five minutes after the call they were headed out the door.

"I'm blocking you in. We'll take my car," he said.

It was easy to see how a major accident could happen. Visibility was hampered by the slash of diagonal rain. Heavy fog added to obscuring vision, and streets were closed due to flooding and fallen trees.

Franklin wanted to fly over the cars and debris. Time was of the essence. This kind of opportunity was rare, and success hinged on surgical skill, focus and maintaining the viability of the donated organ. His patient, Mr. Finch, was barely sixty years old. He'd been on the waiting list for a donor heart for two years. He wasn't the best candidate. Age was a major factor and the fact that he'd already had most of his valves replaced and had suffered cardiac arrest the last time he was on the table weren't the kinds of odds that he would have preferred. But he'd promised Harold's wife, Adrianne, and their daughters, Jessica and Pat, that he would do whatever he could to save him.

"We slept through all of this?" Dina asked more to herself than Franklin as she tried to peer between the rapid swipes of the windshield wipers. Noting his silence she turned to him. His profile was portrait stiff. His focus honed. He was preparing his mind for what was ahead. She needed to do the same.

Darting down the corridor of the third-floor cardiac unit a little while later, they were met by the charge nurse who advised them that Dr. Lorde was prepping the patient and the donor had just arrived by helicopter.

Franklin and Dina hurried to Harold's room.

Anna was adjusting the medication drip. Surprise widened her eyes. She looked from one to the other. "Not dressed for the weather," she quipped.

Dina felt her face heat.

Franklin didn't seem to acknowledge the barb, and walked up to the bed. Harold's wife and daughters were seated along the bedside. He spoke briefly to them, then turned to Anna.

"I'll take it from here, Dr. Lorde. Thank you for stepping in."

"Not a problem." She started for the door, gave Dina a tight-lipped smile.

"Dr. Lorde, scrub in."

Her face lit up. "Yes, Doctor."

She threw Dina a look she couldn't quite read.

"I'm going to get prepped," Dina said to Franklin.

Franklin didn't respond as he took a seat next to Harold's bed and talked with him and the family in low, measured tones outlining the procedure and reminding them of the risks.

"I'm anticipating that everything will go well. The surgery will take at least five hours. So I don't want you to worry," he said, addressing Harold's wife. "Okay then." He stood. "Just relax in the meantime,

Harold." He patted his shoulder, nodded to Harold's wife and daughters, then walked out.

The first team removed the donor heart and prepared it for transplant. Franklin and his team waited behind the glass partition until it was their time to enter the operating theater.

When Harold was wheeled in he was already mildly sedated. Franklin leaned over him, reassured him and promised to see him back in his room. He gave the okay to the anesthesiologist to put Harold under and the transplant began.

Franklin and Dina worked in tandem, often completing each other's moves without a word spoken. Franklin instructed and coordinated every action of the team. Anna oversaw the surgical nurses. Everyone involved worked with the precision of a Swiss clock.

They had been at work for nearly three hours. Franklin made the final arterial preparation for delivery of the heart, lowered it in place and began the long and intricate work of making all the connections.

"Take him off bypass," he instructed, nearly an hour later.

The room went still. Everyone seemed to

hold their collective breath. This was the defining moment of success or failure.

One of the nurses wiped the sweat from Franklin's forehead.

"Paddles."

Anna handed him the paddles.

"Charge."

"Charging."

"Clear."

All eyes darted between the vision of Harold's new heart and the machines. Nothing.

"Charge," Franklin called out again. "Clear."

Then like magic the heart began to beat and audible relief filled the room.

Franklin slowly exhaled and removed his goggles. "Dr. Lorde, would you close, please?"

"Yes, Doctor."

The machines suddenly screamed, that high-pitched wail no doctor wants to hear. Everyone sprang into action.

Franklin stood immobile in the scrub room. The rest of the team had departed. He kept rewinding every moment of the procedure through his head. Textbook. His nostrils flared as he sucked in air. The hardest part was waiting for him on the other side of the swinging doors.

"Frank. Franklin."

He blinked the room back into focus. His jaw clenched.

Dina crossed the space to stand in front of him. She reached out to touch him and he flinched. Her eyes widened in surprise. She took a step back.

Franklin snatched his surgical cap from his head and tossed it in the bin, then brushed by Dina without a word.

Chapter 25

Franklin sat alone in the dark of his office. The tortured faces of Harold's family moved like phantoms across his line of sight. His stomach clenched and un-clenched. What went wrong? Every move he'd made was precise. He didn't miss anything. He couldn't have. But obviously he did.

He rested his head in his hands. As a surgeon he knew losing a patient was inevitable in your career but it didn't make the reality any easier. He could still hear the sobs of Harold's wife echoing in his head. He slammed his fist on his desk rattling everything in its wake.

His desk phone rang. He snatched it up. Listened.

"Yes. Of course. I'll be there shortly."

Slowly he returned the phone to the cradle. *And so it begins.* He straightened his tie, put on his lab coat and headed to the penthouse floor to meet with the hospital president.

Dina sat opposite Anna at a table in the cafeteria, nursing a cup of tea. The aroma of meat loaf, the day's special, filled the air and roiled her stomach. Indistinguishable conversation buzzed around her. Images of white coats and blue scrubs moved in and out of her peripheral vision.

"I'm sure there will be an inquiry," Anna said.

Dina slid her gaze toward Anna.

"They always do when someone dies during surgery. We'll have to testify."

Dina didn't respond. All she could think about was Franklin, what he must be feeling, and she couldn't shake the look she'd witnessed on his face. It was as if his soul had left his body. There was emptiness in his eyes.

"Are you okay?"

Dina focused on Anna. "Yes. I suppose so. I don't know. Still processing, I guess."

"Well, just prepare yourself to get called in." She brought the foam cup to her lips. "Definitely won't be good for Dr. Grant."

"What do you mean?"

Anna looked around then leaned forward, her voice lowered. "Well, there was already buzzing that they wanted to bring someone else in to run the department. Dr. Grant isn't the 'friendliest.' Doesn't play the politics."

"Doesn't kiss ass you mean," Dina said.

"Hey, I'm just telling you what I've heard. This will give them more ammunition while they sideline him during the inquiry." She sipped her coffee.

Losing his position within the hospital after all that he had achieved with revolutionary techniques in heart surgery, and all the hard work and dedication that he devoted to the hospital would completely devastate him. If anyone understood how much what he did every day meant to the health and survival of countless patients, she did.

"Just an FYI," Anna added, cutting into the twist of Dina's dark thoughts, "if I were you I would steer clear of Dr. Grant for a minute. At least until after the inquiry. One of the things the board will look at is whether or not anyone is working together to corroborate their stories. If you get my meaning."

Dina's insides flipped. Her gaze drifted away. She needed to talk with him. "I'm going to head home." She slowly rose to her feet. "Thanks for the information." She pushed her chair under the table.

"Don't forget what I said. For the time being steer clear. For your own good."

Dina didn't bother to respond. She forced a tight-lipped smile and walked away. She couldn't determine if Anna was trying to actually be helpful or was secretly pleased. There was an undertone of satisfaction. But maybe she was being overly sensitive and reading more into what Anna was saying.

Although Anna warned her to steer clear, she went straight to Franklin's office anyway, hoping to find him there. There was no answer when she knocked.

"If you're looking for Dr. Grant, he's gone for the day," the charge nurse said as she walked by Dina.

"Oh. Thanks." She continued down the hall toward the bank of elevators. Part of her wanted to go by Franklin's condo and talk with him face-to-face. But in the weeks and months she'd worked with him and especially since they'd been together, there was one thing she'd learned about Franklin. He validated much of his worth by the quality of his work. And knowing him the way she did, right about now he was questioning his worth, his value and his skill as a surgeon. He wouldn't listen to her until he was ready. She'd give him the night, let him have some space, but first thing in the morning they were going to talk. The hell with the board.

She pulled out her cell phone and ordered an Uber to take her home.

Franklin sat in the waiting area, outside Dr. Freeman's office, who not only served as president of the hospital but as medical director. He knew what was coming and braced himself for the impact. He'd sat in on several inquiries throughout the years. They could be brutal. And if there was even a hint of incompetence or liability on the part of the doctor, there was not much to protect you. Having a patron, someone to speak on your behalf, always went a long way. He'd never been one to cultivate those relationships, and now he feared he would pay the price.

"Dr. Grant, you can go in now."

Franklin gave a short nod of thanks, stood, straightened his jacket and went into Dr. Freeman's office.

The opulent space was outfitted in heavy teak wood, imported rugs, crystal objects on shelves lined with thick leather-bound medical books, plaques on the wall beside framed photos of Freeman with Presidents Obama, Bush 43 and Carter, and numerous entertainment icons.

This was the first time he'd been called to the inner sanctum, although he'd interacted with the president on various occasions. It was clear that the space was designed to overwhelm and perhaps intimidate anyone crossing the threshold. None of that set him back on his heels like seeing Lindsay sitting at the rectangular table with Dr. Freeman.

"Dr. Grant." Freeman rose and extended his hand, which Franklin shook. "Please have a seat. I wanted to have Ms. Gray join us for this discussion."

Franklin gave Lindsay a cursory nod, pulled out a chair and sat. It had been more than a year since he'd seen Lindsay and that was purely by chance. He'd been in Georgetown with the intention of meeting up with Montgomery to look at a property he was thinking of adding to his coffers. He'd decided to get a quick cup of coffee and literally opened the door for Lindsay. She'd been as shocked as he was. The first awkward seconds caused a gridlock in the doorway until Franklin finally stood back and she stepped out. She was still put-together from head to toe, as his mother would often say about women who dressed well and expensively.

Lindsay, how are you? he'd said.

I'm well. She'd reached up and smoothed his brow with a light brush of her thumb in that proprietary way she had that was equal parts sensual and controlling. *I guess this is a day off for you.* She'd smiled up at him.

He'd slung his hands into the back pockets of his jeans to keep from touching her. *Meeting up with Monty.*

Her amber eyes had widened with apparent delight. *What is Mo up to now? Still taking over the world a block at a time?* Her musical laugh trilled in his chest.

He'd half smiled. *Something like that.*

She drew in a breath, placed her hand on his arm. *It was really good to see you, Frank.*

Yeah. You, too.

I've got to run. Meeting. Take care and don't work too hard. She'd squeezed his arm and hurried off, never looking back.

"Can I have my assistant get you anything before we begin?" Freeman asked, jerking him back to the table.

Franklin blinked away the past. "Nothing for me. Thank you."

Lindsay leaned across the table and picked up the silver carafe of water, poured a full glass and sat back down.

Freeman flipped open a thick manila folder, took his glasses from the breast pocket of his navy pinstripe suit and slid the half frames along his chiseled nose. He cleared his throat. "As you know any time there is a loss of life in the operating room that was not directly the result of traumatic injury there must be a full inquiry."

"I'm aware."

"The reason why I asked Ms. Gray to attend is that she will handle the public relations end. The last thing we want is bad publicity for the hospital. As a member of the board, her services are invaluable and she will work with the best interest of the hospital at the forefront."

Franklin threaded his fingers together on top of the high-gloss table, clenched his jaw. His gaze swung toward Lindsay. "I'm sure."

"In the interest of protocol, unfortunately we have no other alternative than to put you on administrative leave until the full inquiry has been concluded."

Even though he knew it was coming it didn't soften the feeling of getting sucker-punched.

Freeman turned the folder around and slid it toward Franklin. "That is the letter detailing your leave and your agreement to the terms. Of course we've had the hospital attorney look it over, but it is our standard letter."

"Once admin leave is in place, we'll need

to sit down and discuss talking points and what any releases to the press will say," Lindsay said.

Freeman took off his glasses and set them on the table. "Sometimes it's better during these . . . times that the doctor under investigation actually takes some time off."

"It's actually easier for you and for the hospital," Lindsay added softly.

"So basically both of you are telling me to *get lost* because I'm bad on the optics!" He pushed back from his seat so forcefully it rocked on its back legs before settling. "What about my patients? What about all the work that I'm doing, my team?" He glared at them both.

Freeman held up his hand. "I totally understand that you're upset, Dr. Grant. But I can assure you that none of your patients will suffer because of this setback. We will put someone in place to take over your caseload and oversee any upcoming procedures."

Franklin's nostrils flared. He knew this was all part of the process. He'd witnessed it happen to others. He'd never imagined that it would be him. He pushed out a breath. He reached for the folder and snatched it toward him.

Freeman offered him a pen. Franklin

declined and took one from the pocket of his lab coat. He scrawled his signature on the required line and slid the folder back across the desk.

"I know this is difficult," Freeman said.

"Do you?"

Freeman's puffed cheeks flamed. He cleared his throat, stood. "We'll be in touch."

Franklin squared his shoulders, nodded. "Who is going to take over for me while I'm on 'leave'?"

"We're considering Dr. Hamilton."

CHAPTER 26

Franklin stood out on his balcony, overlooking the city that he loved. Beyond the dusty-gold horizon was nothing but possibility. Yet, DC, the center of all things good and just, the cornerstone of America's democracy, had cast its vote against him.

He tossed back the last of the bourbon in his glass and braced his forearms on the wrought iron railing, playing and replaying the scene in Freeman's office. He was still rocked from seeing Lindsay in the room. Lindsay, judging and assessing him — determining how the world would see him.

The truth was Lindsay was damned good at her job. That much he knew for a fact. She didn't rise to manage one of the most influential public relations and marketing businesses in DC without knowing what she was doing. She could turn fact into fiction with a simple smile, have you believing crap you knew wasn't true, but it must be because she said so. She was savvy, manipulative and totally driven, and at the same time completely insecure. She operated under the premise that she had to be one up on any and everyone out to get her to improve her sense of self-worth — even when it came to personal relationships.

It had taken him a long time to see through the polished veneer of Lindsay to the fragile woman underneath. But that understanding wasn't enough to hold them together. He was skilled at healing broken bodies, restoring viability to worn and tired organs. When it came to broken souls he was at a loss. Fixing Lindsay was beyond him. An ability to right what was wrong in her soul wasn't in his skill set.

The ringing of his phone severed the trip down memory lane. He turned around and went inside to retrieve his cell. The lighted number was Dina's. As much as he wanted to talk with her, he knew all about protocol. It was enough that they were seeing each other. If it got out that they talked after he'd been dismissed, it could cause all kinds of problems. The phone continued to ring. Finally he gave in to his lesser instincts.

"Hello."

"Franklin. I stopped by your office."

"Before you say anything else, let's end

this conversation now." His stomach knotted.

"But —"

"No. We can't do this. For both our sakes. I'm sure you understand. Thanks for calling, Dina. Goodbye." He pressed the red icon on the phone and disconnected the call. His head lowered as he pushed out a ragged breath, tossed the phone on the couch and went to fix another drink.

Dina plopped down on the side of her bed. She got the whole idea about protocol and tainting the waters, but this was *them* — her and Franklin. She believed that what they were building was real, not something that could get shoved under the rug at the first sign of trouble. Granted, the loss of a patient was a doctor's nightmare, but they should be in this together; if not for the public at least for each other. She knew how much it meant to have someone there for you even when you believed you didn't. When she lost her parents, it was the most devastating, soul-emptying experience of her life.

As an only child she didn't have siblings to cry with or to draw strength from. Living with her aunt wasn't any better, only to wind up in foster care until she aged out of the system. From the age of fifteen she was basically alone. She'd learned to insulate herself from the hurt of connecting with anyone, even as she longed for what she saw around her every day, friends, family.

For the first time in years, she'd discovered that no matter how much she wanted to stand behind her wall of self-protection, she couldn't fight what the heart wanted. Her heart wanted Franklin Grant.

She flopped back onto the bed spread-eagle and stared up at the hypnotically spinning ceiling fan.

When she was a young girl, living with her aunt, she would spend hours staring up at the ceiling fan imagining that it could magically turn back time, return her home before the accident. Before her entire world changed.

Sighing, she pushed herself upright. Wallowing was not going to get her anywhere. Revisiting her past was pointless. Her present was what was important. She would give Franklin the space that he needed. For now.

After a less than restful night, Dina puttered around the apartment preparing for work. Thankfully she didn't have any surgeries scheduled. Her head was still clouded with the events of the previous day. Her thoughts shifted to Franklin just as her cell phone buzzed. She snatched it up hoping that it was him. It wasn't.

"Hello."

"Dr. Hamilton?"

"Yes."

"Good morning. I'm calling from Dr. Freeman's office. He'd like you to come in to see him at ten."

Dina frowned. This must be the first round of inquiries, as Anna said. "Sure. I'll be there."

"Thank you, Dr. Hamilton. We'll see you at ten."

The call disconnected.

Slowly she lowered the phone to the table. Her pulse thumped in her veins. What would they ask her? If their goal was to get her to somehow incriminate Franklin — well the hell with that. She checked the time on her phone. She had an hour and a half to get her game face on.

CHAPTER 27

"Damn, man, I'm really sorry," Monty said. He lifted the mug to his lips. "What happens now?"

Franklin picked up his cup of coffee and put it back down.

The buzzing conversation of early morning hotel guests, the clang of china and clink of silver filled in the background.

Franklin heaved a breath. "The usual, an inquiry by the entire medical staff. The team will have to testify, justify their roles and actions."

"But those things work out, right?"

Franklin started to reply when they were interrupted by one of the hotel staff. "I'm sorry to disturb you, Mr. Grant."

Monty put down his mug. "What it is, Danielle?"

"One of our premiere guests is having a major melt-down at the front desk."

Monty's smooth expression tightened.

"Thank you. I'll be right there." He wiped his mouth with a cloth napkin, stood and snatched his jacket from the back of the chair. "Sorry. I'll be back shortly."

"No problem. Handle your business."

Franklin watched his brother walk away with his head bent toward Danielle. He was truly proud of his brother. Both of them really. They were each successful in their own right, having carved separate paths. The only difference between his brothers and himself was that they found a way to enjoy life, to include love — even elusive love — in their lives. Something that seemed to continually escape him. Even now, this thing with Dina was temporary — actually forbidden and he wondered if maybe that was the reason why he chose her — because she was impermanent.

He sipped his coffee and gazed loosely around at the comings and goings. Everyone seemed to have someone who mattered in some way. What he wanted wasn't so far-fetched. He wanted the kind of bond that his parents had — something real and enduring. Until he could find that, he'd turned to his work. Now he wasn't sure how much longer he would have that.

Dina parked her car in the employee lot and

hurried into the building. What began as a sunny morning had quickly grown ominous with heavy gray clouds looming overhead. The first splashes of rain descended just as she reached the front entrance.

She walked through the emergency entrance sidestepping the rush of orderlies and nurses pushing medicine carts and gurneys, and went straight for the elevators. On the drive to the hospital she'd rehearsed what she would say. She'd gone over every moment of the procedure and there was nothing where she could find fault. That's what she'd tell them. Dr. Grant had performed a textbook operation and the fact that the patient didn't make it couldn't have anything to do with Dr. Grant's ability as a surgeon.

The metal doors slid open on the pavilion level. Her heart beat faster. She followed the signs to the medical director's office and stopped at the desk of Alice, his executive assistant.

"Good morning. I'm Dr. Hamilton."

Alice looked up, smiled. "Of course. Good morning, Dr. Hamilton." She got up from behind her desk. "Please. Follow me."

Dina followed Alice down a short carpeted corridor, stopped when she tapped lightly on the door, then opened it for her.

"Thank you," Dina murmured.

"Dr. Hamilton," Dr. Freeman heartily greeted. He stood, swept his glasses from his nose and came around his desk to welcome her. He stuck out a thick hand which Dina shook.

"Please have a seat. Thank you for coming in."

"Of course." She lowered herself onto the padded chair. She could hear her heart pounding. She linked her fingers together atop her crossed legs.

"I've heard wonderful things about you since you came to us on fellowship, Dr. Hamilton. Nothing but accolades."

"Thank you."

"Here at Jameson we pride ourselves on excellence, on the utmost in quality patient care. Our reputation over the years has remained stellar. As president and medical director of this hospital it is my responsibility to ensure that all the moving parts are well-oiled, for lack of a better analogy, and quite frankly to avoid lawsuits or anything that would tarnish our standing as the number-one hospital in the country —" he pointed a thick finger at her "— or in your department. Our cardiac department has been number one for eight years in a row. Its reputation for cutting-edge surgery cannot be matched."

"I understand Dr. Grant is greatly responsible for that," Dina cut in, mindful of the sales pitch.

Freeman cleared his throat, stroked his mustache. "Yes. However, it is my responsibility to ensure that no matter the circumstances or the personnel involved that our reputation remains sterling."

He flipped open a folder. Dina's stomach clenched.

"You were on the team that performed the surgery in OR 3 on Monday."

"Yes, I was."

"As of yesterday, as is protocol, we have had to put Dr. Grant on administrative leave pending the outcome of the inquiry."

She licked her bottom lip.

"The board met last night and we came to the unanimous decision that until the investigation is concluded we want you to oversee the division. You've worked side by side with Dr. Grant. You know his work and his patients and more important you are highly skilled in robotics. Dr. Grant said as much himself."

Dina blinked rapidly. Frowned. *Before or after you dismissed him?*

"I'll be blunt. We would like you to stay on at Jameson. You are a major asset here.

We can solidify that offer we made to you before your arrival. And when this messiness is done you'll be chief of cardiac surgery."

She hoped the panic didn't register on her face. She gave a short shake of her head. "Why . . . me? I'm sure there are plenty of qualified —"

"We believe that you are the qualified person, Dr. Hamilton. In the interim you would take over as interim chief until the inquiry is completed. And when you've done an exemplary job, which we are confident you will do, the sky is the limit."

Her thoughts swirled in a hundred directions at once. A position like this in a prestigious trauma hospital was what she'd dreamed of. If she took this on, it would only be to hold Franklin's seat warm, because she was confident that he was coming back better than ever. She drew in a deep breath and slowly exhaled.

"Let me just add that with you filling in, Dr. Hamilton, it will maintain care and continuity for our patients and that must be our primary focus."

"I deeply appreciate your confidence in me, Dr. Freeman. Can I think about this?"

Freeman blew out a breath through his nostrils. He linked his fingers and leaned slightly forward. "As the board will now be overseeing the continuation of your fellowship in the absence of Dr. Grant, I would be happy to extend the courtesy of waiting until tomorrow . . . say noon, for your response." He flashed a tight-lipped smile.

Did he just threaten her? Dina nodded, pushed back from the table and stood. She extended her hand. "Thank you for your time, and your faith. I'll be in touch tomorrow."

Freeman rose slowly and shook her hand. "I look forward to hearing from you."

Dina walked out on shaky legs, disturbed, confused and undecided. She was totally aware of corporate politics, and the cover-your-ass mentality of boards of directors. The last thing any hospital wanted was bad publicity and lawsuits. Both things scared away donors. Her pulse pounded in her ears. She pressed the button for the elevator and went straight to her office.

Her dilemma only compounded — or maybe it was her way out. She had the call from Saint Vincent to consider. When it rains it pours.

CHAPTER 28

"So what's the plan, big bro?" Monty asked, picking up the conversation.

Franklin gave a slight shrug. "Wait it out. There isn't much that I can do. I'm sidelined."

"Do you need a lawyer?"

Franklin's brows furrowed. "I'm pretty sure it won't come to that."

Monty signaled the waitress. "Can I get a western omelet and extra bacon, crispy?"

"Sure thing, Mr. Grant." She turned to Franklin. "Anything for you this morning?" She refilled their water and orange juice glasses.

"No. I'm fine. Thanks."

Franklin watched Monty watch her walk away and inwardly chuckled. Old habits die hard. Monty didn't cross the red line with his staff, but it didn't stop him from subtly taking a look every now and then. Even so, his swag and charm seemed to override the fact that he had no real intention of making a serious commitment to a woman. Although all three brothers were career driven, Monty and Zo always found time to add the spice of a desirable woman in the checks and balances and empire building. Franklin on the other hand was tunnel-vision selective as Zo told him on many an occasion. *Man, you know how many women are groomed and nurtured on the notion of hooking a doctor? You got it made and you don't even know it,* he'd huffed during a heated game of one-on-one at the local park. Zo had backed into Franklin on the dribble. *At least play the field. See what's out there.* He'd spun, jumped. Franklin leaped to block the shot but the ball skirted the tips of his fingers, hit the backboard and in. Zo's breath heaved in and out as he pounded his chest in triumph at his move. *All work and no play makes us all dull boys.* He'd snatched up the rolling ball, and was headed to the basket when Franklin stole the ball, whizzed around Zo like a blast of air, leaped, sent the ball soaring and in. *Now that's what I'm talkin' 'bout,* Zo had shouted and given Franklin a fist bump. *All you gotta do is use them skills off the court.* He'd winked and snatched the ball.

Monty swung his attention back to Franklin. "On another topic. Tell me about the superstar you brought to the party. Is it serious? Or was that yet another one-time thing?"

Franklin snorted a laugh. "No, it wasn't a one-time thing, but . . . it will be a short-time thing."

Monty's expression bunched. "Why? What did you do?"

"Why did I have to do anything?"

"Because you generally do. What — she couldn't leap over tall buildings or something?"

"Very funny. No, that's not it."

"So . . . what gives? The two of you seemed really into each other."

"It's complicated."

Monty shrugged. "I got time. I run this joint, remember?" He grinned. "And apparently you have some time on your hands, too."

Franklin lifted his glass of juice but put it right back down. "She's a fellow at the hospital. Brilliant surgeon. Smart. And . . . we've been seeing each other."

"Say what? For how long?"

"Since the party, but we were tiptoeing around each other for a while."

"Is it serious?"

Franklin rested his forearms on the table-top. "I want it to be," he quietly admitted, and the admission seemed to lift a weight from his shoulders.

Montgomery's smooth brows rose. "Whoa. It's been more than a minute that you talked like that."

"Yeah. I know. Just happened." He slowly shook his head in awe. "I've gone out of my way since Lindsay to steer clear of getting involved on any kind of serious level."

"Hmm. I feel ya."

"Somehow Dina got past my radar."

"She must be crazy special."

"She is."

"I hear a *but.* What's the issue?"

He sighed heavily. "Because we work together, I supervise her work, we can't be public about our relationship. She reports directly to me."

"Ouch. That's tricky."

"Yeah, and I'm the one who will sign off on her fellowship. I can't have it seem that there was any favoritism involved. Plus there'll be an opening in a few months for an attending to lead the development of robotics. She's perfect for it. That's why it's so important that our relationship stay under wraps. Barring anything going on with us, she deserves that spot. Jameson will be an even greater hospital with her on board."

Montgomery nodded in understanding.

"And to be honestly selfish, I also want her to stay because I want to be with her. I think we'd make a great team on several fronts. But I'm not going to do anything to jeopardize her chances, even if it means stepping totally out of the picture."

Montgomery pursed his lips. "She knows all this? Cause you can be kinda tight-lipped."

"No," he reluctantly admitted.

"You plan to tell her?"

"Definitely not now. She's going to have to testify at the inquiry. I wouldn't want her to think for a minute that I was trying to play her."

"My advice . . . don't hold your cards so close to your chest. Be honest with her, then let her make up her own mind. But at least it'll be based on having all the facts."

"I'll think about it."

"You care about her, right?"

He nodded his head. "Of course."

"For once stop thinking with your analytical head and listen to what's inside," he said, pointing a finger at Franklin's chest.

The corners of his mouth flickered. "I'll keep that in mind."

The waitress returned with Montgomery's breakfast.

"That looks good," Franklin said and snatched a piece of bacon from the plate.

"Damn, bruh," Montgomery snickered and signaled the waitress again. "He'll have what I'm having."

Franklin hid his smirk behind his juice glass. He set the glass down. "I saw Lindsay."

Montgomery's head snapped up. He stopped chewing midway and set down his fork. "On purpose?"

"Hardly."

Franklin went on to explain that Lindsay was at the meeting and that she would be handling the public relations for the hospital.

"Shit."

"Yeah."

The waitress returned with Franklin's plate.

"Thanks." He shook out a napkin and put it on his lap, then cut into his omelet.

"So basically you're gonna have to deal with her one way or the other," Monty stated more than asked.

"Unfortunately."

"Hey, you know it's over and she knows it's over. Stay focused on whatever you need to do to get back in your spot."

"That's definitely the plan."

CHAPTER 29

Dina shut the door to her office, switched on the lights and sat down behind her desk. She was scheduled for rounds in about a half hour. At least she had a little time to try to process the meeting with Dr. Freeman.

The offer was certainly a great opportunity, one that she had not expected — not like this.

A little more than a year ago while she was presenting a lecture during a medical conference in San Diego, she was approached by Phillip Holloway, a noteworthy surgeon in his own right and Jameson Memorial's chairman of the board. Over drinks he regaled her with all the accomplishments of Jameson Memorial, especially its cardiac unit, and indicated there was a tentative opening for chief of cardiac surgery if she was interested.

"I've been following your research and

your career, Dr. Hamilton," he'd said. "Your robotic techniques could revolutionize cardiothoracic surgery. We could use someone like you at Jameson."

"I'm humbled. Really I am, but I'm doing well for myself where I am."

"You could do so much better. Believe me." He leaned across the table. The green of his eyes darkened with urgency. "Think of it, your own department. Your own budget, and your own staff. You could implement your vision. Is Saint Vincent going to offer that to you?"

Not in a million years. Saint Vincent wasn't a top-tier hospital but they did great work, honest work. She had believed that one day she might be the one to put the hospital on the map. But Saint Vincent didn't have the kind of funding of a hospital like Jameson. The innovations that she envisioned were light-years ahead of what Saint Vincent could afford. There had been rumors that she was being considered for the attending physician position in cardiac. Even so, she knew it was nothing compared to what Jameson could offer.

"I'll think about it."

"Good enough for me. And to sweeten the pot, I'm willing to offer you a one-year fellowship. Use our equipment. Do your research. Get your feet wet, train with the best in the country."

"You're making this very difficult."

"I'm trying to make you an offer that you can't refuse." He smiled a dimpled smile and she could see how easily he charmed, an essential quality for someone in his position.

Dina laughed. She finished her glass of wine, stood and extended her hand. "Thank you for the offer. I'm going to give it some thought. How much time do I have?"

"Take the weekend to think it over." He stood as well and pulled a business card out of his wallet and handed it to her. "I hope to hear from you on Monday. Enjoy the rest of the conference."

She'd taken him up on his offer. Took a sabbatical from Saint Vincent, packed up and came across the country for a chance of a lifetime. She had it all figured out until she fell for the man whose job she was supposed to fill.

Dina frowned, stared off into space. There had to be a way out of this mess without making things worse. If she took over for Franklin during the inquiry at least she would be in a position to champion his return, maintain continuity with the patients and when this mess was all said and done,

Franklin would have his job back, and hopefully she'd get the spot as an attending. Then she could stay in DC, and keep building the relationship with Franklin. It was possible. The murky part was, how would Franklin take it?

Her temples pounded. She leaned back, closed her eyes and massaged the sides of her head with the balls of her fingers while slowly rotating her neck. By degrees the thumping subsided.

Her eyes flew open at the sound of knocking. She straightened in her seat.

"Yes, come in."

The door inched open. Anna stuck her head in. "Hey. I was looking for you on the floor. You okay?" She stepped inside, closed the door halfway.

"Yeah. Fine. Little headache." She rolled her chair away from the desk. "What's up?"

"You tell me. Heard you were up in Freeman's office this morning."

Dina inwardly flinched. "Word travels fast around here."

Anna came around the side chair and sat down. "Soooo . . . what happened?"

"Why did anything have to happen?"

"Nobody gets called to Freeman's office for giggles. What did he say? I'm sure it had to be about the *incident.*"

Dina weighed her response, uncertain of how much or how little she should say. "He basically said what you told me. That there will be an inquiry and that I should have no contact with Fra— Dr. Grant until a decision is made." Dina watched Anna's expression morph from piqued interest to skepticism.

"Really," she intoned. "That's it?"

"Pretty much."

"He could have put that in an email," she said snarkily.

"Hmm. Right about that." She checked her watch. "I have a patient to see before rounds." She stood, signaling the end of the impromptu visit.

"So he didn't say anything about who is going to take over for Dr. Grant?"

Dina's gaze skipped away. She picked up her iPad. "Nope." She could feel Anna's gaze boring into the top of her head. She looked up with a smile. "Off to work."

Anna returned the smile. "Yep." She shoved her hands in the pocket of her lab coat. "Guess I'll see you later." She headed for the door, stopped with her hand on the frame and turned. "Drink after work?"

"Hmm. I don't think so. Not tonight. Gonna need a rain check."

"Sure." She closed the door behind her.

Dina slowly exhaled. She'd be glad when this was all over. In the meantime she had patients to see, rounds to conduct and a decision to make. She pulled her cell phone from her pocket and dialed Franklin's number. Once again, it went to voice mail.

Franklin mentally ticked off what he'd accomplished for the day. He'd had breakfast and a man-to-man convo with his brother, spent two hours in the gym, took his car to the car wash and now was en route to see his parents before they heard about what happened from someone other than him.

He got in his car and looked at his phone before mounting it on the car charger. Three missed calls — all from Dina. He'd hesitated to listen to the voice mail; hearing her voice would only erode his resolve to see her, be with her again. As much as he wanted to see her, he knew it was a bad move. He couldn't risk putting them both in jeopardy. Inquiries into surgical procedure and responsibility were difficult enough without adding any compromising issues to the mix.

He turned the key in the ignition and backed out of his driveway. When he reached the street, his phone rang. This time it was from a number he didn't recognize. He pressed the button in the steering column and the phone call came through his speaker.

"Hello?"

"Franklin?"

His gut knotted. "Yes. Lindsay."

"I wanted to set up a time for us to talk before the inquiry begins. I'm in the process of putting together a statement and I want your input. Would four o'clock today work for you?"

No time was a good time. "Sure. Where?"

"I can come to you, or we can meet at my office. I'd prefer not to do this at the hospital. Too many eyes and ears." She laughed lightly.

The last place he wanted Lindsay was in his house, and she was right about the hospital, the looks and the questions asked and unasked. "I'll come to your office."

"Great. I'll text you the address. See you at four."

"Yeah. Four," he grumbled. He pressed the button and disconnected the call. Whatever momentary mental calm he'd felt evaporated like water on a hot grill. He pulled out into traffic, his thoughts splintering off in different directions. He gripped the steering wheel so tightly that his fingers began to ache. He loosened his grip and flexed.

Since their breakup he'd only seen Lindsay sporadically as she came and went to board meetings or whatever it was she continued to do for the hospital. But they hadn't interacted and had no reason to. The other day in the president's office was the first time he'd spent that much time with Lindsay in over two years.

The dash's dial read out 1:05. He still had time to visit the folks and get into downtown DC to meet up with Lindsay by four. This was going to be a long day.

Ellen Grant covered her son's hand with her own. His father, reclining in his favorite chair, looked into his son's eyes which reflected the same anger and sadness in his own.

"I wanted you both to hear it from me before . . ."

"You listen to me, son, those board people and the inquiry folks are gonna see that this is not your fault."

"Just like before," his mother added.

Franklin's chest tightened at the memory. It was a decade ago, but he'd never forgotten. Although it was totally not his fault and he'd been cleared, the cloud hovered around him. It was like being convicted and then it was discovered that you didn't do it. The retraction isn't what people remember. It was the offense. That loss had pushed him to surpass perfection in himself and everyone around him. And he was pretty sure that when his future was being considered, his past would play a factor.

Franklin pressed his lips tightly together. "I'm sure everything will be fine."

"When will you know?" his father asked.

"It'll be a few weeks at least."

Louis made a noise in his throat.

Ellen offered a smile. "Now that you have some free time you can visit more often," she teased, lightening the moment.

"She just wants you running her around town to her nine hundred club meetings," Louis said, with a shake of his head.

"Well, I wouldn't have to even think about it if you would go."

Louis held his hand up and waved it back and forth. "Oh no!" He leaned forward in his recliner, until he was almost bent in half. "Son, I went to a couple of those meetings, and thought I would lose my natural mind." He laughed. "Never again. No sir."

Ellen rolled her eyes and pursed her lips.

Franklin held back a laugh. This was what he always loved about his parents, the way they bantered and teased each other, understood each other's faults and weaknesses and it didn't matter. They still laughed and smiled like they just realized how much they loved each other. That's what he wanted one day.

"How's that pretty doctor that you brought to the party?" Ellen asked.

"She's . . . good."

"I really liked her. Hope you'll bring her around sometime," she added with a note of hint and hope in her voice.

"Thought I heard her say she was only going to be here for another month or so," his father said.

"That's true. Her fellowship will be over and if she doesn't get a position at Jameson she'll probably go back to California." As he said the words out loud the chance that she would actually leave became a real possibility. A sweeping sensation of emptiness spread through his gut.

"How do you feel about that?" his mother asked.

He looked at her, blinked. "I hope it won't come to that."

"Well," she said on a breath, "things don't just happen. We make them happen." She pushed up from her seat at the table, walked by him and patted his shoulder. "Staying for dinner?"

"No. Thanks. Next time. Promise."

She leaned down and kissed his cheek. "I get the remote tonight," she called out as she left the room. "*Green-leaf* comes on at ten."

"Your mother . . ." He let the sentiment lovingly hang in the air, and a wistful look fluttered around his lips.

"What's the secret?" Franklin asked.

"Secret of what?"

"Knowing that you have the right person."

Louis's right shoulder raised a bit, then lowered. "I have no idea. Guess that's why it's a secret." He chuckled. "You just know when you know. When you realize in that spot deep inside —" he pressed a finger to his chest "— that your days and nights aren't worth a damn without her in them — then you know." He tipped his head toward his son and winked. "I'm gonna step outside and smoke my last cigarette for the day."

"Dad. You gotta stop smoking."

"I know. I will. When I'm ready."

Franklin blew out a breath of frustration. "Try the patch or the gum."

"Nothing fun about that. But I'll think about it." He stood and Franklin followed suit.

"I have to get going anyway."

They walked together outside and stood

for a moment on the front porch.

"No matter what happens with this inquiry, son, I want you to know how proud I am of you." He tightly gripped his shoulders. "Proud for all that you've accomplished, but more important, for the man that you are." He looked him straight in the eye. "You've always defined yourself by what you've achieved, ever since you were a little boy — had to be the best, the smartest, a role model for your brothers. But our work is not who we are, son. It never is. Don't forget that." He patted his shoulder, then pulled out his box of Newports from his shirt pocket. "Never is," he repeated and lit up.

CHAPTER 30

Franklin circled the block three times before finding a parking spot at a meter. He walked back to the building that housed Lindsay's office. It was located in the heart of the downtown financial district. Real estate in the area was through the roof. Lindsay had clearly done well to wind up in these digs.

He pushed through the revolving door and into the gleaming black-and-white marble lobby and over to the security desk.

"Who are you here to see, sir?"

"Lindsay Gray."

The guard turned to his computer screen, hit a few keys and stared. "Tenth floor. ID, please."

Franklin dug in his pocket for his wallet, pulled out his driver's license.

The guard scanned the card, then told Franklin to face the camera. He took a quick picture and returned the license. His picture along with his license appeared on the screen. "Sign please."

He took the electronic pen and signed his name on the screen.

The guard turned the screen back to face him. "Thank you. Go right on up."

Franklin walked over to the bank of elevators. He glanced behind him and watched the slow flow of human traffic navigate their way through security. Many were employees who'd swiped ID cards and pushed through a turnstile. Others were like him who needed to be verified and photographed. Gone were the days when freedom of movement and access were the norm. DC, being the capital of the nation, was always more prone to stricter security measures going into and out of office buildings. The elevator door pinged open. He stepped on. This was the new reality.

When the doors opened on the tenth floor, Franklin followed the signs down the carpeted corridor to the suite of offices at the end of the hall. The words *Media Corp., LLC* were embossed on the glass door in gold leaf.

Franklin drew in a breath of resolve, pulled the door open and strode to the horseshoe-shaped reception desk.

"Good afternoon. You must be Dr. Grant."

"Yes . . . I am," he said with a slow smile.

"You're Ms. Gray's last appointment for today," the young woman said, answering the question that he didn't ask.

"I see."

She picked up the phone. "Dr. Grant is here . . . Sure." She got up from her seat. "Follow me."

They walked down a short hallway. She stopped in front of a closed door, knocked, opened the door and stepped aside. "Go right in."

"Thank you."

Franklin stepped into the room as the door shut behind him. Lindsay rose from behind her desk.

"Franklin," she said on a breath and walked around the desk, a full smile lifting her polished lips. She stepped in front of him, leaned in and kissed his cheek. "Thanks for coming. Please let's sit." She indicated the two chairs positioned on either side of a circular glass table.

Overall, the room was definitely Lindsay, sleek, cool colors, expensive furnishings and a view. He wondered how often she stood at her window and surveyed all that could be hers.

"So." She crossed her legs. Her black-and-white pencil skirt eased up above her knees. "How are you, first of all?"

227

Franklin focused on her face. "As well as can be expected. I'm dealing with it."

"Good." She shifted in her seat and the skirt inched some more.

"You've done well for yourself," he said, taking in the room from the artwork on the off-white walls to the desk that probably cost more than someone's yearly salary. The area rug — definitely imported.

"Took a lot of work." She paused. "But you know that."

His right brow rose briefly. He wasn't going for the bait. She wasn't going to lure him into a conversation about them. "What exactly do you want to talk about, Lindsay?"

She lifted her chin, pursed her lips for a moment. "The board wants to implement damage control. As you know, any time there is a loss of life during surgery there will be some group somewhere that will be up in arms. Not to mention, the lawyers that will invariably whisper into the family's ear about suing you and the hospital."

He rocked his jaw.

"I'll be crafting a press release and some standard sound bites to address any phone calls the hospital or you may receive. Of course, I want you to take a look at the release and if there is anything that needs clarity we can address it." She got up and went back to her desk, leaned over offering a hint of cleavage from the form-fitting white blouse, while she typed something on the keyboard. Moments later the printer buzzed to life and spit out several sheets of paper. She came back to her seat and handed one of the pages to Franklin.

"That's the press release. We plan to have it ready to be approved by the board tomorrow."

Franklin took the paper with the name of Lindsay's firm emblazoned across the top, and read the three paragraphs which pretty much said a lot of nothing: the hospital will fully investigate, the hospital takes patient care seriously, if there is any wrongdoing the person or persons will be dealt with, etc., etc. He'd seen it all before. He'd been here before, but this time felt different and he wasn't quite sure why.

He handed it back to her. "I'm sure it's fine."

She leaned forward and rested her forearms on her thighs. The opening of her blouse like the door to the palace, whispered to him to enter. He ran his tongue across his lips and glanced away.

"There's something you need to know and I shouldn't even be telling you this."

She linked her slender, well-manicured fingers together. Hands so different from Dina's he thought out of the clear blue. He blinked the image away.

"Whatever it is, Lindsay, just spit it out."

"They want you out, Franklin."

He blinked in disbelief. "What?"

She nodded solemnly. "They feel that you may be a liability."

"How in the hell am I a liability?" he thundered and jumped to his feet. The chair rocked backward, then settled.

Lindsay grabbed his hand. "Please, just listen."

He glared at her, as if the root of his current dilemma was all her doing. He pulled away and paced. He ran his hand across his closely cut hair.

"This is the deal. The hospital is under enormous financial stress, especially with all the changes in the health insurance policies. In another six months to a year, at this pace, the hospital will be operating at a loss. The last thing they need or want is a lawsuit or any kind of scandal to hamper any grants or major donor gifts."

He was listening and not listening. Jameson was one of the most renowned hospitals in the country. Part of the reason for that was because of him and the innovations and technology that he'd implemented in the cardiac unit. But apparently none of that meant squat when it came down to him or dollars.

He pushed out a long breath of disgust. "So what's the bottom line here, Lindsay — they want me out and then what? What happens to the department that I built?"

"You don't play politics. You never have. So . . . you have no real allies in high places, I'm sorry to say." She paused a beat. "The board is already tossing a name around to replace you."

His thick brows drew together. "Who?"

"Apparently your protégé and colleague, Dr. Dina Hamilton."

He felt the air get kicked out of his lungs. He started to speak but his thoughts twisted out of shape.

"What is your relationship with this doctor?" She intently watched his expressions.

Franklin's gaze jumped to Lindsay's. Was she asking for business or for other reasons? "There is none, other than professional."

"Hmm. It seems they've been grooming her prior to her arrival."

"What? What are you talking about?" A knot formed in his belly.

"That's my understanding. It came from Phillip Holloway, the chairman of the board. The fellowship was the carrot, so to speak."

He didn't want to believe what he was hearing. Not Dina. She wouldn't do something like this. He slung his hands into his pockets. The knot rose from his gut and settled in the center of his chest.

Lindsay stood in front of him. She gripped his upper arms and looked into his eyes. "If you want me to, I can help you."

His eyes flashed barely contained fury. "Help me?"

"I know how to 'manage' people, especially when it comes to image. It's what I do. I can make them understand that getting rid of you and putting in an outsider would not only be bad for business but a public relations nightmare, especially with all that you have done for the prestige of Jameson."

"Wouldn't they consider any support on my behalf, coming from you, as prejudicial?"

She smiled that smile he remembered when a plan was brewing in her mind. Her doe-brown eyes picked up the light and sparked.

"Frank, this is me, remember? Besides, we were a thing long before I joined the board and before I landed the contract with Jameson. Don't even worry about that. And it's not as if our relationship was broad-casted. It's the way we wanted it. Remember?" she said, her voice dropping a note. She reached out and cupped his jaw in a palm that felt like satin. "I can fix it. I can make it so that not only will you keep your job, but they'll never come after you again. As long as there's nothing going on between you and Dr. Hamilton — so that it doesn't appear like retaliation." Her statement hung in the air.

He stared into her eyes looking for any kernel of truth. One thing he knew about Lindsay was that she was damned good at her job. She could make you believe the sun rose in the north. She was relentless, disciplined and thorough and now she'd added another lovely trait — ruthless. Most of all, she was out for herself. If what she did for others would benefit her in the long run, she was all in.

"Why?"

She took a step back, raised her chin in that defiant way that she had. "Because I can."

Franklin mindlessly walked the two blocks back to his car, mumbling apologies for walking in people's paths or bumping innocent shoulders. He reached his car and leaned on the roof of it for a moment. He needed a clear head before he got behind the wheel. The conversation with Lindsay swirled around in his head. He still could not fully accept what she was telling him when it came to Dina. That was not the woman he knew, laughed with, talked with, made love with. Sure, people were multilayered, and yes, he was certain there were things about Dina that he wasn't privy to. But completely missing that she was with him knowing that she'd been offered his job in order to lure her to Jameson — no — he wasn't going to swallow that.

He unlocked the door and got in behind the wheel. When he turned on the ignition he noticed he'd left his phone plugged into the power source. The screen lit up. Another message from Dina. He stared at the alert until it faded and the home screen reappeared. He put the car in gear and pulled out into traffic.

CHAPTER 31

Dina stepped out of the shower and wrapped up in a towel. She palmed away the mist from the mirror and peered at her reflection. *What are you going to do, girl?* Dr. Freeman wanted her answer in the morning. It might simply be easier to say no and return to California when her fellowship was up. She'd gotten plenty out of the deal already.

She turned out the bathroom light and walked into her bedroom. None of this would matter under other circumstances. The problem was that she'd lost focus. That piece of her that she kept tucked away escaped and left an opening and damn if Franklin didn't step right in it.

She took the bottle of body lotion from the top of her dresser and sat on the side of her bed. There was a litany of reasons why she steered clear of getting involved with coworkers, but mostly she kept to herself because it was safe.

When she accepted the offer to come to Jameson — with chair of the department at the end of the year-long tunnel — she never expected to fall for Franklin. Franklin had been portrayed to her as brilliant but difficult, not one to toe the company line and had been called on the carpet numerous times for circumventing protocol. Yet, from the moment she'd spotted him during the lecture that day, she knew she was in deep trouble. When they began working side by side, she saw the real Franklin Grant, fell for the real Franklin Grant, and day by day, her guilt and her secret sat like an iron ball in her stomach. But she couldn't very well have backed out of her fellowship — untangle the paperwork, and the financing, not to mention what it would do to her reputation was way more than she was prepared to deal with. She'd convinced herself that she and Franklin were simply a fly-by-night attraction after her very long dry spell. She had never been so wrong in her life. Now, here she was, out of the frying pan and into the fire.

Stretching out her legs she massaged in the lotion with long, then circular motions. After the loss of her parents and then abandonment by her aunt the part of her that connected with others was severed. Trust was broken. She never wanted to feel that kind of pain again, that bottomless-pit sensation of emptiness. That could never happen if she stayed focused on her work and kept her feelings tucked away.

Then Franklin Grant bloomed larger than life and revived her heart. He made her feel all wobbly and gooey inside, made her want to take a chance at feeling connected and cared for even if it was just for a little while. So she risked her heart, and for what?

She tossed the lotion on the bed and flopped back against the pillows. He wouldn't even talk to her, as if the loss of life on the operating table was her fault. She sat up. Frowned. Was that what was going on? Did he blame her? Did he intend to sit this tragedy at her feet? It was true that she handled some of the laser incisions, but he was responsible for the suturing, the direction of the entire team, the reconnection and the implanting of the heart.

No. She pushed up from the bed. That wasn't his style. Franklin may be a lot of things but he was not a coward. Maybe it was as Anna said, much like her, he'd been advised not to have contact with anyone. As much as she hated it, the "anyones" included her.

The problem was she needed to talk to Franklin before any decisions were made. She had to tell him everything before he heard from someone else. She needed to explain.

CHAPTER 32

Lindsay stuck her key in the door of the two-story Alexandria, Virginia, town house and stepped into the arms of luxury. She dropped her purse on top of the antique circular cherrywood table in the short foyer, toed out of her shoes and padded barefoot into the open-space living room. From her vantage point she could see directly out onto the back deck through the sliding doors. Hers was one of the few homes in the exclusive community that boasted a pool, which Phillip made a point of using every chance he got.

She smiled as she slipped out of her clothing, dropping each item like rose petals as she crossed the cool wood floors and out to the deck.

Phillip, hearing the sliding doors open, turned toward the sound.

"Honey, I'm home," she purred.

A slow, hungry smile spread his thin lips

as he took in the lushness of her caramel-colored body. His eyes darkened at her catwalk approach. He waded over to the edge of the pool. Lindsay took the stairs and lowered herself into the water to join him.

Phillip slipped his arms around her waist, pulled her nakedness flush against him. "Welcome home, baby."

Later, wrapped in thick terry robes, and stretched out on padded loungers, Lindsay and Phillip snacked on imported cheese, paper-thin crackers, seedless grapes, and sipped white wine on the back deck.

Lindsay rested her hand on Phillip's thigh, chewed thoughtfully on a grape. She had to find the right time and approach. Experience with Phillip taught her that he was most malleable and receptive after exhausting sex — exhausting for him at least.

"Babe," she purred while running the tip of her finger along his thigh.

"Hmm," he murmured.

"This . . . business with Dr. Grant . . ."

"What about it?"

"I met with him today to discuss the public relations aspect." She felt his muscle flex beneath her finger. She spread her hand flat on the warm skin. "I know the board wants to sweep this under the rug and push Grant out."

"And?"

"It's a bad move all the way around. Getting rid of the doctor who has revolutionized the department, brought notoriety to the hospital to be replaced by an outsider . . ." She shook her head. "Very bad move. It would be a PR nightmare and when we have nightmares, the donors do, as well." She let that sit.

"So what are you saying, Lindsay?"

"I'm saying that as the chairman of the board you need to get the rest of the board in line. The last thing we need is a scandal, at worst, or months of bad publicity at best. Those are the only two outcomes."

Phillip reached for the bottle of wine and refilled his glass. He took a long sip. "From what I understand Freeman brought Dr. Hamilton here with the intention of her stepping into Grant's shoes. Grant has never been a favorite of the board. The hospital may do better with some fresh blood at the helm of the cardiac unit."

Lindsay's eyes narrowed. This was not going to be as easy as she'd thought. "Trust me." She squeezed his thigh, ran her fingertips along the sensitive inside, inched higher. "This is what I do," she said, the duality of her words very clear. She turned on her side to face him, while parting the opening of his robe. "Trust me," she whispered again. "I'm working with two new patrons who are almost ready to donate millions." She pressed closer, opened his robe farther. "We don't need any scandal or lawsuit messing that up. If I was Dr. Grant and I was suddenly replaced by an outsider after all I'd contributed to the hospital, I would conclude that it was retribution."

He murmured deep in his throat.

"The last thing Jameson needs is a disgruntled renowned surgeon. The board will listen to you. Baby, it's for the good of the hospital. That deal that Freeman made with Dr. Hamilton should have never happened."

Phillip looked into her eyes. "I've never doubted your instincts." His hand trailed down her arm.

Lindsay heard a *but* and cut if off. "And there's no reason to doubt them now. I know what I'm talking about. Wasn't I right when I said that we should partner with the Forest Foundation, bring Perry Sizemore onto the board with all of his connections to corporate funding, host the intimate dinners for potential partners?"

Phillip pushed out a breath. "Yes, and you were right every time and the hospital benefited immensely as a result."

Her full lips curved into a smile.

He nodded. "I'll go with your idea." He stroked her cheek. "You are so beautiful."

Lindsay leaned over and kissed him softly. *Mission accomplished.*

CHAPTER 33

The sun had begun to set. Dina was restless. She'd been pacing the rooms of her house for the past couple of hours. Moving from the couch to the chair to the bedroom, the kitchen and back again. At this rate she'd never sleep for the night and she needed to be alert and on her toes in the morning when she met with Dr. Freeman. She plopped down on the side of her bed.

She'd made up her mind what she'd planned to say. The decision wasn't easy, but she had to think beyond today.

Her pager buzzed. She picked it up. The number for the hospital trauma unit flashed. She reached for her cell phone on the nightstand and dialed the number.

"This is Dr. Hamilton. I was paged." She listened to the charge nurse. "Yes. I'll be right there."

She shoved her pager and cell phone in the back pockets of her jeans, put on her sneakers, grabbed her purse and rushed out. According to the charge nurse a woman was rushed in after being in a major car accident and was in cardiac arrest.

She knew she had to stay focused and not slip into that dark place where she often went when car accidents and cardiac cases merged. Today she would save a life. She was no longer the helpless fifteen-year-old girl. She was a highly skilled surgeon. With Franklin sidelined she would be responsible for assembling and leading the team. And she would.

Dina pushed through the emergency room doors and ran down to the trauma unit. She stopped at the front desk.

"I was paged. Dr. Hamilton."

"Yes, Doctor. EMT just arrived. The patient is in trauma 2. They have her stabilized, but she arrested en route."

"Thank you." She rushed down the short corridor to trauma room 2 and froze when she reached the glass door. Her heart leaped in her chest. *Franklin's mother. Oh God.*

She pushed open the door and stepped in. The attending on call was by the bedside, along with two ER nurses and an intern. The machines hissed and beeped. Dina sanitized her hands from the dispenser by the door and snapped on a pair of rubber gloves.

"What do we have, Doctor?" Dina asked, scanning the readings from the EKG.

"Sixty-eight-year-old woman. Heart attack. She was pulled from the wreck. Not sure if heart attack was post or preaccident. Scan shows a major blockage and damage to the muscle."

Dina nodded. She studied the scans and the sono. They didn't look good and she wouldn't know just how bad until she operated — on Franklin's mother. She used the stethoscope to listen to Ellen's heart. "Tachy," she murmured. She turned to the resident. "Prep for surgery stat. Page Dr. Lorde, as well." She snapped off her gloves and tossed them in the bin. "Has the family been notified?"

"Yes. It's Dr. Grant's mother," the nurse said.

Dina swallowed over the knot in her throat. "Then we better make sure we get this right." She pushed through the door and into Franklin, with his brothers right on his heels.

"How is she?" he demanded.

"She's being prepped for surgery," Dina said as calmly as she could.

Alonzo let out an expletive.

246

"What about Dad? Where is he?" Monty asked.

Dina gazed from one worried face to another. "Your father?"

"They were together!" Franklin roared. "I need to see her now!"

Dina pressed her hand against his chest and for an instant she was sure he would lift her up and out of his way. "Don't go in there like this. You know better," she said in a harsh whisper, her eyes narrowing. "They're prepping her. I'm going to do the surgery."

"You! Like hell you are. I don't want you anywhere near her."

"Don't be ridiculous. You know good and damned well that I am the best surgeon for anything like this — better than you."

His nostrils flared. "I want to be in there."

"You know that's not . . . possible." She swallowed and stared into his smoldering gaze. Her tone softened. "And even if it was, it's against protocol to operate on family."

"You know she's right, Frank," Alonzo said, and gripped his upper arm.

"Go in. See your mother before they take her up." She paused. "She's not conscious."

Franklin brushed by her. "I don't need your permission."

"We're all stressed," Montgomery said, by

247

way of excusing Franklin.

Dina swallowed hard. "I'm going to have the nurse check and find out about your father. If he was brought in a separate ambulance . . ."

"Thank you," Alonzo said.

"She's going to be fine. I'm going to make sure of it. And your father will be, as well." She offered a tight-lipped smile and hurried off. She stopped at the intake desk to inquire about the car accident victim and if a Louis Grant was brought in, as well.

The intake clerk searched the computer for everyone brought in within the past two hours.

"I'm sorry. Nothing."

Dammit. "Thank you." She returned to the brothers and informed them about what she'd been told by the charge nurse then hurried off toward the elevators and the operating room. All manner of horrible thoughts swirled through her head. If they were together, where was Mr. Grant? Was he thrown clear? Was he taken to another hospital? Was he . . . ? No she couldn't let those thoughts seep into her head and play with her mind. Too much was at stake. She needed to have tunnel-vision focus on Ellen Grant. Period.

■ ■ ■ ■

When she arrived to scrub in, Anna was already there.

"I heard the patient is Dr. Grant's mother," Anna said as she lathered her fingers and scrubbed with a brush.

"Yes," Dina said, and turned on the water at the second sink.

"So you're in charge now."

Dina shot Anna a sidelong glance. "Temporarily. That's it."

Anna mumbled something that Dina couldn't make out. She continued scrubbing.

Anna held up her arms and walked toward the swinging door that led to the operating theater. "Must be nice," she said and pushed through the door with her back.

"They took Dad to Mercy," Franklin told his brothers after being informed by the head nurse after several calls to EMT and the precinct that was at the scene of the accident. He ran his hand across his face and turned in a slow circle. "Look, someone needs to go to Mercy to be with Dad. I was able to speak to the ER attending at Mercy. Dad is stable, but they are running some tests and a CT scan to rule out internal injuries."

"Why did they take him there?" Alonzo asked.

Franklin pushed out a breath. "Mom is critical. This is a trauma hospital. Dad is apparently in better shape."

"I'll go," Montgomery said. "You two stay here. Look after Mom."

"And whatever you got going on with the doc, you need to chill and let her do her thing. You said she's good, maybe better than you," Alonzo said.

Franklin rocked his jaw. They didn't know what he knew. What she'd done. But Alonzo was right. She was the best. "Just go, Monty. Call me as soon as you know anything."

"Yeah."

"As soon as you do, I'll see if we can get Dad transferred here if necessary," Franklin said.

"I'll let you know the minute I find out anything."

Franklin gave his brother a brief nod as they turned and hurried out. "I'm on lockdown," he said, turning to Alonzo. "Look, I'm not sure if they'll let me in the gallery to observe. I'll find out when I get there. In the meantime, I'll take you over to the surgical waiting area." He put his arm across

Alonzo's shoulder. "Come on."

"She's gonna be all right? You can tell me the truth," Alonzo said while they walked down the corridor.

Franklin pushed out a breath. "Based on what I saw on the charts and what Dina told me, there is some major damage, but they're going to repair it. Mom is strong. She'll pull through."

Franklin pressed the button for the elevator. Dina had his mother's life in her hands. He may now have his doubts about her as a person, but he had to trust her as a surgeon. If there was anyone who could heal his mother, it was Dina.

After he settled Alonzo in the waiting area he headed off toward the OR. The interns on cardiac rotation generally tried to get front-row seats for any major heart surgeries. He'd had to turn in his ID but he still had the keys to his office. He went there to retrieve his lab coat. At least if he was able to slide into the gallery he wouldn't stick out like a sore thumb.

Once at the gallery, Franklin eased the heavy metal door closed behind him. The first two rows of the gallery overlooking the operating theater were already lined with white coats. A couple of heads turned in his direction but quickly refocused on the scene unfolding below. One of the female residents he recognized from a rotation earlier in the year came in and sat next to him.

"Dr. Grant," she said softly and gave him a slight smile.

"Dr. Clarke," he murmured in acknowledgment.

"I heard what happened in surgery," she whispered. "I'm so sorry."

He pressed his lips together and gave a short nod. All he wanted to do was focus on his mother's surgery.

"I probably shouldn't be saying anything, but I was selected to sit on the medical committee to review what happened."

The back of his neck tingled. He slid her a look. "I see."

She placed her hand on his arm. "I'm sure everything will work out. I've seen your work." She squeezed his arm. "You're an excellent surgeon." She looked deep into his eyes. "I'm sure you'll be right back where you belong in no time."

Franklin's gaze drifted down to her hand resting on his arm, then slowly back up to her eyes.

"You belong down there," she added, indicating the operating theater with a lift of her chin.

Dina's throaty voice pulsed through the

speakers. "Dr. Dina Hamilton assisted by Drs. Anna Lorde, Paul Vincent and Anthony Moorehouse, and surgical nurses Patterson and Davis and anesthesiologist Gordon. Patient is Ellen Grant, sixty-eight-year-old female. Involved in car accident. Heart attack. Coded twice en route. Scans show extensive muscle damage and arterial blockage. We will attempt to unblock the arteries and use the robotic laser to mitigate muscle damage." She took a quick glance around at her colleagues and received their nodded agreement. "Let's begin." By rote she glanced upward and spotted Franklin.

Her eyes widened for a split second above her mask before focusing on the task at hand. "Scalpel . . ."

The tips of Franklin's fingers tingled, and his body vibrated while he watched the meticulous precision Dina demonstrated as she worked on Ellen. He wanted to get in there, push them all aside and do it himself. It took all his willpower to stay seated. He curled and uncurled his fists. His temples began to pound, and he realized that he'd practically locked his jaws shut when Dina began using the laser to shave down the thickened muscle around the heart. It was painstaking and dangerous. One false move and . . . No, he wouldn't go there, because the most delicate part of the surgery was still ahead.

His cell phone vibrated in his pocket. He took a quick look at the face of the phone. Monty. He didn't want to miss a minute of the procedure, but he definitely could not take a call in the gallery.

He gingerly excused himself and stepped out. "Yeah, Monty. What's going on?"

"Dad is pretty banged up. They are going over him with a fine-tooth comb. Need to make sure there are no internal injuries."

"Yes, of course. So he's awake, talking?"

"Yes. Crazy worried about Mom, of course. Keeps saying he has to get out of here."

"Did he say . . . what happened?"

"No. Not really. He seems a bit confused about the details."

"What are the doctors saying?"

"Basically, that he was very lucky. He'll be sore for a while. No broken bones. But they're still running tests."

"Umm, umm. Okay. Look, be sure to get the name of the attending."

"Yeah, sure. What's going on with Mom?"

"She's in surgery now. So far . . . looks good. It will be at least another two hours."

Montgomery was silent for a moment.

"All right. I'll hold it down over here. Just keep me posted."

"For sure." He slid the phone into his pocket and eased back into the gallery. The next two hours were the longest of his life.

CHAPTER 34

Dina stretched out on the small sofa in her office, lights dimmed, arm thrown over her eyes. The thumping of adrenaline still rushed through her veins and the protective light that radiated around her and through her fingers continued to tingle. Every time she was in the operating room the experience was surreal. It was as if she stood outside herself, looking down, guiding, seeing beyond the now to the next move.

The success of Ellen Grant's surgery was paramount on many levels. First and foremost, the survival of her patient, the mother of the man she was deeply involved with. While she'd worked she fought back focusing on the enormity of what was happening. She could not fail Ellen. There would be no way she could ever face Franklin again. But neither could she downplay the importance of what she'd done today in light of her future at Jameson Memorial. All eyes were on her as she'd led the team of surgeons in her new, though temporary, role. But the only eyes she was truly concerned with were Franklin's. She wanted him reassured with every move she made that his mom was in excellent hands. Being able to face him and Alonzo with the news of a successful surgery was worth every agonizing moment in the OR.

She needed to be with Franklin and, seeing him today, even in the midst of all that was going on, didn't diminish her desire for him. If anything, it only intensified her longing. She sighed heavily, dropped her arm to her side and opened her eyes. Maybe he didn't want to talk to her, but she needed to talk to him. She got to her feet, took her purse from her desk drawer and opened her door.

"Franklin . . ." Her body flushed hot.

He ran his tongue along his bottom lip, shoved his hands into his pockets. "I wanted to stop by and say thank you." His gaze moved in slow circles across her face.

Dina's breath hitched. "Of course. I mean you did already."

"I know. But . . . I wanted to do it away from the intensity of the moment. Face-to-face." He pushed out a breath. "It'll still be a couple more hours before they move her from recovery to cardiac ICU." He shifted his weight. "All her vitals are good," he added, moving between concerned son and seasoned doctor.

Dina offered a halo of a smile.

"I won't keep you. I just wanted to say thank you." He made a move to leave.

"Actually . . . I was coming to find you." She centered herself in his eyes.

The space between his brows tightened. "Here I am."

She reached out and took his wrist, urged him inside and closed the door. "I know we're not supposed to talk until the review is over, but —" she caressed his cheek "— I don't care, Franklin." She took a step closer. "Tell me that you haven't wanted to be with me and I'll back off."

His jaw clenched. "Tell me why you really want to be with me. What did they offer you to come here? Tell me that you weren't lining up for this job — my job — from the beginning."

Dina turned and walked over to the small overstuffed sofa and sat down. She linked her fingers together on her lap. "I was contacted about a year and a half ago," she began.

Franklin slowly crossed the room and perched on the edge of her desk, arms tight across his chest.

"I'd heard all the stories about you long before I agreed to come here. The brilliance." Her eyes widened with admiration. "The arrogance, aloofness and unwillingness to play politics. Heard all that, too. But I had to make up my own mind and from the instant I met you . . . none of that mattered to me. Being with you — in every sense of the word — seeing you with your family, the connection that all of you have, I've always wanted that." She lowered her gaze. "I've spent so much of my adult life steering clear of bonding with anyone. Loss —" she shook her head "— I couldn't bear it again after all that I'd already lost." She looked right into his soul. "But when I met you, when I worked by your side, slept under your heart, I knew that I couldn't keep my feelings on the sidelines anymore."

Franklin lowered his arms and braced his palms on the desk. "I didn't want to be in this space again. After Lindsay." He slowly shook his head. "My work would come first. Relationships — if it happened, fine, if not that was cool, too. And then you came along. All the walls I'd put up, I eased them down for you. I let you in. Every fiber in my being told me not to, but I couldn't help it."

Dina rapidly blinked to stem the burn of tears. "I didn't tell you this, but I was offered to come back to California and head my own department."

His brows rose. "Your own department?" He rocked his jaw, processing the news. "Dina, that's incredible."

She bit back a smile. "Build it from the ground up. It's what I always dreamed of," she said softly.

"But . . . ?"

She glanced away. "The offer came the day of the loss in surgery. I got the call from Saint Vincent the same day I got called to Freeman's office. I'd told them I needed to think about it. I was supposed to give them my answer."

"And you didn't. Why?"

"Everything happened so fast. Freeman offered me your spot — temporarily. The only reason I accepted —" she got up and walked over to him "— is because I want to be the one to hold down your spot. To advocate for you and make sure that the department is the same way you left it when you return." She took his hand. "I had no ulterior motives." Her eyes moved slowly across his face. "It wasn't a coup."

That earned her a chuckle.

Franklin angled his head to the side.

"Holding it down for me, huh?"

"Yes," she whispered and stepped between his hard thighs.

He pulled her close. "I'm not gonna get into all the crazy that's been running through my head thanks to Lindsay."

Dina craned her neck to look at him. "Lindsay?"

He nodded and explained about his meeting and what Lindsay revealed about the board's plan to install Dina, and the PR campaign to keep the hospital smelling like roses.

"Wow," she said on a breath. She frowned. "And you believed her — what she said about me?"

He tugged on his bottom lip with his teeth. "Honestly? At first I did. Yes. If Lindsay is nothing else, she's convincing. And all the crap that was going on with my job being on the line, and the whole lineup of when you arrived had me messed up in the head." He looped his arm around her waist. "But I know better. That's not who you are."

"No, it's not who I am. I want you to remember that. No matter what happens."

He leaned down and lightly pressed his mouth to hers. "I'm a scientist by nature. I need proof."

She wrapped her arms around his neck.

"What kind of proof would you like me to present, Doctor?" She pressed closer against him.

His eyes darkened. "All of you," he said against her lips before capturing her mouth. "Is your door locked?" he whispered hot against her neck.

Dina whimpered as a shiver ran along her spine. "Slam lock," she murmured.

Franklin chuckled and proceeded to relieve her of her white lab coat. "Best kind." He swung them around so that Dina was pressed against the desk.

Dina hooked her legs around his thighs and began to unbutton his navy blue shirt. "Been too long," she said and pressed her lips against his exposed chest.

He reached down and lifted the hem of her skirt, tugging it up above her hips. He cupped her rear in his palms. "Missed you crazy."

Dina unfastened his belt, his zipper. "Show me."

His skilled fingers found their way around the band of her panties and eased them down over her hips, then up her blouse and around her back to unsnap her bra.

Dina's breath hitched, her neck arched back and welcomed the heat of his mouth. His lips hot and sweet trailed down her neck to the swell of her breasts. His tongue teased the warm flesh, flicked across her nipples until they stood firm with longing. He took one in his mouth and suckled until her entire body trembled. Her moans rippled over him, seeped into his pores, fueled him.

Franklin lifted Dina in his arms and walked over to the couch and laid her down. She lifted her arms toward him. "Show me," she repeated.

"With pleasure." He tossed off the rest of his clothes, leaving them in a pile on the floor. He stood over her, devouring her body with his eyes.

"I love the way you look at me."

"I could do that all day, baby."

Dina reached up and encircled his erection in her palm, working him in slow, firm strokes until his ragged groans vibrated in her chest. He gripped her wrist to slow her down. Dina looked up at him and smiled wickedly.

"It's like that, huh?" He grabbed her hips and turned her body so that her feet were on the floor. On his knees he got between her parted thighs. He lifted her legs over the bend in his arms and dipped down to sample the offerings.

Dina's body jerked as if shot with a bolt of electricity. "Ahhh." She grasped his shoulders, hissed in air through her teeth.

Franklin hummed deep in his throat, savored her like an imported dessert, using the tip of his tongue and fullness of his lips to turn her on and out. Her whimpering of his name and full-body tremors every time his tongue flicked around her swollen clit kicked his need for her up another notch. He never wanted her to forget how he could make her feel. He wanted her to remember that he knew every inch of her body and exactly what to do with each part.

"I need you," Dina moaned. "Now."

Franklin peeked up, gave her lower lips a parting kiss and rose from his knees. Dina stretched out. Franklin could feel the waves of heat rising from her flushed body. Leaning over her he said, "I need you, too."

Dina bent her knees and stretched her arms above her head. "All yours," she whispered.

Franklin's eyes narrowed and darkened with desire and happily moved between her welcoming thighs.

Franklin entered her, and the air rushed from her lungs and expelled in a shuddering gasp. He groaned with pleasure as her hot, wet walls closed around him. Wherever his mouth couldn't reach as he moved in steady, deep strokes, his long, slender fingers made up the difference, caressing and teasing every inch of her satiny skin.

Dina lifted and rolled her hips, held him tight between her knees. The thrill of him filling her, moving within her made her mind spin. No clear thoughts formed. She was pure sensation from the soles of her feet to the top of her head. This was what she wanted, to be with him in the most intimate of ways. To feel protected and cared for, and to know that her needs were as important as his. There were no words to explain how he made her feel.

Franklin slid his hands beneath her and lifted her hips higher. She planted her feet deep in the cushion of the couch and met him thrust for thrust.

Their escalated breathing filled the room, creating a sensual turn-on harmony that urged them on — faster, deeper, harder.

Dina's fingertips dug into his broad back. She buried her face in the curve of his neck, moaning his name over and over as the wave of release washed over her, slammed her against the shore and swept her back out to sea again and again until tears slid from the corners of her eyes.

"Yes, yes . . . that's it, baby," he whispered in her ear. "Let go. Come to me." He thrust deep inside making her cry out again.

Dina's reaction to him, the way her insides clutched and unclutched him was more than he could handle. As much as he wanted this to last forever, he knew he was moments from coming full blast. Then Dina did something utterly indescribable with her insides that snapped around him and he exploded — his body shuddering, electrified.

She held him, rocked him, relished in the bliss of sharing her body with his, absorbed his moans of release with pleasure.

Franklin wearily lifted his head and looked down into her eyes. "I'm in love with you."

Her heart slammed between them.

"That's not crazy-good sex talking, either."

Dina smiled, her eyes filled. She cupped his cheeks. "I wondered what was taking you so long," she said, her voice breaking. "I love you, too." She leaned up until their mouths touched.

Dina sighed against his lips as his tongue dipped inside her mouth. Her heart pounded wildly as she gave in to the pleasure of him. She knew they'd crossed that invisible line and exposed themselves to all the ups and downs that come with turning your heart over to another. It was scary and wildly exhilarating all at once. She was finally ready to love and be loved.

"I need to get back," Franklin said as he fastened his pants.

Dina rose from the couch and got dressed. "Your brother must be wondering what happened to you."

They looked at each other and laughed.

"We'll keep this little rendezvous between us," Franklin said and winked.

She stood in front of him, placed her hands on his chest. Her eyes scored his face. "I'm trusting you."

Franklin drew in a breath. His expression softened in understanding. "I know. I'm trusting you, too." He slid his arm around her waist and eased her close. "We'll figure it all out."

She nodded. "You better go."

"Yeah." He leaned down and kissed her one last time, sealing their newfound commitment. "I'll see you later." He turned to leave, opened the door and stepped out into the corridor.

Anna was mere steps away walking in his direction.

"Dr. Grant?" Her tone was as much a greeting as a question.

"Dr. Lorde."

She slid a glance toward Dina's closed door. "Is your mother out of recovery?"

"I'm going to check on her now."

She did a slow nod, tipped her head slightly to the side. "Is Dr. Hamilton busy? I want to go over some test results."

"She was . . . reviewing some X-rays. I need to get over to recovery."

"Of course. All my best to your mother."

"Thanks." He headed off down the hall. His cell phone vibrated in his pocket. He pulled it out, stopped at the elevator and looked at the number, tapped the talk icon.

"Lindsay . . ."

CHAPTER 35

"Franklin, I just heard about your mother. I'm so sorry. How is she?"

"The surgery went well. I'm on my way to recovery now."

"Oh, where are you?"

He cleared his throat. "On the floor. I wanted to thank Dr. Hamilton."

Silence hummed on the line.

"I know this is a difficult time, but I shouldn't have to remind you that *any* contact with Dr. Hamilton or anyone else who was in the OR that day is a major problem and could severely compromise your return. You want to come back, don't you?"

"Of course. Listen, Lindsay, I appreciate your concern. I really do, but I need to go."

"We'll talk. And, Franklin, stay away. I mean it. The only place you should be in this hospital is in your mother's room."

"Goodbye, Lindsay," he managed over a

clenched jaw. He disconnected the call, then shoved the phone back in his pocket before stabbing the button of the elevator.

Alonzo jumped up from his seat when Franklin walked into the waiting room. "Where the hell have you been?"

Franklin held up his hands. "We'll talk about it later. Any word?" He looked over Alonzo's shoulder.

"About ten minutes ago a nurse came out and said they should be moving her to a room in about an hour. She's still asleep."

Franklin pushed out a breath and shoved his hands in his pockets.

"If I didn't know better I'd swear you just tumbled out of the sack. You got that look."

Franklin ignored his brother.

Alonzo's eyes widened. "Wow. For real, bro? Now?"

"Look, it's not like that."

Alonzo sputtered a chuckle. "Yeah, I think it is."

Franklin blew air through his nose, walked over to a chair and sat. He sheepishly lowered his head. "It just happened. Wasn't planned."

"I get it." He sat down next to Franklin. "Might not have been the smartest move you've ever made, though."

Franklin grumbled something under his breath.

"Saw Lindsay a little while ago."

Franklin's head snapped up. "What did she say?"

"Stopped in. Gave me her regards and asked where you were."

Franklin tugged on his bottom lip with his teeth. "How long ago?"

"Half hour. Maybe more. You've been gone for a minute, bro."

Franklin rested his arms on his thighs. "She called me . . . right after."

Alonzo's brow arched. "And, so what? You and Lindsay been a done deal."

"It's not that. Not really. But she asked me where I was. I told her I was leaving Dina's office."

"Does she know about you and Dina?"

Franklin shook his head. "No. But there was something in her voice, even while she was reminding me to stay away from the hospital — except to see Mom."

"Wouldn't stress it then," Alonzo said.

"Yeah, I guess." He rubbed the back of his neck.

The door to the corridor opened and the head nurse stepped in.

"They're moving your mother to her room now. Cardiac ICU Room 2010."

"Thank you," the brothers said in unison. The nurse smiled, nodded and turned away.

Franklin pushed to his feet as his cell phone buzzed. He pulled it from his pocket. "It's Monty . . . Hey, man. What's going on?" His expression relaxed as he listened. "Great . . . Okay . . . Yeah, they're moving Mom to her room. As soon as she gets settled, either me or Zo will come over and relieve you . . . Cool. Later."

"How's Dad?"

"He's sitting up, asking about Mom. They're giving him something light to eat. Scans came back clear. There's no sign of internal bleeding. But there is a cracked rib, a lot of bruising and a very bad sprain on his left wrist. He should be discharged in a day or two. Probably will need a home attendant for a while and rehab for that wrist."

Alonzo pushed out a heavy sigh. "Damn. Not bad but bad enough."

"Dad is as tough as they come. He'll be fine." He put his arm around his brother's shoulder. "Come on, let's go see about Mom."

Alonzo sniffed, gave his brother the side-eye. "When did you start smelling like a woman, bruh?"

"What?" He sniffed rapidly and hard.

Alonzo covered his mouth and laughed. "You smell like something soft and light," he teased. "She's all over you, man. In your pores."

Any other time he wouldn't have given a damn, but that was the last piece of news he needed to hear when he spotted Lindsay coming their way.

"Aww, man," he hissed under his breath.

"Franklin. Alonzo," she greeted, stopping in front of them. "Any updates?"

"She was just moved to ICU," Franklin said.

"That's good news." She smiled, flashing dimples. "Well if there's anything I can do." She rested her hand on Franklin's arm, then frowned, looked at him curiously. "Was Dr. Hamilton here?" Her light brown eyes danced around the space.

"No," Franklin said, almost too fast.

"Oh. Hmm." She shook her head as if to toss away a bad idea. "My senses are working overtime I guess," she said with a half smile. "If there's anything I can do," she said again. "And please — stay away from your department." Her perfectly arched brow rose to emphasize her point. She spun away on five-inch heels that popped like firecrackers against the marble floor.

Alonzo threw his brother a side "I told

you so" glance.

Franklin held up his hand. "Don't say anything."

Alonzo bit back a snicker. He clapped Franklin on the back as they walked out of the waiting area. "Not a word."

The last person Dina wanted to deal with at the moment was Anna. What she wanted to do was sit back and replay that last half hour with Franklin. Damn what were they thinking? They weren't. What they did was crazy risky but beyond thrilling, and it was so good.

"Dina . . ."

Dina blinked, brought Anna into focus. "Sorry." She frowned in faux concern. "Half-dozen cases running through my head at once." She forced a smile. "You were asking me about the rotation?" She linked her fingers together and saw them wrapped around Franklin's incredible erection. She shifted in her seat and squeezed her thighs and knees together.

"Yes, I was hoping to get an earlier rotation for the next day or so, and I'd like to be on the team for the transplant next week. If possible."

"Everything okay?"

"Yes. Fine." Anna's gaze drifted away for

a moment. "Um, I know we're not besties or anything but if something is going on with you and Dr. Grant, I'd be careful."

"What? Why would you think something like that?" she sputtered. Her cheeks heated.

"I'm not blind. I can tell every time you are around each other. The side glances, the little touches, the tone. I've seen the way he looks at you when you're not paying attention. That whole act that he put on of trying to be hard on you when you first got here. Dead giveaway." She half smiled. She leaned forward in a confidential pose. "Listen, I get it. The man is everything and then some. Clearly you were able to get past the hard exterior. But right now you need to think about your own ass, and the rest of the team. Word gets out that something is going on with you two and —" she shrugged "— you're screwed. And Dr. Grant can kiss his job here goodbye."

Dina kept her expression neutral. "I really appreciate the advice and your concern. But neither one is warranted."

Anna studied her for a moment, pushed out a breath. "Okay. But can you take a look at the schedule for me? I'd appreciate it."

"Of course."

"Thanks." She turned to leave and walked out.

Dina squeezed her eyes shut. Who else saw what Anna claimed to have seen? Anna never let on that she saw or felt anything out of the way between her and Franklin. Why? She pushed out a breath. She couldn't think about that now. What she did need was to complete a final check on her patients and go home.

When Dina walked into the ICU she spotted Alonzo standing outside of Ellen's room. Seconds later Franklin stepped out. He seemed to sense her and looked in her direction. Her stomach fluttered. She steadied herself and walked toward the brothers.

"I wanted to stop by and do a last check," she said to them both.

Franklin nodded.

She stepped around them and into the room and closed the door behind her. Once inside she took a breath to steady her own racing heartbeat. Anna's words played in her head, not to mention seeing Franklin again so soon after what had gone down in her office. Add all that to the hospital's offer, and the offer from Saint Vincent which she had yet to give her answer to either, and it was no wonder her pulse was galloping. Her thoughts swirled, but first and foremost she was a doctor and there to care for her patient. She checked Ellen's chart, the dressing and the most recent readout from the machines. Satisfied, she made some final notes for the night staff and started to leave when she heard Ellen's soft moan.

Dina returned to the bed. "Mrs. Grant," she said softly. She placed a light hand on her shoulder. "Can you hear me?"

Ellen's eyelids fluttered, closed and slowly opened.

"I'm Dr. Hamilton. You're in the hospital."

Ellen tried to speak.

"I need you to rest. Don't try to talk. You have an oxygen mask on. You were in a car accident. You had a major heart attack and underwent surgery to repair some damage. But you came through." She smiled down at Ellen. "Your husband is fine, too. He was taken to another hospital, but he is doing well. I promise you. Franklin and Alonzo are outside."

A tear slid down Ellen's cheek.

"Everything is going to be fine," she said gently. "I'm going to let Franklin and Alonzo in, but only for a moment. I'll be back to see you in the morning." She patted her shoulder and walked out.

"She's awake." She looked to Franklin. "You know the routine. Don't get her too excited. I told her your dad is in the hospital but he's fine. You can explain. But she needs to rest. Five minutes. Please. I'll be back in the morning."

Franklin nodded.

"Thank you, Doctor," Alonzo said.

Dina smiled. "Good night."

Alonzo pushed the door open.

Franklin and Dina shared a simmering look before Dina turned and walked away.

"She'll be sleeping for the rest of the night," Franklin said as they walked out of their mother's room. "We probably should head over and check on Dad."

"Yeah. I'll give Monty a call and let him know we're on our way."

"Thanks." While Alonzo was calling Monty, Franklin pulled out his cell and typed a quick text. Expect me later. He hit Send and shoved the phone back in his pocket, then went to join his brother with the thought that there would be pleasure at the end of this day.

CHAPTER 36

When Dina finally crossed the threshold of her town house she was sure her body would crumble. She felt weak. The adrenaline that had fueled and pumped through her veins over the last few hours was slipping away.

She toed out of her shoes and dropped her purse on the hall table. She unzipped her purse, took out her phone and dragged herself inside where she flopped down on the couch. She held up her phone and saw that she had a text. She tapped in her password and the text from Franklin appeared. Expect me later. Her heart thumped. She checked the time. The text was sent nearly an hour earlier. It was already after eight. She was pretty sure he would visit his father. She got up. No telling what time he would show up. Hopefully, she had enough time to get herself together. Thinking about

Franklin coming to see her, sleeping in her bed, and suddenly she wasn't tired anymore.

It was close to eleven by the time her front doorbell rang, jingling her out of a light doze. She blinked against the twilight that her living room had slipped into, sat up, then walked to the door, pushing her loose hair away from her face.

She pulled the door open. "Hey."

Franklin's dark eyes grew soft in the moonlight that peeked from between the treetops. "Hey. Sorry I'm so late."

She stepped aside to let him in. "No problem."

Franklin took her hand as he walked inside, pulled her to him. "I really needed to see you."

Dina moved into his arms, looked up into his eyes. She ran her thumb along the curve of his dark thick brows. "I'm tired as hell but I wouldn't miss tonight for a week of sleep." She tipped up and kissed him lightly on the lips. "Come on in. Hungry? I can whip up something."

"Don't go to any trouble."

"That means you're starving," she said with a grin. "Let's see what I can pull together." She linked her fingers through his and led him into the kitchen. "How 'bout an omelet. Quick. Easy. Filling."

"Sounds perfect. What can I do to help?"

"You can pour us a glass of wine and tell me how your father is doing?"

"Yes, ma'am."

"Glasses are in the cabinet over the sink. Wine is in the fridge."

She took a mixing bowl and dishes from the cupboard, and cutlery and a whisk from the drawer. "Oh, since you're in there . . . can you get the carton of eggs, green and red peppers?"

He chuckled. "Yes, ma'am." Franklin placed all the items on the island counter, then poured them each a glass of wine.

Dina lifted her glass. "To the swift and full recovery of your parents."

"Thank you." He tapped his glass to hers.

"So how is he?"

"He's doing pretty good, all things considered."

"Do you know his doctor?" She went back to the fridge for kale, spinach and mushrooms, and tomatoes.

"Only in passing. But he's very good. We thought we'd get Dad transferred to Jameson, but I don't think it will be necessary. Barring any complications they're going to release him tomorrow or the day after."

Dina nodded. She cracked four eggs into

the mixing bowl and began chopping the mushrooms, green and red peppers. "Makes sense. When I check on your mother in the morning I'll have a better sense of how long we'll keep her, based on her bounce-back from the surgery." She glanced over at him. "You and your brothers might want to consider hiring someone, just to do a weekly wellness check."

He sipped his wine. "Those two are so independent. My mother will have a natural fit. But the idea has crossed my mind. After this, no matter how strong and vibrant they may have been, they will not be the same, no matter what they may think."

Dina took the bowl to the stove, poured the eggs and mixings into the pan. She put her hand on her hip and turned to Franklin. "I have to meet with Dr. Freeman tomorrow. He's expecting my answer."

Franklin's lips tightened. "Know what you're going to tell him?"

She flipped the omelet and adjusted the flame. "One minute I do, the next I don't." She picked up the spatula and folded the omelet, then lifted the fluffy confection from the pan and slid it onto a platter. After setting the platter on the counter she took out a prepackaged container of mixed fruit from the fridge — watermelon, cantaloupe, pineapple slices and grapes — then took a seat opposite Franklin. She looked right at him. "I'm going to stay until the inquiry is over and you're back in place."

He sliced the omelet in half and slid it onto his plate. "What happens if things go sideways with this inquiry? Would you plan to stay in the position?"

The fork stopped midway between the plate and her mouth. She put it back down. "What are you asking me — *exactly*? Because it sounds suspiciously like that BS you were talking about before — me trying to take your job."

He turned his head away for a moment, then looked right back at her. He put down his fork, blew out a breath. "Yeah, you're right. It does. I can't even say for sure that I don't mean it." His brows drew together. "If it came to that —" he rocked his jaw "— I wouldn't want anyone else in there but you." He reached across the table and took her hand. "I guess what I'm saying is, if you are presented with the opportunity — take it."

"That's not going to happen. The inquiry is going to prove that the death was not your fault."

He snorted a laugh. "You still don't get it. This is beyond what happened in surgery.

This is about replacing me, Dina."

"And *you* don't get it. I'm not going to be part of dismantling someone's career." She looked deep into his eyes. "Especially someone I love."

The tight lines around his eyes eased. The beginnings of a smile curved the corner of his mouth. "One of the early lessons in med school is that while we may empathize, as doctors we must think with our heads and not our hearts. We put aside our personal ideologies and make decisions that are in the best interest of the patient."

"What are you telling me?"

"Don't think with your heart." He lifted his glass of wine, tipped it toward her, then took a swallow. "Do what's right for the patient."

Dina slipped into bed next to Franklin and curved her body against his. Tenderly he kissed the hollow of her neck.

"This is very easy to get used to," he whispered, while slowly stroking her hip.

"Very," she sighed. She took his hand and raised it to cup her breast. "I want you."

"Hmmm," he murmured. His growing erection pressed against her belly. "You don't have to tell me twice."

Their entwined fingers moved from the

swell of her breasts, down to the dip in her stomach to between her thighs. With little guidance from her, Franklin gently parted the damp folds and played with her pulsing clit. Dina writhed against his hand, the intense sensation shimmying along her limbs. She sucked in a tight breath when his finger slipped up inside her. She rubbed her derriere against him much to Franklin's groans of delight.

"You gonna get yourself in trouble, woman," he said into her hair.

"Funny, I was looking for trouble." She wiggled onto her back. "Think I found it." She wrapped her fingers around him.

Franklin sucked in air through his teeth. "Yeah, baby, I think you have."

No matter how many times they made love, it always felt like the first time. That first electric shock of having him enter her, fill her, move inside her never lost its power to thrill and surprise. She locked her long legs around his waist, pulling him so close only the faintest stream of air could come between them. She wished that she could absorb him into her pores, make him part of her essence.

Franklin was intense, complicated, brilliant, an incredible lover and a man who lived by his convictions. He was willing to forgo everything that he'd worked for if it was what she ultimately wanted. After the loss of her parents there was no one to care about her like that — not even close. But now that she'd found unconditional love with a man who should be her rival she wasn't sure that she could make that leap — to enrich herself at his expense. Her love for him was equally as benevolent. She knew how much his work, his research and what he'd built meant to him, no matter what he told her.

And that was the impasse.

She held him tighter, planted hot, fervent kisses on his cheeks, his neck, his lips, felt him swell and stiffen inside her. Her heart raced as her hips rose to meet the rising pace of his thrusts. Her insides quickened. Their breathing escalated, met and exploded in a burst of cries and moans that shook them like petals in the wind.

"There's coffee," Dina said when Franklin walked into the kitchen the following morning with only a towel wrapped around his waist.

"Thanks." He poured a cup and sat down.

"I'm going to leave in a few minutes. Rounds. It's too early for visitors so feel free to hang here if you want."

"I need to go home and change, anyway. Check in with Alonzo and Monty. Then I'll come by."

She nodded, but avoided looking at him.

"What's wrong?"

Her lashes fluttered. She gave him a quick look and shrugged. "Nothing. Just thinking about Freeman."

Franklin poured some French Vanilla creamer in his cup. "I'm sure you'll make the right decision."

Dina pushed away from the table, came around, lifted his chin in her palm and softly kissed him. "See you later?"

He nodded.

She turned and walked out.

Chapter 37

Franklin tossed his day-worn clothes in the hamper and went through his closet to find something to put on when his cell phone buzzed.

He padded across the bedroom and picked the phone up from the nightstand. "Lindsay . . ."

"Good morning. I hope this isn't a bad time."

"No. I was getting ready to come to the hospital."

"Can we meet first?"

He squeezed his eyes shut and lifted his face toward the ceiling. "Sure. What time?"

"Actually," she paused, "I'm about two blocks away from your building."

His eyes flew open. He frowned. "Really?"

"Is it okay if I stopped by? It won't take long."

The last place he needed or wanted Lindsay was in his apartment. "You remember the restaurant downstairs?"

"Yes."

"I'll meet you there in twenty minutes." He heard her stifled sigh.

"Fine. See you then."

"Right." He disconnected the call, tossed the phone onto the bed. He wanted to give Lindsay the benefit of the doubt. After all, she did provide him with some options and she did say she would go to bat for him. He was going to have to swallow his pride and deal with her until this mess was over.

He pulled a white cotton dress shirt from the closet, and a pair of gray slacks. Reflexively he reached for his lab coat with his name etched into the pocket and stopped with his hand on the hanging jacket. The jacket represented so much more than a piece of clothing. It was a metaphor for all the work, countless sleepless hours and dedication that it took to earn that coat. Now it reflected everything he stood to lose. He took the shirt and slacks and got dressed.

Before he left he called both Alonzo and Monty and advised them of his plans to see their mother, then head over to see Dad. He left out the part about Lindsay, knowing how they both felt about her. He didn't need to hear their grumbling and griping to add to his own.

He grabbed his lightweight black leather jacket, car and house keys and headed out.

When he pushed through the doors of the restaurant, he was surprised that it was pretty busy with sit-down customers at eight o'clock in the morning. Generally, at this time of the morning he would be in his office, in surgery or on the floors of the cardiac wing. He shoved out a breath, looked around and spotted Lindsay in a back booth. She was on the phone. He took his time walking down the aisle to where she sat.

Lindsay lifted her chin in acknowledgement and ended her call. She smiled broadly. "Thanks for coming," she said, while he slid into the seat opposite her.

"I didn't order. If I remember correctly you don't really do breakfast."

His eyebrow flicked.

The waitress stopped at their table. Franklin ordered coffee. Lindsay did as well along with a toasted bagel.

"So what was so important?" He leaned back in his seat and waited.

"I had a talk with the CEO."

"And?"

"He's willing to go to the board on your

behalf, nix the whole idea of you being replaced. We'll deal with the outcome of the inquiry, but your job is not going to be in jeopardy."

Franklin drew in a long breath and let it out slowly. He linked his fingers together on top of the table and leaned forward. "Why are you doing this?"

"The PC version or the truth?"

"Your call."

"Well, the PC version is that letting you go, with your reputation, would be a nightmare for the hospital, and that will affect the bottom line."

"Okay. And the truth?"

She ran her tongue along her bottom lip. "I owe you, Franklin. What happened with us, the way I handled things was wrong. You didn't deserve that."

He studied her expression looking for any sign that she was doing what she did best, running a game. But that part mattered less than the PC version. If he could get this incident behind him and move on, that was all he wanted — to get back to his patients. Slowly he nodded his head. "And what do I owe you in return?"

The waitress returned with their orders.

"Not that you owe me anything, but . . . dinner would be nice. As friends."

Franklin glanced away. Telling her that he was involved with someone was out of the question. Knowing Lindsay she'd ask questions. And he certainly couldn't tell her about Dina. "Sure. I guess that would be okay. As friends," he added with emphasis.

"Perfect." She stretched her hand across the table and covered his. "How's tomorrow night?"

"Uhh, tomorrow." He eased his hand away. "I'm not sure about that."

"Well, think about it." She lifted the mug to her lips and took a delicate sip.

CHAPTER 38

Dina sat behind her desk and scrolled through the information on the computer screen that detailed the rotation schedule for the day. Thankfully there were no surgeries until later in the week. After her morning rounds she would go up and see Dr. Freeman and give him her decision.

Her first stop was to check on a patient who had a pacemaker replacement and was listed to be discharged. She signed off on the paperwork with at-home instructions, wished him well, then continued her rounds. Her last stop was to see Ellen Grant.

She slid open the glass door to Ellen's room, pumped disinfectant on her hands from the dispenser on the wall, then snapped on a pair of latex gloves.

Ellen's eyes fluttered and a haloed smile of recognition lit her light brown eyes.

"How are you feeling this morning?" Dina asked as she approached the side of the bed, happy to see Ellen sitting up with a light breakfast tray. She set her iPad down on the bedside table. "Making good progress, I see," Dina said. "How did you sleep?"

"I'd rather be in my own bed."

Dina laughed lightly. "I'm sure you would." Dina smiled and lifted Ellen's delicate wrist to check her pulse. "I see they removed the oxygen mask. Are you comfortable with the nostril inserts?"

Ellen gave a slight shrug. "I won't complain."

"I want to check your incision. Okay?" She parted Ellen's gown and inspected the bandage. Delicately she peeled back the surgical tape and the gauze covering. She took a few moments for her examination, then replaced the bandage. "Looks good," she said while taking her stethoscope from around her neck. "Take a deep breath for me." She listened intently to the life-affirming beat of Ellen's heart. "Another deep breath," she said softly. Finally she re-draped the stethoscope around her neck. She placed her hand on Ellen's shoulder. "Everything sounds good, Mrs. Grant. The nurse will be in to run the EKG. As soon as I get the results back we'll talk about getting you out of bed and into a chair. Hopefully, later today." She smiled down at Ellen.

Ellen gripped Dina's hand with surprising strength. "Where's Louis?"

"From what I understand from Franklin, your husband is doing really well. No major injuries, but they were keeping him for a day or two. I'm sure Franklin can tell you more when he comes to see you."

"I want to see my husband," she whispered, taking Dina's hand. "I need to see him."

Dina pressed her lips together in thought. "Let me see what I can do. I'm sure we can work something out." She was immediately thinking of a FaceTime or Skype visit. She was pretty sure that the doctors at the hospital used iPads. She'd text Franklin and ask him to check. "I'll be back to see you later."

Ellen reached out, and with a surprising grip. "Wait. You and my son . . ."

Dina took a quick look over her shoulder toward the door. She stepped closer to the bed. "Yes?"

"He thinks this relationship between you is only temporary. Is it?"

Dina lowered her gaze for a moment then looked into Ellen's eyes. "No. It isn't temporary. At least I don't want it to be."

"Does he know that?"

Dina patted Ellen's hand. "Yes, he does. We talked."

Ellen released a sigh. Her eyes darkened. "Franklin is not only a brilliant doctor, and a wonderful son, he is a *good* man. He doesn't deserve what is happening and he has to come out of this whole on the other side."

"Please, I don't want you to worry. I'm sure that you know your son can take care of himself, no matter what. Finish your breakfast. I'll be back later."

She stopped at the nurse's station and on her iPad added her notes to Ellen's instructions, then exported them to the central computer at the nursing station providing the latest updates for any doctor or nurse who came in to treat Ellen. She put in the request for the EKG.

"I'll be off the floor for about a half hour. My pager is on if you need to reach me," Dina said to the head nurse. "As soon as the EKG results come back, let me know."

She went to her office for privacy and placed a call to Franklin. She was greeted by his voice mail.

"Hey, just saw your mom. She's doing well. Wants to see your dad. So, I was hoping that perhaps when you visit your dad we could set up a Skype or FaceTime so they could at least see each other. Anyway, I'm heading to see Freeman. We'll talk later." She disconnected the call and dropped her phone into her pocket. She reviewed two charts and verified the shift schedule before heading off to see Dr. Freeman.

Dina started off down the corridor just as Franklin, Alonzo and Monty stepped off the elevator. She walked right up to them.

"Good morning," she said, greeting the chocolate trio of delight. "I just came from your mother's room." She looked from one to the other. "She's doing well. I ordered an EKG, and, depending on the readout, we will try to get her up in a chair later today. Then taking a few steps tomorrow."

"Isn't that too soon?" Monty asked, concern deepening the line of worry between his brows.

"It's common practice," Franklin jumped in. "Patients respond much better the sooner we can get them up and moving. But if I don't think she's ready, she's not ready."

Dina's censoring gaze leaped to Franklin. What she didn't need was Franklin riding shotgun on her case, even if the patient was his mother. God forbid anything went wrong, she needed to be assured that she had the confidence of the family. "The test and my assessment will determine if she's ready," she said, directing her very clear position at Franklin. "She's eager to see you all and get an update on your father," she added before Franklin had a chance for a comeback. "I've got a meeting, but I'll be in to check on her later." She stepped around the trio and pressed the Up button.

"Thanks, Doctor," Alonzo said.

"Of course."

The metal doors swooshed open. She stepped on and faced the brothers. "Check your voice mail," she directed at Franklin. She stabbed the button for the top floor and the doors slid shut.

The last thing she wanted to do was walk into Freeman's office agitated. She needed to be clearheaded for whatever he put in front of her and not have her decisions tainted by emotion. Because right now she felt like snatching Franklin up by the collar. How dare he attempt to undermine her decision right in front of his family? She was Ellen Grant's doctor. Her decisions about treatment protocol were her decisions to make. Ellen would be in Cardiac ICU for at least another one to two days, and then to a regular room before being discharged, barring any complications or setbacks. And until she signed off on Ellen being released, what she said went. Period. Franklin was simply going to have to understand that, as difficult as it may be.

She drew in a breath of calm and walked toward the double doors leading to the president's office.

"Good morning. I'm here to see Dr. Freeman," she said to his assistant.

"Good morning, Dr. Hamilton. Dr. Freeman is expecting you, but he has someone in his office at the moment. If you would have a seat, I'll let him know you're here."

"Of course. Thank you." She walked over to the far side of the expansive waiting area and lowered herself down onto the plush lounge chair that felt expensive. On her previous visit she'd been too agitated to pay much attention to her surroundings. Now taking a moment to really look around she was a bit awed. Nothing was overstated but it was clear from the butter-soft off-white carpet to the mocha-toned Italian leather furnishings to the artwork and signed photographs of dignitaries and superstars that hung on pristine walls, that any visitor to the upper echelons of Jameson Memorial's inner sanctum would believe that this was where the real power resided.

The idea reminded her of the first day that she stepped into the surgical theater to lead the team on an open-heart procedure. Giving out commands, making split-second decisions, recalling everything you'd learned and witnessed all came into play. The reality that you had the power of life and death in your hands eclipsed finery any day. The real power was in the hands of surgeons.

That's why she and Franklin melded so well together. Beyond the physical and emotional attraction it was their passion, their often tunnel-vision drive when it came to their work and their patients, their desire to do whatever was necessary to do what was right, even at their own expense. Dina glanced up at a photograph of Freeman shaking hands with President Obama and the photo captured her thoughts completely.

"Dr. Hamilton."

She blinked the space back into focus. "Yes."

"Dr. Freeman will see you now."

Dina stood. "Thank you."

Just as she started toward the door it opened and Lindsay Gray stepped out with Freeman. He stood in the doorway.

"As I said, Richard, this is the best and only way. You'll see." She extended her hand, which he heartily shook with both of his.

Freeman glanced over and saw Dina. "Dr. Hamilton. Please come in."

Lindsay approached. "Dr. Hamilton." She put out her hand.

"Ms. Gray." Dina shook her hand.

"How are you managing in your new role?"

"Fine. Thank you."

"Exactly what I thought." She smiled in a long line. She tipped her head to the side.

"What *is* that scent you're wearing? I meant to ask you once before. I love it." She smiled sweetly.

"It's an oil actually."

"Hmm, very nice. Well, have a good meeting. Enjoy your day, Doctor."

"Thank you."

Lindsay sashayed off with a wave to Freeman's assistant.

Dina drew in a steady breath and walked toward the open door. Freeman stepped to the side to let her in.

"Dr. Hamilton, please have a seat."

Dina stepped around the chair in front of his desk and sat. She linked her fingers together on her lap.

Freeman flattened his hands on the desktop, pinched his lips together, then looked solemnly at Dina.

"Have you come to a decision?"

"Actually, I have. As much as I'm honored by the offer, I couldn't in good conscience take someone's job by default."

Freeman huffed. "We thought you would feel that way." He pursed his lips. "Here is what we are willing to offer. Once the inquiry is concluded — and if Grant is cleared — he would be the one to sign off on the completion of your fellowship." He rocked his head from side to side. "If things don't work out in Grant's favor, I would have to make the decision on your future here at Jameson."

Dina leaned in to interject.

Freeman held up his hand. "Hear me out. I'm willing to offer you an attending position in thoracic surgery and full use of our facilities to continue your robotic research."

Dina's eyes moved slowly across his face, watched his thin pink lips weave his tale. Was this the kind of environment she could work in, let alone flourish in? Did she want to be part of an organization where people were pawns, despite their value, skills and talents? Where all that mattered was the bottom line? She lifted her chin, her gaze level with his. "Why?"

"What do you mean?"

"Why the offer? Why me? Is it really because you value me as a surgeon or because you want to cover up the underhanded offer that was made to me in the first place — with the intention of pushing Dr. Grant out?" She gripped the arms of the chair and pushed to her feet.

Freeman's gaze followed her ascent. His cheeks flushed as if he'd been sitting in the sun too long. His jaw tightened. "I'd be very careful, Doctor. Your insinuations aren't taken lightly."

"I don't want them to be."

"I see."

Freeman stood, as well. He came from around the desk to stand in front of her, expanded his chest in his attempt to intimidate with his height and body.

Dina fought not to roll her eyes.

"I want you to understand that the offer back in California can disappear," he said in a monotone. "Chairman Phillip Holloway is very good friends with the chair at your former place of employment."

Dina's nostrils flared. She licked her bottom lip. She sputtered a derisive chuckle. "So that's how it is? I stay here, build up the hospital with my research, or tell you to go to hell with your 'offer' and lose everything I've spent my career building because you will see to it that there's nothing for me back home. Did I get that right, *Doctor* Freeman?"

He put on a benevolent smile. "As I said, Jameson Memorial would love to have you stay here, build your career, develop your research." He gave a slight shrug. "But if you don't want what we can offer you here . . . I totally understand."

Dina felt her heart bang so hard and fast in her chest she thought she would pass out. She wanted to snatch that smug look off his face, but she really wasn't up for being dragged out of the building by security. She needed a clearheaded minute to think.

"It was good talking with you, Dr. Freeman. Thank you for your time." Without another word she turned and walked out.

She fumed, so angry that she could feel the heat wafting around her. "The freaking nerve!" she spat and stabbed the button for the elevator. Her eyes burned with hot tears of fury that she dared not shed. What was she going to do? If she stayed, she would have compromised all her values. If she left — she had nothing to go back to. Freeman and Holloway would make sure of that.

CHAPTER 39

"We'll be back to see you later, Mom," Montgomery said, then leaned over and kissed her cheek.

"Do what the doctor says." Alonzo wagged a finger at his mother. "And I don't mean this doc," he added, lifting his chin in the direction of his brother.

Franklin's eyes tightened at the corners. "I'll see about getting you and Dad a face-to-face later today." He smiled at his mother, ignored Alonzo's comment.

She reached out her hand to Franklin. He came to the side of the bed. "She's good for you," she said only for him to hear. "And she cares about you, deeply. Don't let that big ego of yours run her off."

He started to respond but held his tongue. He leaned down and kissed her on the forehead. "I'll see you later." He walked out with his brothers.

"She's right, you know," Monty said.

"Right about what?"

"Dina," Alonzo filled in.

Franklin grumbled under his breath.

"Yeah, I saw how you were at the elevator," Monty said. "Ego."

"Whatever," he groused. "My first responsibility is to make sure that Mom gets the best care and the right decisions are made. Just because I've been sidelined on some BS doesn't negate the fact that I'm a damned good doctor," he snapped, burning them both with his gaze.

"Easy, man," Alonzo said, placing a calming hand on Franklin's shoulder. "We're all on the same page."

Franklin pushed out a breath. "I have a couple of stops to make, then I'm going over to check on Dad. Guess I'll see you there." He walked away.

"Hey, Frank —"

Alonzo clasped Monty's arm. "Let him go. He'll be okay. You know how Frank can get when his expertise is put into question. Can't be easy for him to have to be sidelined."

"Yeah," Monty conceded. "True. Anyway, he'll work it out. Always does. In the meantime, I'm starved. Let's grab something, then head over to see Dad."

■ ■ ■ ■

Franklin sat behind the wheel of his car in the visitors' parking lot. He studied the facade of the hospital — the name emblazoned in ten-foot letters above the shiny glass doors. He'd devoted the last fifteen years of his life to Jameson, to his patients. He'd racked up way more successes than failures and put Jameson on the map for innovative heart surgery techniques. None of that mattered. His future was in the hands of others. Something he couldn't abide. Maybe it was finally time for a change. He looked at the email message on his phone. The opportunity presented itself and he was going to step out on faith and take it.

Dina made the last of her rounds for the day. It had taken all of her focus to stay on task and not dwell on the shakedown of a meeting with Freeman. The question now was what was she going to do? How could she make this right? Not to mention that the inquiry was fast approaching and there was no telling how that would turn out based on what she'd experienced so far.

She entered the last of her notes in the system, packed up and headed home. Some wine and a sudsy bath were definitely in order. What she really wanted, she realized as she pulled into her driveway, was Franklin.

She put her key in the door. They'd confessed their love for each other. They promised to be there for each other. She tossed down her bag, stepped out of her shoes and dragged herself inside, suddenly bone weary, and went straight for the wine.

She filled a glass, put her feet up and took a long, quenching swallow. Those declarations of love and commitment — were they up to the challenge that she and Franklin were faced with? Never before did she have to choose between her happiness and her career. For her, career was everything. It filled all the empty spaces left by the deaths of her parents. Falling in love with Franklin shifted that. But did it shift it enough? Was she actually willing to give up everything for love and commitment?

Saying yes to Freeman would secure her future. Period. But end her future with Franklin. She took another swallow of wine, closed her eyes and rested her head back against the cushion of the couch.

His parents were in great spirits after being able to finally see each other, albeit through technology. That lifted some of the weight and anxiety from his shoulders as he eased his car to a stop on the street. While he'd watched his parents' joy at simply seeing each other's faces, and that even in their own illness and injury they only thought of each other and how soon they could be reunited, they reinforced for him what it meant to truly love someone else, to live your life to bring joy to another.

So much of his life had been about being the older brother role model, the scholar, the scientist, the renowned doctor, that he hadn't left time or space for much else. True, the relationship with Lindsay had shaken him, but more than that it gave him an excuse not to turn himself over to anyone else. He, for the most part, could control what happened in the operating room. He couldn't control his emotions, his heart. Good sense told him to fight for his job, his reputation. But his heart wanted more. For the first time in his life, he wanted more than what his career could ever provide. He wanted Dina.

The first drops of rain splashed against the windshield, blurring the outline of Dina's front door. A light came on in the second floor. Her bedroom. He could almost see her moving in that slow but deliberate way of hers, picking up and putting down. Was she going to take a bath or a shower? The image of her naked beneath the pulse of her shower bloomed in front of him. The rain intensified.

Franklin turned off the engine. After what happened between them earlier, he wouldn't blame her if she didn't want to see him. But he needed to see her, tell her what was on his heart and his plan.

CHAPTER 40

Dina paused, frowned in concentration. She turned off the water in the tub. Listened. It was the bell. She dried her hands and pushed up from the side of the tub. She didn't have a clique of friends so it was probably for next door.

She went down the stairs. "Who?" she called out.

"It's Franklin."

Her heart lurched. She ran her hands through the riot of twisting curls on her head, then pulled open the door. Even standing there in the rain, water dripping off his shoulders, he'd brought the sunshine.

"Franklin . . ."

"I should have called."

"No worries. Come in out of the rain." She quickly glanced up and down the street. "When did it start raining," she said as much to herself as to Franklin as she followed him inside.

"I don't want to drip all over your floor." He ran his hand across his hair and wiped his wet palm on his pants.

She laughed. "I'll get you a towel. As a matter of fact, why don't you come with me upstairs? I was running a bath. You can strip out of those wet things."

Franklin's full lips quirked into a grin. "Not a problem."

Franklin tugged his T-shirt over his head. Dina stepped to him and unfastened his pants, then turned on the tub water full blast. He slid out of his pants and kicked them to the side. The room filled with scented steam. Dina shrugged out of her robe and let it fall to the floor.

A slow, desirous smile lifted Franklin's mouth. "I could never get tired of looking at you."

"That's a good thing," she said, her voice growing husky. Her eyes roved over his muscular frame. "And I definitely feel the same way about you." She stepped into his arms, lifted her face to his.

Franklin covered her mouth with his lips.

Their unified sighs mixed with the steam and running water.

"I'm sorry," he murmured against her lips, kneading them tenderly with his teeth.

"About earlier."

"Shh, I know. It's okay." She stroked his cheek.

He scooped her up in his arms, walked over to the tub and lowered her into the water before stepping out of his shorts and joining her.

The heat of the water and their need for each other consumed them. Dina positioned herself between his outstretched legs and leaned back against his hard chest. Her eyes drifted closed as he used the soap to cleanse as well as entice, sliding it across her breasts and down her fluttering stomach.

Dina moaned, caressed his thighs.

Franklin's hand drifted down between her legs and stroked the slick space. Dina trembled, grabbed his hand and pressed it harder against her. "Right there," she groaned.

He was happy to oblige. He kissed the back of her neck. "There's not enough room in here for me to do what I want to do to you."

Dina glanced over her shoulder. Her eyes darkened. "Then let's fix that." She levered out of the tub, snatched a towel from the rack and hooked her finger for him to follow.

Franklin chuckled, grabbed a towel and

followed her into her bedroom.

Dina laid her towel on the bed and scooted on top of it. "Waiting on you," she teased, her thighs spread with invitation.

Franklin crawled onto the bed, starting at her ankles, placing hot kisses along her scented skin, up the inside of her legs, her thighs until he reached the soft down. Her body flexed. She gripped the sheets in her fists when his tongue circled and his lips suckled her.

"Ohhh . . ." Her hips rose.

Franklin slid his hands beneath her and pulled her tight against his hungry mouth.

Dina writhed and whimpered as the thrills rose and set her body on fire. She dug her fingertips into his shoulders; her eyes squeezed shut as she was consumed with sensations she could never name. Her thoughts grew cloudy.

"Yesss, yesss," she cried as the first wave slammed into her. "Oh God!"

Franklin had no desire to let her recover. He wanted her this way, open, willing, shivering with need for him. He entered her, hard, fast and deep, stopping her breath in her throat.

Her eyes flew open. Her lips parted to cry out, but no words formed.

Franklin moaned from deep in his center

when her wet walls wrapped around him and tightened. He lifted her legs over the bend of his arms until they were at his shoulders. Dina sucked in air, thrashing her head from side to side while he moved within her in long, deep thrusts, until they were both on the cusp of release.

"Look at me," Franklin rasped.

Dina's lids fluttered open, focused on his face.

"I love you, Dina."

"I love you," she said, her voice rough and shaky.

Franklin covered her mouth with his, dipped his tongue into her mouth and pushed them over the edge.

Still shaken, Dina curled tightly against him. Her heart was pounding. She felt giddy, deliriously happy. This was what she'd longed for, dreamed of. To have someone like Franklin love her was more than she'd ever imagined.

"There's something I need to tell you," she said into the darkness.

"Me, too. But you first."

She drew in a breath and slowly explained to him what transpired in her meeting with Freeman and his veiled ultimatum.

Franklin spewed a string of expletives.

Dina gripped his hand that cupped her breast. "I decided that I'm not going to take his offer. I couldn't."

"He could ruin you!"

"The work I've done with robotics is too valuable. If I can't stay at Jameson — and I don't want to after this . . ."

"And Saint Vincent will be screwed anyway?"

She turned around so that she could face him. "Too far from you, anyway," she said softly. "I'll find another hospital — maybe Johns Hopkins. I can always do research. It'll be okay. I'll be fine."

"You may not have to worry about any of that."

"What do you mean?"

"Several months ago I applied for a research grant. A big one. I got a message today that it was approved. I'll have the official letter by the end of the week."

"What? Oh my God. That's wonderful! Congratulations." She palmed his cheeks and kissed him.

"The thing is, I'd have to leave DC and move to the Seattle Research Center, and I want you with me. Together we can change the face of cardiac surgery. We'll have the money, the facilities and the support. I'll have free rein to build my own team."

Dina lowered her gaze. "Frank . . . that's a wonderful opportunity, but it's *your* opportunity. I've worked just as hard to get where I am. I had a chance to go back to California and build my *own* team, my *own* department." She flipped onto her back and stared into the darkness. "That may be gone now, but I can't settle . . . take a handout. I don't want to be the woman who rises to the top because of a man."

"Woman, there is no one in the industry that doesn't know of the groundbreaking work you've done. You come to Seattle, you call your own shots, run your own division, just the way you wanted. This is no handout. You deserve and have earned this chance. Take it! Don't let ego get in the way. I can tell you from experience that it's not all it's cracked up to be."

She stifled a chuckle. "I'll think about it."

"Fine."

"Let me ask you something. If you applied for this grant months ago, did you always plan to leave Jameson?"

"I knew it was a possibility. It was one of the reasons why I was grooming you. I wanted you to take my place if it came to that. But it would have been on my terms, not all this bull that's happened with the hospital." He paused. "And I didn't bank on falling in love with you."

She flipped onto her side to face him. "I didn't bank on falling in love with you either." She sighed heavily. "This is big," she whispered.

"Yeah, it is."

"Let's get the inquiry out of the way . . . and I'll give you my decision."

He kissed her forehead. "I'll tell you like a wise woman told me. Let your heart decide."

CHAPTER 41

The inquiry into the possible wrongful death proceeding against Dr. Franklin Grant began on Wednesday, nearly three weeks after the incident. All members of the surgical team were interviewed and questioned by a panel of their peers. Video and audio recordings of the operation were presented, discussed and dissected. It took the panel seven days to come to a unanimous conclusion that Dr. Grant was not responsible for the death, and nothing that he did or instructed his team to do contributed to the loss of the patient. Autopsy results confirmed the panel's conclusion that the patient's heart simply failed and that all measures had been taken to save him. The panel determined that Dr. Grant must regain his full status and return to duty.

Franklin sat at the long table, facing the panel. "I want to first thank everyone for their time and diligence. I am relieved of course by your findings. But what I came to discover in the past few weeks is that whether I was found guilty or innocent, Jameson Memorial is no longer the place for me." He pushed to his feet. "Thank you." He walked out leaving everyone with their mouths open.

He strode down the corridor toward his office for the last time, feeling better and lighter than he'd felt in longer than he could remember. He had a chance to do great work, work that he was destined to do — without the strings and hypocrisy that ran rampant at Jameson.

"Franklin!"

He stopped, turned to see Lindsay hurrying down the hallway. She stopped in front of him.

"What the hell was that? You're leaving?" Her eyes were wide in disbelief.

He half smiled. "Yep."

"But why? Everything worked out. You got your job."

He tipped his head to the side. "Thank you for everything, Lindsay. Really. But what I do — it's more than a job. And if you know me like you think you once did, you'll understand that, and understand why I can't stay here. I have a chance to do truly

important work, and I'm going to take it."
He leaned down and kissed her cheek.
"Take care of yourself." He started to leave.

"She's good for you, you know."

He stopped midstride, frowned in question.

Lindsay winked. "See, I do know you."
She spun away in the opposite direction.

Franklin shook his head and chuckled.
"Go figure," he murmured.

CHAPTER 42

"Well it's about damned time," Monty said, then tilted the bottle of beer up to his lips. "You're too good for that place. It would have sucked you dry."

"My sentiments exactly," Alonzo echoed. "There's nothing like being your own boss."

With their parents out of the hospital and on the road to a full recovery, the family returned to their routine dinner gathering.

Louis put his arm around his wife's shoulder. "When are you planning on leaving, son?"

Ellen sniffed and pressed her lips tightly together.

Franklin snatched a look at Dina and took her hand. "Right after the new year. We figured that would give Mom and Dad enough time to fully get on their feet and . . . plan a small family wedding." He burst into a grin that lit the room.

Dina giggled like a schoolgirl, then boldly

held out her left hand to showcase the blazing diamond.

Monty jumped, covered his eyes. "Whoa! I'm blind," he teased.

Alonzo slapped his thighs. "Congratulations, bruh." He got up and grabbed Franklin in a bear hug before doing the same to Dina.

"Hey, watch it, man," Franklin playfully scolded. "That's my wife-to-be you squeezing on."

Monty pushed Alonzo out of the way, lifted Dina off her feet and spun her around. "Welcome to the family!"

"Oh, Franklin," Ellen cried, tears of happiness streaming down her cheeks. "I prayed for this day for you."

Franklin walked over to where his parents sat on the couch and hunched down in front of them. "I have the best examples in the world in both of you. I let my work fill the spaces until the time was right and the woman was right." He stretched out his hand for Dina. She came and bent down beside him.

"I haven't had a family in a very long time," she said, her voice unsteady. "I thought it was out of my reach." She looked to Franklin with love blooming in her eyes. "And then Franklin brought me into his world and his heart, and I started to believe that family for me was possible."

"Oh, sweetheart," Ellen said. She cupped Dina's cheek. "You have a family now."

"I hope you'll be adding to the numbers real soon," Louis said with a wink.

"Dad!" the brothers chorused with laughter.

Franklin and Dina sat out on the porch of his parents' home, under the light of a sky sprinkled with stars.

"I'm really happy that Anna was offered the attending spot. She deserves it. I hope she realizes that," Dina said.

"She'll do just fine."

Dina rested her head on his shoulder. "Seattle, huh. Hear it rains a lot."

"Might have to spend a lot of time indoors."

"In bed," she whispered.

"I like the sound of that."

"Yeah, me, too."

She lifted her head to meet his lips and they sealed their future.

ABOUT THE AUTHOR

Donna Hill began writing novels in 1990. Since that time she has had more than forty titles published, which include full-length novels and novellas. Two of her novels and one novella were adapted for television. She has won numerous awards for her body of work. She is also the editor of five novels, two of which have been nominated for awards. She easily moves from romance to erotica, horror, comedy and women's fiction. She was the first recipient of the *RT Book Reviews* Trailblazer Award and won the *RT Book Reviews* Career Achievement Award. Donna lives in Brooklyn with her family. Visit her website at www.donnahill.com.

■ ■ ■ ■

SEALED WITH A KISS

NICKI NIGHT

■ ■ ■ ■

This book is dedicated to my heartbeats

—

Les, Milan & Laila.

ACKNOWLEDGMENTS

Lord! Thank you. We did it again. This journey has been such a blessing. There are many people who helped bring this story together. Thank you to my editors, Glenda Howard and Rachel Burkot. To my agent, Sara Camili, thank you for everything. As always, to my author girlfriends who help keep me sane — Zuri Day, Lutishia Lovely, Tiffany L. Warren, Victoria Christopher Murray, ReShonda Tate Billingsley, Leslie Elle Wright, Sheryl Lister, Brenda Jackson, Beverly Jenkins, Donna Hill and so many more. Thanks for the cocoon of your creativity, sanity, insanity and warmth, and thank you for always being the wonderful women that you authentically are. I adore each of you. To my street team, thank you for helping me spread the word — Priscilla Johnson, Michelle Chavis, Rowena Green Winfrey, Shavonna Futrell, Cheryl McClinton, Deidre Young, Yolanda

Rigby-Wilson and Shannon Harper. To my heartbeats, Big Les, Little Les, Milan and Laila, you are my inspiration. I hope I impress you forever. To my siblings, my gals, readers and book clubs nationwide, thanks a gazillion! Where would I be without your support? I dunno! However, if I failed to mention your name, please know that I thank you and love you, and that you rock!

Dear Reader,

I hope you will enjoy getting to know the talented Kendall Chandler and the handsome entertainment mogul Tyson Blackwell. Have fun taking this journey as their love affair unfolds.

Kendall is ready to take her acting career to the next level. Love is the last thing on her mind. Besides, she's not interested in mixing business with pleasure, since that has never worked out well in the past. However, when Tyson Blackwell comes along, neither can manage to help themselves, despite each of their vows to steer clear of dating others who also share the spotlight.

Find out if the spotlight creates more distance for these two who seem adamant to stick to their vows, or if the spark that crackles between them is just too strong to be ignored. Enjoy the ride!

Ciao,
Nicki Night

CHAPTER 1

Kendall promised herself she wouldn't spend any more time or energy taking in what those meddlesome bloggers wrote. Yet she found herself clicking her way right into that rabbit hole from the alert from Google that appeared in her emails. How did she get sucked in again?

"Ugh!" Her hard groan reached the rafters of her spacious home. She bounced back against her chair and huffed.

Despite almost a year passing, her and Storm Sanders's highly publicized breakup was still a hot topic in the social media stratosphere. Bloggers weren't tired of writing about it and the public didn't seem tired of hearing about it, so the scandal lived on like a sitcom in a syndicated afterlife. But Kendall was tired — tired of the media, tired of being questioned if she still loved him, tired of being mentioned by bloggers whenever Storm was spotted with another woman, tired of Storm. Kendall wished everyone could move on like she had. Storm's betrayal had lingered for too long. The lingering had prolonged the hurt until she'd finally become numb. She was so glad to be over that ordeal.

The media enjoyed debating whether or not she and Storm were over each other. No one bothered asking either of them directly. Paparazzi caught snapshots as they moved about separately, and somehow the pictures ended up side by side in celebrity gossip rags. They'd ask intrusive questions, printing whatever they chose despite their answers, so Kendall stopped responding to them altogether.

Buying a place outside of Los Angeles was the best decision she'd made in a long time. Kendall's secret sanctuary in Temecula, Southern California's wine country, was more than an hour away. The residents there didn't meddle so much. Even as a well-known pop star, she could shop and dine practically undisturbed. It's not like the people in Temecula didn't know who she was, but it was void of paparazzi at every turn, and the town was much more mellow in the presence of celebrities. Kendall would sign the occasional autograph but had yet to find people with cameras lurking in her bushes.

Kendall still kept a condo in a gated community in LA, but when she was done with work, she'd trek back to Temecula where she could enjoy a semblance of a normal life in her lakeside home. Her heart lived in Chicago with her family. She also kept an apartment in New York on the West Side overlooking the Hudson for those times when business brought her to the East Coast.

But East Coast or West, her life belonged to her public. Minimal privacy came with her line of work, but every now and then, she wished she could remove the famous parts of her and live incognito.

Kendall left her laptop in her study, went to the kitchen to make a cup of tea and sat in the room that had made her fall in love with the house. Folding her legs underneath her, she curled up in her favorite wing chair and took in the unobstructed view of the lake at the end of her yard and mountains in the distance through the wall of glass doors. Kendall did her best thinking here. She'd done her best everything here — crying, laughing, writing, reading. It was in that very chair that she'd mapped out her goals in her journal. She was going to be more than just a singer. Both sides of the big screen called her name. Kendall was going to make it in front of and behind the camera. She'd already visualized herself acting, directing and producing films.

Kendall's first attempt at film didn't go so well and nearly tainted her name in Hollywood. She shook her head to get rid of those memories. She was at peace and didn't want to go there. It was time to show the world how serious she was about taking her career to new heights.

Kendall heard a faint ringing and realized she'd left her phone in the kitchen. Placing her tea on the small round table next to her cozy chair, she jogged to the counter to answer.

"Hello."

"Kendall!" Her agent sang her name. Kendall smiled and prepared herself for good news. "Are you sitting down?" Randi asked.

Kendall hopped on the countertop. "I am now."

"Are you ready for this?"

"Randi. Spill it! I can't take the suspense."

"I just got a call from the producers of that new biopic that rumors have been swirling about, and guess who they want to play Jocelyn James?" Randi squealed.

Kendall slid down from the counter. Her mouth fell open. Seconds ticked by before she could speak. "Me?"

"Yep. Can you believe it?"

"Oh. My. Goodness! Are you *serious*!" Kendall felt like she could leap ten feet into the air. "They want me?"

"They want you, baby girl!" She called Kendall a range of pet names.

Kendall screamed. Stomped. Screamed again. "Wooo! This is huge, Randi. Huge!"

"It's your time, my dear! We're going to show this world what you've got! So, it's a go?"

"It most certainly is."

"Woo! Great. I'll get all the deets and get right back to you."

"I hope I can do her justice. She is one of my dad's favorite artists."

"For sure! I think you can do Jocelyn James superior justice. She was gorg, you're gorg, your voice has a jazzy flair . . . you'll rock at playing her." Kendall could hear Randi suck her teeth and imagined her waving her off. "So, Pops was into jazz, huh?"

"He loves it. He's going to be so excited to hear about this."

"Okay. I'm gonna jump off here and call them back to let them know you'll take the role. You'll have to come out of the woods, babe," she said, referring to Kendall's Temecula home. "They'd like for you to come and do a read sometime this week."

"Not a problem. I was coming up to LA to meet with some friends this weekend anyway."

"Cool. Come up earlier and we'll do lunch."

"You got it."

"Later, doll — and congrats!"

Kendall hung up the phone and shimmied. She threw her hands in the air and squealed. "This is happening!"

Kendall's plan to reinvent herself was coming to pass. Now, if only the other areas of her life could come into alignment.

CHAPTER 2

Saying goodbye was never easy, but this time, Tyson Blackwell was ready. He almost looked forward to life without Tiffany Reddick. The whirlwind they'd lived had become tiresome, and it was obvious that she loved the frenzy more than him. Tiffany had used him to gain more spotlight than she'd ever experienced. Tyson chided himself for not seeing the truth right away. Instead he was taken by her beauty, her zest and her sense of ambition. That was before realizing their adoration for one another wasn't reciprocal — Tiffany was an unapologetic opportunist.

Tyson stepped back until the mirror reflected the fullness of his tall frame. Tugging on the lapels of his tux, he turned to one side and then the other. He looked good — ready. Tyson looked forward to tonight's movie premiere and the dance he and Tiffany would do for the cameras. The world wasn't aware of their breakup yet. They wanted the movie to be the big news, not their relationship status. Everyone who wasn't close enough to keep their secret would find out after opening weekend, and they were determined to control the narrative.

Despite what he knew of her, Tyson never let the truth pass his lips. He wouldn't dare muddy her public's view of Hollywood's newest rising star, their new sweetheart and the star of the biggest movie of his career as a producer, a role he enjoyed in addition to the title of CEO soon to be passed down from his father. Instead, he was sure her true colors would eventually burst through her as if she'd swallowed a rainbow.

Tyson saw his phone light up before it rang.

"Ready for the big night?" his brother, Turner, asked.

Tyson squirted a splash of cologne onto his neck. "Yep."

After a few moments passed, Turner asked, "Are you okay?"

Tyson didn't answer right away. "Yeah. I'm ready." Soon the sting would be gone. Talking about their failed relationship would be less burdensome once they were really done. He was tired of playing charades. That day hadn't come yet.

"You sure?"

"I'm sure. You're bringing what's-her-name . . . Kimberly?"

"No. You'll meet this one tonight."

Tyson chuckled. "You rascal, as Dad would say."

"Hey! I'm a single man. I'm entitled to my pick of women."

"I can't argue with that." Tyson was single now too. He remembered the fun and lure of dating but hadn't expected to get back into it so soon. Hopefully dating hadn't lost its luster. This time, he'd stay on the market awhile, have some fun, push serious dating off for some time and finish getting Tiffany's betrayal completely out of his system. She hadn't cheated with another man. She'd simply cheated him out of a genuine connection under false pretenses. Tyson had to give it to her. She was a hell of an actress.

". . . best that I get it out of my system now." Tyson pulled himself from his thoughts and focused on what his brother was saying. "That way," Turner continued, "when and if I decide to settle down, I'll only have eyes for my wife. By then, my oats will have been sowed and harvested. Ha!"

"Probably cooked too." Tyson laughed with him. "See you at the theater."

"Cool. Are you coming with Tiffany?"

Tyson hesitated again. "Yeah."

Turner sighed. "I'm sure you can't wait until this is over."

A sharp inhale followed by a loud exhale was his initial response. "Let Dad know that I'm on my way."

"You got it."

Tyson ended the call and stuffed his wallet in his pocket. Without looking at his watch, he knew his driver would arrive soon, and sure enough, he did.

At Tiffany's home, they waited fifteen minutes for her to emerge from the house. If each of those minutes went into putting the finishing touches on Tiffany's gorgeous look, they were all worth it. Tyson knew she'd be stunning, but he hadn't expected his own breath to hitch. A single wide braid wrapped around the edges of her hairline and blossomed into an elegant bun in the back of her head. The soft flair of her ivory gown and the way it embraced her curves made her look both angelic and sexy at the same time.

Tyson cleared his throat and sat up straighter in his seat. Why couldn't things have been different? *It takes much more than beauty.* Remembering his gentlemanly ways, he stepped out of the car to greet Tiffany, hugging her in a friendly manner and then helping her into the car. The driver shut the door and rounded the vehicle to return to the driver's seat.

"Don't you look handsome?" Tiffany said with a wink.

"Thank you. And you look quite stunning yourself."

"I might have to keep our breakup quiet for a while longer just to keep you off the market."

"Tiffany."

She waved her hand. "It was a joke, Tyson." She sucked her teeth. "When did you become so serious?" She turned to look out the window.

"Ready for tonight's performance?" Tyson asked, referring to the two of them acting like they were still together.

Tiffany turned to look at him. She narrowed her eyes for several moments before scooting closer to him. "Maybe," she whispered, running the back of her index finger down the side of his face, "we should rehearse."

"Tiffany." Tyson sighed her name. Before he could speak again, she kissed him.

The kiss happened in slow motion. Tyson became aware of her lips on his when he felt her softness. He kissed her back, waiting to feel that surge of excitement from before. He remembered when her kisses would soften him, entice him, release waves of wild passion inside of him. Things were different now. The effect wasn't there.

Tiffany pulled back, her hand still on his cheek. She stared into his eyes for a moment, blinked. Focusing on her dress, she brushed away imaginary lint. "I would say that required another take, but I don't think it will get any better."

Tyson sat straight, but let his head relax against the headrest. He assumed that, like him, Tiffany expected more from their kiss. Both seemed to wait for some kind of surge or shift. It didn't happen. Tiffany retreated to her side of the car, stared out the window. They clung to opposite sides of the backseat, taking in the blurred scenery of the passing landscape until they reached the theater.

The car pulled to a stop. Lights flickered against the dark tinted windows. Once again, his driver exited, and seconds later he pulled Tyson's door open. Tyson unfolded himself from the rear, attempting to look lean, fit and refined. He reached back, took Tiffany by the hand. She cooed and cast dreamy eyes on Tyson. He smiled back, pulled her to him. They kissed, broke apart to stare into each other's eyes and pecked lips again. Tiffany ran her thumb across his moist lips. He took her hand, and on cue, together, they turned toward the flashing cameras. Tiffany leaned into him, cooed again, smiled and waved to their fans — her fans.

"Tiffany!" someone yelled from the sidelines. More cameras flashed. "We love you!"

Press waved for their attention. Fans lined up behind stanchions, loving them. Loving their chemistry. Every other step they snuggled and posed for the cameras. She ran her hands down the front of his tux, touched his lips, his cheeks. Tyson never let her other hand go. More pictures were taken. She pressed her body against his, rested her head on his shoulder, leaned back and tossed carefree laughter into the air. The cameras illuminated the red carpet.

"We love you, Tyfany!" Their fans had given them a power couple nickname, like Brad Pitt and Angelina Jolie's Brangelina or Kanye West and Kim Kardashian's Kimye.

Inside the premiere, Tiffany hardly left his side. They smiled for more cameras. Tyson was charming and Tiffany was lovable, becoming America's next sweetheart. Together they were adorable. Their public feasted on their chemistry.

The audience was on their feet at the end

of the movie. Tiffany aced her starring role as a historical figure in a tale of overcoming odds.

"Oscar-worthy, don't you think?" she leaned over and whispered in Tyson's ear.

He raised both brows. A small grin played at the corner of his lips. That wouldn't be a bad thing, but he knew Tiffany well — had seen all of her personas, from the sweetheart to the sex kitten to the key one she kept hidden, but when it had emerged, it became the weight that broke the relationship. The manipulator. If she rose to the top too fast, she'd become a diva of the worst kind.

Tiffany and Tyson maintained their ruse through the reception that followed the movie. By the time his driver pulled up to Tiffany's stately home, Tyson was exhausted.

"Come inside." Tiffany's gaze was direct. Her words hit Tyson's ears like a command.

They'd been here before. Dozens of times. Tyson remained quiet, holding her gaze. Torn.

Tiffany sighed. "I guess it's really over."

Before today, Tyson would have already told his driver to come back for him later. But this dance with Tiffany had already lingered far too long after the music stopped playing. Tyson was still attracted to her. Any man with reasonable eyesight would be. And as a man who enjoyed spoiling his woman, he'd given in to her more than he ever should have. But Tyson didn't like the feeling of being strung along and continuing this routine with Tiffany made him feel like he was dangling from the end of her puppet strings. This needed to end.

"Good night, Tiffany." Tyson stared directly at her, fighting the temptation. He could give in just one last time or he could stand his ground.

Tiffany's mouth hung open slightly. She blinked, surprised by his response. He could feel coolness emanating off her because of his rejection. Tiffany blinked a few more times, cleared her throat and then sucked her teeth. Without another word, she fumbled with the lock, jabbing the button until she heard the door click. Yanking the lever, Tiffany swung the door open and threw it back so hard, the sound of metal bending squawked in the air. A second later she was out of the car and slamming the door behind her.

"Let's make sure she gets in." Tyson's voice was even. He let his window down and watched Tiffany stomp her way up the walk and enter the house. He sighed again and rolled up the window. The driver pulled away. Tyson watched the house until he could no longer see it, confident that it would be the last time he'd set eyes on Tiffany's home.

CHAPTER 3

"Kendall!" Randi sang in her usual way.

"Hey, Randi." Kendall stood, knocking over the water the waitress had just placed on her small bistro table, and hugged her agent and friend. Water streamed between the slim slits in the bistro table onto Kendall's toes. Randi grabbed a napkin and dabbed at the water. Kendall waved the waitress over. Despite the little mishap, alfresco dining was Kendall's favorite. A cute hat and sunglasses helped keep her identity at bay when she was out, but Kendall even dined outside when she was at home alone.

"You ready, darling?" Randi's eyes widened with excitement. She rubbed her palms together before taking a seat opposite Kendall. "This is just the beginning, babe."

Kendall put her hand to her chest. "I'm more than ready. This is going to be it. Nothing like the last time."

"Oh yeah." Randi pursed her lips. "And that sleazebag is still in the business. Can you believe it?" she said, referring to the producer of the last movie Kendall had played in. "There needs to be a special place for jerks like him. One that girls like us get to hold the key to." A look of disgust deepened the lines in her face.

"I still can't believe he spread rumors about me being difficult to work with." The mere thought of Henry Douglas made Kendall shudder. "Jerk! I can just imagine the poor girls who fell for his crap."

Randi wrapped her arms around herself, scrunched her nose and shivered in the 80-degree weather as if it were cold. "And he was old enough to be your father. Yuck!"

Randi laughed, thankful for her friend's ability to lighten the tension. It had only lasted a moment, but the memory of his sleazy advance made her feel as if slime were sliding down her skin.

"That's why this project is so important. That fool had the editors cut most of my parts out of that film. People barely remembered that I was in the movie. That was supposed to be my debut to the world, helping me launch my acting career, and he ruined that because I wouldn't let him kiss me." Kendall shook her head. "That's total bull—" Kendall swallowed the expletive positioned at the end of her sentence.

Randi covered Kendall's hands with hers. "And you handled yourself like a champ, sweetie. I hope he learned something after you put him on his ass — literally!" Randi leaned back so the waiter could place a bottle of sparkling water and a glass full of ice on the table. "I bet he never expected all that strength to come from little ole you." Randi sat, folding her arms in front of her.

"Yeah. I thanked my dad for forcing me to take those karate lessons. Never knew how well it would serve me. Anyway." Kendall waved her hand. She was done with those memories — for now. If she continued talking about that ordeal her mood would be soured, and she had an audition to ace.

"Yeah, anyway! So, did you rehearse?"

Kendall brightened, sat up taller. "Of course I did. I have every one of Jocelyn's albums and have been singing her songs since you called me last week. I'm more than ready. They need to be ready for me."

"Have some tea with honey." Randi turned toward the approaching waiter. "Can she get a tea with honey, please, and I'll have the quinoa burger with sweet potato fries. That will be all."

Kendall's mouth fell open. She stared at

Randi. "Randi!" she scolded. "I'm hungry." She laughed.

Randi wagged her finger. "No, no, no. Tea now, and food after the audition. My treat. Cool?"

Kendall looked at her watch and huffed. She had to meet with the producers soon. "Ugh! Okay. Cool. Get your wallet ready because my appetite is growing as we speak. By the time this audition is over, I'll be *hangry*!"

Kendall and Randi entered the modern glass building and were directed to the tenth floor. The doors opened to a glass lobby with the BCG logo in large metal lettering. The receptionist smiled and scurried from behind the desk.

"Oh my goodness. Kendall Chandler!" She shook Kendall's hand as if she were trying to remove her entire arm from her body.

"Hello." Kendall smiled.

"Wow. Wow. Oh wow. It's so great to see you." She was still shaking Kendall's hand.

Kendall chuckled. "It's great to meet you too, uh . . ."

"Uh. Um. Kim! Yes. My name's Kim. I have every single one of your albums. All of them are my favorite." Her laugh morphed into a squeal. "Oh goodness. Okay." Kim ran around to the other side of the desk. "I'll let them know you're here."

"Tell 'em I'm here too," Randi teased. "The name's Chopped Liver. Ha!"

Kim slapped her forehead. "I'm so sorry. It's just that —"

"I know." Randi dismissed the woman's apology. "Happens all the time. I'm just teasing."

"Whew! I'll tell them you're here."

Kendall and Randi took seats in the sleek, gray chairs along the wall. Moments later, a young gentleman with the sides of his head shaved and a pile of curls on top ushered them through shaded glass doors, down a corridor into what appeared to be a conference room. They were greeted by the project's producer, executive producer, director and someone from the casting team. Cordialities were exchanged, Randi took a seat, and the crew asked Kendall a few questions about Jocelyn James. She read a few lines, mimicking Jocelyn's Tennessee drawl before being asked to sing something for them.

"What should we play for you?"

"Oh, I don't need music," Kendall said. She saw Randi wink and nod from where she sat. "I've got this."

The crew looked at one another, nodding.

"Okay," the director said doubtfully. "Go for it."

Kendall took a deep breath and began singing. It was her father's favorite — a deep, sultry love song that she'd sang a thousand times. She felt the music in her flesh and disappeared into the rhythm. Kendall let the song carry her away, as if she were floating along with every note. She belted the end and closed with a sweet whisper just like Jocelyn had been known for. When she finished, the room was completely silent. Everyone stared at her, some with mouths hanging open. Randi quietly clapped in her corner, smiled and thrust her fist forward. From that, Kendall knew she'd aced the audition.

The director's clapping finally broke the silence. He nodded. "That was incredible."

"Thank you!" Kendall's cheeks burned from blushing.

The door opened, stealing everyone's attention, including Kendall's. She felt the smile slide from her face as she took in the long strides of the man she recognized as Tyson Blackwell. They had been in the same circles, but never actually met before. Kendall mostly knew of him through the media's obsession with covering his every move as if he were an A-list actor or entertainer as opposed to someone behind the scenes. She took in his designer shoes, jeans that must have been all too happy to cover his most prized possession, white button-down shirt that fit like it was made specifically for his taut chest, five o'clock shadow framing the most luscious lips she'd ever laid eyes on, skin so smooth it looked like chocolate-colored glass and dark eyes so commanding, she thought she'd levitate just by staring into them.

Kendall had always thought Tyson was good-looking from a distance, but up close, he was a work of art. Kendall's eyes started at his feet. Italian handmade shoes covered large feet. Long legs gave way to a taut torso that pressed against his expensive, cuff-linked dress shirt. His suit was stylish and fit well, obviously custom-made. Strong masculine fingers darted across the screen of his cell phone. She imagined what he might have been capable of doing to women with those fingers. The feel of them had to drive women wild. Smooth jet-black hairs framed a luscious pair of full lips in the form of a goatee.

When he smiled, Kendall caught a glimpse of perfect pearls for teeth. The deep brown hue of his supple skin sunk in at his cheeks, creating dimples that could have been mistaken for craters. They made his smile sexy and adorable at the same time. Lastly, those eyes — dark, hooded, mysterious and piercing. Kendall looked away so as not to get lost in them. Tyson Blackwell was male perfection.

No wonder that actress Tiffany Reddick clung to him the way she did in public. If Tyson were Kendall's man, she might never leave his side. Kendall shook her head and laughed. He wasn't single, and she wasn't looking anyway.

Tyson joined the men at the table.

"One moment." The executive producer held up a finger to Kendall. They chatted amongst themselves for several moments.

"Ty. You need to hear this," the director said, turning back toward Kendall.

"Beautiful and unfiltered," said the one who'd introduced himself as the producer. He slapped the table, stressing his point.

Kendall's cheeks burned again. She'd heard from plenty of people that she had a beautiful voice. Why was she blushing so much now?

"Can you do that just one more time?" the producer asked. "Please?"

"Sure." Kendall shrugged, took another deep breath and began to sing again. No one stopped her, so she sang the entire song.

"See," the director said, holding his hand out as if he were presenting Kendall.

"Whoa." Tyson clapped. "That was amazing." He walked over to Kendall and held his hand out. "Tyson Blackwell. I'm a huge fan." He wrapped his large but incredibly soft hand around hers and shook.

Kendall wanted to melt into a puddle right there in front of everyone. *Stop it! He's taken. The industry is already full of trifling man-stealers,* she scolded herself. *Like the one who slept with Storm.* "Hello, Mr. Blackwell. Thank you. I'm quite flattered." Kendall banished those thoughts and focused on the work of art holding her hand, which had started to grow warm and moist.

"Please call me Tyson. I'm definitely not old enough for you to address me so formally."

Kendall's cheeks heated. "Thank you. Tyson," she added his name almost as an afterthought. "I'm glad you like my music." He flashed that sexy smile, but the fact that he was still holding on to her hand made her question his loyalty. Didn't he have a girlfriend — a famous one at that? Kendall pulled her hand from his grasp, hoping that he wasn't proving to be another Hollywood cheater. Of all arenas, this playground was way too small.

"Thank you for coming today, Kendall. We'll be in touch with your agent shortly." The producer's words burst into her consciousness.

Kendall wiped her hands along her maxi dress. "Great! I'll be waiting to hear from you. Thanks for giving me the opportunity to audition for this part. Jocelyn James is a family favorite."

"You're welcome," he said. "Believe me, it was our pleasure." He looked among his colleagues, who cosigned with nods.

Kendall and Randi said their goodbyes. She felt the warmth of Tyson's gaze on her as she headed toward the door. She refused to look back, though it was hard not to peek. Kendall couldn't feed into what he was putting out. His relationship with Tiffany was very public — just the kind of public she preferred to stay away from. Tyson was like a masterpiece at the Smithsonian — amazing to look at but perpetually untouchable. It was best for her to put distance between them now. She wasn't a cheater, and the last thing she needed was to give the blogs a new scandal to chew on for the next couple of months.

Besides, she'd come for business and that's what she planned to stick to. There was no way she'd let another man get in the way of her budding film career. It didn't matter how gorgeous he was.

CHAPTER 4

Tyson's phone rang, but instead of picking it up, he simply rolled over in his bed. The past few days had been long and arduous — pretty much nonstop since the premiere the week before. Tiffany had been featured on just about every news and talk show promoting the opening of the film. The media reported record-breaking ticket sales the first night and spread rumors that Tiffany's performance was potentially Oscar-worthy. Now that the weekend was over, they would find out just how well the movie had done. All of this was great. Great for Tiffany. Great for BCG. And great for Tyson. So why was he so bummed?

Tyson's phone rang again. He didn't bother checking who was calling. That way he wouldn't feel guilty for not answering. Normally Tyson would be at work by now, even though the sun had just made an appearance a short while ago. But this ordeal with Tiffany had him in a flux. The breakup was bad enough. Tyson prided himself on being able to gauge people, and the fact that he hadn't realized he was being used until it was too late bothered him sorely.

There was no doubt that Tiffany was an amazing actress. Her performance the night of the premiere proved that point even more. The public ate up their fake doting on each other. Tyson couldn't help but wonder how much acting she had been doing during the good times in their relationship.

Tyson decided to avoid dating actresses going forward. He thought back to a few days before, when he'd met Kendall Chandler for the first time at the audition. She was even more beautiful up close than she was on TV. They'd attended a few industry events together, but never actually talked. Plus, Tiffany was usually right on his arm. But she was an entertainer and a budding actress too. He'd flirted a little, holding her hand extra-long when they shook, but later tossed aside the idea of seeing more of her. He needed a new dating pool. No more celebrities — at least for now. He hated painting them with a broad stroke but didn't like being played and feeling vulnerable.

Worse, Tiffany was neither apologetic nor ashamed about her intentions. *This is Hollywood,* she'd tossed out in response to his inquiries about whether or not she'd dated him just because he was producing the project she wanted so badly to work on. She'd acted like he shouldn't have made such a big deal about it all. Then she'd chided him for being sensitive. After all, she'd remarked, he had been known in the industry for being a player. As a very eligible bachelor, Tyson was entitled to date whomever he wanted and do as he wished. He had always been honest enough not to falsely lead any of his lady friends on, or at least that had been his intention. He would make sure not to, going forward.

A clean break from Tiffany was what he needed, especially now that the movie was out. Their breakup would have stolen the spotlight from the prepromotion. Truthfully, announcing their breakup before the premiere probably would have helped sales, but this project was too important to muddy with scandal.

His joy in their relationship had expired months ago. That's why he refused to stay with Tiffany when she beckoned the other night after the premiere parties. There was no need to allow anything between them to linger. It was time to have the conversation with her about how they would communicate their breakup to the public. Getting in front of the story was important. If bloggers caught wind first, they would blow everything up with speculation about scandals. Tyson didn't want either of them to come out looking bad, despite the things she had done.

Tyson's phone rang again. He rolled onto his back, let his hands fall alongside of him and sighed. He wasn't ready to talk to anyone. He let it ring and wondered if he and Tiffany should discuss their strategy over the phone or in person.

When his phone rang again, he silenced it. It rang once more.

"Really!" he yelled at the phone but still reached for it. There was some obvious urgency. The picture and number of his sister, Tory, flashed on the screen. "Hey, Tory."

"Turn on your TV." The urgency in Tory's voice made him sit straight up in his bed.

Tyson grabbed the remote and pointed it at the television. It glowed to life. "What channel?"

"Seven."

Tyson tuned in just in time to hear the anchorwoman say, "We will be back with more on Tiffany Reddick and her devastating breakup with media mogul Tyson Blackwell after this commercial break."

Tyson's lower lip fell at the same time the remote slipped from his grasp. "What?"

"It's everywhere — social media, the news, the radio. She's telling the world how you dropped her after the filming and forced her to keep quiet about it until after the movie came out so that this news wouldn't impact movie sales."

"Are you freaking kidding me?" Tyson felt his face heat up.

"I can't believe she did this."

"Unfortunately, I can." Tyson whipped the sheet back and hopped out of bed. He paced the plush white carpet of his expansive bedroom. His thoughts were a barrage of angry utterings thrashing around in his head. If he were a vengeful person, he'd have her blacklisted, but that wasn't like him. And at this point, he would look like nothing more than a bitter ex.

"It's back on," Tory said.

The anchorwoman appeared on screen again. She announced their exclusive interview with Tiffany Reddick, the lead of the weekend's record-breaking movie opening. Tyson sat on the edge of his bed with the phone still pressed to his ear.

"Tiffany, tell us how you managed to keep this secret all these months. The two of you seemed so happy on the red carpet at last week's premiere."

Tyson's breath hitched. He watched Tiffany's smile fade. She sighed. Dropped her shoulders, pursed her lips and shook her head. A woeful look fell across her face.

"I don't even know, Gail. All I know is that it hurt . . . so bad. I felt . . . used. But I don't blame Tyson. After all, this is Hollywood. Love can be as fickle as the air we breathe."

Tiffany sighed again. Another award-winning performance, Tyson thought. She had thrown him under the bus and he knew exactly why. Tiffany was strategic. In another week, the success of the movie's opening weekend would be old news. But talk of their scandalous high-powered breakup would linger, keeping her in the public eye. The least she could have done was let him know what she'd planned to do. By the end of the day, the news of the film, and more importantly their breakup, would be broadcast on every major media outlet from California to London and everywhere in between.

"Tyson? You there?"

"Yeah." He slapped his hand against his

forehead. "I'm here," he said in an almost whisper.

"What are you going to do? You *could* let me handle her. I'd enjoy it."

What could he do? Following up the story would make him appear sour or weak, and he was neither. Tiffany needed to secure the spotlight much more than he did. She was determined to gain it, and now that she had it in her clutches, she would do anything to keep it.

He was done with her. There was no need to pursue this any further. Tyson would never work with her again. That was certain.

"It is what it is, sis."

"Are you okay?"

"I'm fine."

"Want me to meet her in a dark alley and blacken both eyes?"

Tyson's laugh was sudden and sharp. "No, Tory. I can fight my own battles, and this one really isn't worth the energy."

"If you say so. Let me know if you change your mind."

"I won't."

"This is just so wrong. So, so, so wrong."

"I know."

"But don't worry, Ty. You know what they say about karma. Her day will come."

"I'm sure it will, sis. I'm sure it will."

CHAPTER 5

Kendall practically leaped out of bed, jarred from her sleep by insistent knocking. Disoriented, she squeezed her eyes shut, blinked a few times and looked around the room. The bright rays of the already scorching sun assaulted her sight. She squeezed them shut again. The banging continued. In the distance, she heard someone calling her name.

Kendall threw the covers back, jabbed her bare legs into a pair of lounge pants and headed toward the door. On the way, the broom caught her eye and she snatched it, holding it like a bat, ready to swing in case what met her at the door presented a threat.

"Kendall!" Boom. Boom. Boom. "It's me, Randi. Open up." More banging.

"What the . . ." Kendall snatched the door open. "Randi! What the hell? Something wrong?"

Randi pushed past Kendall. "Wrong? Heck no! Everything is right. It's all so very right!" Randi noticed the broom in Kendall's hand, halted and reared her head back. "Uh. What's that for?"

"What was all that banging about? This isn't LA It's quiet around these parts." Kendall set the broom against the wall. "Speaking of which, why are you here so early?" Kendall shuffled to the kitchen to see the clock on the wall. Randi followed her, pouncing on her heels like an excited puppy. "Whoa! It's seven o'clock in the morning. What time did you leave LA?"

"Just after five. It took you longer to answer the door than it took for me to get to Temecula." Randi was right at Kendall's back and stopped just behind her when Kendall stopped moving.

Kendall turned toward the refrigerator and bumped right into Randi. She raised her brow. Randi smiled hard, pressing her lips into a line to keep whatever joy she was containing inside.

Kendall widened her eyes and tilted her head. Laughter broke her questioning gaze.

"You're scaring me, girlie! What is it?" Kendall felt excitement welling up in her belly, feeling like a gang of birds had taken flight. Randi hadn't driven this far for nothing. Whatever it was, she'd insisted on delivering this news in person. Calls, texts or emails obviously wouldn't have sufficed.

"This thing is really happening!" Randi jumped up and down. "I woke up early this morning and I just happened to check my phone. Last night I fell asleep early. Missed Trice's album launch party and all. I need a vacation. Anyway. So, I wake up at, like, four a.m., right? I just know Trice probably left me a dozen and one crazy messages, wondering what happened to me. So, I'm checking my messages, Facebook, Instagram, you know."

"Oh. My. Goodness, Randi! Land the freaking plane already."

Randi giggled.

Kendall narrowed her eyes, glaring. She knew Randi was teasing her.

"And there was a message from BTV inviting you . . . to . . ."

"Randi!"

"They want you to perform at the BTV Awards!" The words rushed out. Randi screamed and stomped like she was running in place.

Kendall's mouth fell open. "What did you just say?"

"Yes, girlie! You're going to perform at this year's BTV Awards!" Randi screamed.

Kendall screamed too. Facing each other, they screamed and jumped together.

"There is no way I could have told you that on the phone. I had to see your face when I broke this news. Tyson Blackwell produces that show, and I think after hearing you sing the other day, he decided to add you to the roster."

Kendall sat on a stool near the kitchen island with her hand on her heart. "This is amazing." She sprung right back up. "I have to call my dad. My cousin. Jade is going to lose it. This is . . . this is . . ." She searched her mind for the right words. "So freaking epic!"

"Sooooooo." Randi stretched the word like a melody. "Freaking. Epic! You're a superstar, baby girl! It's really happening."

Kendall had enjoyed a steady rise up the pop charts, gained a sizable fan base, status, respect and popularity, and even received a few nods for music awards but had never actually won. She sold out concerts across the US, Canada and throughout Europe, but there was still so much more to accomplish. This was the first time she was being asked to perform at an awards show.

"What am I going to wear?"

Randi looked down at her cell phone. "When a decent hour arrives, we'll get Mica on the phone to get started on that."

Mica, Kendall's lead stylist, was going to

make sure Kendall's look was as epic as the opportunity.

Kendall and Randi gushed over the details for a while longer before Randi stretched out across the couch in Kendall's great room to take a much-needed nap. In the meantime, Kendall called her family to share the news. Her last call was to her best friend and first cousin, Jade.

"Jade!" Kendall put the phone on speaker and placed it on the granite countertop. "Guess who is going to perform at this year's BTV Awards?"

"No way!" Jade screeched.

"Yes way! This girl!" She pointed thumbs at herself even though her cousin couldn't see.

Jade screamed. "That's epic, Kendall!"

"I know!"

"I'm coming. I will not miss this."

"For sure. We'll hang out all week. You know how Hollywood gets down during red carpet season. It's going to be bananas!"

"I'm so proud of you. This is amazing. Okay, you're forgiven for waking me up at this ugly hour on a Saturday. Usually I can't even speak until way after the sun comes up. But you've got me up *and* talking."

"I couldn't wait to tell you. You can go back to bed now."

"Uh . . . I'm sure you know that's not going to happen, right? There aren't enough sheep in dream world to help me fall back to sleep. That's okay. I'll call Chloe, Jewel and Chris, wake them up and share the news. They'll be mad but happy, just like me."

They both laughed and chatted a few minutes more before hanging up.

Exhilaration coursed through Kendall's veins. With Randi napping, she didn't know what else to do with herself. She'd told everyone in her family, from her dad in the Midwest to her grandparents and cousins on the East Coast. Besides Randi, she didn't have solid friendships out West, and none of her family lived there. She missed having them close, but California was where she needed to be to take her career to new heights.

Kendall thought about the fact that Tyson was possibly behind the decision. Her excitement waned slightly. She hoped it wasn't some kind of attempt to get close to her, and she hoped he wouldn't expect something from her. And what if he did? What if he was like Henry and wanted her to give in to his perverted whims for the sake of this opportunity? Kendall would have to turn it down. She was going to be all business. Ready to sacrifice the biggest opportunity of her career rather than subject herself to indecent intentions. She had paid her dues and was a solid artist. She didn't care if her climb up fame's ladder took longer because she had principles. So be it. She'd have to find out Tyson's intentions before she got too excited. There was no way she'd become part of his Hollywood harem just to get a gig.

She truly didn't know if Tyson was that kind of man, but the industry was full of those types, and no matter what, her soul wasn't for sale.

CHAPTER 6

Tyson hadn't heard from Tiffany since the interview. Every text, call and voice mail remained unanswered. After three days, he stopped trying. More days passed. The news about their breakup stirred, picking up momentum. Paparazzi were everywhere, shoving cameras and microphones in his face. Tyson felt that the less he said, the more the media speculated. Despite being contacted several times about his side of the story, he refused to weigh in, leaving the on-camera frenzy to Tiffany. His best work had always been done behind the scenes.

Now it was one of those rare Saturdays when he didn't have a calendar full of commitments, and Tyson felt like he wanted to go for a run. His mind needed the activity more than his body. Tyson dressed in comfortable gear, set an app to track his run, put on his favorite workout playlist and strapped his cell phone to a holder on his arm. Luckily his community was heavily secured. He wouldn't have to deal with paparazzi until he passed through the gates on his way out of the area. In the kitchen, he downed half a bottle of water, then headed to the door, pulled it open and froze.

Tiffany stood on the other side, finger out and ready to press the bell.

"Oh . . . Uh." She blinked.

Tyson felt his lips tighten. He expected anger to surge through him, but it didn't. "Tiffany." He offered a tight greeting, stepped over the frame. Tyson joined her outside and locked the door behind him.

Tiffany cleared her throat, seemingly understanding that he had no plans to let her in. She sighed, dropping her shoulders in sync with her exhale. "We should talk."

Tyson pulled his bottom lip in and gnawed — an involuntary action when he retreated into his own thoughts. Assessing his real feelings again, he realized he wasn't angry at all. He expected to be, was ready to feel the irritation warm his blood, but . . . nothing. He inhaled deeply, waiting to feel the weight of the situation settle in his chest like a boulder, ready to feel the heaviness pass through his lungs into the atmosphere and add to the tension already waiting there. Yet he felt nothing. Just air. Tyson inhaled, exhaled again. Still nothing. Next, he felt relief. Tyson was done with this, with Tiffany and her antics. He was over it and over her.

Tyson looked at her forlorn expression. She could have been acting for him, but it didn't matter this time. He scanned her beautiful face, large brown eyes, skin reminiscent of the richest dark chocolate smoothed over perfect features. Tiffany was still beautiful to him, but not *for* him.

Tyson watched her swallow and slowly lift her eyes to meet his.

"Tyson, I —"

Tyson held his hand up, stopping Tiffany before she could start. "Don't." He couldn't stand to hear the lies he knew would come.

Tiffany's brows creased.

"No explanation needed. I understand you. We're good. Okay? We're good," he repeated for good measure.

Tiffany's mouth opened but she said nothing. Tyson gently placed his fingers on the bottom of her chin and closed her mouth for her.

He smiled and felt that smile spread throughout his body like clean, fresh air. The remnants of Tiffany had left his system. "I wish you well," he said, meaning it. "I'm going for a run now. I'll see you around."

Tyson leaned forward and planted a soft peck on her lips and another on her cheek. There was no spark, nothing that compelled him, made him want to go back for more. He watched Tiffany touch her own lips, the same spot where he'd just kissed her. After another smile, Tyson stuffed an earbud in one ear, let the music begin to soothe him and took off for his run, leaving Tiffany on his step where he'd found her.

Three miles and a half hour later, Tyson returned to a small envelope sticking out of his mailbox. Inside, he found the key to his door and the fob to get past the security gates at the entrance to his community. He'd forgotten that Tiffany still had those. Months had passed since they'd been an actual couple, so there had been no need for her to use them. With the key, she'd left a note.

Tyson,
I know you're angry with me. It will all be fine. I wanted to wait to make the announcement with you, but my agent insisted I do it during that big interview. We knew it would get more press for the movie. I know you understand that. You're a businessman, and at the end of the day, it's all about business. No PR

equals bad PR, right? I'd still like to talk. Let's do dinner soon.

Tif

Tyson read the letter, shook his head and hoped that someday Tiffany would be able to put agendas aside and allow herself to feel. Tyson decided right then that the next woman he dated would have to have more substance. The superficial, looking-good-in-public, power couple illusion would no longer do. There was too much of that already going on in the industry. He wanted a woman capable of stealing into his soul and capturing his heart, not making a business arrangement.

One thing he knew for sure was that the woman he would fall in love with was not going to be a celebrity. And he was especially done with actresses.

CHAPTER 7

"It's official!" Kendall cheered as she maneuvered in and out of traffic on the 605. The ride from Temecula was mostly spent inching along with hundreds of other cars along the route. "The contract is signed and I'm on my way to meet with the studio to finalize a few details for the awards show."

"Congratulations again! I'm so excited for you," Jade squealed. "What did Uncle Booker T. and the boys have to say about this?" she asked, referring to Kendall's big brothers, whom everyone always addressed as "the boys." "I'm sure all of Chicago knows his little princess and their little sister is moving on up even higher in the entertainment world."

"I don't doubt that. They're all pretty thrilled."

"What family wouldn't be?"

Kendall rode along with the quiet for several moments. "It's times like this that I wish Mom was alive." She swallowed hard to push back rising emotions.

"I'm sure she's cheering you on from her diamond perch in the sky. She's probably got lavender and glitter all over heaven. Ha!"

Jade was right. Kendall's mom had loved all shades of purple and pink, and anything with frills and bling. Grace had been a refined woman with a zeal for anything that radiated femininity. Had she been alive, she would have already been in LA to give Kendall's stylist some very personal advice on her attire for the performance.

"Enough about that." Had Kendall not changed the subject, she would have begun to cry. After every accomplishment, her mom would have been her first call. "Try to stay a few days after so we can hang. I'll be too busy before the event."

"Great idea!"

"Okay. I'm here." Kendall maneuvered into a parking lot. "Call you back later?"

"Yes. I want to hear every single detail, big and small."

"Ha! You got it."

Kendall ended the call, slipped on sunglasses and headed inside the same Blackwell Communications Group building that housed the offices of Blackwell Television which she'd come to for the Jocelyn James audition. She may have looked like she had it all together, but excitement had her insides rumbling. Kendall had achieved mainstream success in her singing career, but this would be a first. *Excitement* was too subtle a word to describe how she felt about this opportunity. She'd perfected her ability to keep her cool. Head up, shoulders back, Kendall stepped into the building as if she had these kinds of meetings every day.

Tyson came to mind the moment she hit the door. He must have really liked her singing that day. It wasn't long after that Randi had told her about their invitation to have her perform for the awards. The feel of Tyson's hand on hers came to mind also. Kendall remembered how long their handshake had lasted. She remembered the strong feel of his hand, his smooth skin. She recalled his sexy smile, perfect teeth and deep dimples making him even more gorgeous.

Yet as attractive as Tyson was, and he was undoubtedly attractive, Kendall wasn't letting him get in the way of her career. She'd seen the recent interviews about Tiffany and Tyson's breakup and knew that Tyson was single now, but she wasn't interested in him. If she had to let him know that in no uncertain terms, then so be it. This performance was a pivotal move for her, but she was more than willing to sacrifice it if Tyson was looking for anything more from her than a solid business arrangement and a great performance.

Kendall checked in at the lobby, entered the elevator and took a deep breath. She needed to rid herself of those thoughts. Tyson and BCG's interest in her performance could be strictly professional. And she hoped for everyone's sake that it was.

Kendall's phone rang just as she reached her floor. The screen displayed Randi's number.

"Hey, chickie. Did you make it?"

"Yep, I'm stepping out of the elevator as we speak. Are you on your way?"

"Yes, but I'm extremely late. If they can't wait, I need you to conference me in, cool?"

"Ugh!" Kendall always felt better with Randi by her side. "If I must."

"Be there as soon as I can. Traffic is a beast."

"Fine."

Kendall greeted the receptionist, the same one from the day of her interview. She was much calmer now.

"Ms. Chandler, what a pleasure to see you again. Right this way." She waved for Kendall to follow her lead. "Mr. Blackwell and his staff will be right with you. Can I get you something to drink? Coffee, tea, water?"

"Water would be great."

"Gladly. Be right back!"

Kendall took a seat in the conference room that provided her a clear view of the glass wall separating the space from the corridor. The room was adorned in a sleek gray-and-white palette. Charcoal-colored chairs with chrome hardware surrounded the massive white table in the center, with phones and speakers near each end. A large TV screen hung on one wall with tall, wide, stately shelves boasting books, awards and plaques on the opposite end. Promotional posters of BCG movies and shows hung along the long solid wall. Kendall looked back toward the phone and remembered to call Randi.

"Hey! Did the meeting start?"

"Not yet. I'm in the conference room waiting on them now. How far are you?"

There was a pause. "The GPS says I'm ten minutes away."

"GPS? Why are you using GPS when you know the way?"

"To gauge the time. See you when I get there."

"Okay." Kendall ended the call, put her phone on the table and looked around the room again. She picked up the cell phone and looked at the time. Punctuality was vital to her. Several minutes passed and she was still sitting there alone, waiting on Tyson and his staff.

The receptionist showed up with a bottle of water and a few lemons on a saucer covered with a paper towel. Kendall thanked her and watched her disappear through the door. Several more minutes passed, and still no one showed. She was starting to get annoyed. Kendall went out to the receptionist.

"They know I'm here, right?"

"Yes, Ms. Chandler. No one came yet?" The receptionist looked genuinely surprised. "Let me check to see what's happening. Can I bring you more water in the meantime?"

"No." Her response was sharp. She hadn't meant to take out her frustration on the receptionist. This wasn't her fault. "Thank you. I'm fine." Kendall softened her response and strutted back down the hallway and into the conference room, trying to keep her attitude in check. The task became more difficult with each passing minute.

Randi still hadn't arrived. The ten minutes had come and gone. Kendall called her but only reached her voice mail, which was full. Forced to wait, Kendall walked around the conference room looking at more of the images. After twenty minutes had passed, she still hadn't heard a peep from Tyson and his crew. Her next call to Randi went to voice mail again. Annoyance blossomed even more now.

Kendall picked up her purse and headed for the door. Just as she reached the frame, she heard Randi's voice and a second deeper one that sounded like it could have been Tyson's. Kendall paused, inhaled and exhaled a sharp breath and pondered whether or not she even wanted to stay for this meeting.

"Ms. Chandler." Tyson's deep voice bellowed.

Kendall could have sworn she felt it rumble in her belly. Had his voice just gone through her? Instead of responding, she looked at her arm as if there were a watch there and looked back up at him. Her face was set tight with agitation.

Tyson held his hands up as Randi and several others stepped in the room behind him. "Our apologies. We had a crisis that required our immediate attention. I'm really sorry. Please, let's get started." Tyson gestured toward the chairs surrounding the large conference table.

"Hey!" Randi was breathless, as if she'd

run up to the tenth floor. She placed her hand on Kendall's shoulder, a calming gesture. "Sorry I'm late." She addressed the room and quickly returned her gaze to Kendall. "Let's sit down," she said to Kendall quietly.

Tyson and his team settled into seats, but Kendall stood just as rigidly as she had been. Randi patted her shoulder and led her toward two open seats, but Kendall remained standing.

She took another deep breath and thought about the best way to voice her displeasure at how unprofessional it was to leave her waiting so long. But Tyson started before she could speak.

"We hope you will accept our apologies and that we can move forward with the meeting."

Kendall bit back the sharp response she wanted to give and remained professional. "I understand that things happen. I would have appreciated it if someone would have advised me that you were dealing with a crisis, giving me the option to wait or perhaps reschedule. My schedule is quite full."

"Yes, and we thank you for your patience. If you will accept my apology . . ." Tyson pressed the palms of his hands together and nodded. Wordless, he kept his eye on Kendall until she relented with a dismissive toss of her hand before finally taking a seat. Tyson nodded again and smiled. "Now if we can get started." He placed a file folder on the table and flipped it open. "We wanted to speak to you about the run of show. We know you agreed to perform one of your latest songs. However, we're giving Carolyn Johnson a lifetime achievement award and would love if you would perform one of her tribute songs during that presentation, along with some of the other artists we believe would truly do her music justice."

Kendall's mood went from annoyed to elated so fast she was sure her heart fumbled a few beats. She held her expression and cleared her throat. "I'd be delighted," she said evenly. In her head she was screaming. "Which one of her songs are you interested in having me sing?" she asked coolly.

"As I mentioned, you'll be joined by a number of other artists. We'd like to begin rehearsals in the next few weeks. We'll have a more solid layout by then."

"Who are the other artists?"

Tyson rattled off the names of several major entertainers. Not only would she sing a tribute song to one of the world's most iconic R & B artists of all time, but she'd get to do it alongside today's most renowned singers, ones whose careers she aspired to emulate. Her irritation had completely dissipated. She sat back coolly and folded her hands. She had to, in order to keep them from twitching. She pretended to think it over as if it were something she would ever refuse. Kendall looked at Randi. Silently they shared the same cool expression, masking their unbridled exhilaration. This was big for both of them.

Kendall's agency had pinned Randi to her when her career began to take off. She was green but as eager as Kendall. Seasoned agents were assigned to bigger names. Together they navigated the hills and valleys of the entertainment industry, sharing all of Kendall's milestones and weathering the setbacks. This was Kendall's biggest highlight to date, next to her chart-topping release the year before that had earned her new levels of recognition and a nomination but hadn't gotten her the award. In that time, Randi became more than her agent. Both had traipsed to LA in hopes of living out their industry dreams, and together, they'd realized those dreams.

Randi nodded discreetly. Kendall had passed the baton. Randi turned and looked around the room, making eye contact with each of the BCG employees around the table and settling her sight on Tyson. "Nice. It sounds like we need to negotiate a new rate and a new contract. Can you have your new offer on my desk by tomorrow morning?"

Tyson looked at his team. Each agreed through nods and shrugs. "We can do that."

"Great! I'm glad this worked out."

"Me too." Tyson responded to Randi but directed his gaze at Kendall. He smiled. She shifted a little, hoping it wasn't enough for him to notice.

Kendall wasn't uncomfortable under his gaze. Not at all. His eyes were too dreamy for her to be uncomfortable. In fact, something in her core had shivered when she'd looked back into those gorgeous brown eyes of his. But Kendall was serious about being all business in the presence of Tyson Blackwell. She had enough media drama with Storm. Her next relationship, whenever that happened, would be with someone outside of the industry, someone who wasn't a spotlight magnet. Besides, Tyson had been a known ladies' man before dating Tiffany, with a litany of A-list celebrities on his arm, and now the media was speculating that foul play on his behalf had caused their breakup. They were the topic of every blogger's conversation of late. Tyson and Tiffany's newly publicized relationship status had placed her own scandal on the back burner, making her and Storm old news. She was almost grateful, and certainly wasn't looking forward to gaining that spotlight back.

They discussed a few more details that would be part of the revised contract and then ended the meeting. On the way out, Tyson reached forward to shake Kendall's hand. "Again, my apologies for the delay. We look forward to working with you."

Kendall shook Tyson's large masculine hand, taking note again of how soft it felt. Just the way Kendall liked her men's hands. Quietly, she admonished herself for that thought.

"Thank you." She wanted to say more, wanted to tell him that she intended to keep her interactions strictly business. Wanted to let him know she was a professional. That his dreamy eyelashes that spread like a fan, full lips, toned body and deep sultry voice would have no effect on her . . . because she was focused on her career and her career only.

Kendall pulled her hand from his a little too quickly and turned on her heels. "Good day," she said and headed for the exit, not stopping until she hit the elevator, leaving Randi in her wake.

CHAPTER 8

While everyone fanned out of the conference room at the end of the meeting, Tyson stood, puzzled, pondering Kendall's exit and wondering what had just happened. He'd apologized multiple times for being late for the meeting. She seemed fine after he'd told her and her agent about adding Kendall to the tribute.

Kendall's actions demonstrated exactly why Tyson was done with actresses. He understood her initial irritation but didn't get her behavior before her abrupt exit. Women were already complex puzzles. Actresses raised that complexity to extreme levels.

Tyson wasn't one to buy into rumors. He knew how Hollywood worked. Swelled egos were easily bruised. If something didn't go someone's way, they were ready to label you. Women were tagged as divas. Sometimes it was true; many times, it wasn't. Tyson always gave people the benefit of the doubt, let them prove their own character. He wasn't sure what the deal was with Kendall. She wasn't the same woman he'd seen at the audition the week before. Regardless of that, she was talented, and that's why he wanted her added to the tribute. The award show was his project. He wanted this year to be epic, and Kendall fit the vision he had in mind.

The latter part of his day was better than the earlier part. The employee that had taken ill and caused him to be late to the meeting with Kendall was recovering in the hospital. That scare shook the entire office, but he saw no need to share that with Kendall. It was company business. Even the emails from various media outlets didn't bother him. He delved into his work, enjoyed a dinner meeting about a new project idea and made it home through the throngs of paparazzi at a decent hour. His main distractions were recurring thoughts of Kendall that kept sneaking up unexpectedly.

Kendall had popped into his mind while he deleted interview requests via email. Her face had flashed across his mind's eye as he prepped for his dinner meeting and once again as he settled into the quiet of his spacious home. Tyson shook his head and made his way to the wine cellar in search of a great red to usher him off to sleep.

Why was her image haunting him? She was beautiful and sang like the gift of song was solely designed for her. Such power emanated from her small frame. But he was in the entertainment business in LA. Beautiful women were as common as coffeehouses and yoga studios. What was it about Kendall that kept pulling his mind toward her? He couldn't be attracted to her. She was an actress and potentially a diva. He'd had enough of those.

Tyson poured a glass of wine, plopped on the sofa in the family room and pointed the remote to the seventy-inch television above the fireplace. He settled into the cushions, letting the weight of the day seep out of him and into the softness. That same heaviness pulled on his eyelids. Tyson flipped through channels, not paying enough attention to any show in particular. The remote grew slack in his hand. He pointed it at the television again, repeated his search and settled on an old rerun of a sitcom that had been resurrected in syndication heaven. Tyson blinked and realized he'd missed a few seconds of the show, possibly even a few minutes.

Adjusting himself on the couch, Tyson placed his wineglass on the ottoman in front of him and sat back. The cushions seemed to embrace him and he let the full weight of his fatigue go.

Kendall stepped into the room, dressed in all white, with soft lighting illuminating her frame. Tyson squeezed his eyes shut. What was she doing there? How'd she get in?

A sexy smile played on her lips. One perfect foot crossed in front of the other in the fashion of a runway model. She sauntered toward him, her gaze fastened to his. Tyson sat up straight, seemingly held in a trance by her beauty. She drew closer as if she were floating. Tyson held his hand out and she disappeared.

What? He shook his head and suddenly felt as if he were falling.

Kendall's abrupt disappearance jolted him from the dream. Grabbing handfuls of the couch cushion, Tyson steadied himself and sat up. He blinked, looked around and blinked again. The television was still going. His glass of wine, half-full, still sat on the coffee table and he was alone. He didn't know how long he had slept, but the image of Kendall's sexy approach made him want to go back to whatever realm of sleep she showed up in.

Laughing at himself, Tyson stood, took his glass to the kitchen and headed to his bedroom. Kendall was off-limits, no matter what his unconscious mind drummed up. No more actresses. No more entertainers — especially ones whom he'd have to work closely with over the next few weeks, or ones who acted like divas — and especially no more blog magnets. He was getting to the point where being the focus of every blog was no longer fun.

Yes. Tyson was done with women like Kendall. They were all the same. Weren't they?

CHAPTER 9

This first rehearsal had Kendall in awe. Entertainers that she'd followed since she was a little girl were alongside her singing Carolyn Johnson's iconic songs. She'd met a few of the other singers and tried her best to contain the fangirl inside of her while they worked. Kendall was one of the three younger or newer entertainers. To her surprise, the atmosphere wasn't ripe with arrogance, competitive tension or entitled attitudes. Everyone was friendly.

"Okay! From the top." The choreographer snapped his fingers.

The fellow singers moved to the sides of the stage, remaining out of sight until their cues. The music started and a new soul artist with a voice full of old soul, who had just taken the charts by storm, came out first, belting out one of Carolyn's old sultry songs. Kendall closed her eyes, allowing the girl's voice to flow through her. She swayed to the music. Katia held the last note of the first verse until the next artist, Crisis, joined her.

Crisis was a multiplatinum, multigenre singer and rapper who surprised her with his soulful rendition of Carolyn's next verse. Kendall's eyes popped open to make sure it was him singing. He didn't sound like that on his R & B records. The two of them sung the last verse as a duet with everyone cheering them on. Their last note was a high one that reached the rafters and caused applause to erupt from the others.

Katia and Crisis's bow was Kendall's cue to move to center stage. They stepped back as she entered, starting with a low, sexy crooning of one of Carolyn's most popular songs about love and heartbreak. Kendall felt as if Carolyn moved through her, egging her on. She relaxed her shoulders and allowed herself to fall into the rhythm until she felt it all over her body. She ended her part with a long note that moved up several octaves. More applause, a few hoots and shouts of "go girl" rang out from the sidelines. The choreographer barked instructions throughout, clapping his hands and snapping his fingers. He moved swiftly, like lightning. One moment he was next to her, moving her toward the *x* that she was supposed to use as her marker, and the next, he was downstage, waving his hand at the singer who was supposed to come up next.

Each singer put their own stamp on Carolyn's songs without departing from the sultry jazzy essence that she was known for. For the last number they all moved center stage, forming an arc, and riffed together, connecting their voices like a rhythmic puzzle. The performance was intoxicating. The last note left them all huffing, but also laughing, feeling good and nostalgic.

"Great! Now let's do this one more time but save your voices. That was beautiful, but this time I need you to focus on where you're supposed to end up on stage. Please pay close attention." With that, the choreographer took each one of them by the hand and marked where they were supposed to stand before, during and after their part. "Okay, take a break."

"Thank you!" Kendall trotted down the steps in search of her purse. She drank a few sips of water and headed for the restrooms.

Pushing her way out of the theater, she ran straight into the taut chest of Tyson Blackwell. She nearly bounced off his firm torso. Tyson caught her by both arms, helping to straighten her up on her two feet. A tickling squirm squiggled through her. Kendall straightened her back and stood rigid.

"Hello," she said after clearing her throat. The coolness of her tone defied the heat that shot through her when her body connected with his.

"Hi."

For several seconds, both remained quiet. Kendall allowed him to lock gazes with her for just a moment before averting her eyes.

"Uh. Bathroom?" She pointed her finger from one side to the other as if she needed to be told the direction.

"Yes. That way." Tyson pointed to her right.

His voice . . . "Thanks," Kendall said, then turned on her heels and headed off quickly. Inside the bathroom, she checked to confirm that she was alone. Kendall looked in the mirror, rolled her eyes upward and shook her head. There was something about that man. Kendall hoped he didn't plan to frequent their rehearsals, because he proved to be a delicious distraction. He was off-limits but that didn't mean she'd lost her senses. She wasn't blind and her nose worked well enough to take in the musky scent of his cologne that now lingered on her chest after running into him.

Kendall remembered how annoyed she had felt when he'd left her waiting at their last meeting. Yes. That would be her strategy. Every time she felt affected by how incredibly attractive he was, she'd remind herself of how disrespectful he had been in keeping her waiting. She'd give him attitude. It seemed childish, but it was the most mature thought she could conjure up because being around him made her feel like a teenager again.

"All business!" Kendall admonished herself. "No more drama for me." She looked in the mirror and told her reflection, "It's not worth it." Kendall handled her business in the bathroom and returned to the mirror. Despite not being interested in Tyson, she checked her hair, putting a few strands back into their place before heading back to the theater. Part of her hoped Tyson was gone, and another part wished he was still there.

When she got back inside, Tyson was off to the side of the stage chatting with the choreographer. Several singers were scattered across the theater with cell phones pressed to their ears.

"Okay, people, we need to make a few minor changes. Back on stage, please!"

Everyone made their way back to the stage

to receive new instructions and rehearse one last time. Instead of leaving, Tyson sat in the center of the front row. A nervous burst of air blossomed in Kendall's chest. What was that? Since her first few months of performing, she almost never got nervous. Kendall took her place and couldn't help but steal glances from her spot offstage.

The dim lighting in the audience contrasting the bright lights from the stage cast angles across Tyson's face, highlighting his stellar cheekbones and strong jaw. Kendall allowed herself to stare, to take him in from the shadows where she couldn't be detected. She couldn't do this from across the conference table.

She let her gaze linger until she found him staring back at her through the contrasting shadows. He smiled, and something fluttered in her stomach.

Kendall turned away. She was ready to sing.

CHAPTER 10

Tyson hadn't missed Kendall's glances because he'd been discreetly watching her eyes from the moment she'd reentered the theater. He couldn't help it. Sleep hadn't come easy the night before, and Kendall was part of the reason why, but when they'd collided at the door and her body met his, it was like a shot of espresso. She'd energized him with her touch.

No woman had ever affected him this way before, and he hardly knew her. All he knew was the woman the media and blogs talked about, the singer who had recently begun to top the charts and take the world by storm with a voice that could do unimaginable things. Her quality and range were the talk of the industry. When he'd heard her live during the movie audition, he knew he had to have her in the awards show. Her quality was authentic, not created in a music studio. But he quickly found that having her around

405

was dangerous. She represented everything he wanted to stay away from, yet something magnetic compelled him to her, into his thoughts and even his dreams.

Tyson finished up early at the office so he could catch part of the rehearsal. He wanted to hear her sing. He needed to hear her voice again.

Kendall's stare set his body temperature on high. He felt her looking without having to turn and meet her eyes. In fact, he purposely didn't turn in her direction, and when he finally did, he smiled — a smile that let her know that he knew she was watching. She turned away. That made him chuckle. The least he could do was have some fun.

Antoine clapped his hands. "Okay, people. Let's make this the last one." He lifted his lithe arm high and slashed his index finger through the air. Music flowed through the theater. R & B artist Katia came out first, sounding like a jazzy angel. Moments later, singer and rapper Crisis joined her. His deep, soulful voice reminded Tyson of the songs his parents listened to. Closing his eyes, Tyson bobbed his head to the rhythm. The duet faded, the music flowed behind them and shifted, and so did something in Tyson.

He felt Kendall even before she hit the stage, felt her voice flow through him before she sung her first note. His eyes snapped open. Kendall was center stage holding the most beautiful note that ever graced his hearing. His presence in the theater felt surreal. Tyson felt as if he could float from his chair and be carried away on the melody Kendall sang. Her voice flowed through him, claimed him, held him captive. It pinned him to his seat, cajoled him, charmed him. Tyson couldn't take his eyes off her until she had sung her last note. What beautiful sound emanated from her small frame? It was even better than what he'd heard at the audition. Air swirled in his chest, and he felt like a teen crushing on a schoolgirl. Suddenly he was aware of how compelling her singing was, as if it could take him over, seize him like hypnosis.

Tyson stood and exited the theater through the back to avoid running into any paparazzi. He had to extract himself from the charming web she was slowly wrapping around him with her singing. He didn't stop until he was inside his luxury sports car. Turning the key in the ignition, he started the car but sat back without shifting gears. What had just happened? Had he stayed, he felt like he could have lost control. Tiffany was stunning, yet he never felt like a spell was being cast over him when he was with her. This wasn't lust. Tyson had long since learned to control his urges. In Hollywood he had to. He certainly didn't want to appear disrespectful to women.

This was something different. Something that, despite the fact that Kendall represented everything he wanted to avoid, he felt the strongest desire to explore. What if she was a spoiled, entitled diva? What about the annoying media? What about his father's pleas for Tyson to represent the company appropriately now that he was going to be CEO? He had to honor his father's wishes. They planned to announce the transition the night of the awards show, making Tyson the youngest CEO of any major media conglomerate. Tyson needed press that would help build his image as a respectable businessman, not scandalous gossip that made him seem like nothing more than a frivolous player.

There was more at stake. Tiffany was already putting his efforts to task. Could he stand more scandal? Because an affair with Kendall would lead to just that. The media would have a field day. People would assume she got the movie role and the tribute due to their affair. It would probably also fuel the stupid rumors that he'd been cheating on Tiffany, which supposedly caused the breakup.

No. Tyson needed to lie low. He recalled some of Tiffany's behavior and decided it probably wasn't worth it. Just more of the same of exactly what he didn't need in his life. Kendall was a blog magnet too.

Tyson's phone rang. He answered without bothering to see who was calling.

"Tyson. Uh . . . where are you? Listen."

Tyson sighed. Whenever Tiffany started a conversation with "listen," things never turned out well.

"Hello, Tiffany, I'm well. What can I do for you?" He braced himself, trying his best to sound cheerful, unbothered.

"Um . . . has anyone from the media tried to call you?"

"What media, Tif?" He pressed the phone closer to his ear as if it would help him listen more keenly.

"Sweetie, just remember, there's no such thing as bad PR. Okay?"

CHAPTER 11

Kendall didn't get nervous often, but this would be one of the biggest performances of her career. Watching Randi run around tapping her wrist where a watch would have been seemed almost surreal. So did the frantic scene of the makeup artist and hairstylist finishing her makeup and hair at the same time. They had to get her into the dress designed by the same iconic designer that had become famous for styling the former First Lady.

"Come on! Get that dress on, chickie! We're pressed for time." Randi's bark was without bite and always good-hearted. She smiled after and hadn't stopped pacing since she'd arrived hours before.

"I'm coming." Kendall found herself smiling too. A mixture of nervousness and sheer excitement made her giggle. Then laughter tumbled from her lips and she covered her mouth, but that didn't stop the chuckle from spilling through her fingers and blossoming into a full-out, hysterical, back-bending laugh that she couldn't contain. The only thing that kept her from feeling like she was stuck in a dream was the smooth, sultry sounds of Carolyn Johnson's music playing in the background. Kendall had secured the starring role in the movie and was chosen to perform at the awards show and almost couldn't believe her luck. Kendall made it a point to listen to both Jocelyn and Carolyn until their music became a natural part of her existence.

"What just happened?" Randi looked puzzled. "What's so funny?" Randi's hands were out at her sides.

Kendall threw her hands up and let them slap against her sides. "I can't believe this is happening. I literally dreamed of this . . . and now it's happening. I could scream." Kendall laughed again. She put her fingers over her lips and snickered. "I can't help it."

At first Randi's face was blank. A moment later, she joined Kendall, laughing along with her.

"You're nervous!" Randi tilted her head. "You're actually nervous."

"I know!" Kendall snickered, shrinking into her shoulders. "Can you believe this?

Randi." She walked over and held Randi by both shoulders. "I've been so wrapped up in rehearsing and getting ready that the enormity of all of this escaped me. It literally just hit me. I'm performing at the BTV Music Awards!" Kendall squealed. "Me! Kendall Chandler! Not once but twice. The only thing that could make this night better is if I actually won one of the awards." Kendall threw her head back and laughed again.

"Oh my goodness! Ken. This. Is. Huge!" Randi pulled Kendall into her arms and squeezed tight. "Come on." Randi pulled away, still laughing. "We need to get you in that dress."

Kendall headed to her bedroom with Randi and her stylist. When she slipped on the black formfitting number and gold stilettos, she turned to look in the mirror. Her stylist fussed with a few curls and stepped back. Randi smiled wide. Hair and makeup had done a stunning job. She looked flawless from head to toe. It reminded Kendall of the days playing dress-up in her mother's closet. The memory brought on a flash of sadness. Kendall wished her mother could have been there to witness this.

"Look at me, Mom. It's happening."

"Oh no you don't!" Randi snapped. "Get me a tissue." The stylist hurried away and came back just as quickly. Randi stuffed some of the tissue in Kendall's hand and dabbed at her glistening eyes. "Do not ruin all this makeup."

Kendall took a deep breath. "Okay. Okay." She fanned her eyes with her hands. "I'm not going to cry. Let's get going." Kendall gathered the bottom of her dress and headed for the great room.

"Ken! Ken!"

Kendall whipped her head toward the door in time to see her cousin Jade whirl into the room like a rush of wind.

"Jade! You made it." Kendall held her arms out for her cousin to step right into.

Jade halted. A hand flew to her gaping mouth. "You look . . ." Jade seemed at a loss for words. "Absolutely amazing! Look at you!" Jade walked a circle around Kendall. "Sexy!" Jade stretched the word out, teasing, pointing to the high slit starting at the top of Kendall's thigh and growling. They all laughed again.

"You look pretty stunning yourself, darling." Kendall whipped her head with Old Hollywood flair.

Jade shimmied. "Thank you. Nixon picked it out. He's downstairs. Come say hello."

Jade grabbed one hand, and with the other, Kendall gathered the bottom of her dress and met Jade's fiancé at the bottom of the stairs.

"Nixon." Kendall nodded and hugged him.

"You look great, Kendall! Knock 'em dead tonight."

"Oh, I plan to." Tyson came to mind just then for some reason. Kendall shook her head.

"We need to get going, people." Randi clapped her hands. "Is that car here yet?"

Jade shuffled to the window in her formfitting gown and held her hands over her eyes, shielding the glow of the bright afternoon sun. She watched the sleek black car ease to a stop in front of Kendall's condominium. "Looks like it's just pulling up."

"Let's go!" Randi commanded.

Kendall, Randi, Jade and Nixon piled into the limousine and headed to the theater where the awards were being held. The second Kendall exited the car, cameras began to flash in her direction. She insisted that Randi, Jade and Nixon walk along the red carpet instead of entering through the other doors. Fans, journalists and bloggers yelled out over the noise to Kendall as she walked along the famed scene, stopping in front of the step and repeat for a mini photo session. Posture erect, Kendall whipped her head this way and that, turned from one side to the other and thrust her leg forward through the high split, taking in the pop of the flashing cameras. Entertainment networks asked questions, prompting brief interviews. Kendall talked about how excited she was to perform tonight. One asked about Storm, which didn't surprise her. Kendall offered only a pleasant smile.

"We've moved on. I've been so busy I haven't had a chance to speak to him lately, but I'm sure he's doing great," she said coolly.

"So, the two of you still speak?"

Kendall smiled, waved at more fans and continued walking along. She was done answering questions about Storm.

From the moment she exited the car, time moved in fast-forward. Her performance was a blur. When they called her name as a nominee for best album, she waved the nomination off because she was up against several heavy hitters.

"And the winner is . . ."

Kendall's heart raced, still holding on to hope for the possibility, despite thinking there was no way she'd win. The pause made the announcer's words seem to last an eternity. Kendall's heart thumped. "Would she announce the winner already?" she whispered to Randi, who was sitting next to her with fingers crossed on both hands. Kendall looked down at Randi's fingers and how rigidly she sat, and chuckled.

"Hey. A girl can dream right?" Randi shrugged. "You should be crossing yours. Come on. Do it!" Randi instructed.

Kendall shook her head. Randi nudged her with her elbow. Kendall shook her head again and crossed her fingers.

"Kendall Chandler!"

The sound of her name appeared to penetrate her hearing from a distance. Confusion settled in for a brief moment. Time paused. Randi screamed beside her, grabbed her arm and yanked her up.

"Randi." Kendall wondered what Randi was doing.

"You won!" Randi was jumping up and down.

The haze dissipated. Kendall looked around. All eyes were on her. The large screens reflected her puzzled expression as realization hit. Kendall's mouth fell open. Her hands flew to her face and tears sprang to her eyes. Randi grabbed her arm and led her toward the stage. On the way, Kendall snapped back into the moment, joining reality. Her chest filled with air.

"Oh my God! Oh my God!" she repeated over and over. She had won. She had actually won. Onstage, the actress handed her the beautiful gleaming statuette. Kendall took it, noting that it was much heavier than she had anticipated. She placed her hand under it, securing her grasp on the coveted metal. The microphone seemed to beckon her. A wave of déjà vu flashed over Kendall. She had been here before, but only in her dreams. This felt better than her dreams, though. This was real. Time slowed as Kendall looked out over the crowd. A tear rolled down her face, tickling her cheek. She swiped it away.

Kendall opened her mouth and had to think of what to say. She wasn't prepared, because she hadn't expected to win.

"Good evening." Whew! Kendall had actually gotten two words out. She pressed on. "This is such a wonderful surprise." Randi stood by her. She looked over the mass of people, hoping she could spot Jade. Her father hadn't been able to make it. "Being in such amazing company, I hadn't expected to win." She could do the humble response. "They are all incredible artists. Whew. Okay." Kendall took a deep breath.

A collective chuckle emerged from the crowd. "There're so many people I want to thank." Kendall scrolled through a mental list and thanked Randi, several people from her family, the record company, artists who came before her and had inspired her, and then Tyson. She thanked Tyson and the BCG family for giving her the chance to perform at the awards and closed out by dedicating her award to her mother.

Overwhelmed by the excitement of the day so far, Kendall left the stage as a walking bundle of emotions. Backstage, she gathered herself. It was time to change and get ready for the tribute.

"You go get ready," Randi said. "I'll take care of this, baby."

Before handing over the award, Kendall looked at it, smiled and kissed it. "Take good care of my baby."

Kendall joined the backstage crowd and changed into an elegant red ball gown, Carolyn's favorite color. Offstage, she waited for her cue before joining Katia and Crisis back onstage. She walked out singing. The audience was on their feet, including Carolyn. Kendall hit center stage, directed her attention to Carolyn, smiled, waved and serenaded her as if no one else were there.

Unlike rehearsal, the energy was electric. Carolyn looked stunning and graceful — and even a little tipsy. She danced and sang along with each of them as they sang her songs. During the finale, when all of their voices blended together, Carolyn cried, holding her hand to her heart. Her tears flowed as she received her lifetime achievement award and gave a heartfelt acceptance speech.

The show closed out with Tyson's father, Benjamin Blackwell, handing the reins of the company over to Tyson, announcing him as the new CEO of the Blackwell Communications Group. There was a standing ovation by some. The night seemed a complete success.

Kendall, Randi, Jade and Nixon headed over to the first of several after-parties, starting with the official one, hosted by BCG. Entertainment shows from the network interviewed winners and performers in small spaces outfitted with cameras and adequate lighting. The rest of the space was illuminated with turquoise lighting. Champagne fountains were posted in every corner. White-gloved waiters and waitresses walked around with canapés and cocktails. The dance floor was filled to the edges.

Kendall finished up her interview and

went searching for Jade. She spotted Tyson seated at a high table alone. Kendall remembered seeing him backstage earlier. A wave of gratefulness flooded her. Despite not wanting to get too close, she wanted to thank him for choosing her for the tribute.

Tyson looked incredible in his tux. She hadn't seen much of him since he'd made that swift exit at rehearsal. He must have thought she was either a diva or a weirdo. She wasn't the nicest toward him, and when she wasn't being not so nice, she was staring at him. After tonight, she'd probably go back to not seeing much of him at all. That would be for the better. Filming for the movie was due to start in the coming weeks, but now that he was CEO, she was sure he wouldn't have time to hang around the set.

Kendall decided to go over to say hello and thank him. She'd keep the encounter brief. As she got closer, she noticed he seemed deep in thought. His brows were knitted together, and his jaw appeared tight.

"You'd think the new CEO of BCG would look a lot happier." Kendall took the stool across from him at the round table.

The moment she sat down, she realized she didn't really want to keep it brief. There was something about being in Tyson's presence. She didn't understand what it was, but she liked the way it felt.

CHAPTER 12

"I don't look excited?" Tyson feigned a wide-eyed cheesy smile in response to Kendall's comment.

Kendall raised a brow. "Uhhh." Both of them chuckled. "Are you happy with how the evening went?"

"Actually, yes." Tyson smiled a genuine smile. The night had been hectic, but successful. The past few days had given him hell.

"Well, I won't bother you. I just wanted to thank you for selecting me for the tribute. It was a pleasure to be a part of that." Kendall slid down from her stool.

Tyson reached for her arm, stopping her. "Don't leave." Tyson paused. He heard the need in his own voice. "How about a drink . . . to celebrate."

It took a moment for Kendall to respond. "Sure." She eased back onto the stool.

Tyson waved over one of the waitresses

holding a tray of champagne glasses and took one for him and one for Kendall. "To your performance and your win!" Tyson lifted his glass.

Kendall lifted hers as well. "Thank you. And to your promotion!" She nodded. They clinked glasses and sipped.

"Listen." Kendall took a breath. "I didn't mean to be callous or . . . weird. It's just that I take my work and opportunities seriously, and I wanted to be respected for what I bring to the table."

Tyson sipped. "Nothing wrong with that. No explanation needed."

Kendall smiled. Silence settled between them for several moments.

Tyson smiled back at Kendall. He liked being in her presence. She gleamed with positive energy, which he needed right now in the same way he needed air for his survival. The weight of Tiffany's most recent betrayal still clung to him. It took sufficient work for him not to allow the bitterness to overtake him.

Tiffany's call a few days before had been her attempt to soften the blow of what was probably happening on television as he sat at the after-party with Kendall in her beautiful award-wining afterglow. Buzz around their breakup continued to dominate headlines, which Tyson had to admit continued to fuel ticket sales of the movie they'd just dropped. A competitive entertainment show called to ask her for an exclusive interview to discuss Tiffany's life and the success of the movie. Tiffany admitted to Tyson that, all for the sake of PR and high ratings, she had allowed the *interviewer* to paint Tyson as a relentless playboy who had reeled in an unsuspecting and promising star, only to betray her in the end. Of course, she made no mention of her own salacious trysts that she'd been found guilty of numerous times during their courtship. "There's no such thing as bad PR." Her words had played in his mind on repeat since their conversation. He was furious beyond words and hadn't seen or spoken to Tiffany since.

Instead, he braced for the potential impact this interview could possibly have on him in his new role as CEO at a time where scandalous behavior against women could ruin reputations and careers. He'd already seen a few long-standing Hollywood execs' careers derailed by the exposure of their inappropriate actions. Not that Tyson had done anything like the horrible acts some of these men had committed, but there was no telling how this would play out. The company could come under scrutiny, and their reputation could be marred. His father would be disheartened. And most of all, Tyson would never want to be known as someone who didn't treat women with the utmost respect. He'd never condoned these men's behavior, and the possibility of being grouped in with them due to Tiffany's desire to gain exposure made him downright angry. Even worse, she kept saying it wasn't a big deal.

"Tyson . . ." He thought he'd heard his name. "Tyson." This time he recognized Kendall's soft voice, looked down and noticed her hand gently on his forearm. "Are you okay?"

He turned to look at her, wondering how much time he'd spent drowning in his thoughts. He felt the rigid set of his jaw and loosened it. "I'm sorry . . . yes . . . I'm fine."

"Okay. I didn't mean to bother you." She stood. "I need to find my cousin anyway. She's probably looking all over for me." Kendall let out a nervous laugh.

"Wait!" Tyson stood. "I'll help you find her." He didn't want to be alone with his thoughts anymore. He needed to be around her. "I didn't mean to space out. This week has been hell."

Kendall cast him a look filled with pity.

She eased back onto her stool again. "Need to talk, maybe?"

Tyson pulled in his bottom lip and gnawed on it. "Maybe I do."

Kendall looked around and back at him. "All the couches seem to be taken. This stool will have to do."

That made Tyson laugh, a genuine laugh. "I'll take it." Tyson wasn't sure what it was, but something told him he could trust Kendall. He wouldn't spill all of the beans, but just enough to offer a deserving response to why his attention had just wandered off in the middle of their conversation. "I love the media, but sometimes I hate it."

"Who are you telling?" Kendall slapped the table and leaned in closer. "Especially the blog monsters. They're like hungry, little vicious animals constantly clawing at you for a morsel. Ugh. They'll take any little thing and run with it, not caring if there's any truth to it or not. I can't stand it, and the most frustrating part is, there's not much we can do about it."

Tyson laughed. He'd obviously hit a nerve. "Yeah, I'm getting dragged through the media mud as we speak."

Kendall's gaze was sympathetic. "I know."

"There's more than you know."

"Oh. I'm sorry." She put her hand on his arm again, and he felt something like an electrical current ripple from his arm straight to his core. Tyson cleared his throat and continued, grateful to have a listening ear. He hadn't uttered a word about this to anyone since Tiffany's call.

"Most people don't realize that Tiffany and I broke up almost a year ago. We were supposed to wait until after the release of the film to make the announcement. We . . . or I guess now I should say *I* didn't want the media to run with stories about the breakup and water down the promotions we planned around the release. However, Tiffany took it upon herself to let the cat out of the bag because she thought it would increase exposure. And it did, in both good ways and bad."

"Oh." Kendall frowned. "That's . . . interesting." Tyson felt like there was more to her expression and comment.

"Yes. Like many, she believes no PR is bad PR, but I don't feel the same. Not a day goes by without people contacting me for my side of the story. I refuse to be pulled down that path, so I've been trying to lie low as far as the media is concerned."

"Good luck with that." Kendall playfully rolled her eyes.

"It was going okay until . . ." Tyson paused, wondering how much more he should reveal. In his silence, Kendall leaned in. He was sure she hadn't even realized how her body involuntarily responded to the suspense he'd apparently created. "Tiffany gave an exclusive last week that airs tonight, right after the awards."

Kendall looked at her cell phone. "That means it's on now!" The realization made her eyes stretch wide.

"Yeah." Tyson felt the heat of anger rise again. A deep breath helped him suppress it, and one look in Kendall's concerned eyes doused the sparks of whatever remained. "She allowed the media to insinuate that I'm this scoundrel who feeds on women's desires to make it in Hollywood for my own pleasure." Tyson shook his head. "She called me after she'd done the interview, and when I got upset, she asked me what was the big deal and insisted that no PR was bad PR."

"Oh, Tyson. That's horrible."

"My family doesn't know yet. I don't want the world to think I'm one of the jerks who use, abuse and toss women away. That's just not who I am, but after what I've seen the media do to me because I wouldn't add to their crazy discourse about our breakup, I can only imagine what could happen after this interview airs. I'm just bracing myself for the questions, accusations and anything else that the media and the industry will throw at me."

Kendall sat back and sighed. "I'm so sorry, Tyson. I truly wish there was something I could do."

Tyson took in her thoughtful gaze. He noticed her caring brown eyes, slender face framed by high cheekbones, beautiful bright red lips and the soft sensual lines of her shoulders exposed by her strapless gown. Kendall was gorgeous and didn't ever appear to be absorbed by her own beauty.

Despite being an entertainer, Kendall seemed sincere and authentic. Something about her was different. He remembered her tears onstage as she received her award. Her excitement wasn't an act, and her genuine nature seemed to compel her in everything she did.

They continued to sit in silence for a few moments.

"Hey! What did you have planned after this reception?" she asked suddenly.

"Nothing really. I knew that interview would be airing, and I thought I might catch a bit of it, but I'm really not up to it."

"Deal with that later." Kendall slid off her stool. "Let's go have some fun." She grabbed his hand.

What did Tyson have to lose? He'd already toasted with the staff about his promotion. At this point of the reception, many had already started to go off to other parties or head home, including his parents and siblings. Hopefully his dad hadn't been watching a lot of TV and had missed the previews for Tiffany's interview tonight. Tyson hadn't turned on his television since he'd spoken with Tiffany, just to avoid the teasers.

Hanging with Kendall was much more enticing than going home and pondering the possible backlash of the exclusive.

"Let's go!" Tyson agreed and followed Kendall's lead.

CHAPTER 13

Kendall probably shouldn't have invited Tyson to hang out with her, but she couldn't leave him to stew in his feelings. She knew what it felt like to be dragged around by the media. Tiffany and her actions reminded her a lot of Storm and his careless disregard for how the things he did impacted others. Maybe she should arrange for an introduction between the two of them. They seemed to have a lot in common. It crossed her mind that Tyson could have been making his role in this ordeal seem light, but something in her believed otherwise. Tyson was telling the truth. She felt it.

They found Jade, Nixon and Randi sitting on white sofas sectioned off by lush, white curtains.

"You guys want to go over to Time Record's after-party? I heard it's one of the best in the industry. We have VIP tickets." Randi waved the tickets back and forth.

Kendall looked at Tyson. He shrugged. "Jade, Nixon. Are you up for it?"

Jade looked at Nixon, who shrugged just like Tyson had moments before. "Let's go," he said.

Tyson called for a car, and within fifteen minutes they were walking into a trendy nightclub and lounge owned by an A-list entertainer. Since its grand opening a year before, the unassuming warehouse had become the hottest go-to for exclusive events. To regular people, it was a legend, but to Hollywood insiders, it was a welcome respite from the public's demand for selfies and autographs. In fact, cell phones had to be stored upon entering, and photos and videos were strictly prohibited.

They just happened to step in while Kendall's newest hit was playing. Kendall threw her head back and laughed. Hearing her music being played for everyone to listen to took her right back to her tiny little room where she'd grown up in Chicago and stood before her mirror singing into a hairbrush. Her life, despite her recent media debacle, was purely a dream come true. Up until the moment she passed, Kendall's mother, Grace, had indulged her dreams, buying anything that would encourage her. Until her parents had bought her that karaoke machine when she was eleven, she and her mother would play music, dance and sing at the top of their lungs into anything with a handle — hairbrushes, utensils, whatever. The living room had been her stage.

Kendall looked over at Jade, who flashed a proud smile and winked. She turned to Tyson, who was bobbing his head to the beat.

"You dance?" Kendall leaned toward Tyson and yelled over the music.

"Pft! Do I dance?" Tyson waved her off.

Kendall twisted her lips and then smiled. "Are you telling me you've got skills?"

"I've got more than skills." Tyson did a two-step, stopped abruptly as if he didn't want to give his *audience* too much and brushed his shoulder off before winking.

Kendall gave him a raised-brow glance before laughter spilled from her amused lips. "Then show me what you're working with."

Tyson took her by the hand. "Let me know if you need me to slow down for you."

Kendall shook her head. Surely Tyson didn't think she was incapable of keeping up. He was present for her performance earlier at the awards. Those dance classes that Grace kept her in weren't for naught.

Kendall was no amateur, and her skill could only be matched by a few contemporary artists. Outside of work, Kendall simply enjoyed dancing. It was fun and often made her feel free.

Tyson led her to the dance floor in time to catch the second half of her song. He sang the lyrics as he twirled her around on her toes and pulled her in to his torso. When her back connected with his chest, she felt a light surge shoot through her. Kendall swallowed. *It's all in good fun.*

Tyson wasn't joking when he said he had moves. He was a great dancer and moved easily, as if he had elastic in his bones. His steps were smooth, rhythmic, masculine and incredibly sexy. Kendall didn't even believe he was trying to be sexy. Somehow it simply exuded from him.

They danced nonstop through the next four songs. Nixon and Jade were right by them. Randi had secured herself a partner and worked her way to the other side of the floor. The DJ spun a popular song that got the entire crowd worked up. Tyson and Kendall joined in with others as they pumped fists in the air and sang aloud. Sweat trickled down the center of Kendall's back. Heat emanated from the crowded dance floor and enveloped them. Kendall kept dancing, not wanting to ever stop.

Tyson took her hand in his and spun her around. His sensual two-step enticed her. Kendall continued moving to the beat but closed her eyes. She had to. Getting pulled into Tyson's gaze felt carnal and dangerous, made her body temperature rise even higher. She could lose control of herself in his eyes alone. She couldn't glare upon the raw sexiness in those brown orbs without feeling like she could be taken over by some naughty version of herself.

Tyson looked happier than he had earlier, but besides the sexiness, she could still see the heaviness of the issue he'd been facing. The music changed again and the DJ began playing popular clips of songs from the sixties through the new millennium. He allowed just enough of the record to play to elicit excitement from the crowd before switching to another popular sound, creating a joyous uproar.

Tyson, Kendall, Nixon and Jade launched into dance moves matching each song and era, bending with laughter after many of their routines. They kept going until Kendall's hair became slick and stuck to the sides of her face.

"I need water!" she shouted over the

music and grabbed Jade. "Let's go get some water."

Tyson took her by the hand, led them all through the crowd to the bar. As they waited for their drinks, a gentleman in a black suit and white shirt with several undone buttons leaned in to say something in Tyson's ear. Tyson turned to Kendall, gesturing for her to follow him. Together, Tyson and Kendall followed the guy with the stringy blond locks. He led them to a VIP area with bright-colored couches against a wall that was backlit with muted colored lights. Moments later, waiters showed up with their drink orders. Randi was still somewhere in the sea of dancing people, but Kendall had ordered a water for her and placed it on the cocktail table in front of them.

"Whew!" Kendall fanned herself. "That was so much fun."

"Wasn't it?" Jade said. "I know one thing . . . my feet are getting pretty angry with me. I'm ready to come out of these shoes. I haven't danced that much since Chloe's wedding!"

Kendall tilted her head and smiled at Tyson. "How are you feeling, dude?"

"Pretty good."

Kendall couldn't help but feel a little

proud for being responsible for the change in his mood. They locked eyes for several moments before Kendall looked away. His gaze could cast spells. Instead of focusing on his magnetism, she texted Randi and told her where they were. They hung out for a while longer, chatting, laughing, singing to popular songs and sipping an endless flow of cocktails.

Kendall pulled herself from the chatter to take in the moment. Three short years before, she'd been in Chicago still helping to run the family's financial services business, spending her nights and evenings as an underground artist trying to be discovered. Now she sat at a party filled with celebrities, many of whom were household names. She sat as one of them, as part of their tribe, as the winner of a BTV award after her first performance at a major awards show, and as a singer in an incredible tribute to one of the world's most renowned veteran entertainers. Kendall closed her eyes and breathed in long and deep. Slowly she released that breath through slightly parted, smiling lips.

Slander, betrayals and failed relationships hadn't taken her down. She was here now, proud of all the hard work and sacrifice she'd put in and ready to work harder to get to the next level. Hollywood was her next conquest, and she was ready to take that world on. That's why she'd moved to Los Angeles. She could be a singer from Chicago. But to become a true movie star, she had to travel to the movie mecca.

She opened her eyes and found Tyson staring at her. Then the most interesting thought entered her mind: What would it be like to navigate this new world with a man like Tyson at her side?

CHAPTER 14

Tyson could feel the heat from his father's rage through the phone. "Your mother was so upset. She sat there in total disbelief at the lies that came from that girl's mouth. She couldn't tear herself away from the TV. And you knew nothing about this?"

Tyson patted the moisture from his body with a towel and tossed it across the marble vanity. White, plush carpet absorbed his steps with a light thud. Sunlight bathed the room through a tall wall of windows overlooking at least an acre of lush greenery beyond Tyson's deck and infinity pool. Tyson stood in front of the window, enjoying the warmth of the sun's rays on his exposed skin. In his usual fashion, he allowed the rest of the moisture covering his body to be licked dry by the air.

"Not before she did the interview, Dad. I only found out a few days ago."

"This is not a good look." Benjamin

huffed, sounding exasperated. "Have you spoken to her since then?" Tyson could imagine him pacing back and forth, shaking his head.

"No, sir." The last thing Tyson wanted to hear was Tiffany's excuses.

"Maybe I should give her a call."

"No. Don't waste your time, Dad." Tyson didn't want to subject his father to Tiffany's malicious manner.

"I don't understand. Did you do something really bad to her, son?"

"Dad!"

"I'm sorry. Why does she do these things? I just don't get it."

"What we need to worry about is how you want to respond to the media, if at all."

"Geesh!" Benjamin breathed. Tyson imagined him palming his forehead before parking one hand on his hip, his go-to gesture when he was frustrated beyond words. "Let's see how this goes before we make any statements. I don't like the way she put you out there as if you're preying on young actresses, dangling opportunities in front of them in exchange for . . . who knows what!" Tyson knew his father would avoid saying anything that implied sex. "Maybe it will blow over. And in the end, if we need to take legal action, we will. I built this company with my own hands and I won't stand for anyone trying to tear down the reputation we've built here. Right now, let's see which way the tides roll. I've seen this before, and sometimes it's better not to give the scandal any energy. But I'll tell you one thing. She'll never work on another BCG production as long as I'm alive. Trust is important, and she's broken our trust for the last time. That girl has got to understand that she isn't in this world alone."

Tyson nodded as if his father could see him agreeing with his words. Tiffany didn't realize she was leaving a trail of friends behind who could have been in her corner for life.

"You let me know if you hear anything else, okay?" His father continued. "And don't talk to those paparazzi people."

"You don't have to worry about that, Pop. I'll call if something else comes up."

"Right away, son. I want to know immediately. No more keeping anything from us, worrying about how we're going to deal with it. We're in this together."

"Yes, sir." Tyson would communicate as much as he could, but lately, he hadn't been in control of what had hit the media at all. Getting in front of the story seemed impossible these days.

Tyson had gotten so used to paparazzi that he blazed trails through their intrusive microphones, cameras and questions as if they were a gang of gnats. Since this started, their presence had multiplied. They were everywhere, at his home, outside of his office, at his favorite eateries. It was like someone had posted his schedule on the paparazzi hotline. One even attempted to climb his iron gates but was swiftly apprehended by security. That one faced trespassing charges. Tyson didn't want to ruin him, just teach him a lesson. Despite never being afraid of the spotlight, Tyson chose to move about more stealthily, sticking to his exclusive circles. That wasn't his preferred choice, but it was what he needed to do at this time.

Speaking of exclusive, he thought about how much he enjoyed Kendall and her friends' company the night before at the awards festivities and after parties. He was glad he hadn't refused Kendall's offer to hang out. Most of his family had already dispersed, and he had planned on torturing himself by going home to watch Tiffany's live interview with a great bottle of red wine or a good Scotch at his side. He was curious as to how much she'd actually said. Now it really didn't matter. The media was on it. Articles and video clips had already made their way through the viral stratosphere, being shared and viewed faster than trolls could muddy the feed with their unscrupulous comments.

As angry as the whole ordeal made him, he didn't stay mad at Tiffany. He'd learned that this way of hers was all she knew. Despite the lifestyle she'd been able to acquire, her childhood had set her up that way, forcing her to fight for everything she could get her hands on, right down to the few pieces of bread her foster mom placed before her and her slew of foster siblings. She'd been fighting for position and attention ever since. The impact on others was never something she paid attention to. Survival didn't allow that luxury.

Tyson slipped into a pair of jeans and a T-shirt. Kendall and the stunning red grown she'd so elegantly worn during the tribute flashed across his mind. The funky thigh-high leather boots, sequin shorts and bustier from her performance flashed through his brain as well, followed by the sexy dress she arrived on the red carpet in. He picked up his phone to call her, to thank her for getting him out of his funk last night. Except Tyson personally didn't have her number. His assistant had only communicated directly with Randi. He'd never asked for it.

"Dammit!"

Tyson needed to thank Kendall. The fact that yesterday was a monumental day for her wasn't lost on him. There was so much for her to celebrate: a successful performance resulting in the standing ovation, an amazing tribute and her first BTV award. Instead, she seemed more concerned about helping him forget his problems. Tiffany would have never done that. That would have required Tiffany to think of someone's needs besides her own. She probably would have pouted and yelled at him for not praising her accomplishments enough.

He wondered what Kendall was doing. The cable box reflected an early afternoon hour. It was typical for him to wake at such a time after a late night out. Was Kendall a night owl or morning person? Was she just rolling over, blocking the sunlight with an eye mask and fluffy pillow, or had she been up for hours? Was she a wild sleeper? Did she sleep in silky lingerie, comfy cotton loungers, footie pajamas? Or in the nude? Tyson wanted to know these and other intimate details.

The next time he was graced with the privilege of being in her presence, he needed to exchange numbers with her. But now that the awards show was over, when would that happen? Before this their paths had hardly ever crossed. Filming would start for the biopic in a few short weeks, but he was no longer the producer. As the CEO, there was no real reason for him to be on set. Besides, the studio was in a different part of the city from his office.

All Tyson knew was that he had to see her again. He'd find a way.

CHAPTER 15

Only a sliver of the sun had made its way over the horizon when Kendall woke. Jade and Nixon had made it back to New York, and it was now the first day of filming for the Jocelyn James biopic. Kendall wanted to get to the studio early. Word of her being selected to play Jocelyn had been carefully rolled out to the media, and Randi was already fielding requests for interviews. This, along with the rave from all the great reviews of her performances at the awards several weeks ago, her win and the fashion critics' praise of her ensemble on the red carpet, had replaced the speculations surrounding her breakup with Storm. Once again, Kendall was happy to see her name in the headlines.

Kendall just wished she knew who her new costar was going to be. Now that Tyson was CEO, a new producer had taken over the film project. Right out of the gate, he made several casting changes. She assumed that was his way of making his mark as the new guy in charge. Several people whom she'd looked forward to working with had been cut. Such was the nature of Hollywood.

Curiosity nagged at Kendall. She wanted to know who her new costar was going to be. Based on the script, Jocelyn had one hell of a life story, riddled with family drama, tragedy, scandal and heartbreak. It was a boyfriend with friends in the music industry who'd encouraged her to use her beautiful voice to escape the tribulations that life had dealt her. When it looked like her career would actually take off, he became jealous and abusive. She'd fled to the respite of her manager, who'd secretly loved her. Their story was one of a deep, hard love that helped Jocelyn overcome her tumultuous life.

Kendall knew the love scenes would be intense, and this was her first major role, so she had to give it her all. It would be awkward for her at first. This she knew, but she'd have to work on becoming comfortable in her role rather quickly in order to master it and give her best performance. She hoped to have good chemistry with her costar and the rest of the cast, but she'd be sure to let him know, whomever he turned out to be, that she was all business. Their on-screen romance would cease to exist once the cameras stopped rolling. She intended to make that undoubtedly clear.

Kendall was happy for Tyson's latest accomplishment, becoming CEO, but was admittedly equally disappointed that he would now have less involvement with the film. She had looked forward to seeing him pop in on the set and wondered if he would have accompanied them to the on-location shoots in New York, Paris and the village in Africa where they were scheduled to film.

Thinking of Tyson made her think of the night they'd hung out at the lounge after the awards show. She hadn't spoken to him since, but now she wondered how he was doing. She'd watched Tiffany's interview in its entirety and had to admit that it didn't paint Tyson in a very kind light. From the way Tiffany answered the interviewer's questions, she could tell that she was a master manipulator. She allowed the host lots of room to plant seeds of speculation, and instead of setting any records straight, she let those very seeds fester and grow like weeds. Not once had Tiffany defended any of the crazy conclusions the woman drew. At times, her only response was a Cheshire

Cat smirk. When she wasn't smirking, she played the wounded victim, fat crocodile tears dripped from her beautiful face. Kendall couldn't deny that Tiffany was gorgeous. Had she been born with those boobs that stood at attention right under her chin? What did it matter? The camera loved her, and so did the media. And Tiffany loved the camera right back.

At the point where Kendall began to pay more attention to Tiffany's beauty and less to what she was saying, she looked down at her worn but incredibly comfortable tank top, boy short panties and bare legs as she sat cross-legged in the center of her bed. She laughed but put down the cup of ice cream she'd been enjoying and never went back to it.

Off camera, Kendall wasn't the glamour girl that her public might have expected. Though she relished the finer things in life, she equally appreciated many of the simplicities life had to offer. The greater public probably didn't even realize that she had freckles, ones that she absolutely adored because she had inherited them from her maternal grandmother. They hadn't seen the natural curls that settled just past her shoulders, since her tresses had always been covered by overzealous wigs and weaves or pressed to perfection to hang sleekly down the sides of her oval face. Making the shift to the public's Kendall was easy and she liked keeping the *real* Kendall to herself, just like her sanctuary in Temecula. Those sacred spaces were hers and hers alone.

Thinking back to the interview, by the time it was over, she had felt for both Tiffany and Tyson. Tiffany because she assumed that something tragic must have led to her unscrupulous ways, and Tyson because he'd allowed her a glimpse into the pain that Tiffany's dodgy behavior caused. Hopefully, she'd see him soon enough. He had been fun to hang with. Maybe they could actually become real friends.

The sun had yet to make a full ascent. Kendall took a long shower, made a green smoothie and bulked it up with flax seeds and vanilla-flavored protein powder. That would keep her satisfied until she'd need a snack and it was much better than ice cream. Of course, there would be plenty of food on set for the actresses. And since she was playing the lead, she'd surely have her very own trailer and people ready to serve at her every beck and call.

"Look, Mama! I made it!" Kendall held her arms out at her side and spun around. Grace was smiling down at her from heaven.

She was sure of it.

The drive over to the famous studios was quick. The guard at the security gate took her ID, examined it and handed it back with a smile.

"Welcome, Ms. Chandler." She pulled out a map and directed Kendall to the appropriate set for the film, congratulated her on her win at the BTV Awards and sent her off with a cheerful smile.

The drive into the studio felt like she was rolling along through a dream. The haze was real, though, compliments of the fog that had yet to be burned off by the fullness of the sun. She was a child riding through the adult version of Disneyland. That's what the studio resembled, with immaculate structures done so well they actually looked like the real locations from across the country. Kendall pulled up to a parking lot and immediately noticed a spot with her name posted on a sign. She gasped, covered her mouth and blinked several times to keep the tears at bay. She hadn't expected to be overcome with emotion. Kendall was used to VIP treatment, but this was new — this was part of a lifelong vision. It was one thing to imagine something so much that it felt real, but it was a whole different thing to actually experience it happening in real life.

Once again, she wished she could pick up the phone to tell her mother all about it. Dad would be excited too of course, but it wasn't the same.

Several other actors had arrived as well. The crew was setting up, gathered in groups discussing design and whatever else they talked about. Adrenaline rushed through her veins. Kendall wanted to skip but managed to hold her posture. A stagehand approached and greeted her.

"Hi, Ms. Chandler. Congratulations on your win." The petite brunette with the pretty face held out her hand. Her shake was firm, all business.

"Thank you and good morning."

The young woman smiled in a way that let Kendall know she hadn't expected her response.

"You're very welcome and very nice. I love your latest album, by the way. I've been following you since your first release."

"Oh. Well, thanks again."

The woman's smile grew wider, if that were possible.

"I'll show you to your trailer."

"Thanks." Inside she squealed, but outside she was as dignified and cool as a smooth cocktail. This would be the first time she'd have her own trailer. Kendall couldn't wait to see inside.

The young woman opened the door to let Kendall in.

With one foot on the step, Kendall turned back to her. "I'm sorry, I didn't get your name."

"Wow. Maddie. My name is Maddie. I don't usually get asked."

Kendall sighed. "Really?" She never wanted to become one of those celebrities who made people feel invisible.

"I'll go ahead and get out of your way. Let me know if you need anything at all, Ms. Chandler."

"Thank you, Maddie. I will."

Kendall entered the large trailer with her name scribbled on the door. Inside, the decor was a contemporary mix of chic simplicity, almost as if she'd designed it herself. In the rear there was a queen-size bed covered with a pale blue-and-cream duvet. A plush, gray area rug spread under the bed, extending on both sides. Kendall plopped down on the bed and fell back.

"Oh!" she moaned. "So comfortable."

Back toward the front was a corner dining table large enough for about four people topped with a vase filled with white lilies, Kendall's favorite flower. Besides being beautiful, they were the only flowers whose sweet scent didn't remind her of her mother's funeral. Next to the table was a small kitchenette, two sleek love seats with pillows that looked like the stuffing was wrapped in an eclectic piece of art, and basically a full-size refrigerator, not a minifridge like in the trailer she'd shared with fellow cast members on the other film she'd worked on briefly.

Kendall opened the refrigerator and saw that it was filled with fresh fruit, containers of mixed greens, a bag of spinach, a bottle of French vanilla creamer and glass bottles of alkaline water. The freezer held bags of frozen fruit. *Interesting.* All of these were things Kendall would have packed herself. When she turned around, she noticed a high-speed emulsifier on the counter and a beautiful wooden box filled with small canisters of exotic loose-leaf teas. It was like someone had set up the trailer with all of her favorite things.

Just then her phone rang. It was Randi.

"Hey!"

"What's up, chickie?"

"Things are great. I see you had them add all my favorite things to my trailer. Good job, Randi."

"Get used to it. We're going all the way to the top, doll!"

"Yes, we are, dammit! Ha!" A knock at the trailer door interrupted their laughter. "Hold on a sec, Randi."

Kendall opened the door, expecting to see Maddie. Instead, she came face-to-face with Tyson.

Chapter 16

Tyson paused when he looked at Kendall. He could read the surprise in her eyes. She wasn't expecting to see him.

"Um . . . let me call you back." Kendall said and touched her screen before looking up at Tyson. "Hello." Kendall's greeting sounded more like a question.

"Good morning, Kendall."

Both fell quiet for several moments. In those seconds, Tyson took Kendall in again. It had been a while since he'd last laid eyes on her. She wore no makeup this time. He hadn't noticed her freckles before. The brown specks sprinkled across the bridge of her nose and over her cheeks all seemed perfectly placed. Her hair, which was usually perfectly coiffed without a single strand out of place, was pulled into a loose bun piled at the top of her head. Several loose waves hung down around her neck and temple, giving her a sexy, messy appeal.

Clear gloss made her full lips look slick. Tyson fought the urge to press his lips against hers. Standing before him in a fitted T, jeans and sandals that glittered, Kendall looked just as sexy as she had in a floor-length fitted gown. He couldn't ever remember seeing Tiffany without makeup.

"Oh. Uh. Come on in." Kendall stepped aside. "I'm glad you came by. I thought about you."

"So, you were thinking about me?" Tyson couldn't help his smile.

"Oh!" Kendall rolled her eyes. "Don't let your head get all big. These trailers only have so much room. Come on." Kendall led him to the lounge area. They sat on the sofa. "What's up?"

"I wanted to say thank you."

Kendall held up her hand. "Hold that thought for just one sec. I'm a horrible host." She shook her head at herself. "Would you like something to drink? I have water, coffee, tea?"

"No. I'm fine. I won't be here long at all."

"Okay. Now, you were saying . . . thank you? For what?"

"For helping me to get out of the funk I was in that night. I appreciate your concern, and I'm glad I hung out with you and your cousin."

"Yeah! That was fun, wasn't it? It's been a while since I just simply had fun. It's always work, work, work. I think we both needed it."

"I think you're right." Tyson paused, letting his next question marinate for a moment. "I'd love to hang out with you again."

Kendall sat expressionless. She let his statement fall into the silence. Tyson watched her swallow and then clear her throat. He waited, refusing to rescue her from the quiet that thickened and filled the space around them. He wanted an answer, even if it was no.

Kendall sighed. "Tyson." He knew where this was going. At least he would know he tried. "I . . ." she started and paused again. "I really enjoyed myself that night and I'm glad you were feeling much better after, but . . ." She inhaled again, exhaled slowly. "My career is really taking off right now. I'm in such an amazing place, and I have you to thank for part of that." Tyson's brows furrowed. Kendall waved off the inquiry in his expression. "I'll come back to that. This is not a good time for me to take on new friends. I'm trying my best to be focused on my career, my dreams. I'm doing well in the music world, but I want to also make it in

Hollywood, and I want to do it on my own merit."

"I see." Tyson wasn't completely sure if he did. Had she seen and believed some of the craziness Tiffany had been dishing about him misleading aspiring actresses? Was Tiffany ruining not just his image but also his chances at dating other women?

"Are you sure you understand? The expression on your face just changed." Kendall tilted her head a bit. "What are you thinking, Tyson?"

"Does my situation with Tiffany have anything to do with your decision?"

Kendall shook her head vigorously. "Oh, goodness no. I want to make it and be respected for my hard work and dedication to the craft. I want it to be clear that I earned my place in Hollywood."

Tyson pulled in his bottom lip and gnawed lightly. "I can understand that. I earned my position of CEO at BCG. My dad made me prove myself over several years. He didn't just hand over the reins of a billion-dollar company to someone incapable of running it, yet there's lots of speculation about me getting the position just because I was his son. So, I can respect how you feel, but that doesn't mean we can't be friends."

Kendall grunted. "What will people think?"

"Frankly, I don't care what people will think. If I did, I'd be in a mental institution by now because I would've driven myself crazy. I care about getting to know you better." Tyson shifted in his seat. "I'm not going to waste any time. When I first met you, I thought you were beautiful, of course, and incredibly talented. I also assumed you were just another arrogant, self-absorbed, superficial entertainer. Just the kind of woman I said I would never date again, thanks to Tiffany." Kendall's eyes widened. "But you proved me wrong."

He wasn't ready to say everything. It was too soon to tell her that she showed up in his dreams and he thought about her all the time. Tyson didn't want to scare the woman off completely. "I've gotten to know you a bit more and really like who you are. I want to know more. I can respect your desire to be acknowledged for the hard work you put into being successful, but I also believe you can do that whether you're dating or not. In fact, we don't have to date. How about we just get to know each other as friends."

"You just want to be friends with me, Tyson?" Kendall cocked her head sideways and glared at him.

"No. But I'll settle for friendship for now, and we can see where this takes us." Tyson stood. "You've got a big day ahead of you. I'll get out of your way. And even if you decide that you don't want to be my 'friend' —" Tyson curled his fingers into quotes "— at least let me take you out as a token of my gratitude for just being there for me after the awards. For being a 'friend.' " He exaggerated the air quotes again and smiled this time.

Kendall tilted and shook her head. She looked up at Tyson. "So, we're already friends?"

"Looks that way to me. And you started it."

Kendall rolled her eyes and laughed. "Fine. Let's continue to be friends — but on one condition."

Tyson raised one brow. "What's that?"

"Can we keep the damn media out of our friendship?"

"I wouldn't want it any other way."

"Good!" Kendall flopped back on the sofa.

"Now, about me taking you out." Kendall looked at Tyson sideways again. "To show my gratitude . . ." She raised her brows. "You'll be shooting most of the week, so how about Saturday?"

"As long as there's nothing on my calendar, I guess Saturday is fine. Where can we go without the paparazzi tagging along?"

"Oh. Don't worry. I've got that covered." Tyson winked. "See you Saturday."

CHAPTER 17

Kendall had a blast the first few days of filming. Getting into Jocelyn's character was exhilarating, and the studying she'd done to prepare for the role was definitely paying off. By the time she came out of hair and makeup each day, she felt like a young girl playing dress-up in the exquisite outfits from the fifties and sixties. The old Hollywood glam transported her back in time.

The first few scenes were easy to get into. More intense scenes were on the horizon, with depictions of the abuse and violence Jocelyn suffered and how she'd almost been taken over by drugs and alcohol in her attempt to escape the madness that had been her life at times. Kendall shed tears as she read some of the scenes, but she was ready to go *there* to bring Jocelyn's character to life, transport the pain and make the audience feel. It wasn't far from what she'd done with singing. Kendall had been taught to inject her emotions into the music. Her mentor had told her that if she didn't feel it, the people wouldn't feel it, and if she failed to make her audience feel something, the beauty of her voice would be lost.

Maddie had escorted her throughout the set on the first day, where she met several other cast members, a few of whom she'd met before and some she was meeting for the first time. Jocelyn's stepfather's role was being portrayed by an iconic actor with more than eighty films to his credit. Kendall had grown up watching this man on television and in films and tried not to be star struck. His down-to-earth personality and quick wit made her feel immediately at home in his presence and infused the set with a sense of family. Great chemistry between the actors was already developing. His innate warmth made her wonder how he'd make the transition to portraying the harsh man who had done such wicked things in Jocelyn's life.

The entire project made Kendall appreciate Jocelyn's talent and accomplishments even more. Kendall didn't believe that everyone was built tough enough to overcome the obstacles people like Jocelyn overcame and still end up being legends. The new actor playing her love interest had yet to arrive. They'd begun by shooting scenes that he wasn't a part of. Apparently, he'd been held up due to canceled flights out of some part of Europe where he had just finished up another project. Everyone wondered who it was going to be, betting on some of the industry's most talented actors. The producers were being quiet on the issue, which only fueled the speculation.

Kendall had arrived early again this morning and was greeted by a cheerful Maddie, who had already taken note of some of her favorite things. She'd had a smoothie prepared and sent to Kendall's trailer. Kendall sipped and lounged inside the trailer, taking in a few quiet moments before the day started.

A knock on her door, followed by Maddie yelling, "Hair and makeup in ten!" alerted Kendall to get ready. She dialed her father.

"Dad!" she sang. Kendall had gotten in the habit of calling him every morning and evening, giving a play-by-play of her day. He seemed to relish the stories about what was happening on set.

"Morning, baby girl! What's on the agenda for today?"

"I get to finally find out who my costar is going to be. They've been so hush-hush about it. You know how Hollywood is. They love stirring up a buzz."

"You have any idea?"

"I sure do. I think it's Elgin Alba. He's the hottest actor in Hollywood right now."

"You'd love that, wouldn't you!" Booker T. chuckled.

Kendall giggled. Her dad knew how much she'd fawned over that man even before she became famous herself. A few years her senior, he was the perfect person to play opposite her role. Kendall hoped she'd be able to contain herself, especially after performing love scenes with him. "Ha! But this is work, Dad." She'd also heard all the rumors about Elgin's many trysts with costars. And she was no floozy. This was business. As gorgeous as he was, there was no way she'd allow herself to get caught in his web. Actors performed love scenes with gorgeous costars all the time. And this was her new world. She thought about Tyson. He was her new friend, and she couldn't deny that she was as interested in exploring their new friendship as he was.

Kendall chatted with her dad for a few more minutes, asking after her brothers and promising to call them. Kendall ended the call, looked at her cell phone and jumped up. She was supposed to be in hair and makeup by now. Way more than ten minutes had passed. She downed the rest of her now-lukewarm smoothie and high-tailed it out of the trailer.

Tyson called while she speed walked toward the building.

"Good morning, friend." Tyson's deep voice poured through the phone like hot lava, warming Kendall more than the brisk walk. That and the tone he used on the word *friend* made her blush.

"Good morning to you." Her voice had lowered an octave or two. She smiled and shook her head at herself. She couldn't keep Tyson's sexiness from affecting her.

"I hear you're crushing it over there. Might you be a better actor than singer? Is that even possible?"

Now Kendall's cheeks burned from blushing. "You sure know how to make a girl feel good early in the morning." The second that sentence left her mouth, Kendall palmed her forehead.

"Well! I'm not quite sure how you'd want me to answer *that*!"

Kendall laughed. "Don't!" She held her hand up in a halting motion as if he could see her. "Please, don't answer that!"

Tyson's laugh was sharp, piercing the line. "I'll go ahead and keep that response to myself. I just called to wish you luck and let

467

you know I look forward to seeing you on Saturday."

Kendall tilted her head. A warm smile eased across her lips. "I must say that I'm looking forward to it as well. So where are we going?"

"Uh, uh, uh," Tyson objected. Kendall could almost picture him wagging his finger at her. "It's a surprise."

"What if I told you I don't like surprises?"

"Then I'd tell you where we're going. I wouldn't want to upset you."

"You would?" Kendall couldn't keep the excitement out of her voice.

"Nope."

"Tyson!" she chided.

"Got ya."

Kendall couldn't help but laugh. "I walked into that, didn't I?" Kendall slowed her gait as she reached the room to get her hair and makeup done. She stopped right outside the door to finish her conversation with Tyson.

"Yes. Did you really think I was that easy? I'm insulted."

"You're a mess."

"A little of that too."

"I can tell. Sorry, but I've got to go. I need to get my Jocelyn James on."

"Ha! I'd love to see you in character."

"Maybe you could stop by the set one day."

"Maybe I will."

"That would be nice. In the meantime, I've gotta run. See you Saturday."

"Looking forward to it."

Kendall ended the call, took a deep breath and slowly dropped her shoulders as she let it out. The more interactions she had with Tyson, the more she confirmed that there was something special about him. It had been over a year since she'd been on a date. This was going to be interesting. Thinking about how much fun they'd had the last time they hung out together made her anticipation for Saturday shoot up a few notches. Right now, she had work to do. Kendall took another deep breath, exhaled and tilted her head from one side to the other, stretching her neck as if she were preparing for a boxing match. With her chest up and shoulders back, she stepped into the makeup room.

Kendall emerged nearly two hours later totally transformed. She looked and felt like the Jocelyn James of the fifties, with a head full of tight curls, long luscious lashes, a fitted dress set low on her shoulders that by today's terms would be too much coverage for an artist, but back then could have been deemed just a little scandalous. The dress was so narrow at the knees that she was forced to take small steps with one foot directly in front of the other. It gave her an old-school kind of sexiness that infiltrated her being. In this getup, Kendall wasn't *playing* Jocelyn James. She *was* Jocelyn James.

Maddie emerged and escorted Kendall on set. All eyes were on her as she strolled through the studio.

"Ah yes. Here she is!" Jack Baker, the producer, clasped his hands and walked over to her. "Stunning, absolutely stunning, and such perfect timing. Your co-star has finally arrived. Of course, you've met before."

Jack turned slightly. Excited, Kendall turned and stood face-to-face with her ex, Storm. The smile melted from her face.

"Kendall." Storm's lips eased into a smile that resembled more of a smirk. He reached out to shake her hand.

"Storm," she said, tight-lipped, and left his hand hanging.

CHAPTER 18

Hearing Kendall's voice made Tyson long to see her face. He chuckled at himself. He couldn't believe how he'd begun to fall for her. As a man who could always be counted on for standing by his word, Tyson wasn't the kind to backtrack. Yet his vow to eliminate actresses from his dating pool had lasted no time at all. His reasoning was that Kendall was different: beautiful, unselfish, sexy . . . talented, and she had substance. Tyson could go on.

Tyson almost never pursued a woman. There were always plenty at the ready, from groupies to celebrities to executives. Tiffany had pushed herself to the front of the line when she decided she wanted to be with him. She'd made her intentions clear and run off any other woman trying to get his attention. Besides being attractive, Tiffany had ambition that he admired. But ultimately, it was that same ambition that drove them apart.

Tyson called his assistant.

"Good morning!"

"Good morning, Mr. Chandler," Brianna chirped.

"Just confirming that my schedule is clear of meetings for the morning. I need to make a stop before coming in."

"Sure. Let me check." The phone went silent for several seconds. "Okay. Yes. You have a conference call at eleven with the New York office. I'll text you the call-in number and set an alert on your calendar."

"Perfect. You're the best. See you this afternoon."

"Okay. You're going to be back in time to meet with the PR team, right? Or would you like for me to reschedule that meeting?"

"No! Don't reschedule. I'll be back in time. Thanks." That was one meeting Tyson was not going to miss.

The fuss created from Tiffany's interview hadn't died down. Instead, it started burgeoning into a larger monster. BCG had engaged their PR team to develop a strategy for addressing the public, and part of that was to have Tyson do an exclusive interview with a competing network so it wouldn't seem as though BCG was holding back or hiding something. Entertainment shows privy to the fact that Tyson was ready to speak were clamoring for the exclusive.

"See you later, Mr. Blackwell."

"Take care." Tyson ended the call and made a U-turn at the next light. The prospect of seeing Kendall lifted his mood.

Being in Kendall's company would be a welcome respite from all that he'd been juggling. The work of a CEO wasn't easy. After just a few short weeks with his new title, his respect for his father had skyrocketed. There was so much to do. So many people counted on him, needed his leadership, sought his approval. The fate of the entire company rested on him. The level of responsibility was staggering, and Benjamin Blackwell had made it all look so easy. Not to mention the media frenzy that Tiffany had handcrafted. She was still interviewing, giving exclusives and relishing the spotlight. It was sickening. She was in so deep that she hadn't bothered to notice that some of their mutual friends had begun to distance themselves from her. A few even called to check on Tyson to see how he was dealing with it all. It was clear to everyone but the media and Tiffany that she was taking this way too far. The public were hungry piranhas, and Tiffany happily dangled the bait.

Tyson navigated his Porsche through the

heavy Los Angeles traffic toward the other side of the city, arriving at the studio much later than he'd anticipated. He had less than an hour to see Kendall before finding someplace quiet to take his conference call.

He handed over his ID at the security desk, and the guard directed him to the lot near the studio where Kendall was filming. The closer he got, the wider his instinctive smile grew. He couldn't wait to lay eyes on Kendall, especially in character. Tyson wanted to see her in action. Now that he was no longer the producer on this project, there was no real reason that he needed to be on set. Yet BCG was one of the companies invested in the film, and there was nothing to stop him from visiting.

Tyson parked and made his way through the normal rush that existed on set. Throngs of people from the crew, including set designers, maintenance people, production assistants, engineers, security, actors, directors and extras, milled about doing what they needed to do. Tyson waved at several familiar faces and made his way inside to where they were shooting the current scene.

Tyson put his phone on vibrate and quietly stepped into the shadows on the set of a smoky lounge where Kendall — as Jocelyn — sat at a bar looking disheveled. Mascara darkened the space under her eyes. She took a frustrated drag from a cigarette before smashing it into an ashtray. Her elbow rested on top of the bar. She held her forehead in her hands, sat up straight, shook off her angst and swatted away tears. Suddenly, she threw back the entire contents of a tumbler containing some amber-colored liquor and slammed down the glass. The entire set was silent, sucked in by the anguish Kendall exuded. Tyson was caught up, wanting to know what had caused the pain and at the same time wanting to run to Kendall to make it all better.

But she wasn't Kendall at all. Everything about her was Jocelyn. Kendall had transformed into Jocelyn James and dragged everyone around them into the illusion, pinning them in a trance until the director yelled, "Cut!" At the sound of his voice, Tyson shook his head, willing himself back to reality. Just as he had anticipated, Kendall was a remarkable actress.

"Beautiful! One more time from the top."

Tyson leaned against a wall and settled in, ready to take in this scene from the start. A makeup person hurried to Kendall, dabbed her forehead and cheeks, fluffed her hair and jetted away.

"Okay. Quiet on the set . . . aaand . . . action!"

Leon loomed over Kendall. Threatened her with his presence.

"Leave me alone, Leon!" she demanded. "I can't do this no more."

She picked up her drink. He snatched it from her hand. Slammed it down on the table.

He looked around, drew closer to her "So you too good for me now. If it wasn't for me, you wouldn't even be here. I should have left you in the gutter where I found you."

"Don't forget you come from that same gutter, Leon!" she spit.

He grabbed her shirt. Pulled her so close that the tips of their noses touched. She stood and glared right back into his eyes, challenging him, not backing down.

She snarled, "Go ahead. Hit me if it'll make you feel like a man."

Leon drew his free hand back, poised to bring down a slap so hard it was sure to bring her crumpling to her knees. Nearby, several breaths caught audibly.

"Hey! Hey!" Benny ran in from the opposite side of the bar. He got there just in time to catch Leon's hand midair, before it landed on her face. "You wanna hit on someone? Try me, punk."

Leon wrangled his hands from Benny's

476

clutches. Jerked his hand away from the front of Kendall's dress. Tugged on his suit jacket and adjusted his hat.

"Get out of here," Benny demanded through clenched teeth. "And don't let me see you around here again." His gaze narrowed on Leon even more.

"Humph!" Leon grunted, looking at Jocelyn's rescuer and then back at her, sucking his teeth. "I'll see you later, Jossie." He sneered. "You need me." He tugged on his suit one more time. Walked backward until his heel hit the door. All eyes, from the bartender's to the patrons', followed him out. Kendall glared at him as he backed out the door.

"You okay, Jossie?" Benny asked quietly.

"I didn't need your help, Benny." Shame sent her eyes darting throughout the seedy bar. Pride lifted her chin. "I know how to handle myself."

He held his hands up in surrender. "Well, I'm here when and if you ever need me." His smile carried pity, sincerity and a slight gleam. "Just call." He backed away.

Jocelyn sat and puffed her cigarette long and hard. Her lips popped at the end of the drag.

Kendall finished the scene as emotion poured into the space, thickening the air. The director yelled, "Cut!" again. Tyson let out a breath that he hadn't realized he'd been holding. He wanted to clap, yell "bravo," but this wasn't the setting. Everyone around him moved along as usual, performing their duties. The three main actors from the scene joined the director in reviewing a replay on the monitor. They held a brief discussion about it. Tyson remained in the shadows, still seized by her stellar performance, until something hit him. The second man, the rescuer, Benny — that was her ex — Storm. When had he become part of the cast?

Tyson moved out of the shadows and walked over to where they stood discussing the scene with the director.

"Tyson! My man. How's it going? I didn't expect to see you down here," the director said, pulling him into a masculine embrace.

"I just stopped by to see how everything was going. Looking good." He spoke to the director, but his eyes were on Kendall.

"Tyson." She nodded, released a small smile. He nodded back.

In his periphery, he could see Storm look back and forth between him and Kendall.

"Tyson Blackwell," Storm interrupted, holding out his hand. Tyson shook it, even though something in him didn't want to.

"We've never actually met. I'm Storm Sanders."

"Good to meet you, Storm." Tyson's tone was neutral. Storm's grip on his hand was tighter than necessary. Was he claiming territory? Even though Storm addressed Tyson, his eyes ping-ponged between Tyson and Kendall.

"Great meeting you too." Storm turned back toward the director and then Kendall.

"Like I said, I just stopped in to see how things were going and to say hello." He smiled at Kendall. She smiled back, but there was something unreadable in her expression. "I'd better get back." Tyson looked at his watch. His conference call was due to start soon. "Looks like this is going to be a real blockbuster." He nodded politely toward Kendall and said his goodbyes to the others. "Have a great day, everyone." He gave a general wave, and as he turned away, he could feel Storm's gaze boring into his back.

"Tyson!" He turned to find Kendall walking toward him. "Can I have a word with you?"

"Sure. I have a call I need to jump on in a bit, but I'm happy to talk until then. I'm sorry I don't have more time."

"That's fine." Kendall glanced back before

heading toward the exit.

Tyson looked back as Kendall did and found Storm's eyes still on them, only now his focus was more intense.

Outside, they kept walking until they were a few feet from the entrance of the studio.

Kendall's expression turned serious. "Why didn't you tell me they had cast Storm in this film?"

Tyson held up his hands. "I knew the producers made changes when I left the project, but I didn't know that was one of them."

"Well, is there anything you can do? I don't think it's a good idea for us to work together."

Tyson sighed. "That . . ." He paused. "That's not normally how we do business in Hollywood, and my interference at this point would be frowned upon."

"But you're the CEO of the entire company." Kendall's arms flailed. Her voice elevated a few pitches.

Tyson shook his head. "Unfortunately, it doesn't work like that. BCG is not the only company investing in this project. There are boundaries that we have to respect."

Kendall crossed her arms, closed her eyes for a moment and huffed out a breath. "I'm sorry. I shouldn't have asked that."

Kendall's frustration was clear to Tyson. For his own benefit, he was happy to see that. It confirmed that she was no happier to see Storm on the set than he was. He understood. Had Tiffany showed up somewhere he hadn't expected, that would have bothered him too.

"Listen." Tyson touched her arm. He opened his mouth to speak and saw movement from the corner of his eye. He turned slightly to find Storm standing in the entryway, not being at all discreet about watching them. "I'll talk with a few people and see what I can do, but I can't make any promises. It sucks, I know."

"Thanks!"

"See you Saturday?"

"Yes." Kendall gave him a weak smile.

Tyson wanted to kiss her right there in front of Storm, take her frustration away, but that would be out of line. They were only friends, and he wouldn't allow his ego to reduce him to inappropriate behavior. He had nothing to prove to anyone, especially not Storm. He wanted Kendall and would be able to legitimately claim her as his lady soon enough. Tyson wasn't about to engage in a match of flaring egos. He was too far above that and refused to cheapen their friendship with that kind of behavior.

Despite the slight pangs of jealousy that crept up when he saw Storm on set, Tyson wasn't concerned about losing Kendall to any man — except himself.

CHAPTER 19

"Tyson, this sounds like much more than an appreciative dinner." Kendall wondered what he was up to.

"Oh, you'll appreciate this. I'll admit, it's not average, but then again, I'm not an average kind of friend. Are you dressed comfortably like I asked?"

Kendall looked down at her stylish ripped jeans and glittering sandals. Her fitted T-shirt had the word *Dope* scribbled in silver across her breast with a tilted crown. Any more comfort, and she'd be in sneakers or barefoot. "I guess." She shrugged even though they were on the telephone. This wasn't what Kendall had envisioned when Tyson offered to take her out. Even with their stance about being "friends," she'd at least anticipated a romantic dinner or something close to that. She'd had the perfect dress in mind. Tyson's request for her to wear something comfortable — he had also specifically told her *not* to wear heels — doused any speculations she'd had about what their first time out as friends would be like.

"And this early hour? It's seven o'clock in the morning. This is just ungodly for a Saturday." Laughter bubbled from her before she could finish her sentence.

"Ha!" Tyson said. "I'm not saying any more. This is supposed to be a surprise, remember?"

"I thought I told you I don't like surprises." She was sure the smile in her voice was evident.

"I'm still not telling. The car should be there to pick you up in fifteen minutes."

"So, there's nothing I can do to get you to talk?"

"Nothing. Don't forget to bring a sweater just in case you get cool."

Now Kendall was really confused. California was experiencing a heat wave. Kendall assumed it would be her protection against the frigid temperatures inside some of the area's restaurants that kept their air conditioners on full blast.

"I'll see you soon."

"Okay," she said with a moan, and then pouted.

Kendall went to her closet and grabbed a

light sweater, folded and tucked it inside her tote. She ran her fingers through her hair, which was flat-ironed bone straight and cascaded down the sides of her face from a center part. A single coat of red lipstick popped against her fair complexion. Eyeliner and a little mascara were her only cosmetics. Kendall never felt the need to pile on a full face of makeup on a daily basis. She had enough of that during interviews and shows.

Kendall checked her appearance in her bedroom mirror, and then checked it again. Excitement surged through her. Kendall knew this concept of friendship was a farce. Tyson was into her and she was into him. Her face had lit up when she saw him on set the other day. It wasn't until he showed up that she realized how much she'd longed to see him again. Still, it was important for her to make it in Hollywood on her own merit, so she'd have to contain herself. And if anything were to really come of it, she'd demand they keep their interactions discreet. At the very least, she was willing to have some fun with Tyson whether something more blossomed from their friendship or not. She could tell by the way he had been handling his breakup with Tiffany that he wasn't the kind to kiss and tell.

Kiss. Kendall tilted her head and narrowed her eyes pensively. Would Tyson kiss her today? Was he a good kisser? A great kisser? She imagined his lush lips covering hers and the feel of being wrapped in his strong arms and she shuddered. "Stop it! We're going out as friends," she admonished herself and giggled.

Kendall's curiosities continued to venture off into wonderland. How was Tyson as a boyfriend? Was he considerate and kind? Did he spoil his women? She assumed yes, because she couldn't imagine a woman more spoiled than Tiffany. And from what she had seen of her in interviews, Tiffany seemed a bit of a brat. Kendall hated the fact that she had negative thoughts about Tyson's ex. She wasn't the kind to trash-talk other women. She let thoughts of Tiffany flutter away and shift back to Tyson — Kendall liked the qualities she'd seen in him so far. He was a gentleman; he seemed grateful and professional but knew how to turn on the fun and seemed to value his privacy, which was extremely important to her. And despite his incredibly good looks and the fact that he hailed from a famous and wealthy family, he didn't seem the least bit arrogant.

Just as she walked to the refrigerator to

retrieve a bottle of water, her cell phone released a muffled rumble. Since she spent so much time in the recording studio and now filming the new movie, Kendall had come into the habit of keeping her phone on vibrate.

"Hello."

"Your car is waiting outside." The deep sound of Tyson's voice sent an electrical current up her spine.

Geesh, that man's voice is sexy. Kendall was recalling all the things she had to pretend not to notice: the succulent lips, pearly white teeth, muscular chest perfectly straining against his stylish shirts, his commanding height, strong hands and athletic build. "Whew." Kendall shuddered as if she'd caught a chill. Tyson Blackwell was a masterpiece.

"Coming down now."

Kendall grabbed her tote and headed out of her condo, past the paparazzi stationed outside of her complex ready to snap pictures of her and the few other celebrities who lived there. Now that the frenzy around her failed relationship with Storm had died down, there weren't as many photographers camped out front as there used to be. She had Tyson to thank for that. As much as she loved her condo, she found herself wondering how much longer she'd keep it. Her other home was her respite, but it was a bit far for handling business in LA on a regular basis. The more private areas of LA came with a much higher price tag. She was doing very well and hadn't come from humble means as a Chandler, but she was very smart with her money. Besides, she'd already splurged on her home in Temecula, and when she wasn't working, she preferred to stay there.

Kendall quickly closed the space from the gate outside of her complex to the car waiting for her at the curb. Inside she expected to see Tyson, but he wasn't there. She dialed his number.

"Hey. Where are you?"

"You're in the car?"

"Yes."

"Great. Then I'll see you soon."

Kendall pressed her lips into a smile. "Okay, Mr. Secretive."

"Yep. Bye for now." Tyson ended the call.

"Wha—" Kendall looked at the phone as if the device had offended her. "This guy." She shook her head and laughed. She used her time in the car to scroll through her social media profiles. She wasn't one to post much, but she liked seeing what other celebrities put out in the world. Some of her fellow entertainers posted constantly. If someone were looking for them, they'd know exactly where to find them.

Within twenty minutes they'd arrived at LAX Airport. Kendall was greeted by an escort who led her through the remote entrances reserved for private air travel. What was she doing at the airport? Where was Tyson taking her? Several nearly empty corridors later, they came to a desk where security personnel asked for her ID. A few people sat around scrolling through their phones and sipping wine, coffee or tea in a small glassed-in waiting area. It looked less like a public airport and more like the lobby of a contemporary boutique hotel.

Kendall knew what was to be expected. This wasn't her first time flying privately, even though she or her family had never owned a plane. After clearing security, an attendant escorted her through the Jetway onto an airplane with *BW Force One* elegantly scripted over the door. The pilot and attendant offered a warm greeting and indicated with grand arm sweeps for her to walk down the aisle. The interior was outfitted with several large white-leather seats that were able to recline and black, plush carpet. The attendant led her beyond white curtains to another area with leather benches along the walls and bistro tables positioned equally apart in front of them. At the end of the benches stood a polished wood bar and another attendant with a warm, welcoming smile.

Tyson, in all his masculine glory, leaned his elbow on the bar as he chatted with the bartender. He looked up at her, and she swore she saw a gleam in his eye.

"There she is!" Tyson met her as she walked, gently grabbing her arm and planting a friendly peck on her cheek.

"Hello, Tyson. We must be having dinner in Athens somewhere because I've never had to leave this early to get to a reservation on time."

"Ha!" Tyson tossed his head back and released a sharp bark of laughter. "I'll reveal this much to you — we're doing a little more than having dinner."

"Finally!" Kendall grunted. "Some details."

Tyson laughed again. "Make yourself comfortable. Can I get you a drink?"

"It's not even nine o'clock in the morning," she chided.

"Okay, then. Orange juice?"

Kendall scrunched her nose. "How about a mimosa?" This time the attendant joined in on their laughter.

The voice of the pilot filtered through the speakers, announcing that they were preparing for takeoff. Tyson sat next to her on the thickly cushioned bench, strapped himself in and leaned over to help Kendall buckle her seatbelt.

"How long is the flight?"

Instead of answering, Tyson pressed his lips together, pretended to turn a key and then tossed the imaginary key away.

Kendall jokingly rolled her eyes. "Okay, okay. No details. I'll just stop asking questions."

"Now we're talking," Tyson said. "Or not," he added.

Kendall swatted him playfully.

"Just relax, my friend. That's what today is all about."

Kendall rolled her eyes at Tyson again, but couldn't keep herself from smiling.

CHAPTER 20

Tyson loved seeing Kendall's smile and thought about what he had in store for the day. There would be more smiles to come. He knew Kendall was used to luxury and he wanted to impress her. She had plenty of material things, and he was sure she had eaten at some of the finest restaurants around the world. Tyson wanted to give Kendall something more meaningful, something that showed he was more than his last name or just another rich bachelor. In his bones, he felt that Kendall would appreciate things that required thought and offered a little more substance than an expensive dinner. He wanted to give her an experience that would give her a much-needed reprieve from the busy life she lived.

Filming could be exhausting for actors. They often started working early in the morning before the sun made its appearance and usually didn't leave the set until well into the night. This could go on for five to seven days a week and several weeks at a time. Acting required stamina. Tyson also knew that the crew would soon be on the road to do some shoots on location. He'd miss her then. Stopping by the set on a production that he'd invested in already generated questions but showing up on set in a whole different country would cause curiosities to pique. He was trying his best to minimize attention on himself, and he didn't think Kendall would be into that either.

Tyson found her easy to talk to and appreciated her sense of humor. As they flew to his surprise destination, he listened intently as she expressed her frustration about having to work with Storm on the movie. Kendall didn't want Storm getting any ideas, especially with all the love scenes they had to shoot. Tyson didn't want to hear any more about Storm but let her vent anyway.

Tyson had done his research to see how Storm ended up being in the movie. The new producers thought it would create great media buzz. They wanted to keep it quiet until it was time to begin promoting the release in theaters. He hadn't liked the sound of that, knowing first-hand what it felt like to be used as a promotional pawn. Kendall wouldn't like it either.

As an executive producer and head of one of the companies making a major investment in the film, he wanted to pull rank and tell them to find another costar. But he'd decided against it after a conversation with his father. Benjamin warned that interfering would not only be heavily frowned upon but would raise questions. Tyson couldn't say he wanted Storm off the project because he was falling for Kendall. That would really make it appear as if Kendall had gotten the part because he was interested in her, which could sabotage her desire to be respected for making it on her own. Besides, with Tiffany allowing lies to fester, painting him as a womanizing opportunist, this could make both him and Kendall look bad — and neither of them were interested in any more negative press. He wanted to come to her rescue, but professionally his hands were tied.

The entire ordeal made Tyson even happier about what he had in store for Kendall. Their day would be spent far away from paparazzi, media, bloggers and all things Hollywood. As much as he loved his work and the industry, that lifestyle could be extremely taxing.

Halfway into their flight, they'd recapped the awards show and talked about the movie, other BCG projects, Kendall's upcoming album and what was on the horizon professionally for both of them. Now Tyson was ready to shift the conversation. He wanted to know more about Kendall.

"You stopped asking questions about our plans today," he commented.

"You're not going to give me any answers. How about a hint?" She smiled. Something swirled in his chest. He cleared his throat.

"Nope. And I think you lied when you said you didn't like surprises."

"Whatever!" She swatted his arm. "Truth is, I love surprises. People put a lot of thought into them. I think that makes them special."

"So, you think I'm special?" Tyson fished for the compliment.

Kendall pressed her lips together, holding in her smile. "I said surprises are special."

"Well, wouldn't that make the person who put all the work into creating the surprise special too?" Tyson teased, raising a brow.

"Yes. Okay." Kendall blushed. The urge to run his finger over her heated cheeks hit Tyson hard. He kept his hands to himself. "You're special too," she said.

"Thanks. I knew there was something

special about you when I heard you sing that day in the office. No one would have made a better Jocelyn James."

Kendall beamed. "Thank you."

"You're welcome." Tyson's voice gained a husky tone.

Moments passed with them simply looking into one another's eyes. Tyson wanted to pull her in for a kiss right then.

Kendall cleared her throat, broke the gaze. "So . . . how much longer is our flight going to last?"

Tyson shifted in his seat. "We'll actually land soon."

"How far is our destination from the airport?"

"Not far at all." Tyson looked into Kendall's eyes. "Tell me about Kendall Chandler."

"What would you like to know?"

"Everything."

The pilot told them to fasten their seat belts for the next half hour. They did, and he listened intently as Kendall shared stories of her family, being the only girl with two brothers, growing up in New York and then moving to Chicago, spending summers with her grandparents and helping out in their small restaurant and bakery on Long Island, her Southern roots through her grandparents, and her dreams of wanting to become a singer. Tyson took note of every detail as if he would be quizzed on the answers later.

Finally, after more than two and a half hours of flying, they landed. Tyson took Kendall by the hand and led her through the plane. Kendall stepped off and looked around, surveying the lush, flat greenery surrounding the landing strip.

"Whoa!" Her voice was like a whisper.

Pride filled Tyson's chest. He watched as she continued to scan the vast property, trees, lake and mountains in the distance.

"Beautiful. This doesn't look like any airport I've ever seen."

"This isn't the airport. It's one of my homes. This one is called Serenity Ranch. It's where I come when I need to get away from everything and everyone."

"Wow." Kendall's mouth dropped. "I love it already. What else is here?"

"Just in time." Tyson pointed to an approaching Jeep. "I'll show you. It's always better when you see it for yourself."

The Jeep pulled up. Tyson greeted the driver and introduced Kendall, and the two climbed in. For the next twenty minutes, they drove around the three-hundred-acre Montana ranch, passing horse stables, groundskeepers' residences and massive, beautiful greenery cushioned by thick walls of trees. A tennis court was set up next to the expansive log home. Before going inside, Tyson showed her around the back, where a multilevel paved deck stretched into a single wood path jutting out over the lake. Mountain vistas painted the backdrop in the distance.

Kendall remained quiet for most of the tour. Inside, Tyson led her around the first floor, which was filled with large windows and rustic charm that blended beautifully with opulence and fine furnishings.

"This place is amazing." Kendall walked in a slow circle. "My place in Temecula is my sanctuary, but pales in comparison to this. Where are we?"

"Montana."

"Montana? Is your family from here originally?"

"No. DC."

"Really? So how do city folk come across a gem like this?" Kendall walked to the windowed wall and peered out over the lake and mountains.

"A friend of my dad had a place out here. We visited one day and I fell in love. I had to have one of my own."

"This is absolutely amazing."

"And the best part about it . . ." Tyson said, pausing. Kendall widened her eyes in anticipation of the rest of his sentence. "No paparazzi!"

"Yes!" Kendall pumped her fist. "No freaking paparazzi!" They shared a hearty laugh.

Tyson closed the space between them. He could smell the sweet scent of her perfume.

"Hungry?" he asked. He was, but not for food. His voice was low again. He hadn't meant for it to happen. His body did involuntary things in her presence. "What would you like to do first?" A strong urge to wrap her in his arms came over him. He walked over to the sofa and sat, just to put a safe distance between them. "Here we can go horseback riding, play tennis, go out on the boat or just chill out. Other than that, we can take a ride into town. Before the day is over, you have to have a slice of huckleberry pie. No one makes it like the local folk."

"Let's start by going into town. Then let's come back and do everything you just said!" Kendall giggled.

"We can, but that will take more than one day. I planned to get you back before your curfew tonight," he teased.

"Then we need to get moving. I want to

experience everything this sanctuary has to offer."

Tyson stood, clapped his hands and rubbed his palms together. "Let's do it." He took Kendall by the hand and led her to the kitchen to retrieve the keys to the SUV he had stored in the garage.

"Tyson."

He loved the way she called his name. "Yes."

"Thank you so much. This is just what I needed. It's perfect. The perfect first date."

"Ah. So, we're on a date now?"

Kendall cut her eyes and gently punched his arm. "Show me the town, dude."

CHAPTER 21

Kendall faced the window, taking in every bit of the scenery as they rode through town. The beauty of Serenity Ranch and its surrounding area had her smitten. They pulled up to a cozy little strip of shops in a town that looked like it had been painted for a film set. It hardly looked real. A few people strolled along the sidewalk looking as if they were in no hurry at all. Couples held hands, kids chased one another around the legs of their parents, and a few bike riders navigated paths alongside slow-moving cars.

Kendall opened her window, sat back in her seat and let the mountain air caress her skin. It felt and smelled different from the air in Los Angeles. She closed her eyes and let the free strands of her hair billow out in the wind.

"We're here!" Tyson jumped out, rounded the SUV and opened her door.

Taking her by the hand, he led her inside a quaint restaurant. It looked like a bakery, with several bistro tables covered in large red-and-white-checkered tablecloths. A bell dinged as they walked through the door. The smell of fresh pastries permeated the air, making Kendall's stomach rumble and her mouth water. She felt hungrier than she had a moment before.

"Hey there, Tyson buddy." A small, elderly man with a head full of wiry, gray strands greeted him from behind a counter. "Back in town for a while?"

"Just today, Sam. How's Millie?" Tyson shook Sam's hand.

"Mouth still works!"

"I heard that!" came a voice from the back.

"Oops!" Sam said then winked at Tyson and let out a laugh that sounded more like a wheeze.

Kendall and Tyson laughed as a woman with a full head of white silky curls that almost matched her fair complexion came from the back, wiping her hands on a towel. She walked toward Tyson with her arms open wide.

"How ya doing, sweetie?"

"Great, Millie," Tyson said, stepping into her embrace. He had to bend low in order to hug Millie. She cupped his face and planted a loud kiss on his cheek. "Muah!"

"Don't get jealous." Millie pointed back at Sam. "And who's this pretty lady?" Millie peered over her glasses and swept her gaze over Kendall from feet to head.

"This is my friend Kendall. Kendall, meet Sam and Millie Meadowbrooks."

"Nice to meet you." Kendall held out her hand.

Millie swatted her hand away. Before Kendall could take offense, she said, "Aw girl. We hug around here," and wrapped her arms around Kendall.

Caught off guard, Kendall didn't know what to do. She looked over at Tyson, and he nodded and smiled. She returned Millie's embrace.

Sam came from behind the counter and hugged Kendall too. He gave Tyson a fatherly pat on his back.

"You hungry?" Millie asked.

"Yes, ma'am."

"Good! I just whipped up a fresh batch of honey biscuits. Sammy, how about a nice cup of coffee or tea to go with their biscuits?"

"That sounds wonderful. It's been a while since I've had one of your biscuits," Tyson said.

"Well, get comfortable. Let Sammy here know what you want to drink and I'll be right out with a biscuit for each of ya." Millie started toward the back of the bakery. "Whipped butter cream and preserves for you, Tyson, right?"

"Yes, ma'am."

Moments later, Kendall and Tyson sat across from each other at one of the small tables, with steaming cups of tea and coffee in front of them. Millie came out a while later with saucers carrying two oversize biscuits.

"There you go, honey. Enjoy!" Kendall and Tyson thanked Millie, and she turned to walk back toward the kitchen. "Oh." She paused midstep. "I baked fresh huckleberry pies this morning too. Wanna carry one back to the ranch with ya?"

"Sure do!"

"You got it. Now dig in."

"This is the largest biscuit I've ever seen in my life," Kendall whispered.

"I'll bet it's also one of the tastiest."

Kendall twisted her lips in doubt. "Not better than Momma used to make."

"Maybe not, but it's damn good. They make their own whipped butter. Try it on the biscuit."

Kendall tore off a piece of biscuit, spread

a little butter on it and dabbed a bit of the preserves. She put it in her mouth and thought her taste buds would explode. Closing her eyes, she moaned. "Oh my goodness!" She covered her full mouth as she spoke. "This is delicious!" she mumbled over the food.

"Told you!" Tyson winked and stuffed a large piece of the biscuit in his mouth. His eyes rolled back. He plunged two fingers in his mouth to lick off the remnants of butter and preserves.

Something about Tyson's down-home gesture tickled Kendall. She'd always seen him in his professional mode but liked seeing him this way — relaxed. His guard had been tucked away.

They finished up their meals. Millie boxed up one of her famous pies and sent them off with best wishes. They perused a few more shops on that block before getting into Tyson's SUV and heading back to the ranch.

While Tyson put the pie in the refrigerator, Kendall walked to the den to see the view of the lake through the wall of windows. The water was calm. A small boat and two kayaks swayed near the edge. Mountains stood handsomely in the distance beyond the lake. She opened the double doors and stepped out onto the deck. Looking at the scenery wasn't enough. She needed to be a part of it. A light breeze flowed from the lake, offering a cool but bearable chill. Its light touch felt great washing over her body. It wasn't cool enough for a sweater, but the breeze was still nice. Moments later, Tyson met her out back and stood by her side.

"This view is amazing."

"It's one of the main reasons I bought the house. You play tennis?" he asked.

"Do you cry when you get beat?"

"What?" Tyson reared his head back. "I don't get beat."

"Humph! There's a first time for everything," Kendall teased.

"We'll see about that!" Tyson warned.

An hour and a half later, Tyson had beat Kendall three times.

"Who's gonna cry now?"

Kendall waved him off and tossed her racket into the bin with the others. "It's the jet lag."

Laughter erupted from Tyson like bubbling lava. He shook his head. "The flight was only two hours. How could you possibly have jet lag?"

Kendall threw her head back and laughed. She had no comeback. Tyson had won fair and square. "You should have let me win at least one game. I'm the guest!"

"I would have if you hadn't talked so much smack!"

"Whatever!" Kendall smiled. Even after that intense game and trying to chase down the balls Tyson served, she felt relaxed. "Come on." She grabbed Tyson by the arm. "I want to see the horses."

Tyson and Kendall jumped into a golf cart and drove over to the stables. He introduced her to his horses by name and let her choose which one she wanted to ride. Kendall choose one with a coat so shiny and black it looked as if it had been oiled with tar. He was beautiful. They spent the next hour trotting around the ranch.

To Kendall's surprise, they returned to the house to find a spread of fresh fruit, finger sandwiches, mixed green salad and bottled waters sitting in a cooler of ice. She wondered how it had gotten there. Of course, there were other people on the property. Someone had to maintain it, yet she hadn't seen another soul other than the man who drove them from the jet to the house earlier. Where was he? What about the pilots, the attendants? Was the airplane even still on the property? She couldn't see it from where they were. It was like everything they needed just magically appeared

— tennis balls, rackets, saddles, food.

"You're so full of surprises, Tyson."

Kendall was delighted. She hadn't had this much fun in . . . Kendall had to think. She'd never had this much fun with a man before. She'd had good times, but with Tyson, Kendall felt like she could be completely free. What was it about him that made her feel so comfortable? Eating to their fill, they downed their food quickly and then sat on the porch for a while.

"We can't leave without going out on the lake," Kendall said.

"Are you ready to check it out?"

A wide, toothy smile spread across Kendall's face. She felt like a child at Disney World. She wanted to try every ride, eat all the candy, take pictures with all the characters. She couldn't leave with anything undone. She almost didn't want to leave at all. The place was beautiful. Tyson was fun and sexy. Kendall shook her head. *Focus!*

Tyson led Kendall down the wood plank to the small speedboat. He stepped in the wobbly vessel first and held his hand out to help Kendall get in. While Kendall took a seat, he started up the boat and took off. She held her arms out to the side and her head in the air, letting the wind whip at her hair. After a few minutes, Tyson shut off the engine and allowed the boat to drift along. He sat beside Kendall.

"I'm glad you're enjoying today."

"Today was amazing so far. Just what I need. Thanks."

Kendall was so grateful, she wasn't sure if a simple thanks could express the weight of her gratitude. Tyson could have easily taken her to some fancy restaurant back home. Instead, he thought about what she needed. She loved a considerate man. No matter what happened between them, she'd never forget this day.

Kendall's cheeks ached from smiling so much. She couldn't help it. The water, the view, the mountains — it was all so breathtaking that it summoned her to relax. She leaned against Tyson's arm. Kendall knew closing in on the space between them would insinuate a new level of intimacy. They'd been passing searing gazes back and forth all day, yet still keeping things at a friendly distance. She wanted to get closer to him, had desired to get closer since he had touched her hand to help her out of the car earlier. The tension between them started with a low sizzle and grew increasingly until it crackled like bolts of lightning. Neither could ignore the chemistry. It was thick and alive.

Leaning on his hard body made Kendall grow warm inside. The intimate parts of her awakened. Her hand lay across his knee, and Tyson covered it with his hand. They floated on the water, bobbing with the ripples. No words passed between them. The silence was welcome, comfortable, right. A fresh, full breeze washed over them, cooling Kendall's skin. She'd grown warmer against him. Soon after, Kendall pulled back and looked at Tyson. He turned to face her as well.

"Thank you," she said again.

Tyson smiled. It was half-cocked and sexy as hell. The muscles at the meeting of her thighs tightened.

"You're welcome." His voice was low and husky. He didn't take his eyes off her.

Kendall grew warm under his gaze. She swallowed. He continued to stare, searching her eyes. She looked deeper into his, as if she could glimpse his soul. Tyson leaned in, closing the space between his lips and hers. His eyes were still fastened to hers. Instinctively, Kendall's chin lifted, readying itself for what was to come. Tyson drew nearer slowly, as if asking permission along the way. Kendall felt her lips part. Her body was acting of its own volition. Tyson closed in, pressing his soft lips on hers. Kendall felt like she was being kissed by clouds. Her lips parted more, receiving him. Tyson's hands roved around her back. Kendall's encircled his neck. Pulling one another closer, they drank each other in, kissed each other's breath away. When they came up for air, both were panting. Kendall's body was aflame.

"Let's go back." The warm breath from his husky whisper caressed her lips. It was like a brush of warm wind.

Kendall nodded. She couldn't speak.

Tyson started up the engine and sped back to the house. He anchored the boat, steadied it and helped her out, then pulled her straight to his chest right there on the dock. Tyson wrapped his arms around her, grasped and caressed her back, breasts and behind. Kendall's hands roamed, explored as much of his tall, strong body as she could reach. She pressed herself against his pelvis. A moan rose in his throat. The quick ride back had done nothing to douse the inferno that had been ignited on the water.

Together they walked toward the house, bodies and lips still locked as if letting go could stop them from breathing. Tyson twisted the knob, pushed the door open with his foot. He lifted Kendall in his arms, carried her across the threshold and gently put her down on her feet. She tugged at his shirt, popping a button, then tugged at his belt. Tyson helped her. His pants fell to the floor with a clink from his buckle. Kendall rubbed her hand over his erection, released it from the hold of his boxer briefs. It sprang forward, striking her. She giggled but didn't stop. Tyson lifted her T-shirt over her head, freed her breasts and filled his mouth with one.

Kendall pulled away, breathless. She looked at him. The question transmitted subliminally. Tyson nodded, tore himself away from her long enough to retrieve protection. He returned and handed it to her. Kendall ripped open the package, slid it over his erection and held his hardness in her hand. It filled her palm. The walls of her center pulsated in anticipation. Tyson slid her jeans down her hips, then peeled them and her lace panties past the heels of her feet.

Tyson lifted Kendall in the air. His strength made her moist. She wrapped her arms around his neck and her legs around his muscular back. Tyson eased her down onto him, entering slowly.

"Ah!" Kendall's moan was involuntary. It was her body's response to the deliciousness of Tyson gently filling her to capacity.

She squeezed her muscles around him, clenching him, and then watched as his head and eyes rolled back.

Slowly at first, Tyson lifted and lowered Kendall onto his erection as he stood. Kendall moved her hips in a circular motion, tightening her walls around him. The friction they created was exhilarating and severely intense. Kendall knew she wouldn't last long and figured Tyson wouldn't either. They moved into each other faster until they slammed against one another. Kendall's legs trembled, and her body followed with a shudder. Her peak began with a low rumble, and burgeoned until it exploded through her. Kendall screamed and milked Tyson's still-erect member. She felt him swell inside of her and jerk a few times. Tyson moved faster, and she held him tight. He grumbled and grunted, closed his eyes. Grunting again, his breath shortened and then he roared. Kendall collapsed against him. Still holding her, he slid to the floor.

She lay in his arms, cuddled against his chest. Together they watched the sun set. After the magnificence of its descent, Tyson began snoring lightly.

CHAPTER 22

"You've got this, Ty." Kendall had taken to shortening his name since their escapade at his ranch in Montana.

"Thanks for your encouragement, but I still don't want to do this."

"I completely understand. Don't let them trip you up. Some journalists are good at that, especially the ones who dish celebrity gossip."

"Are we still on for tonight?"

"I wouldn't miss it. Meet you there, and I want to hear all about the interview."

"Oh, you will. See you later, pretty lady."

Kendall tittered into the phone. Tyson knew she was blushing. She did it every time he called her some kind of endearing name. He couldn't see her smile, but it felt good to him just the same because he was the cause of it.

Tyson didn't think he'd ever get enough of her smiles. He'd awakened to her smiling face after they'd made love at the ranch. Kendall's smiles had returned that night when they made love again in his oversize custom bed. They were supposed to fly back to Los Angeles but weren't ready to return to the paparazzi-infested town. Frankly, Tyson hadn't had enough of Kendall to himself. It didn't take much to convince her to stay until the next day. There was more boating, horseback riding, eating, shopping and then the hot tub.

Tyson sat back in his office chair, closed his eyes and willed his body to remain calm. Thoughts of what they had done to one another in that hot tub nearly gave Tyson a fresh erection. Kendall was an incredible lover, unselfish and indulging. She didn't lie around like a wet fish waiting for him to initiate everything. She took charge, and that excited him to no end. Kendall didn't just stimulate his body. She invigorated his mind. They talked about everything from their childhoods to politics to current goals and aspirations. Tyson shared his ambitions, and she encouraged him. His conversations with Tiffany had always centered around her own desires. If Tiffany was ever asked, she probably couldn't name a single thing that Tyson wanted from life. But Kendall was different. Not only did she ask Tyson about his wishes, they engaged in discussions about how he could achieve those desires.

Their conversation took on a more intimate turn when she talked about her mother's death a few years before and expressed how much she missed her. Tyson held her in his arms, wishing he could siphon the pain from her heart. He kissed her tears away and they made love again with a passion so intense it felt like an out-of-body experience. It was surreal.

Tyson appreciated the fact that as famous as she was, she was still grounded and unspoiled. Admittedly, he hadn't expected any of this from Kendall and was more than pleasantly surprised.

"Mr. Blackwell. Your car is ready." Tyson's assistant, Brianna's voice jerked him from his thoughts of Kendall.

It was time for his interview. After a deep breath, Tyson stood, straightened his tie and headed down to his awaiting limo. Brianna, someone from BCG's marketing team and the head of PR joined him. During the ride, they prepped Tyson again. He felt like a witness getting ready to testify for a big trial. The closer he got, the more he wanted to back out. He definitely wasn't camera shy but contributing to celebrity gossip wasn't something he'd ever wanted to do. This felt gimmicky, and Tyson wasn't the type to engage in gimmicks. His reputation as well as the company's were on the line.

They arrived at the studio in less than fifteen minutes. Their car pulled to the curb and the second the door swung open, they were swarmed with reporters and their cameras. Stations that hadn't gotten the exclusive, along with bloggers and paparazzi, filled the sidewalk. With their arms held out, his team had to carve a path for Tyson to get from the car to the building. He walked with his head high, only offering a professional nod and tight smile for the many cameras, ignoring the microphones shoved in his direction. Tyson wanted to get this over with. He wished he were back in Montana with Kendall. He would have liked for her to attend the interview with him and could picture her coaching and encouraging him from the sidelines. But she was filming, and that would have raised even more questions.

Inside, he was quickly ushered to the greenroom to get camera ready and then into the studio where the interview would take place. Reina Roberts, the host of her self-named show, greeted him with a firm handshake. Reina was approved for the interview by his team because of her reputation for being a fair and unbiased host. She had interviewed many of the world's most powerful people in entertainment and beyond.

Reina sat directly across from him, separated only by a small accent table. Both received microphones, and once the sound was checked, they were ready to begin. A hush fell over the set.

"I have some tough questions for you. Are you ready, Mr. Blackwell?"

"Ready, Ms. Roberts." Tyson gave her a confident nod.

The director counted backward from three and pointed to Reina. A green light flashed on one of the three cameras. Reina faced it and began her standard introduction, then announced Tyson as her guest.

"Thank you for joining us today, Mr. Blackwell."

"Please call me Tyson and thank you for having me."

Reina started in with rapid-fire questions, addressing all the rumors and insinuations that had been circling since Tiffany's last interview. Tyson kept his cool, knowing what to expect.

"Okay, Tyson." Reina nodded. "Tiffany has been pretty vocal about your breakup while you've been very quiet. Why haven't we heard from you?"

Tyson folded his hands and looked pensive for a moment before answering. His PR team had encouraged him to make sure he came across in the sincerest manner and to give thoughtful answers. "Our relationship meant a lot to me — still means a lot to me. Tiffany is a . . . talented, smart . . . and beautiful woman. Our breakup was a great loss and very personal. I needed to deal with it on my own — privately. It wasn't easy. I've also seen how quickly things can get misconstrued, and I didn't want to say anything that would place Tiffany in a bad light. Sound bites go a long way with social media these days."

Reina chuckled. "I know what you mean." She tilted her head. "So why speak out now?"

"There's been a lot of speculation, and I think it's important to let people know that despite our breakup, I have a lot of respect for Tiffany and I truly wish her the best. There are still rumors swirling, and I know I may not be able to dispel them all, but at least I can put some to rest, especially any that may potentially be harmful to her."

"You still care about her?" Reina looked somewhat surprised.

"I do, and I wish her well. When you break up with someone, you don't just turn off your feelings like a switch. We may not have worked out, but I'm still very proud of her for what she's been able to accomplish."

"Interesting." Reina hummed, looked at Tyson through a narrowed gaze. "What about the accusation that you'd taken advantage of her being an actress on the rise?"

Tyson spoke calmly, in a comfortable but measured tone. "Not only am I a mama's boy, but my sister would kill me if I ever took advantage of Tiffany or any woman in such a way. Tiffany earned every role she's ever received simply because she's a great actress. I can tell you firsthand that she gives her all to every role, making sure she delivers her best possible performance." And that was true. Tiffany was by far the most determined actress he'd ever dated. She was going to make it to the top or die trying.

"Is it true that you cheated on Tiffany?"

"I never cheated on Tiffany." *Even though she cheated on me.* Tyson was mindful to maintain a sincere expression.

Reina looked at him sideways. "Never?"

"Never. I've never cheated on any woman I've been in a serious relationship with." Reina still looked skeptical. Tyson smiled

520

and shook his head. "I give you permission to speak with any of my exes. Not one of my relationships ended because of me being unfaithful."

Reina hit Tyson with a few more questions. "Could you see the two of you ever getting back together?"

"No. But we'll probably always be friends."

"Anyone new in your life?"

Kendall's beautiful face flashed before him. "Not at this time." His smile was purposely mysterious.

"Thank you for joining us today, Tyson." Reina turned to the camera. "Well, there you have it. Tyson Blackwell's side of the story. That's all we have for today. See you next time on *Eye on Entertainment with Reina Roberts.*"

The lights on the cameras went off, and the once-quiet set buzzed with chatter and moving equipment. The interview seemed to end abruptly. A man rushed to Reina and helped extract her microphone from the back of her dress. She walked over to Tyson and shook his hand.

"Thanks again for the interview. I have to admit, I was expecting something . . . juicier. Sounds like you genuinely cared about Tiffany. That says a lot."

Tyson wanted to ask exactly what it said to her but held his tongue. He was glad that it was all over. "You're welcome. Thanks for hearing my side," Tyson said.

Tyson thought the conversation was over, but Reina didn't move. She looked at him pensively for several moments.

"So, you're not seeing anyone at this time, huh?"

"Uh. No. Not at this time." He thought of Kendall.

"Then maybe we should have dinner sometime soon."

Reina was a beautiful woman, but Tyson wasn't interested. Not to mention Reina's line of work would keep him steeped in the world of celebrity gossip, and that was the one thing he wanted to get as far away from as possible. Most of all, nothing and no one interested him more than Kendall Chandler. She was his perfect fit and had him completely smitten. Tyson had eyes for no other woman.

"That would be nice. Unfortunately, my schedule doesn't allow for much social interaction, and my wounds might still be a little fresh." Tyson definitely wasn't still pining over Tiffany but didn't mind using her as an excuse. He had to let Reina down easily, not wanting to hurt her feelings. Egos were fragile in Hollywood and could be troublesome if attached to someone bitter from rejection.

"Oh. Yes. I understand. My apologies. I should have thought about that." She flipped out her card anyway. "After you've given yourself some time, give me a call."

Tyson took the card. "Thank you."

He couldn't wait to get back to Kendall.

Happy to be done with the interview, Tyson left with his team and treated them to lunch. They laughed about how uneventful it seemed to have gone. Even in fairness, Reina had been fishing for scandalous details, but Tyson refused to feed the monster. His team hoped the interview would come across exactly as they planned, showing the human side of Tyson — a man like any other, dealing with the effects of a failed relationship without painting his ex as a trifling, attention-hungry opportunist.

Back at the office, it was business as usual. With Kendall heavy on his mind and the fact that she was leaving to shoot on location in another country the next day, he had to see her. Finishing up early, Tyson headed over to the set, arriving just in time to see Kendall and Storm entwined in each other's arms right in the throes of a heated love scene. He knew they were acting, but it seemed so authentic. He felt like he was spying on real lovers.

After a few short moments, Tyson left the set. Jealousy burned in his chest. He couldn't help it. It was clear to him that he was over Tiffany — but was Kendall done with Storm?

CHAPTER 23

Kendall couldn't wait for Tyson to arrive. When she left the set, she headed straight for the freeway. She wanted to make it to Temecula in time to get ready for her night with Tyson. Her sanctuary would give them the privacy they needed to really enjoy each other's company away from the prying lenses of the paparazzi. She imagined he'd be stressed about the interview, and she planned to help him ease the angst.

Whatever they had between them was their delicious little secret. It had to be. Kendall was going to get credit for her own advancement in the entertainment world. If word about her seeing Tyson got out, that could muddy her credibility, and she couldn't have that. She hadn't even told Randi.

The second she got in the house, she showered, removing Storm's touch. She had to dig deep into her character and her acting lessons to get through those scenes with him. How had she gotten to the point where his touch made her want to recoil? When they weren't shooting, Kendall avoided him. She usually retreated to her trailer. Storm acted like they didn't have a messy past. Maybe he thought if he acted like he hadn't betrayed her, she'd act like it never happened.

Feeling refreshed after her shower, Kendall put on a tank and leggings. She looked much more comfortable than sexy, and she knew it and loved it. She pulled her hair into a bun on top of her head. Even though it was her go-to when she lounged around the house, she remembered that Tyson thought the bun and her freckles were sexy.

Kendall's mind went back to Montana, when Tyson had kissed those freckles under the midnight sky. The stars had seemed to twinkle a little brighter that night. Knowing he was driving, she fought the urge to text him to find out how close he was, and instead started dinner. Tonight, she was cooking soul food — deep-fried fish, greens, buttery corn on the cob and her grandma's famous lemon pound cake. She hadn't cooked like that in ages.

Kendall spoke to her voice-controlled speaker system and asked it to play R & B soul. After getting most of her meal on the stove, she lowered the music and called Tyson. She'd fry the fish when he arrived so it would be piping hot.

"Hey!" Kendall couldn't contain her excitement. The anticipation of another night with Tyson made her giddy.

"Hey." Tyson's tone was even.

Kendall's brows furrowed. "You okay?"

"Oh. Yeah. I'm fine."

Kendall looked at the phone and placed it back to her ear. "You sure?"

"Yes, I'm sure. It's been a long day, that's all."

"Oh. I can imagine." She plopped on the sofa in the den and folded her legs under her, then looked out into the night covering her backyard. The landscape lighting kept the patio and pool in view. "What's your ETA?"

"Uh . . . half hour?"

"Okay." Kendall looked at the clock on the cable box. She decided to drop the fish in the grease in twenty minutes. That way it would be ready around the time he arrived. "We're going to have to get up and run in the morning after tonight's dinner. I haven't eaten like this in a long time." She laughed.

Kendall chatted with Tyson for a little while longer before ending her call to tend to the meal. Even on the phone, he didn't seem like his usual self. She credited his low energy and light conversation to his rough day. What had happened during that interview? Whatever it was, Kendall would help him feel better.

Just as she had hoped, Tyson arrived right around the time that the fish was ready to come out of the pan.

"Hey you!" Kendall swung open the door and practically jumped into his arms.

Then they did something they'd never do in Los Angeles — kissed right in the open doorway. Yet Kendall felt like his kiss was void of its normal passion. Tyson usually kissed her like he required her lips for survival.

"I left a washcloth and towel for you in the bathroom. Why don't you freshen up and get comfortable? We'll have dinner and I'll show you around my Wine Country Shangri-la." She giggled.

"That sounds good."

"It will be good. Now go." She pointed him toward the guest bathroom, then headed back to the kitchen.

Minutes later, Tyson emerged from the restroom in a T-shirt that must have been ecstatic about being so close to his muscular chest, and jeans that showed off his long legs, sexy stride and strong thighs.

"Mmm!"

"What'd you say?" he asked.

Kendall hadn't thought Tyson would hear her moan. "This food smells great." She blamed it on the aroma of their meal. "Ready to dig in?"

Tyson clapped his hands and rubbed them together. "Absolutely."

"Come on," Kendall said, spooning greens onto two plates. "We're going to eat outside. I love it out there."

Kendall surprised herself at how open she'd been with Tyson. After Storm, she hadn't wanted to be bothered with any man — especially one from their industry. Tyson had gotten past all of her defenses, and although she enjoyed laying eyes on a sexy man like any woman would, it was his internal qualities that she'd come to admire most. Tyson was proving himself to be a man of character. He was considerate and smart. That was more attractive than any gorgeous face or athletic build. Kendall was enticed by his mind and heart. He'd proven himself a man of integrity by the way he had responded to the ordeal with Tiffany. Tyson had always spoken about her with care, no matter how many scandalous television appearances she'd made.

Kendall's flight to Paris was due to leave the next night, giving her about twenty-four hours of Tyson to herself. The film crew was preparing to shoot in Europe and were all scheduled to fly out throughout the day.

Kendall and Tyson planned to spend the night and day together. Then he would drop her off at the airport in San Diego before heading back to LA. She knew this time would be as magical as their time together in Montana. Her home in Temecula wasn't as big as Serenity Ranch, but they could surely have just as much fun.

They sat under Kendall's gazebo. Tyson ate like it was his last meal and went back for seconds. His obvious enjoyment of her cooking made her feel great. She loved cooking but didn't get around to it much. It connected her to her family, even though she was miles away. She loved when people enjoyed her food.

"More?" Kendall asked.

"No!" Tyson wiped his mouth with the napkin. "That was delicious. Where'd you learn to cook like that?"

"My mom, dad, grandma. All the kids and grandkids are pretty good cooks. It's a Chandler thing. Wait until you taste my dessert. It's one of my grandma's best recipes."

Tyson held his stomach, closed his eyes

and dropped his head back. "Dessert?"

"Yep. You have to taste a little." Kendall went inside and came back with a slice of pound cake on a saucer and two forks. "We'll share."

Tyson's eyes widened. "Okay." He picked up a fork, cut into the cake and put a sizable piece into his mouth. Tyson closed his eyes and shook his head vigorously. "That's ridiculously good. Is that one of the ones your family sells in supermarkets?"

"Not that one. You have to know someone in the family to get this cake."

Tyson polished off the rest of the cake, and the two sat in silence, listening to the sounds of the Southern California night. Tyson seemed himself while they ate but went back to being a little distant once they were done. He'd been up and down since he'd arrived. Kendall figured the stress had a pretty decent grip on him.

"Tell me about the interview," Kendall said so he could get that off his chest.

Tyson shared some details. "I don't think it's going to qualify as must-watch TV. She basically told me it wasn't juicy enough."

"You've got to be kidding me." Kendall shook her head. "This industry, I swear."

Conversation lulled again and didn't run as smoothly as it had the other times they were together.

Tyson asked about the progress of the film. Kendall told him things were going well. She didn't want to talk to him too much about Storm. Plus, she didn't want him to think she was unprofessional if she mentioned how much she had to push herself to get through the love scenes with him. No one wanted to talk to their new beau about on-camera sex with their ex anyway, so she kept the details to a minimum.

It was quiet again. Kendall stood from her lounger, removed her leggings, tank top and bra. "An hour has passed," she said, reaching for him. He sat up and took her hand. She pulled at him, and Tyson stood. She removed his T-shirt, bit her bottom lip at the sight of his rippled chest and hard pecks. She didn't have to loosen his belt. By the time she got his shirt off, he was already on that. Tyson's pants fell to the pavement. He stepped out of them and let Kendall lead him to the pool. Even though he hadn't said much, Tyson's erection had grown to its fullness by the time they reached the water.

Kendall giggled, jumped in and paddled to the other side. Tyson jumped in after her, and together they swam several laps before meeting up in the center of the pool. Tyson took her into his arms and they kissed under the stars. The coolness of the water did nothing to douse the heat rising in Kendall's core. Tyson held her as he made his way back to the edge of the pool. Her nipples were as hard as his rigid erection. Steam rose from his caramel skin.

Gently, Tyson set her on the edge of the pool, laid her back and buried his face in the soft folds between her legs. Kendall hissed and spread her thighs wider, giving Tyson greater access. He feasted on her like he had on their earlier meal, sucking and nibbling ravenously until Kendall felt her bud swell so deliciously, she thought it would explode, shattering her entire body into a million tiny pieces. She thrashed about. Tyson wouldn't let go. He lapped at Kendall's center until the pinnacle of her pleasure poured out in one long, sensual scream. Breathless, she was unable to string together audible syllables. Kendall simply panted his name over and over again, trying each time to get the full word out.

"Ty . . . Ty . . . Tys . . . Tyson." His name lingered on her tongue.

Tyson replaced his tongue with his thumb, stroking her until she could no longer stand his touch. Her legs tightened around his hand. She ushered him away. Rolled over and closed her legs snugly. Tyson caressed her trembling legs, which were too weak for her to stand on. Her entire body tingled as if someone had touched it with raw, exposed wiring. When she calmed, she was able to move again. She stood, watching him emerge from the pool. Water cascaded from his perfect body, washing over his well-sculpted torso and arms. He glistened like a god. Kendall touched him. She had to. Her hands fanned out over his chest and she grabbed his strong arms. Tyson pulled her into those arms, kissed her, let her taste her own nectar. Kendall moaned into his mouth. His erection pressed against her.

He picked her up, carried her to the chaise on the patio and laid her down gently. He found his strewn pants, pulled out protection and sheathed himself. Tyson stretched himself over her, kissed her some more. Kendall wanted to feel him. She reached for him, held him in her hands. He filled her grasp and she guided him toward her canal. He didn't oblige her right away. Instead, he held himself over her writhing body, gazed into her eyes. Kendall saw more than lust there. She touched his lip with her finger. Caressed his face. Was that worry?

Tyson blinked but held her gaze as he

lowered himself. With his eyes still locked on hers, he lifted one of her legs, held it in the crook of his arm and entered her slowly. Still a little sore from their insatiable appetite for one another since Montana, Kendall winced slightly from the sweet pain of him filling her up again. The pleasure quickly overtook the soreness and her head fell back. Moving in sync, they met each other stroke for stroke. They fit together perfectly. Their rhythm was natural. It was like their bodies were kindred spirits that knew one another through time and space. Initially, they started with a slow grind that gradually rose to a fevered pace. Tyson's grunts became a measured chant. Kendall knew he was close to going over the edge. She tightened her walls around his perfect thickness, clutching, milking, coaxing his climax from him.

He squeezed his eyes shut and shook his head. Kendall cushioned him in her softness. She slammed against him. He thrust himself harder, deeper. She took all of him in and moaned. The pleasure was almost too much for her to bear. A rumble started in his core, tumbled through his torso and escaped his throat in a guttural groan.

"Ken-dall!"

She felt his release ripple through him,

felt his erection pulsate and jerk. The motion touched something deep inside of her, causing a release to gush and drench him in her juices. Tyson collapsed on top of her, gentle enough not to cause discomfort. Kendall felt the wind of his short breaths on her neck, felt his erection begin to soften. She wrapped her legs around his back. Pulled him closer.

Kendall was sated, and despite Tyson seeming a bit stressed, she was still hungry for more. She'd never been so greedy, but the delectable way Tyson loved her made her gluttonous. But she'd let him rest — for now.

CHAPTER 24

Tyson was still angry with himself for letting his jealousy get the best of him. As he made love to Kendall the other night, he tried over and over again to flush from his mind the scene of her and Storm lying next to each other. This wasn't the first actress he'd ever dated and, as a producer, it definitely wasn't the first time he'd watched someone he was interested in do a love scene. This was different.

Tyson had to make up for his lack of focus that night at her beautiful home. He was a little better the next day, but it annoyed him to know that she was about to spend a week in Paris, the world's most romantic city, with Storm, shooting more love scenes. If it were possible, he would have kept her from making her flight to Paris and stayed with Kendall in her Shangri-la for at least a few more days.

He'd missed her ridiculously since she'd

been gone, and with her filming schedule and the time difference, they only had a small window each day for video chatting. It bothered him daily that Storm was there with her instead of him. He hadn't been seeing Kendall long, but felt it was necessary to solidify what they had together. It would have to be their secret. He didn't mind, but Kendall had to know where he stood. Tyson wanted to be with her for the long haul, plain and simple.

Tyson's phone rang and he was surprised to see that it was Tiffany. They hadn't spoken since she'd called with the news about her outrageous interview. She must have seen his air the evening before.

"Hello, Tiffany. What can I do for you?"

"Tyson!" She sounded angry. "Why on earth did you do that horrible interview? You've ruined everything."

"What?" Tyson scrunched up his face.

"My press has dried up because of your boring interview. What's wrong with you? Have you lost your gall? I had the media eating out of the palm of my hand, and I was getting calls from every network. The movie was in all the headlines, and ticket sales were through the roof. The blogs were clamoring for my story, and you went and doused my fire."

"*Your* fire? Have you ever stopped to think about the fact that all this press you're getting was affecting someone other than you?"

"Tyson, please. You're as much of a media whore as I am."

Tiffany's words struck a chord. That wasn't a lie. At least before Kendall, it wasn't. Being so far in the spotlight made him more popular with the ladies. They wanted to be seen right along with him. He didn't want all that attention anymore. He was a CEO, but more importantly, he had Kendall. He no longer needed the spotlight.

"You know what, Tiffany. I'm in a different place now. Enjoy your media spotlight but keep me out of it."

The loud sound of Tiffany sucking her teeth came across the line crisp and clear. "You've gone soft now that you're CEO."

"Tiffany." His voice was surprisingly even. It seemed that she recognized the seriousness in his tone and quieted down. "I'm done with this whole 'play the media' game. Finished. Have all the fun you want, but I'm warning you. Keep my name out of your mouth or else."

"Or else?" she questioned. "You're serious?" Then, in the silence that followed, it sounded as if the realization of how serious Tyson was finally hit Tiffany. She sighed.

"Whatever, Tyson!" she said before hanging up.

Tyson called his lawyer and had him draw up some paperwork ordering Tiffany to stop mentioning him in the media or he'd sue her for defamation. Her thirst for media attention had become a dangerous obsession. He couldn't allow her to drag him down with her. Not now.

He was serious about his feelings for Kendall. Someday their relationship would be out in the open. But Kendall valued her privacy. If he didn't stop Tiffany now, her antics would reach all the way to Kendall. He couldn't risk having her walk away.

When Kendall got back to the States, he was going to plan a special evening for them and tell her how he felt. It hadn't been long, but he'd never felt so sure about a woman in his life. He didn't mind keeping their relationship under wraps for as long as she desired. Kendall would be his sweet little secret. In the meantime, they'd continue to enjoy each other's company off the grid.

Tyson looked at his desk calendar. It would be at least five more days before she returned to the States. He didn't want to wait that long before seeing her again.

Tyson spoke with his parents, told them he was taking two days off and then let his staff know he would be out. Next, Tyson called the family's pilot and had him prepare for his flight.

By the time Kendall got off from work the next evening, Tyson was in France. Needing to sleep off the jet lag, he decided to call her before catching a few hours of sleep. He couldn't wait to surprise her later.

"Hey! How was work today?"

"Great. I love Paris. It's such a beautiful city. Jocelyn James was a troubled soul but a lucky woman. I didn't realize how much she impacted music here."

"That's cool. What do you have planned for tonight?"

"Not much. Probably dinner with some cast members. I might get out to see more sites. I went up to the top of the Eiffel Tower at sunset. The view was amazing."

"That sounds like fun. Have you seen any other parts of France?"

"An old friend of the family had a château in the countryside. I went there once."

"Ever been to Nice?"

"Actually no. It would be . . . nice to visit there. Ha!" Kendall laughed at her pun.

Tyson shook his head and laughed with her. "Cute. Wanna go?"

"I might try to make it before we leave here."

"How about tonight, for dinner?"

"What? Tyson, what are you talking about?"

"I want to take you to dinner. Tonight. In Nice."

"How are you gon—Tyson! Are you here? In France?"

"Maybe!"

Kendall squealed. "I can't believe you. Does anyone know?" she whispered.

Tyson laughed again. "Just my pilot. My dad will find out eventually."

"Oh! My goodness. I kind of missed you, dude. You're unbelievable. I have to work in the morning."

"Don't worry. I'll have you back in time. Send me the information for your hotel. I'll send a car for you and let me know what time you'll be ready."

"I can't believe this. Okay. I'm going to be exhausted on set tomorrow." Kendall giggled. "But it will be worth it!"

Tyson picked her up at seven o'clock. By ten, they'd arrived in Nice and were sharing an exquisite meal at one of the most renowned restaurants along the Mediterranean Coast.

After several glasses of wine, both had

loosened all the way up. Kendall was giddy and laughed at everything Tyson said. They walked along the beach, then headed back to the room and made love well into the early morning, falling asleep in each other's arms.

Despite such an adventurous night, Tyson rose well before the sun. He propped himself up on one arm and watched Kendall sleep. She was curled into his frame. Tyson ran his fingers through her wild sex-strewn hair, outlined the curvature of her perfect naked body and relished her beauty before kissing her awake.

Kendall moaned and stretched.

"Good morning, beautiful."

"Mmm." Her eyes fluttered. "Good morning," she groaned. "What time is it?"

"Just after four thirty."

"You're so bad, Tyson. I'm not going to be any good on set today. They're going to have to put extra makeup on me."

Tyson kissed her forehead. "You don't need makeup."

A lazy smile spread across Kendall's lips. "You're so sweet."

"It's true." Tyson winked.

"They're still going to have to slap on some extra foundation under these eyes."

"Listen. I need to talk to you."

Kendall's expression turned serious. "About what, Ty? Everything okay?"

"Hopefully everything is perfect."

Kendall looked perplexed. She shifted to face him, also propping herself on one elbow.

"We haven't defined this yet." Tyson pointed back and forth between the two of them. "It hasn't been that long but I'm ready to. Kendall, you're not just good, you're good for me. You make me want to be better. I want to be with you and only you. This can be our dirty little secret for as long as you'd like." Tyson stopped speaking and looked into her eyes. She opened her mouth and he placed his finger on her lips. "I don't want an answer now. Think about it. I'll wait."

Kendall blinked several times. "Wow," was all she said.

"As for right now, we need to get out of here." Tyson planted a quick peck on her forehead. "Move, lady!"

Leaving Kendall to absorb what he'd just dropped on her, Tyson headed for the shower.

"Are you coming in?" he yelled after turning on the water. "Or do I have to come and get you?"

"Maybe you should come and get me,"

she purred.

With that, Tyson quickly exited the bathroom, scooped Kendall off the bed and carried her to the shower, laughing all the way.

CHAPTER 25

Kendall was the last one to meet the crew in the lobby and hoped her sunglasses hid the effects of her love hangover. She could hardly keep from smiling. If only the crew knew who she had been with hours before.

Our dirty little secret. She heard Tyson in her head. The mystery made things more enticing. Kendall felt like she was part of a sexy covert operation. But was she ready for this? A new relationship? Tyson was another media magnet. Did she really want to be with him, or was she caught up in the fun and mystery of their discretion? Kendall felt like she was indulging in forbidden fruit — and she liked it.

If no one knew, they couldn't assume she hadn't gotten the part on her own. There was so much to consider. One thing was for sure — she wasn't ready to give Tyson up. The fun had just begun.

Storm eyed her suspiciously. He was probably wondering why she had ditched them the night before. What did he care? She didn't owe him any explanations.

"The cars are here!" one of the production assistants yelled. Everyone piled through the hotel doors toward the waiting vehicles.

"Ken."

Kendall turned. "Hey. What's up, Storm?"

"There's something I'd like to talk to you about. What are you doing later? Are you joining us for dinner?"

"Yeah. Sure."

Kendall continued toward one of the cars that had yet to be filled.

"What did you do last night?" Storm persisted.

"Nothing."

"Oh. I came to your room when we got back from eating. You didn't answer. I figured you were out."

"Oh."

Kendall climbed into the small car. Unfortunately, Storm climbed in with her, and another actress, Mila Canton, climbed up front. The only noise in the car was the driver's music. Kendall tried to mentally retreat back to her and Tyson's time together, but it didn't work. She couldn't concentrate enough to bring Tyson back —

not when she was focusing on trying to ignore Storm's blatant stares. Kendall looked at her phone. She had told Tyson to let her know when he landed. He had at least six more hours of flying ahead of him, but she couldn't wait to hear his voice again. In a few more days, she'd be back home and in his arms. She put her head back, closed her eyes and pretended to be asleep until they arrived at the location for the day's shoot.

Just as she had anticipated, the makeup artist had to add extra touches around her eyes.

"Somebody partied hard last night, huh?"

Kendall smiled inwardly. "Just super tired. Didn't sleep well," Kendall said. It was true. They'd hardly slept a wink.

Finally, it was time to shoot. Kendall's psychedelic dress and wig, teased high and flipped upward at the ends, made Kendall feel like she had become the Jocelyn James of the sixties once again. She'd taken her seat at the Parisian café, pretended to puff on a cigarette and waited for Storm's character to enter the scene. He did as he was instructed, sitting directly across from her and engaging in a painful interaction where Benny Dickson, the man who had become Jocelyn's late husband, pleaded with her to forgive him for his betrayal. The heartfelt scene caused a dense silence to descend upon the set. Tears flowed from both her and Storm's eyes. She looked at her costar. She couldn't deny Storm's talent. In that moment, he was Benny. She believed, as Jocelyn had all those years before, that Benny was truly sorry. He looked into her eyes, pleaded with his soul. Kendall blinked. She saw Benny one minute and Storm the next.

Had Storm actually been sorry for his betrayal, the scene could have felt more like déjà vu. Instead, it felt surreal, and ended with Storm on one knee before her, holding and kissing her hand. He slid a velvet ring box from his sports jacket, and then his shaky voice asked for her hand in marriage. She swatted at him. Wanted to dismiss him. Kendall took a long drag of her cigarette, slammed it into the ashtray and swiped at the tears falling down her face. Storm stood to his feet, pulled her up with him, gently took her face in his hands and kissed away those tears.

Before the director could say cut, the cast and crew applauded. The thunder of their applause snapped Kendall from the recesses of her character. She had to agree that they had just created one of the most intense and beautiful scenes of the movie. She and Storm. Again, Kendall wished they had chosen another costar. The beauty of the scene made her uncomfortable, reminded her of Storm's real betrayal. Even then, she wasn't sure if he was acting or had been sincere.

They'd filmed into the night, shooting several more scenes packed with raw emotion, and were ready to head back to their hotel. Kendall was hungry and tired, looking forward to a shower and a good meal. After that she'd talk to Tyson until she fell asleep. That had become her evening routine. When she thought about Tyson, a smile radiated from the inside out. Kendall texted him a simple Hey as she headed to the cars.

"Kendall!"

She turned in the direction of the voice calling her name. Storm jogged toward her.

"Yes?" Her voice was formal, even. She was back to her normal, cool self with him. The warmth exuded in the scenes they'd shot earlier had evaporated.

Storm caught up with her and looked at her for a brief moment, wearing an inquisitive expression. "Can I talk to you?"

What's this about? "Sure."

"Over dinner? I'm hungry."

Kendall shrugged. "Sure. Me too."

The two climbed into one of the waiting cars with another actress. There was minimal conversation on the ride back. Kendall spent most of the drive fighting fatigue and looking out the window. She couldn't get enough of the Parisian landscape. When they arrived at the hotel, the driver had to wake all three of them.

Kendall stretched, maneuvering her body in catlike movements. The driver opened the door and helped her out. Storm waited by the side of the car.

"I'm gonna go freshen up a little. Meet you back in about twenty minutes," she said to him.

Inside the restaurant twenty minutes later, Storm was the perfect gentleman. After they placed their orders, he turned to her.

"So, what's up?" Kendall wanted to get right to the point. Had they been in America, she never would have agreed to dinner. Paparazzi would have been all over them. She could see the cheesy headlines now: Storm and Kendall, Rekindled?

"You're not wasting any time." Storm chuckled and reached for her hand. Kendall recoiled slightly. Storm sat back, letting his hands slide back into his lap. "You hate me that much?"

"I don't hate you, Storm."

He leaned closer and spoke almost in a whisper. "Then why do you seem so uncomfortable with me on the set?"

"What?" Storm was right. Having to pretend to love him, sleep with him and dote on him wasn't easy considering their past. But she at least thought she was giving a good performance. She wanted to give this role her all. Had anyone else noticed? "But —"

"I know you. I can feel it," Storm replied, answering the question in her mind. Kendall exhaled, sat back and dropped her shoulders. She didn't like him claiming such an intimate connection with her.

Their food arrived. Kendall leaned aside so the waiter could place her steaming plate down. Storm ate in silence while she pushed her food around, taking a bite here and there. Her appetite had waned.

The quality of her performance was foremost on her mind. Kendall would have to work harder to keep her character authentic.

Storm closed his lips over a forkful of roasted duck and looked at her. He put his utensils aside, reached across the table and took her hand in his.

Once again, Kendall recoiled just a bit. Her reaction was instinctive. She looked up to find Storm's eyes right on her. Had she been doing that on set?

"We need to at least be friendly."

Kendall huffed. "We are friendly." She really didn't want to have this conversation with Storm. This was about as friendly as she was capable of being with him. Had he forgotten his betrayal? She was no longer angry with him, but she certainly wasn't interested in rekindling any kind of friendship with him either.

Storm peered at her as if he were looking over glasses. "Like *real* friends." After several moments of quiet he added, "Or maybe more."

Kendall threw him a sharp look. He'd actually looked hopeful. "That's not going to happen."

"Are you seeing someone?"

Kendall narrowed her eyes at Storm. "That's none of your business."

It was Storm's turn to look exasperated. "We could have gotten past that, you know?"

Kendall wasn't going to do this. The wounds from his infidelity had been healed. The bitterness was gone. She wasn't going backward. "We did get past it, Storm. We broke up."

Storm looked annoyed for a moment, as if the reminder had stung. "We were good together — we looked good together." He leaned forward over the table, close to her. "Our reunion would be the hot topic of every rag and entertainment show. The exposure would be amazing."

Kendall felt her jaw tighten. Storm still hadn't gotten it. If Storm knew her — really knew her — he'd know that wasn't the kind of spotlight Kendall desired.

She stood, and Storm stood as well, his expression confused. Kendall dug in her purse and dropped enough money on the table to cover her meal. Storm caught her arm as she rounded the table. Kendall stopped walking. He moved closer to her, close enough for her to feel his breath on her cheek. For a few moments he didn't speak, but he rested his forehead on her temple. Kendall remained still, hoping to avoid a scene. She glanced around the restaurant. They hadn't attracted too much attention. A few patrons looked and turned away. To them, it could have seemed as if Storm were whispering in her ear.

"Kendall." There was more breath in his voice than volume.

"What, Storm?"

"I'm sorry." He kissed her cheek. She felt nothing. "For everything," he added.

554

"Good night, Storm." Kendall walked out of the restaurant without looking back.

CHAPTER 26

Tyson couldn't wait to lay eyes on Kendall. He waited as patiently as possible while his driver went to get her from the exclusive airport in Burbank. This was one of Los Angeles's top seven terminals for private jet travelers. The rest of the crew would fly out together the following day.

She'd only been filming in France for a week and a half, but that was far too long for Tyson. He'd missed Kendall. Somehow, she had fastened herself to his soul, and he needed to see her, touch her, kiss her as soon as possible. Her absence left a hole in his existence. No one had ever left him craving her presence the way Kendall did.

The last time Tyson talked on the phone to someone until he fell asleep was when he was a teen with a crush on one of the cheerleaders in prep school. The entire time Kendall was away, her sweet voice lulled him to sleep every single night. They never ran out of topics to talk about. Tyson had laid his feelings on the line and was ready to move swiftly in sealing their relationship. He didn't mind the secrecy at all. In fact, he welcomed it. It proved to be less distracting because it allowed him to always have Kendall all to himself.

Tyson heard a commotion and rolled the window down slightly. Several people ran toward the terminal exit. Some had cameras and microphones; others held cell phones high in the air. Tyson wondered what poor soul would be the next to be inundated by the media's attention. Obviously, someone had been tipped off to some entertainer or famous politician's life. The scene made him curious, but Tyson pulled up the window anyway. He had his share of media attention for the time being and was still getting some of it.

A moment later, the car door was yanked open and Kendall was stuffed inside. Tyson's eyes widened. He reached for Kendall and pulled her into the car.

"What's going on?"

Kendall sat back with her hand across her heart and panted. "I don't know. As soon as I came through the door, they surrounded me. Carl had to practically fight them off."

Tyson could hear his driver still yelling at

them to back off. He was confused. "How did they know you were coming to this airport? What were they asking?"

"I couldn't even tell. I just kept walking. Some asked about me and Storm getting back together, but that's what they usually ask. I don't know what's happening. Did something happen here in the States?"

"Are you okay, Ms. Chandler?" Carl asked, turning toward the back of the car.

"Yes. I'm fine, Carl. Thanks!" She turned her attention back to Tyson. "Were there any announcements about the movie?"

"Not really. They're working on some promotional stuff now, but nothing has been released."

Kendall finally caught her breath and huffed. Tyson felt the car moving and was glad to get away from the frenzied scene. Kendall was definitely the type of woman who could handle herself, but he suddenly felt the need to protect her.

"Come." He scooted closer and placed his arm around her. She rested in the crook of his arm. Kendall's breathing slowed, returning to a normal rhythm as they drove. "You must be tired."

"Exhausted."

Tyson kissed her forehead. Kendall's eyes fluttered. His lips craved more, but he resisted his own urges so she could rest. He caressed her arms and watched as her breathing found its sleeping rhythm. In his arms was where she belonged. Tyson was ready for the long haul.

They rode silently for a while before Kendall's phone rang, startling her awake. Tyson wished she had placed it on vibrate. She fished for it.

"Hello." She sounded sleepy. "What!" She sat straight up, listening to the caller. Tyson recognized Randi's voice through the phone. "No. No. No. No. No! This can't be happening." Kendall grunted. "He's right here." Tyson's brows furrowed. She looked at Tyson but quickly averted her eyes.

"What's wrong?" Tyson asked. Kendall frowned and huffed over and over again. The suspense wore at him. "What's going on?"

Kendall held up a finger to him, listening to Randi, who seemed to be talking a mile a second. She slapped her free hand onto her forehead. "Okay . . . yes . . . I'll try . . . tell me what she says. I'll be in the car for at least another hour . . . I will." Kendall hung up the phone, looked at Tyson and dropped her head again. She massaged her temples.

"What!" Tyson barked. Kendall flinched. He hadn't meant to startle her, to be so sharp with her, but he needed to know what the hell was going on.

"Someone leaked photos of me and Storm in Paris."

Tyson paused and took a breath before asking, "What photos?"

Kendall groaned. "Randi is texting them now."

Kendall's phone buzzed and Tyson forgot his manners. She typed her pin number and hit the message icon. Tyson turned her hand so he could see the screen as well. Ping after ping, followed by photo after photo flashing in her texts. Pictures of what looked like Kendall and Storm tangled in bedsheets, holding hands across a table inside of a restaurant, standing close with Storm's head against hers. Each looked more compromising than the last.

"What is this?" Tyson couldn't hold back the anger in his voice. Were these from scenes they'd shot or something else? The temperature of his skin rose a few degrees. Though it felt like someone had shoved a dagger through his heart, Tyson didn't want to overreact. He asked another question in a softer tone. "Where are these from?" He realized they could have been old pictures that resurfaced. "When —"

"Paris," Kendall said and closed her eyes.

Inside he yelled. *Paris!* Had she cheated on him in Paris? Could he even consider this cheating? He had to give her the benefit of the doubt. "I don't understand."

Kendall took a deep breath. She started talking even though her eyes remained closed. "Some of these photos were taken while we were shooting, and someone snuck pictures while we were at dinner."

"Dinner." Tyson felt air circulate in his chest. "You and Storm went to dinner together — alone?"

"Yes." She sighed and still hadn't looked at Tyson. Her eyes were open now.

Tyson shifted, putting some space between them. "You went to dinner with Storm by yourself."

"He . . . he asked if he could speak to me. I figured since it wasn't LA we'd be safe, so I said yes. Someone must have been watching, possibly following us."

"Why did you go with him?"

"It wasn't like that."

"Then what was it like?" He couldn't contain the sharpness of his tone.

"Tyson!"

He looked at her directly and tilted his head, refusing to back away from his question.

"I know you don't think I was fooling

around with Storm!" she charged.

Tyson held her glare.

Kendall shook her head. "I can't believe you." It was clear that she was angry too, but he needed answers.

It was hard enough to watch her and Storm folded in each other's arms when he had visited the set. He could tell by the way Storm looked at her that he wanted her. It was harder to know that they would be in Paris together for ten whole days, while he waited for her back in the States. Men knew when other men had an eye for their women.

Yes. Kendall was his woman. He'd made his intentions clear before leaving France. If she didn't agree, she would have ended it there. This was what he wanted, and he knew she wanted it too.

"Tell me what to believe, Kendall."

"There is nothing between me and Storm — nothing!" She swiped her index finger across the air as she spoke. "I'm insulted by the fact that you even question that. I don't owe you any explanation, but I have no problem telling you that I've done nothing wrong."

Tyson reared his head back. "You don't owe me anything?"

Kendall balled up her fist and growled.

"It's not like we've even defined this . . . this thing that we're doing."

He turned to face her directly. "Before I left you in Paris, I made it very clear what I wanted from you, and I didn't receive any objections. So as far as I'm concerned, this thing — is solidly defined. If you don't feel that way, then let me know now. I know what I want. I've never been clearer in my entire life, but I'm not going to force you into anything."

Kendall held her head in her hands. "I can't believe this is happening right now."

CHAPTER 27

Kendall was torn. She was angry with Tyson for assuming the worst of her, yet she understood. Had she seen pictures of Tyson and Tiffany like the ones that had just flashed across her screen, she would have been upset as well. But the fact that he had immediately jumped to conclusions irritated her to no end. What kind of woman did he think she was?

Yes, she'd been harsh when she said she didn't owe him any explanations. Her intention wasn't to hurt him, but she was right. She enjoyed his company immensely, loved making love to him, felt completely comfortable and free in his presence. He had become her hideaway, part of her sanctuary, but they weren't officially an item — yet. He'd placed the proverbial ball in her court when he'd left France and told her to think about it and respond when she got back to America. She hadn't been home an hour and they were arguing about why she had accepted Storm's invitation to dinner. He was questioning her integrity when he should have been backing her up. Tyson was thinking of himself, while she had to find a way to once again navigate through another probing media frenzy. Maybe this thing with him wasn't going to work after all.

"You know what. Don't worry about taking me home. I'll get there." Kendall pushed her tote aside and learned forward. "Carl. You can just drop me off at the next exit. I'll get home."

"That won't be necessary, Carl. We're taking her all the way home."

Kendall sat back hard and folded her arms. She couldn't sit in the car for another forty-five minutes with Tyson.

"Carl, can you pull over, please?" Tyson's tone was calmer than it had been since Randi's upsetting call.

Carl did as Tyson asked. The second the car came to a stop, Kendall jumped out and began pacing the shoulder. Tyson got out and joined her.

She couldn't find the words to explain what she felt. Her fingers had balled into fists. She marched circles into the pavement on the side of the freeway. Heat radiated from the inside out, and not the sexy kind of heat. She was hot with irritation. It rose so quickly, she thought her head would combust just to let the steam out. Tyson leaned against the back of the car with his arms folded. Kendall stopped pacing, closed her eyes and took several cleansing breaths.

"Look," Tyson said. "I'm sorry. I saw those pictures and got instantly upset."

Kendall looked up at the bright afternoon sky and then down toward him. "I didn't mean to snap at you. I'm dealing with a crisis here, and you're grilling me as if I'd purposely done something wrong to you. If I had anything to hide, I would have never opened those pictures in front of you." Kendall ran her fingers through her hair, sure that she still looked a mess.

"Sorry. That was selfish of me. I was wrong. I'll deal with my feelings. What do *you* need from *me*?" Tyson walked toward her.

Not only had he admitted to being wrong, he had put his feelings aside and availed himself to her. The closer he got, the more Kendall could feel the kinetic energy drawing them to one another. She wanted — needed — to feel herself wrapped in his arms, and at that moment realized there was no place she'd rather be. She understood his anger now and felt bad for saying she didn't owe him an explanation. Whether or not they'd officially marked their boundaries with declarations, she'd already belonged to him. He just knew it before she did.

"I need you to believe me . . . and support me."

Tyson gently pulled her into his arms. His warm chest against hers gave her comfort like she'd never known from another man besides her father. Despite the tautness of his chest, she felt cushioned and safe. He rubbed the back of her head. Kissed her forehead.

"I believe you. You got through this before, and you'll get through it again. It's frustrating at times, but this is our world. You were born to sing, and I know that no meddlesome media is going to run you off from doing that. This time, I'm here. I'm with you."

Kendall offered up a weak smile. Tyson was right; she loved her life and wasn't giving that up for anyone. More seasoned artists told her not to pay them any attention. She hadn't mastered that yet but was determined to get better at it.

Tyson was with her and would be with her through this. The last time, she'd dealt with it alone, wanting to crawl into a cave and hide away. She was an artist. Media wasn't *all* bad, but she still valued her privacy.

"Let's get back in the car. Your Shangri-la is waiting. We'll turn off our phones and just chill."

"That sounds wonderful." She exhaled away the rest of the weight she'd been holding in her chest.

Tyson held her face in his hands and pulled her into a kiss. Gently he pecked her lips once, twice, three times. With his tongue, he teased her mouth open and entered, tasting her sweetness.

Instinctively, Kendall wrapped her arms around him, pressed into him and rose onto her toes. She relished how supported she felt. Then she remembered they were on the side of the freeway, in broad daylight. Someone could recognize them.

"We really need to get in the car."

He took her by the hand and led her several feet back to the limo. He opened the door and climbed in after her.

Carl pulled off and Kendall lay back on the headrest. She was already beginning to care less about what the media had to say. Why should she waste her energy? She would never be able to control what they reported. Had she never pursued her dream, they wouldn't be interested in her love life.

She felt Tyson lace his fingers between hers. He held her hand. It felt good. Felt like more than just a touch. Kendall felt as if she were literally being carried. Leaning over, she rested her head on his arm. He lifted it and placed it around her. She snuggled against his chest. The adrenaline that had previously coursed through her like a raging river had finally subsided.

She had gotten through this before, would get through it this time and again in the future just like any other celebrity. As long as she was determined to live her dream, she would have to deal with the media.

She reminded herself that this time, she had Tyson.

CHAPTER 28

Tyson and Kendall had become inseparable. Several weeks of filming had ended and rehearsals for Kendall's next tour wouldn't start for several weeks. Her tour would be over by the time the movie aired on television in a few months.

Things at BCG had gotten busier. Their last movie, which Tiffany starred in, was now going to pay-per-view channels and online movie outlets. Tiffany had found a beau and no longer focused on using Tyson to stay in the spotlight. Everything had seemed to come together perfectly for both Kendall and Tyson like a puzzle.

Tyson and Kendall's quarrel had in fact been a turning point in their relationship. They undoubtedly belonged together. Reporters had speculated that the pictures of Storm and Kendall had been leaked by some Parisian blogger, but Kendall wasn't buying it. She wanted to know how that blogger could have gotten so many pictures of them on set. And why? She was convinced this had to be an inside job. The issue still made the list of hot topics for daytime shows. Kendall was getting better at ignoring negative media exposure, but she'd told Tyson she couldn't completely ignore this one. Something wasn't adding up.

Tyson, meanwhile, enjoyed the mysterious nature of their relationship. They'd spent weekends in Temecula, which they officially nicknamed their Shangri-la. When they weren't there, they retreated to Serenity Ranch in Montana, far from the spotlight. On several occasions, they'd even escaped to exclusive beach resorts to hide and flirt under the tropical sun. His siblings had started questioning him about his discreet disappearances, but he wasn't ready to give up any information.

The only person who knew about their relationship was Randi, and she was a vault. Kendall insisted her secrets could be buried with her friend. Even during the times Tyson visited the set, Randi gave no indication that she knew anything. Tyson attended the wrap party and was careful to keep his distance. He even tried not to look in her direction so he wouldn't get caught gazing. It was hard because Kendall looked stunning that night. They'd left in separate cars and met up in Temecula to celebrate the completion of her first television film project.

Tyson's phone rang with a video call. He closed his office door, quickly returned to his chair and pressed Accept. Kendall appeared on the screen. Her hair was just as messy as it was when he'd made love to her that morning before heading into work. The long drive from Temecula just as the sun fractured the darkness of the sky gave him time to come down from his Kendall high. He'd arrived at work early, exhausted, sated and as happy as a kid going to Disney. Kendall was the chocolate to his sweet tooth. His desire for her was like an addiction. Not just her body, but her grounded nature, and definitely her mind.

"Hey there, Mr. CEO. How are you feeling?"

"Tired!"

"I thought so." Kendall rolled around on the bed. Tyson instinctively licked his lips at the sight of her in that camisole with no bra and a pair of lace panties. Her messy hair made her look sexier. "Come back tonight?" Her tone was sweet and pleading. "I can't wait until the end of the week to see you again."

"Hmm." As much as he wanted to, Tyson knew he wouldn't be able to make the drive. He'd had almost no sleep the night before and a long, busy day today. Driving back to Temecula after work would take hours, and he couldn't imagine staying up for the ride. However, he didn't want to wait days before seeing her either. Both of them had places in LA, but that was paparazzi territory.

"Can Carl drive you?"

Kendall was hard to resist. "Let me make sure my calendar is clear. Maybe I'll even work remotely or just take the day off tomorrow. I doubt I'll get any sleep tonight anyway."

"Yay!" Kendall giggled. "You'll get all the rest you need."

"I bet. I didn't say it was a definite. I need to check my calendar. I'll let you know for sure right after this meeting."

Tyson checked his calendar as soon as they hung up. The evening was open. He maneuvered a few appointments around on his calendar to free up his schedule the next day. Then he arranged to be at the heliport at four in the afternoon to head over to Temecula. He couldn't sit in three hours of rush hour traffic. Instead of telling Kendall, he kept her in suspense. He'd surprise her by arriving earlier than expected and planned a great evening together before indulging his own desires.

Tyson put out the usual fires and headed out of the office by two o'clock to pack a small bag. He finally let Kendall know he was coming on the drive over to the heliport. The joy in her squeal made him wish he could snap his fingers and be with her instantly. He couldn't wait to see her face.

Tyson stopped at one of the local wineries and picked up an exquisite bottle of Cabernet. He made a second stop for flowers and made a reservation at one of the neighborhood's finest restaurants. When he arrived at Kendall's place, he was the one surprised. Kendall opened the door and jumped into his arms. He gave her a passionate kiss right in the doorway.

Kendall had transformed the backyard into a private spa oasis. There was a massage table draped in white linen. Soft music played through the outdoor speakers. The sound of water flowing through a ceramic fountain blended perfectly with the music, and there was a sweet soothing scent wafting in the atmosphere. Not to mention something delicious flavoring the air inside the kitchen.

"Wow!" was all Tyson could manage. He placed the wine down on the console table in the foyer. "These are for you." He handed Kendall the flowers.

She pushed her nose into the center of the bouquet. "These smell absolutely amazing. Put your bag down in the bedroom. We're starting in there, okay?"

"I'm following your lead." And he did, for the first time ever. In all his years of dating, Tyson was the one who had always initiated the dates, trips and surprises. He didn't mind spoiling his women, but he never knew what it felt like to be the one spoiled. He had a feeling he was going to enjoy himself more than he could have imagined. No restaurant for them, unless that was part of Kendall's plan.

Upstairs, he placed his bags down. Kendall curled her finger, beckoning him to her. He practically floated in her direction.

"Thank you for coming."

"You don't have to thank me." He kissed her nose.

"I know. But I know you were tired. You're always taking care of me and I wanted to do something special for you. So tonight is your night and tomorrow we go on an adventure."

Tyson lifted his brow and winked. He liked the sound of that.

Piece by piece, Kendall peeled his clothes

off and walked him to the shower. She washed him between kisses. He washed her between nibbles on her breast. After, she dried him, wrapped a towel around his waist and led him to the massage table outside. Kendall kneaded every muscle, including his erection. Tyson touched her lower back and caressed her bottom. She kept removing his hand from her.

"No touching yet."

Tyson yearned to feel her even more. After the massage, she had him in the lounge chair under her gazebo and fed him a hearty dinner of collard greens, steamed snapper and herb-infused basmati rice. Tyson made her put the plate down and pulled her on top of him. He positioned her to face him, sitting on his growing erection. He wanted her, appreciated her and was finally starting to put a name on the other thing he felt for her.

He was falling in love with Kendall.

CHAPTER 29

The heavy petting that Kendall and Tyson started on the patio caused their hunger for one another to almost consume them. Kendall was so happy to be able to take care of Tyson for once and make him feel good. He'd nurtured and indulged her since they'd been together, filling every crevice of her life with sheer satisfaction. She simply wanted to give him a taste of what he'd consistently given to her.

As much as she wanted to continue doting on him, need mushroomed inside of her as she kissed and ground on top of him outside on her patio. Her center heated dangerously, thinning the juices moistening between her legs. Kendall's skin became sensitive to his touch. She hungered for him, had to have him. Kendall could hardly breathe. Tyson rose, lifting Kendall in his arms. He carried her to the massage table and drew the curtains around them. The only thing visible were the stars twinkling above them.

Tyson laid her on the table facedown and returned the earlier favor. He massaged her back, behind, legs and feet. Then he turned her over and kissed her from her lips to her toes, paying special attention to her breasts and the heated core between her legs. Tyson tortured her, taking his time, caring for and kneading every part of her. When she could no longer wait, she clamored for him, scooted to the end of the table until her center met his erection. She lay on her back and he stood between her legs. Tyson took her hands in his. Laced his fingers in hers. He called her name and made her look directly into his eyes as he entered her, rocking her back and forth. Kendall hissed. Her back arched hard. She shut her eyes, unable to keep them open.

"Kendall." Tyson called her name gently. "Look at me," he whispered.

She opened her eyes and fastened them to his. Locking their gazes on one another, they rode to a decadent rhythm until both their bodies trembled uncontrollably. Tyson's head fell back; veins protruded in his neck. He grunted, sounding at first like he wanted to control the roar trying to thunder through him. He growled. Kendall felt his erection pulsate within her walls. She squeezed her eyes shut. The very edges of her skin grew sensitive. She shuddered. Her climax ripped through her. Both of them howled and collapsed, her back to the massage table, his chest to hers. Kendall felt her eyes roll back. She had never been loved so indulgently before in her life. They lay panting for some time.

"Kendall." She opened her eyes to Tyson holding himself over her, he looked straight into her eyes. "Do you feel loved?"

She did, wholly and completely. Kendall nodded.

"Because I love you."

Wow. This could be forever.

Relaxed, sated and happy from the inside out, Kendall led Tyson to the bedroom and curled into his arms.

The next morning, they rose, prepared breakfast together and returned to bed to enjoy it and another round of each other. They lay around for another hour after, chatting, laughing, touching and teasing.

"Do you realize that you said you love me last night? You weren't just sex drunk, were you?"

Tyson leaned onto his elbow and raised a single brow. He tossed his head back and laughed. "Sex drunk?"

Kendall giggled. "Yes. Sex drunk. You know, when the sex is so good it's intoxicating, and you do and say things that you don't mean just like when you've had too much to drink."

"Ha! Oh yeah. I was sex drunk. You know what they say, right? Drunk people tell the truth."

Kendall stopped laughing as Tyson's words sank in. He loved her. He really loved her. Did she love him? What she felt for Tyson seemed a lot like love. This was more than a feeling. It was physical and moved through her bones. It filled her, found its way to the crevices of who she was, making her whole like never before. It complemented her being and made her feel invincible.

"Good. Because I think . . . I love you too." There. She'd said it, didn't let it die on her tongue. Tyson pulled her into his arms and rolled her onto his body. He kissed her long and passionately. She rolled back onto her side, facing him. "So now what?"

"We love on each other." Tyson kissed her again.

Kendall couldn't help her giggles. She felt light and bubbly.

"Do you want kids?" he asked her.

"One or two."

"Damn." Tyson snapped his fingers. "I was thinking more like seven or eight!"

"What?" Kendall shot straight up in bed. Her heart felt like it was palpitating rapidly. Tyson burst out laughing.

"Kidding! Just kidding." He laughed again, holding his hands up in surrender. "You should have seen your face."

Kendall hit him with a pillow. "I almost had a heart attack. This was about to be over before it started."

"Bailing already! Ha!"

Kendall watched him laugh. She loved the way his lips curved. "Okay. Top three things that are most important to you?"

Tyson shifted himself in the bed. "That's easy — family, friends and my work. I love what I do. What about you?"

"God, my family and my dreams. I've always been a dreamer."

"Nice. Speaking of family, I want you to meet mine — soon."

"You want me to come out of hiding?" Kendall winked.

"I don't care if we never come out of hiding. I love having you all to myself." Tyson kissed her nose. "Eventually, and only when you're ready, I want the world to know that

I love you."

Kendall felt something swell in her chest. It was her heart.

"What are your dreams?" he asked.

"To bring joy to people through song, make it big as an actor and open up my own foundation to help fund arts for kids who don't get it."

Tyson nodded. "I can respect that." He moved close to her. "Can you do me a favor?" He kissed her lips.

Kendall felt her core warm all over again. She couldn't fall for his charm — she'd made plans for the day. If she didn't get out of bed with Tyson soon, they could end up lying there all day.

"What's the favor?"

"Sing to me."

A smile eased across her lips. She sat up in the bed again. "What would you like me to sing?"

"A love song."

CHAPTER 30

Once again, Tyson had caused Kendall to be running late. She couldn't blame only him, though. Both of them had trouble keeping their hands off one another. Tyson stayed overnight at her condo in LA, and they took much longer to get dressed than they should have. Late but sated, they rushed to get ready for Kendall's magazine interview with her fellow cast members. *Entertainment and Style* magazine wanted to shoot a series of pictures of the cast representing the several decades that spanned Jocelyn James's career. This issue of the magazine was scheduled to come out around the same time the television movie was being aired.

"Come on. You're going to be late!"

"Tyson." She gave him a sideways glance. "You're the one who made me late."

"Well, if you don't hurry . . ." He slid his arms around her waist and planted a kiss on her lips, "then you're going to be even later."

Kendall shook her head and waved him away. "Pass that jacket, please." He grabbed the garment she pointed to. Fall temperatures in Los Angeles dipped just low enough for jackets and sweaters. "Okay. I'm ready."

"I'll meet you downstairs." Tyson went to get his car from the parking garage.

Kendall watched him walk out of the condo and couldn't help but smile. She was lucky — no, blessed — to have such a great guy in her life. Tyson was such a departure from her previous boyfriends. Speaking of which, she wasn't looking forward to seeing Storm. She'd had very little verbal interaction with him since they had finished shooting, even though she kept bumping into him in the oddest places.

Kendall grabbed her purse. As she made her way to the parking garage connected to her building, she reminisced over how much had changed these past several months. She'd started the year single and had become one of the media's hot topics. It was almost Thanksgiving, and so much had happened. Kendall was able to cross off several items on her list of things to accomplish, and the movie was one of her biggest accomplishments to date. She'd performed at her first awards show, won her very first award, begun working on her third album and was preparing for another tour. Best of all, she had Tyson. His presence made everything she'd been able to achieve that much sweeter, and she wasn't stopping anytime soon.

By the time she got downstairs, Tyson was waiting right near the exit. Although they still hadn't made any official announcements about their relationship, they no longer went out of their way to hide it. There was no more of that completely-avoiding-each-other-in-public stuff. They'd even dined at a few local restaurants, but kept the hand holding and snuggling for when they were safely behind the privacy of closed doors.

When they arrived, the six other cast members were all there and were in different phases of hair, makeup and costume. The team at the magazine ushered Kendall inside the moment she arrived. Tyson intended to take a few calls and knock out some emails until she was done, but one of the editors insisted he join them inside the studio.

Kendall spotted Mila and the two other actresses who played her backup singers in the movie perched in makeup artists' chairs with their chins held high. Kendall headed over for air kisses before noticing the men on the other side of the room. Storm and the actors who played her first boyfriend and estranged father were getting cleaned up as well.

Kendall felt Storm's eyes on her before she ever turned around.

"Hey, guys!" She clumped their greetings together so she wouldn't have to address Storm individually.

"How's it going, Kendall? Any new music coming?" one of the men asked.

"I'm back in the studio starting next week. Can't wait."

Storm finally spoke. "Hello, Kendall. Looking lovely as usual."

"Thanks." Kendall turned to her makeup artist. "Make me look just like Jocelyn," she teased and laughed. Her remarks generated a few laughs from those within earshot.

Kendall felt eyes on her and was surprised, but this time it wasn't just Storm who kept glancing in her direction. For some reason Mila kept looking her way. Kendall wondered what that was about. Kendall tried her best to be inconspicuous and turned to look in her mirror to see if Mila was still staring. Mila looked at her then Storm and glanced away quickly. Something was up.

One by one, as their faces were done, each of them headed into wardrobe. For the first shoot representing the sixties, Kendall was front and center wearing a white period-inspired gown with her cast members surrounding her. The backdrop was psychedelic and changed with each decade. The cast members were dressed in five different eclectic variations of popular styles from each decade, with the last being all-gold attire representing Jocelyn's fifty-year career. For that last decade, Kendall donned a formfitting gown that shined and cascaded over her curves like liquid.

Throughout the entire shoot, Kendall noticed Mila staring oddly. Maybe she had become jealous of the attention Kendall received as the lead. Kendall hated to think that Mila could have been envious of her. They'd gotten along well during filming, but Kendall did recall Mila becoming a bit distant after they'd returned from Europe.

The actors changed back into their regular clothes and met the editorial staff in the conference room, where the actual interview would take place.

Storm hung back a bit. "How's it going?" he asked as she passed by.

"Going well, thankfully."

"Good." Kendall kept her eyes on the

door to the studio instead of looking at Storm when they spoke.

Tyson had walked into the hallway to take a call. Kendall checked on him, finding him walking in small circles as he spoke on the phone. Kendall waved. He lifted his chin, winked and kept talking.

"Can I talk to you for a moment?" Mila's voice startled Kendall.

She gasped and swung around with her hand across her heart. "Of course. What's up?"

"Sorry to startle you." Mila looked around. "Can we talk privately?"

"Uh. Sure." Kendall furrowed her brows.

Mila led her down the hall, away from everyone else.

"What's going on?" Kendall asked.

Mila sighed. "I'm not sure how to start."

"The beginning always works." Kendall chuckled, but when she noticed Mila hadn't joined her, the smile disappeared from her face. "Mila, is everything okay with you?"

"No." Mila put her head down and let her shoulders slump. She appeared even shorter than her already short frame.

Kendall felt herself walking closer to Mila. Growing impatient, she placed her hand on Mila's forearm. "What's the matter, Mila?"

Mila dropped her head. When she lifted it

and faced Kendall seconds later, her eyes glistened with tears. Kendall felt her throat tighten. She was the type who cried when she saw others in pain. Right now, she fought back her own tears and rubbed Mila's arm.

"Kendall. I'm sorry. I'm so sorry."

Kendall stood erect. She stopped rubbing Mila's arm. "Sorry for what?"

"I did it. I helped Storm. I shouldn't have."

Kendall narrowed her eyes and held them on Mila. "What are you talking about?"

"I took the photos — the ones in the studio and the ones of you and him at the café in Paris. Storm is the one who leaked them. He said they would help create more buzz about the movie. I believed him. It didn't feel right, but I wanted him to like me, so I did it anyway. He was nice to me then, but afterward, he wouldn't speak to me. Once we were done filming, he never answered my calls. This is the first time I've seen him since we wrapped. Now I realize he was using me the entire time, and I probably hurt you in the process."

Kendall felt like she had been sucked into a vacuum. Pressure encircled her temples. She felt her cheeks grow warm. Mila continued to apologize and explain why she had aided in this betrayal. Inexperience and naivety were to blame. Kendall's anger at Storm drowned out Mila's words. She saw her lips moving, was sure that sound accompanied what she was saying, but she heard none of the words that came out of her mouth.

Kendall thought back to Paris. She remembered Storm taking her hand across the table, coming close enough for her to feel his breath on her cheek when they stood. That was all staged. Storm had known the toll media frenzy had taken on her when they were going through their problems before breaking up. He knew she didn't like the negative exposure. The only reason this latest viral scandal didn't bother her was because Tyson had helped her develop thicker skin. The speculation, being at the center of hot topics and paparazzi invading their lives didn't affect her the same way it might have once, but the fact that Storm had set her up infuriated her.

"Kendall, Mila! They're wait —" Storm was approaching them.

Kendall's glare stopped him in his tracks. Mila wiped her eyes.

Kendall marched up to him. "You conniving, selfish . . ." Kendall couldn't decide what to call him next. She stuttered over the heat of her words.

Kendall's voice rose and traveled a bit too far. Mila looked at her. Tyson looked up and started walking her way. Storm seemed stunned. It took a moment but realization set in — Kendall could tell by the way his expression transformed from confusion to understanding. He couldn't hide. Storm glared at Mila, then looked back at Kendall with pleading eyes.

"Can we talk about this later?" Storm held his hands up in surrender.

Tyson arrived, towering over Storm. "Is everything okay?" His eyes were on Kendall. "Babe, are you okay?"

Tyson had just called her "babe." He was staking his claim, leaving nothing for speculation. Storm's brows creased. He looked at Tyson and then back at Kendall.

"I'm fine, babe." Kendall smirked. "Mila." Kendall said her name with the authority one would use with a direct report. "Thank you for your honesty. I forgive you, but we could never be friends." She turned Storm and felt Tyson at her back. "And you — if you see me walking down the street, do yourself a favor and cross over to the other side."

Kendall was determined to let her anger subside. She had become what she'd always wanted to be. Kendall was a star. People were interested in stars, in the very details of their lives. She was relevant. They could have their hype. It came with the territory, but when she was ready to move out of the spotlight, she had her Shangri-la. She had her family. She even had Montana, because now she had Tyson.

Kendall looked into Tyson's eyes, felt his support. She rose to her toes, and Tyson leaned down. Their kiss was quick and defining. Lacing her fingers between his, without looking back, Kendall sauntered away with Tyson at her side. She straightened her back, lifted her chin and entered the conference room where the interview was being held with a smile.

CHAPTER 31

Tyson was so wrapped up in work and Kendall that he hadn't realized how close they were to Thanksgiving. He scrambled to finish up at the office before picking up Kendall and flying to Serenity Ranch. He'd arranged for both of their families to fly in, meeting them there on the morning of the holiday.

Tyson lay in bed, soft sheets covering his naked body. Kendall slept in his arms, her wiry hair strewn across the sheets and his shoulder. Tyson shook his head. It was almost hard to believe what had become of them. He felt blessed. She was beautiful, smart, ambitious, grounded and sincere. And she was an actress. Tyson chuckled. He'd ended up with an actress after all.

Tyson saw a flash of orange through the window. His bed faced a wall made of glass. The undisturbed view of the lake and mountains in the distance was breathtaking.

"Kendall." Tyson nudged her. "Wake up!" Kendall shifted but didn't wake. "Ken. Babe," he whispered. "Babe," he repeated. He slipped his arm from under her.

Kendall groaned and scrunched up her face. Her eyes opened and closed slowly several times before landing on Tyson. She stretched and smiled. "Hmm?"

"Look!" He pointed toward the window. They sat up in bed. Tyson put his arm around her again. She nestled against him. Together they watched the sun dawning over the mountains — a spectacular ombré light show with reds, yellows and oranges splitting the sky in half. The deeper blue above the gradually blending colors gave way to fresh baby blues below. The sun was showing off, and they enjoyed every second of its boast.

"We should get dressed. Our family will be here soon. My mom was going on and on about getting the turkey in the oven early." Tyson had offered to have their holiday dinner catered, but the parents insisted on making it themselves. Tyson imagined the chaos that was sure to fill the kitchen.

"You're right. And remember what I told you. Don't take the things my dad says personally. Okay?" Tyson sucked in a long, deep breath. Kendall laughed. "Really, he's harmless."

The bell rang just as they finished dressing.

"Baby girl!" Kendall's father, Booker T., held his arms open wide. Kendall ran into them.

"Daddy!" She squeezed him tight. He kissed the top of her head. "I sure do miss you, baby girl."

"I'll be home for Christmas."

Booker T. pouted. "I have to wait that long?"

"I'll try to get up there before then."

"It's my turn," Shane said, nudging his father out of the way. "Hey, lil' sis." Kendall squeezed her brother and then went to the waiting arms of her oldest brother, Lincoln.

"Guys. This is Tyson Blackwell." Kendall presented him.

Kendall's brothers shook Tyson's hand and ended the greeting with a friendly embrace.

"Great meeting you," Lincoln said.

"I've heard good things," Shane added, nodding approvingly.

"Mmm-hmm." Booker T. lifted his chin, raised a brow and examined Tyson from head to toe. "Mmm-hmm." He walked around Tyson and scanned what he could see of the first floor from the foyer. "Mmm-hmm." Kendall held her breath during her dad's assessment. "Mr. Tyson Blackwell, huh?"

"Yes, sir." Tyson gave a respectful nod.

"Let's go have a talk." Booker T. placed his large hand on Tyson's shoulder.

"Let's do that." Tyson turned and shook Mr. Chandler's hand.

Leading them into the sunroom, Tyson offered them seats. It was the next best thing to being outside with flawless views of the water and mountain terrain. He'd grabbed a few flutes, a bottle of champagne he'd been chilling and a container of orange juice. When each of the men held a mimosa, they toasted, sipped and settled into the plush chairs. The newly risen sun warmed the space perfectly.

Booker T. held up his glass. "You're off to a good start," he said, referencing the drink. "That's how you welcome a man into your home!" The men laughed. Booker T. turned to Tyson, his expression growing serious. "How did you meet my daughter?"

Tyson didn't miss the way Booker T. laid protection over Kendall. He was reminding Tyson that he cared deeply for his daughter's happiness and well-being. "I'd known of her, but we officially met when she came in to audition for the role of Jocelyn James. She told me James was one of your favorites."

"She is indeed. My wife and I listened to her often, even saw her in concert a few times." Booker T. sipped his mimosa. "Hollywood is rough on the love life." Booker T. tilted his head and raised a brow at Tyson. "My baby girl has been through a lot."

"I know . . . and I understand." Tyson decided to put it all out there. "Mr. Chandler." Booker T. nodded, giving him license to continue. "Hollywood isn't easy on life, period. I'll admit I've made my mistakes. I'd even given up on dating celebrities because of how rough relationships were to maintain. I too have been dragged through some of the harshness that being in the spotlight served up. My last girlfriend was an actress, and that relationship ended badly and quite publicly. When I first met Kendall, it was all business, but as I got to know her, not the entertainer but the woman, I'd fallen for her before I realized I was no longer on my feet. She's smart, feisty and beautiful. She restored my faith in the fact that there were still good women in my line of business. I understand how much of a gem she is, and I can only imagine how much she means to you all." Tyson made eye contact with each of them. "You have my word that I will take great care of Kendall. I have her back, and I plan to be around for a long, long time."

"Well, my son. You've said the right things. You seem to be a man of your word. We will certainly see how this all plays out. Fair enough?"

"Fair enough." Tyson shook each of their hands again, sealing their unspoken pact. He cared for her and wanted to protect her as much as they did. They'd see for themselves that he was great for Kendall.

The men returned to the kitchen, where they met Kendall. She was taking the veggies she'd chopped the day before out of the refrigerator. The pies and cakes she'd baked sat in glass cake dishes along the counter.

"Move on over, girl. The chef is here," Booker T. teased.

"Oh no, no, no! The chef has just arrived!" They all turned around to see Tyson's mother, Eva, standing firm with one hand on her hip and the other filled with bags. Tyson's father, Benjamin, and his siblings, Turner and Tory, stood beside her, carrying bags as well. Benjamin shook his head and rolled his eyes toward the ceiling.

Eva was decked out in a beautiful blend of autumn colors with burgundy stilettos to match. She stepped over to the island and put down the bags, then clapped the residue from her hands and parked them on her hips.

"Now, who is this gentleman claiming to be the chef?"

Benjamin shook his head again.

"Mom's at it already," Tory said, putting her bags on the table.

Booker T. stepped forward confidently and tugged on the lapels of his suit jacket. "That would be me, Booker T. Chandler," he announced smugly, saying each part of his name as if it were a statement in and of itself. He ended with a huge smile and held his hand out for her to shake. Eva shook it, eyeing him as if she was accepting a challenge he was presenting.

Tyson and Kendall looked at each other and laughed. Everyone else joined in. Booker T. greeted Benjamin next, and the two embraced in a masculine hug. Tyson knew right then that their families would fit together like pieces of a perfect puzzle.

"Pleasure to meet you, Booker T.," Benjamin said.

"Likewise," Booker T. responded.

Tyson took over the rest of the introductions. The ladies hugged and the men shook hands. Eva winked over Kendall's shoulder when she embraced her. Having his mom's approval made him smile deep on the inside.

Somehow, each of them fell into place as if their families had been gathering for the holidays for years. Kendall, Eva, Booker T. and Tory headed to the kitchen. Benjamin, Turner, Shane and Lincoln found their way to the large TV in the family room. Once everyone was settled in, Tyson ping-ponged back and forth between both spaces, making sure everyone was okay.

"You sure you know what you're doing over there with that bird? No experimenting on Thanksgiving Day now. You hear?" Tyson heard Booker T. say to his mother.

"You worry about that macaroni and cheese you're tending to, or do you need me to come show you how it's really done?"

"You're a feisty one! Ben!" Booker T. yelled through the kitchen, reducing Benjamin's name. "How do you deal with this one here?"

Laughter flowed between the spaces. Over the next few hours, the kitchen crew laughingly prepared a delicious feast, leaving the setting of the tables to the ones who sat watching television while the food cooked.

"Dinner is ready!" Eva announced, still in

her stilettos. "Gather around and let's say grace."

"Speaking of grace." Booker T. looked toward Kendall. "May I?" His eyes glistened.

"Please." Kendall nodded. Her eyes watered as well.

Booker T. went to his bag and pulled out a frame. He cleared his throat. "If you all don't mind, I'd like to have my lovely late wife join us." He turned the frame around to reveal a picture of a beautiful woman with a salt-and-pepper bob. Tears rolled from Kendall's eyes. Shane and Lincoln cleared their throats. Tyson was sure that all that rapid blinking was meant to hold back their tears. "She would have loved to be here and see her Kendall joined with such a beautiful family."

Eva smiled and walked over to Booker T. "May I?" She held her hands out. Tyson wondered what she was about to do. Booker T. handed the picture to Eva and she looked at it for a moment, pursing her lips together. "She's beautiful! I can tell she was strong." She exhaled and looked into the eyes of Kendall, Shane and Lincoln before settling her gaze on Booker T. "We women usually sit near each other so we can chat." Her nod was a request for permission.

Booker T's nod was permission granted. Eva walked over to the table and placed Grace's picture next to the chair she'd claimed for herself. Then she reached for her husband's hand. His chest swelled. Tyson wasn't sure if it was pride, or if Benjamin was trying to hold back his own emotions. Kendall's tears now flowed stronger. Shane and Lincoln didn't hold theirs back. A proud, loving smile spread across Booker T.'s face as the rest of the family gathered around the table.

"Mom. Would you do the honors?" Tyson asked.

"Gladly, son." And she did. "Heavenly Father, we stand before You with grateful hearts, thanking You for bringing our families together — all of us. We have so much to be thankful for. Please bless the food we are about to eat for the nourishment of our bodies and bless the hands that prepared it. Bless the pathway of these two wonderful people, Tyson and Kendall, and may we share many more holidays together just like this. Amen!"

The "Amens" were a chorus. Everyone released hands and hugged. Tyson's heart felt like it could overflow, filling his chest cavity with warmth.

"Dad, would you carve the turkey?"

"Absolutely, son."

"Yeah. And put a piece on my plate so I can taste it and see if she did a good job!" Booker T. teased.

While everyone laughed, Eva squinted her eyes at Booker T., pressed her lips together and then leaned toward Grace's picture. "Girl, how did you deal with this one?"

Everyone laughed even harder. "I guess the same way I deal with you," Benjamin whispered loud enough for everyone to hear, and stepped out of Eva's reach just in time to avoid getting hit.

The instant camaraderie confirmed that Tyson had made the right choice. He turned to Kendall, took her face in his hands and kissed her like they were the only ones in the room. He floated away, only to be brought back to the present by the teasing whistles, hisses and claps of their family members. Kendall shook her head, chuckled and rested her cheek against his chest. Tyson wished that moment — and what he felt — could be frozen in time.

CHAPTER 32

Life had changed significantly for Kendall.
After Thanksgiving, she made it a rule to
see her family more and spent more time
traveling back and forth to the Midwest.
She spent Christmas with her father and
brothers just as she'd promised and rang in
the New Year with Tyson by her side. Much
of their free time was now spent together
with their families.

Their relationship was public now. Kendall
no longer minded the flash of the cameras
or what the media had to say, whether good
or bad. She'd chosen this life. There was no
way to have a life in the spotlight without
dealing with them, but Kendall no longer
let it get the best of her. She hardly noticed
paparazzi anymore, and she spent less time
in her condo where they usually camped
out. Instead, she was spending more time in
LA at Tyson's home, which was protected
by a security gate far down at the end of a

private road.

It was red carpet season and the anniversary of her first award show performance. In the year that had passed she'd finished touring and the Jocelyn James biopic aired. Kendall had begun racking up the accolades. Her new album was on schedule to be released in the summer, and she'd just wrapped up her second film project. This one was going to be in theaters. She was performing at the BTV awards again and had also been asked to announce other nominees and winners as well.

"You're not done yet?" Tyson burst into the bathroom, snapping Kendall out of her daydream. "You've been in the tub for almost an hour. What's going on in there?"

"Thinking about you."

Tyson widened his eyes, looked at his watch and huffed. "Ugh! We don't have enough time!"

"Ha!" Kendall's laugh bounced off the marble walls. "Okay. I'm coming out now."

"Ayanna just arrived."

"Shoot! Okay, tell her I'll be right down." Kendall finished up efficiently. She didn't want to keep her hairstylist waiting. The makeup artist would be arriving soon after.

Two hours later, Kendall was slipping into her gown, a formfitting, pale yellow, strapless number with an epic bow on the side, cinched by a sparkling broach. Tyson complemented her with a matching yellow shirt under his black tux.

"Come on, Kendall! We have to go," he chided. She was used to him rushing her and kind of liked it.

They reminded her of Booker T. and Grace before she'd passed. Kendall sighed. She wasn't going to get sad. Instead, she kissed her hand and pressed it to her heart. "I love you, Mommy. Hope I'm making you super proud."

"Ken! Babe! Come on!" Tyson yelled from downstairs.

"I'm coming, I'm coming!" Kendall grabbed her evening purse and shoes, gathered the bottom of her dress and trekked down the stairs.

"The driver has been waiting for twenty minutes!" Tyson yelled as if she were still upstairs and wouldn't hear him.

"I'm right here."

He swung around, mouth open, no doubt ready to complain about how long it had taken her. Instead, he froze, blinked, and his features softened. Tyson's shoulders relaxed, and he shook his head slightly. Slowly he walked toward her, took her by the hand and kissed it gently.

"You look . . . absolutely . . . stunning." It seemed he had to search for the words.

Kendall felt the love in his statement. Her cheeks burned, and she blushed. "Thank you." She twisted from one side to the other. Tyson walked a circle around her and then slid his arms around her waist. He pulled her in for a kiss. "I love you."

"I love you too, my knight in handsome formal attire."

Tyson kissed her through her giggles. "We need to go." He took her by the hand and led her out to the car.

He didn't wait for their driver. After tucking her in safely, he rounded the car and jumped in on the other side. The driver got back in and pulled off smoothly. In the back, Kendall held his hand.

"Like my dress?"

"I love your dress. Can't wait to get you out of it."

"Ha! Behave, Tyson."

They kissed, touched and giggled through half the ride. Neither of them had ever been successful at keeping their hands off each other. New love felt amazing, and Kendall hoped that she and Tyson would be like this forever.

"I can't wait to hear you sing," Tyson said. His expression changed suddenly, going from adoring to something that looked alarming.

"Carl. We have to go back!"

"What? Why, Tyson?" Kendall became nervous.

"I forgot something I need for tonight."

"Carl." Tyson looked at his watch and cursed. "We need to hurry."

Carl turned the car around and drove several minutes back to the house. Tyson barely waited for the car to stop before he jumped out. Kendall wondered what was so important that they had to go back for. Was it his speech? She had a version of it on her phone. She'd helped him with it and had a copy in her emails.

Tyson leaped through the car door he'd left open. He was breathless. "Okay. Whew. We're good now."

Kendall didn't see anything in his hand. "What did you have to go back for?"

"Something I needed to bring with me on stage."

"Okay." Kendall shrugged. Tyson was being vague.

"Now, where were we?" Tyson leaned over and kissed her again.

His sweet kisses pushed any more questions right out of her mind. A while later they arrived at the red carpet. Cameras began snapping the second they emerged from the car. Kendall took Tyson's hand, and together they confidently strode toward the red carpet. Kendall felt herself glowing with Tyson by her side. Photographers clamored to take their picture. Tyson gave them a show, squeezing her in his arms, kissing her for the cameras and waving at their fans. Kendall enjoyed every second. They looked at each other, nodded and then suddenly morphed into a series of silly poses. Kendall puckered her lips, turning from side to side, and they both folded their arms in hip-hop stances. They held those poses and stood back-to-back, winking for the cameras. Tyson dipped her as if they'd ended a perfect waltz, and then they dabbed. The cameras snapped away, catching their genuine laughs and loving kiss at the end before they moved on toward the entrance. They knew their antics would be the talk for a while. It was so much fun.

Inside, they greeted friends and took their seats just before the lights went down, the music came up and the show began. Kendall announced her nominees in the first part of the ceremony and went backstage to prepare for her performance. She came out in a sequined bodysuit, a matching sparkling blazer and thigh-high gold boots with sequins coming up the sides. Soon she had the entire theater on their feet, singing and swaying with her.

At the end, the entire audience stood clapping. Kendall's chest heaved, both from the performance she'd just given and from being filled by the audience's response. She stood there absorbing the applause and the spotlight, feeling proud as she scanned the crowd. Kendall waved, bowed and waved again. She turned to exit the stage and halted. Walking toward her was Tyson, his parents and his siblings. Behind them were her dad and brothers. She'd had no idea her family would be there. Her hands flew to her mouth. She even hit herself in the face with the microphone.

Kendall bounced up and down. "What are you doing here?" She was so excited to see her family she'd forgotten that she was onstage. She hugged her dad and brothers and squeezed Eva, who had become like the mother she'd been missing, in her arms. Kendall noticed they were all still onstage and looked at Tyson suspiciously. *What is happening right now?* She kept smiling for the cameras and wondered why no one else moved.

The lights went down, and the large screen behind them flashed. Music flowed through the theater. Kendall recognized the song. It was the one she'd sung to Tyson the night she'd told him that she loved him. He had asked her to do him a favor and sing him a love song. A collective "ah" came from the audience. Pictures of them flashed on the screen — selfies of them in Paris, Temecula, Montana, their parents' homes. Suddenly those changed to the silly ones they'd taken on the red carpet when they had arrived. Kendall covered her face in her hands and laughed. She wagged a finger at Tyson.

The lights came up. Applause erupted in the audience once again. Kendall grinned hard. She kissed her hand and sent it out over the entire theater. She reached for Tyson's hand but didn't feel him next to her as she had the moment before. She turned and noticed that Tyson had dropped to one knee.

She gasped. Tory took the microphone from her and handed it to Tyson. One of Kendall's hands flew to her mouth. Tears sprang to her eyes. The other hand covered her heart. Kendall pulled her lips in, gnawing on the bottom one to keep from crying audibly.

"Mama always said people are going to talk. You might as well give them something to talk about," Tyson said and took Kendall's left hand. "Kendall Marie Chandler . . . will you make me the happiest man in the world and —"

"Yes!" Kendall yelled. Then she pulled him to his feet and wrapped her arms around his neck. "Yes!" She plastered his face with kisses. "Yes, I'll be your wife!"

Kendall kissed her husband-to-be passionately, as if it were just the two of them. Turner patted Tyson's back and cleared his throat. Kendall and Tyson laughed into each other's lips before breaking away. He took Kendall's hand and slid the huge ring on her finger. She held it up for the audience to see and giggled. There was more applause. The love song played louder. Tyson swept her off her stilettos and carried her offstage.

"I guess we gave them something to talk about." Kendall kissed him again. Her heart felt like it could explode.

"And write about."

"And post about!" Kendall threw her head back. Her belly shook as they laughed.

"I knew this felt like forever. I'm not going anywhere," Tyson said.

"Our kind of forever. And neither am I," she said.

Then they sealed their promise with a kiss.

ABOUT THE AUTHOR

A born-and-bred New Yorker, **Nicki Night** delights in creating hometown heroes and heroines with an edge. As an avid reader and champion for love, Nicki chose to pen romance novels because she believes that love should be highlighted in this world and she delights in writing contemporary romances with unforgettable characters and just enough drama to make readers clutch a pearl here and there. Nicki has a penchant for adventure and is currently working on penning her next romantic escapade. Nicki is a member of Romance Writers of America (RWA) and the New York City Chapter of Romance Writers of America.

The employees of Thorndike Press hope you have enjoyed this Large Print book. All our Thorndike, Wheeler, and Kennebec Large Print titles are designed for easy reading, and all our books are made to last. Other Thorndike Press Large Print books are available at your library, through selected bookstores, or directly from us.

For information about titles, please call:
(800) 223-1244

or visit our website at:
gale.com/thorndike

To share your comments, please write:
Publisher
Thorndike Press
10 Water St., Suite 310
Waterville, ME 04901